Readers love *My Fair Captain*
by J.L. LANGLEY

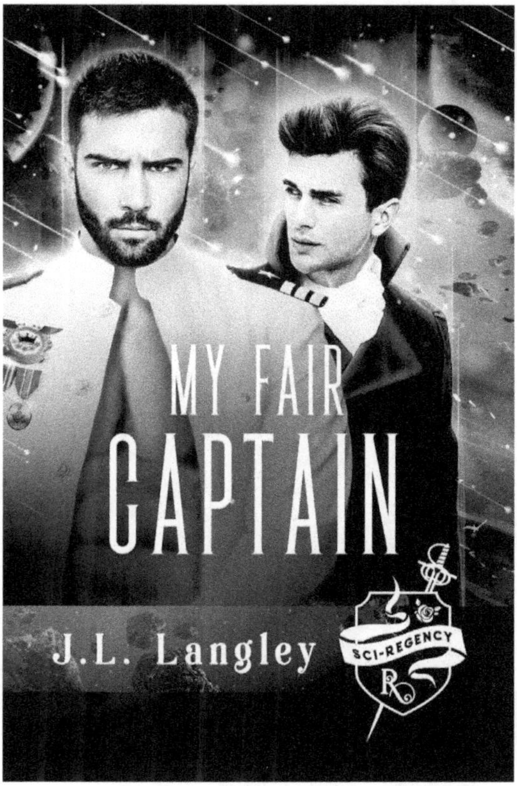

"I simply adore this book and I can't recommend it highly enough…. If you love highly romantic tales that will live with you long after you finish the book, then *My Fair Captain* is the book for you."
—Top 2 Bottom Reviews

"I highly, very highly recommend to all of you!"
—OptimuMM

"In the end, I adored this re-release more the second time around."
—The Blogger Girls

By J.L. Langley

THE SCI-REGENCY SERIES
My Fair Captain
The Englor Affair
My Regelence Rake

Published by Dreamspinner Press
www.dreamspinnerpress.com

MY REGELENCE RAKE

J.L. Langley

DREAMSPINNER PRESS

Published by
DREAMSPINNER PRESS

5032 Capital Circle SW, Suite 2, PMB# 279, Tallahassee, FL 32305-7886 USA
www.dreamspinnerpress.com

Trade Paperback ISBN: 978-1-64080-691-7
Digital ISBN: 978-1-64080-690-0
Library of Congress Control Number: 2018907626
Trade Paperback published November 2018
v. 2.0
First Edition published by Samhain Publishing Ltd., October 2012.

Printed in the United States of America

This paper meets the requirements of
ANSI/NISO Z39.48-1992 (Permanence of Paper).

Chapter One

September 13, 4830: Planet Regelence
Dinmore House, the Marquess of Crestview's residence in Classige, Pruluce

HIS YOUNGER brother was right. Life was like a book, but instead of the romance novel Tarren professed it to be, it more closely resembled a Greek tragedy.

In all fairness it probably wasn't as bad as that, but Colton was having a hard time seeing the good at the moment. He glanced out over the busy ballroom and zeroed in on the love of his life waltzing with that… that… light-trousers. What could Wentworth possibly see in Lord Biltmore's second son? Eugene Collis might be of age, but he was a wanton. A wanton and a buffoon. No one had ever caught Eugene in flagrante delicto, but there were rumors, lots and lots of rumors, even before he'd turned twenty-five. Maybe that was the problem. Wentworth had a reputation for his attraction to easy men, and Colton wasn't easy.

Colton sighed and absently lifted the crystal cup to his lips. Galaxy, Viscount Wentworth made his heart ache.

Wentworth's sable hair looked windblown and elegant at the same time. No surprise—his hair always appeared as though he'd just come in from riding. His perfect jaw sported a beard shadow. Anyone else would've seemed scandalously unkempt, but not Wentworth. On him it represented an air of mystery and added to his rakish appeal. His breeches should be outlawed, the way they emphasized his muscular arse and thighs. Really only his legs, since his coattails covered his backside, but Colton knew the man had a splendid arse. Sebastian Hastings spent nearly as much time in the saddle as Colton himself. It was one of the many reasons Colton adored him.

"Are you going to actually drink that, or are you pretending?"

Colton lowered his glass and contemplated his brother's stepson. "What?"

Trouble waved his hand absently and turned to watch the dancers. "You've put that cup to your lips at least three times in the last five minutes without taking a drink."

They both stepped to the left to allow a couple to exit through the open patio doors. Couldn't people go to one of the other open doors? Everything was getting on his nerves tonight it would seem.

Colton sipped his lemonade, then set it on the small table next to the door. "I don't particularly like lemonade."

Trouble chuckled. "It took you that long to decide?" He studied his glass, winced, and downed it in one gulp. "I don't either, actually, but Hawk took the glass of champagne I filched." He stepped past Colton, deposited his empty glass on the table, and situated himself back in front of the exit leading to the veranda. "Why are you hiding on the edge of the ballroom? I thought you liked these shindigs."

Colton shrugged. Trouble wouldn't understand; he was infatuated with his betrothed. All Trouble had to do was wait, and one day Rexley would be his. Although, why anyone would want Colton's stuffy oldest brother completely boggled him. "I like them just fine, but I'm tired of dancing." And tired of being fawned over by everyone but the one man he wanted to dote on him. If only Wentworth would notice him….

"Oh, speaking of dancing…." Trouble pulled his dance card from his waistcoat pocket and began looking around.

What Trouble was searching for, Colton had no clue, so he continued trying to locate Wentworth. Where was he? He'd been here only moments ago. Normally Wentworth stood out in the all-black evening wear he favored.

"You've got it bad." Trouble shook his head and put his back to the ballroom to gaze out the french doors. "Come on, we need to go outside."

"We can't go outside. We don't have a chaperone."

Trouble growled and huffed out a breath. "Fine." He cocked his arm and threw his dance card.

"Oh my stars." Colton turned in time to see the black card sail over the veranda railing, past a strolling couple, and into the fountain.

A chuckle came from their right as Lord Bannon Thompson sidled up next to Trouble. “You definitely win for originality, Winstol.”

“I win first to dispose of that ghastly thing too.” Trouble snatched the dance card from Bannon’s hand and chucked it out the door as well. It too landed in the fountain pool.

Bannon laughed. “Why, thank you.”

“Quite welcome.” Trouble brushed his hands together. “Good riddance. I hate dancing.” He exaggerated a shudder. “Guh, there should be an age limit to the men who can ask you to dance.”

“I concur.” Bannon leaned forward past Trouble, making a hank of auburn hair fall into his eyes. “Colton? Don’t you usually dance?” Scrunching his face and rolling his eyes upward, Bannon blew at the hair.

Colton shrugged. “I don’t feel like it.”

“He’s pining away for Wentworth.” Trouble turned around, facing the dance floor again.

Discreetly, Colton elbowed Trouble in the ribs.

“Oof. Whaaat? I’m just saying….”

“You should join the DCDC,” Bannon said. “It will take your pining to a new level. Maybe it will make Wentworth notice you and do something about it.”

“What is the DCDC?” Colton studied the crowd. Wentworth nearly always came to events late and retired from them early.

“The Dance Card Destruction Crew.” Trouble grinned, showing off the charming dimples in his cheeks. Grins like that made it hard to remember why he was called Trouble.

“We lost Aiden and Payton, but we’re still going strong. Winstol is our newest member,” Bannon explained.

“Who are the other members?” Colton asked. Was that Wentwo— no. Colton’s shoulders slumped. Apparently the viscount had already quit the rout. What time was it? Shouldn’t they all be leaving soon?

“Just me and Winstol.” Bannon shrugged. “Rupert says he can’t flirt as well without dancing, so he still refuses to join.”

Colton chuckled. “Sure. Why not?” He didn’t want to dance with anyone but Wentworth anyway. He pulled his card out of his waistcoat pocket.

Trouble confiscated the card. “Bombs away.” He tossed it out the patio door just as he’d done the other two.

"Uh-oh." Bannon touched Colton's shoulder. "Is that the admiral coming this way?"

Colton squinted. It did look a bit like his brother-in-law headed toward them.

"What?" Trouble swiveled so fast he practically jumped around. "Nate will throttle me. He said I had to dance tonight. Let's go." He grabbed Colton's arm and dragged him out the patio doors with Bannon laughing behind them.

"Trouble…." Stumbling down the steps toward the garden, Colton nearly plowed into Lord Girton. "Beg your pardon, Girton."

"Sorry, Girton," Bannon yelled and grabbed Colton's other arm to help usher him away.

Caught as he was between Trouble and Bannon, Colton had no choice but to follow. They dodged around hedges and tall perennials, another fountain, and several benches. The garden was a maze of alcoves, faux Greek ruins, and plants. In the daylight it was probably beautiful, but at night it was a little spooky. Too many spots where people could hide.

They came to an arbor that resembled a cave with the mass of climbing vines and fairy lights strung over it. Trouble and Bannon flopped down on the bench, cackling like a couple of loons.

Trouble tugged at his cravat. "Do you think Hawk saw us?"

"I'm not even sure that was Nate." Colton smiled and sat between Trouble and Bannon. That was fun. He couldn't remember the last time he'd done something so carefree. Since Aiden and Trouble had been abducted at the end of last year, he and Tarren had been the very epitome of respectability. They'd been absolute angels. No more sneaking out, no more balancing on the edge of propriety only a hair away from scandal.

Speaking of propriety…. "Cut that out." Colton knocked Trouble's hands away from his cravat. The kid always fussed with them, complaining they were choking him.

Trouble growled but let go of his neckcloth. "Idiotic torture device," he mumbled.

The weather was refreshingly cool with stars twinkling above. Nice for fall. Cool but not freezing. There were no flowers in bloom, but plenty of evergreen plants dotted the landscape. Best of all, no one stared at Colton.

Closing his eyes, Colton slouched back on the bench like Trouble and Bannon. The sway of leaves and the tinkling of water from the fountain made for a lovely lullaby. The tension riding him for the last three hours, since arriving at the ball, seeped out of him. A soft breeze tickled his face.

Bannon groaned.

"What?" Colton frowned.

"What?" Bannon asked.

Colton cracked open one eye. "Why are you groaning?"

"It wasn't me."

"Shhh…." Trouble sat up.

Colton and Bannon leaned forward.

Cocking his head, Trouble raised one platinum brow.

The groan, or rather moan, came again.

With eyes wide, Trouble bit his bottom lip and grinned.

Bannon slapped a hand over his mouth and pointed toward their right. The back of a vine-covered arbor, like the one they sat under, lay beyond a large grouping of bushes. The perfect spot for a lovers' tryst.

Hopping to his feet, Trouble put a finger to his lips.

"Oh no. Get back here," Colton whispered and made a grab for the scamp, but Trouble evaded him.

Trouble tiptoed, which was ridiculous because he was on grass, toward the moans. He disappeared from sight for all of thirty seconds before he returned with a blank look on his face.

Uh-oh. A lump settled in Colton's stomach.

"Who was it?" Bannon wanted to know.

Trouble shrugged and sat on the bench. "Just a couple of lords."

Normally Trouble would be smiling and cracking jokes or encouraging them to go check it out themselves. It must be someone they all knew, participating in a clandestine meeting. Was it one of their friends? Or perhaps family? No, it couldn't be. Father and Cony were one hundred percent devoted to each other, as were Aiden and Nate. Rexley would never do something so careless. And Tarren—

Colton shot to his feet. Tarren was reckless and a hopeless romantic.

"No!" Bolting from his seat, Trouble shook his head. "It's nothing. Come on. We should all go back. It's getting chilly. Aren't you getting cold?" Taking Colton by the arm, Trouble motioned for Bannon to get up. "I'm cold. Bannon? How about you?"

Colton freed himself and started around the bushes.

Trouble darted in front of Colton, placing a hand in the middle of his chest.

"Jeremy, if it's Tarren—"

Trouble sighed. "If it were Tarren, I'd have told you. Let's just go back to the ball. Please?" He gave Colton a weak smile.

Colton should've been relieved, but instead his heart raced and the hair on the back of his arms stood on end. He walked around Trouble.

Behind him, Trouble began whispering to Bannon.

Colton crept past tall ornamental grasses and a knot garden. The alcove appeared completely concealed from the back. Surely Trouble had not gone around to the front or parted the vines. He'd have been noticed if he had.

Slurping noises and deeper but quieter moans filtered through the greenery.

There, in the right corner of the mass of foliage, halfway toward the bottom, was a clear space. Colton bent and peered through the hole in the spindly branches and leaves. He wasn't going to like what he saw. Nervous flutters tickled his insides, but he forced himself to look.

A man reclined on the bench with his head thrown back. The angle concealed his face, and the night hid the color of his clothes, but his hair appeared to be dark. Colton let his gaze drift down the long, toned body. The man's evening coat was undone and his shirt untucked. *Oh.* His trousers were open. There was a nest of dark hair and—

Colton gulped. The man's prick was in the mouth of—

No! It couldn't be….

Colton's gaze shot back to the man's head. Still, he was unable to make out the man's features, but he didn't need to. Turning away with his heart in his throat, he took a deep breath and then another. When he brought his hand to his face, it shook, so he lowered it.

Bannon caught his wrist. When had Bannon gotten so close? He pulled Colton away from the arbor and down the aisle.

Trouble kept pace beside them.

Colton couldn't look at either of them… not yet. He stared at the ground, focusing on putting one foot in front of the other. His composure was fleeting, trying to abandon him altogether. But he wouldn't let it. He couldn't.

They walked for several seconds, and Bannon came to a halt. He turned Colton and pushed him down on a bench.

Trouble sat next to him, grabbed his hand, and squeezed. "I tried to keep you from looking."

"It's quite all right." He patted Trouble's hand and gave him a weak smile. Glancing up at Bannon's concerned gaze was almost Colton's undoing. "Seriously, everything is fine." He'd never get the image of Eugene Collis's lips stretched around Wentworth's thick cock out of his head, but he would not break down over it.

Wentworth was nothing to him, not really, and this was probably for the best. It was the eye-opener he needed. All the flirting he'd done over the years had never amounted to anything. Wentworth was *not* interested in him. Colton had always known it, but he'd hoped one day....

"Why should I care what he does?" Standing, he wiped his sweaty hands on his breeches. "We have to return to the ballroom before anyone notices we're gone."

Bannon frowned and cut his attention to Trouble, who returned the gesture.

Colton took both of their arms and led them toward the mansion. If they didn't believe he was over Wentworth, he couldn't blame them. He wasn't so sure he believed it himself, but he was determined for it to be the truth.

ALONE IN his bed, Colton stared up at the sapphire-blue canopy. It fit his mood. Funny how sometimes the blue could seem peaceful and other times it depressed him. No, he wasn't melancholy. He was disillusioned. He shouldn't be, because as he'd told Bannon and Trouble, Wentworth was nothing to him.

He'd spent the past few years flirting and doing everything he could, short of declaring his love outright. Wentworth always ignored him. Deep down Colton had known there'd never be anything between them, but the scene in the garden had walloped him upside the head. He'd built so many dreams around Wentworth. Silly, childish dreams. All the while the viscount was out living his life with other lovers. Colton had heard the rumors, but seeing the proof made it real.

He teased Tarren unmercifully about his romance novels, but Colton was every bit as fanciful as his younger brother. Wentworth was not going to come to his senses one day and ride up to steal Colton away in some grand romantic gesture. It was time he faced the truth.

After heaving himself out of bed, Colton went to the window and opened the heavy brocade curtains. He peered past the carriage house, pasture, and the rolling fields. The moon was bright tonight, but he still couldn't see Wentworth Park from here. Colton rested his forehead on the cool pane. How many times had he stared out this very window trying to catch a glimpse of the viscount riding? Wentworth came to work every day through that field.

Colton sighed. He had to get on with his life. If his future didn't include Wentworth—and it so obviously didn't—he needed a plan. He was done pining for a man he'd never have, a man who had no interest in him whatsoever.

Something moved closer to the castle, drawing Colton's attention.

His new filly, Apollonia, frolicked in the pasture; her mother grazed a good ten feet away. Since it was a mild evening, the horses had been left out. Apollonia was such a pretty thing. He hadn't meant for her to be conceived and would've chosen a different mare as her mother, but he was pleased. She had the sorrel coloring—technically the Jockey Club considered it red chestnut, but he'd always thought it more of a sorrel—and the spirit of Apollo, her father.

With a clump of grass in her mouth, Apollonia tossed her head and strutted around her mother.

Colton chuckled. "What a show-off you are."

She flung the grass in the air and let it fall before running in a circle and back to her mum. Her antics were not so different from her father's. She might make a fine racehorse one day. Galaxy knew her father would be. Apollo was fast. And he loved to run.

There was nothing like being on Apollo's back and feeling the wind whip past while racing through the countryside. The first couple of times had been frightening, but Apollo was so surefooted and graceful it hadn't taken Colton long to appreciate the experience. Too bad he didn't have his brother Payton's small frame. Colton would love to be a jockey, but he was way too big. He took after both his parents, getting Cony's height and Father's build. Not a bad combination—he was rather pleased with his looks—but not jockey material.

He wasn't bad at polo, and he was fairly certain he could become better with practice, but his heart just wasn't into the game.

Apollonia nipped her mother's leg and dashed away. Her mum raised her head and nickered, admonishing the filly, but Apollonia pranced in a wide circle.

Colton grinned. *My little hoyden.* Even though her mother belonged to Rexley, he had not so much as batted an eye when Colton claimed the foal. It had been assumed by everyone she'd be Colton's. He even helped their head groom, Cecilia Brooks, deliver her. And Colton would train her to a saddle when she was ready. He smiled. The lost feeling he'd carried around since he'd stumbled upon Wentworth and Eugene Collis had vanished. His life was about to take a new direction. It all seemed so clear now. He'd always had an eye for horses. And he was good with them. Breeding racehorses was his calling. It was something he'd love and be smashingly good at.

Giving one last glance in the direction of Wentworth Park, Colton let the curtain fall back in place. "So long, Wentworth."

He climbed back into bed and closed his eyes. He was going to be okay.

Chapter Two

September 14, 4830: Planet Regelence
Townsend Castle in Classige, Pruluce

"Good morning, milord."

Sebastian swung his leg over Maximilian and smiled down at the stableboy. "Good morning, Denny. How are you this fine day?" Hopping to the ground, Sebastian handed over the reins.

"I'm good, milord. Cook made cinnamon buns this morning." Holding the reins in one hand, Denny rubbed Max on the neck with the other.

The big stallion nuzzled his nose into Denny's side in greeting.

Sebastian had been hesitant to turn such a spirited mount as Max over to the boy when he first started working in the stables, but Denny had quickly proven himself to be capable.

"Did she? Well, then, I think I'm going in through the kitchen today." Sebastian patted his horse on the shoulder, marveling at how the sunlight made Max's black coat shine.

Denny chuckled. "Better watch it, milord. Mrs. Studdlefield was in there when I left."

"Thanks for the tip." Sebastian tousled the kid's hair and strode toward the side entrance. With any luck, the housekeeper was long gone from the kitchens and there were still plenty of cinnamon buns.

"My lord, Captain Wentworth!"

With his hand, Sebastian shielded his eyes from the sun.

Miller, one of the uniformed guards, had come around the side of the castle and was heading straight toward him. Sebastian didn't groan, but it was a close call. Jeffers must've alerted the guards to his arrival.

Miller stopped in front of him. "Captain, Johnson and Blake are under the weather, and all the princes have outings planned. We don't have enough men to cover duties. Hendricks accompanied Prince Rexley, Lady Muffin, and her nurse to the modiste early this morning. His Majesty King-Consort Raleigh has an appointment with the haberdasher later this morning, and Prince Aiden is leaving at thirteen hundred hours to have lunch downtown with the admiral, and—"

Cutting the man off with a raised hand, Sebastian changed direction toward the front entrance. So much for cinnamon buns for breakfast. "I'll figure it all out when I get to my office. No one leaves until I get back to you." He supposed he should at least be glad the princes were relating their schedules to the guards now. That had taken Sebastian months to accomplish.

"You want me to stop the royal family?" Miller sounded outraged.

With all the things that had happened lately, Sebastian didn't trust just any guard with the security detail. "Yes, Miller. Is that clear?"

They stopped, and Miller resumed his post. "Yes, sir."

Sebastian opened the door. "Did Admiral Hawkins by any chance take an escort with him when he left for the base this morning?"

"I don't believe so."

Bloody hell. Sebastian nodded, stepped into the foyer, and closed the door behind him. What was he going to have to do to get Nate to take a guard with him? It was an ongoing argument. "Jeffers, is the king available?"

"Yes, my lord. He's awaiting you in his study," the castle butler answered.

"Inform him I'll be there directly." Sebastian headed to the breakfast room. He needed a cup of tea in the worst way. He'd been expecting this problem. So far, with the newly increased security, they'd managed to have enough staff to cover outings, but today their luck had run out. He was already looking into hiring more Royal Guards, but he wanted to speed up the process. "Jeffers, ask His Majesty if he'd like a cup of tea."

Sebastian turned the corner and caught a glimpse of black hair as he collided with a brick wall. "Oof."

There was a grunt and the sound of crumpling paper.

Tears sprang to Sebastian's eyes as his face smashed against a hard skull. Stumbling backward, he grabbed his nose.

"Begging your pardon, my lord." Stepping back, Colton rubbed his forehead. In his hand, he held a bookreader and daily newspaper. He shook out his wrinkled paper and began reading it again.

Sebastian pulled his hand away from his nose. No blood. "Quite all ri—"

Without making eye contact, Colton stepped past Sebastian and continued down the hall.

What in the—

Frowning, Sebastian continued to the breakfast room, then turned to watch Colton leave. Colton never looked back. Why didn't he say good morning and ask how Sebastian was doing? *Dust*, he hadn't even let Sebastian apologize. What was with the bookreader and newspaper? Colton did not read. Unlike his brothers, he seemed to have a real aversion to it. *He's up to something.* Thank galaxy he was Steven and Raleigh's problem.

Sebastian had enough headaches of his own.

He went to the sideboard and poured himself a cup of tea, then added a dash of milk and six cubes of sugar. If he accompanied Aiden downtown, that would leave them only one guard short. Now, who could he call in on their day off?

"Lord Wentworth, His Majesty would love a spot of tea," Jeffers announced.

Taking another cup, Sebastian poured some more. *Wait a minute.* He set the teapot down. What was with Colton calling him "my lord"? Colton always called him Wentworth. Sebastian shook his head, plopped two cubes of sugar into the king's cup, and grabbed two spoons.

When he reached the study, Steven was sitting behind the desk, looking over something on the computer. "I brought you tea, Your Majesty."

The king lifted his head and smiled. "Ah, Wentworth. Thank you."

Sebastian set the cup, saucer, and spoon in front of Steven. He took a seat in one of the two chairs. "You're welcome. I wanted to talk to you about some things, and Jeffers said you were waiting for me."

With pursed lips, Steven stirred his tea. "Yes."

Sebastian sipped from his cup and studied his king. He'd known the man long enough to tell when Steven was hedging.

"You go first."

Sebastian chuckled. "Need more time to plot?"

Blinking up at him, Steven smiled. "Not at all."

Sebastian arched a brow, not sure he believed the professed innocence. "Okay, in that case, we've got to hire more guards. I don't have enough men to cover the family on their daily jaunts without compromising castle security. And speaking of security detail… once again Nate left without an escort."

Steven sighed. "Yes, I know. Nate thinks it will look suspicious if he has a Royal Guard escorting him to the base, but I worry about him. Do you know any IN soldiers stationed here in Classige whom you trust?"

Did he? Sebastian took a drink. He kept in touch with the men who had served under him. Unfortunately they were Regelence Special Regiment, not IN. However, both his two-year term in the IN and his four-year term in the Regelence Navy as RSR—Regelence Navy's special forces—he'd been stationed here in Classige, so he might still know some IN soldiers who were native-born Regelens. "Let me ask around."

Steven nodded. "Good. Perhaps if I can get Nate some names of trustworthy men who are loyal to Regelence, he'll use them. He inherited Admiral Jenkins's aides. I trust Admiral Jenkins's judgment normally, but with our recent… shall we say, questions about the IN's loyalty, I'd much prefer Nate had his own men. He says all the soldiers he trusts are on the *Lady Anna*, and he wouldn't dream of asking them to landlock themselves."

Admiral Jenkins was one of the most exceptional men Sebastian had ever known. If it weren't for him, Sebastian wouldn't be here now, but he wouldn't vouch for the man's old aides, only the man himself. "You know that *is* a good idea. I need more guards, better guards, with all the stuff that has happened. And while I don't know many IN soldiers, I do know several retired Regelence Navy men. I'm going to call some of my old regiment who are retired and see if they would be interested in working for me again."

Steven's eyebrows rose. "Does this mean you're going to hire hunky ex-RSR men for bodyguard duty?"

Sputtering, Sebastian nearly choked on his tea. He set his cup and saucer on the table beside him and gave Steven a mock glare. "Not if you let Raleigh hear you call them hunky. He'll throttle me. I'll find you the oldest and fattest one I can, who is still capable."

Steven stuck his tongue out in a very unkingly gesture. "I wasn't actually talking about for me. Although a comely escort would be appreciated. I was thinking about the boys. And if I get an old fat one, so does Raleigh. It's only fair."

Sebastian laughed. "Galaxy help me." What kind of bumblebroth had he gotten himself into? He could see it now. Raleigh and Steven were going to drive him insane trying to get the most out-of-shape bodyguard assigned to each other. It was baffling what the two of them could make into a game. As for the boys…. "Why does it matter what they look like? Are you matchmaking?"

"Would I do that?" When Sebastian just stared, Steven continued, "I was actually wondering if it was a good idea. You of all people know what it's like to be the object of my boys' attention. I don't want them getting in the way of the men trying to protect them."

"A very good point. I shall find unsuitable men. Perhaps heterosexual or—"

"Portly ones?"

They both laughed.

"I will try. And if I fail, I'll enlist Cook's services to help round them out."

"Except for the one you assign me, of course." Steven smirked. "Offer them triple what they made in the RSR."

"Capital." Sebastian stood and reached for his cup.

"Not so fast. I've a favor to ask of you."

"I knew you were plotting." Returning to his chair, Sebastian kept his cup in hand.

Steven grinned and sipped his tea. "I'm not scheming. I just have an assignment for you."

"Oh?" Sebastian would do anything for his king, and his king knew it, so why the hesitation? It must be something Sebastian wasn't going to like.

"Have you seen Colton this morning?"

"Yes." Sebastian frowned. His nose still hurt from the impact of Colton's hard head. "He was acting peculiar."

Steven's brows pulled together. "How so?"

"He ignored me."

Steven surged forward in his seat, his eyes wide and a smirk on his face. "Upset you, did it?"

"What? No." Sebastian winced. He'd spoken a little too clipped and a bit too fast. "I'm not complaining. Just stating it was unusual."

"Yes, it is. Which means it's worse than I thought. He's determined to do this."

"Do what?"

"He cornered Raleigh and me while we were still abed this morning with plans for a new stable. He's decided to breed racehorses. And given that he's not plaguing you with attention, it means he's thrown himself into this."

That explained Colton's preoccupation this morning. One thing Sebastian had learned over the years was whatever Colton did, he did wholeheartedly. "Steven, one can't just up and decide to start a stud. There is a matter of licensing and regulations. The Jockey Club has to approve the stables. Racehorses have to be licensed and added to the breeding register. A respectable lineage is a must. Any ole horse will not do. Not only will the Jockey Club not license it, but who's going to purchase the offspring of a horse without a pedigree?"

Steven was already nodding and waving his hand dismissively. "I know, I know. And so does Colton. He's going to set up the stables first, then petition for approval."

"It's not at all proper for him to be involved in breeding horses." Young lords did not involve themselves in something so vulgar. They were supposed to pretend they had no knowledge of where foals, or babies for that matter, came from. Even if the foal or baby in question was artificially procreated.

"Brooks will help manage the stables. She's already agreed. Colton will have to work behind the scenes until he's of age or married."

Apparently, Colton had thought of that argument when presenting the scheme to his parents. "Yes, but what about horses? He'll have to purchase some good racing stock."

"He will, but for now he has Apollo. And he's planning on having his new filly trained."

Ah yes, Apollo. He was beautiful and very fast, but—"Apollo is not a racehorse."

"He's the progeny of Beaumont's Beauty. He was listed in the breeding register at birth."

Sebastian blinked. Had he heard correctly? He wasn't a part of the racing set, but he knew enough about racing to recognize the name. "Beaumont's Beauty? The horse that won the Roseglen Stakes four years in a row? That Beaumont's Beauty?" No other horse had won that particular race more than twice except the Earl of Beaumont's horse. Though dead now, the horse was a legend.

Steven dipped his head. "That's the one."

"Bloody hell. Why have you never raced him?"

Shrugging, Steven said, "He's Colton's," as if it explained everything.

"You bought the offspring of Beaumont's Beauty to be ridden about town as an everyday mount?"

"Colton wanted him. You shouldn't be surprised. The boy was riding before he could walk and has always had an exceptional eye for horseflesh."

"Regardless of Apollo's parentage, everyone is going to want to see him race."

"That shouldn't be a problem. However, what I need your help with is Colton. He's determined to find a location on Townsend property today for his stables. You're fairly knowledgeable about horses, and you'll know the best places from a security standpoint. I'd like you to help him."

Sebastian groaned. "I'm already short guards today. Can this not wait until tomorrow?"

"Fine with me." Folding his hands over his stomach, Steven smiled. The smile was downright evil. "But one of us needs to tell him. And by one of us… I mean you."

"Why me?"

"Because he likes you."

SEBASTIAN STEPPED out of the study into the hustle and bustle of the central hallway. Why couldn't Steven just tell the boy no? Sebastian didn't have the time or patience to coddle Colton today. All of the princes were impossible to discourage once they set their minds to something.

Heading toward his office in the basement, Sebastian sighed. He needed his earpiece to connect him privately with Jeffers. Then he'd look into calling some of the off-duty guards. Colton and his pet project were going to have to wait until after castle business was taken care of, or longer if Sebastian could possibly manage it. Spending time with Colton, even to pick a good spot for his business, would likely encourage him to increase his flirtation toward Sebastian. And that was the last thing Sebastian needed. He had enough problems with Eugene.

Sebastian groaned. Eugene's temper tantrum when Sebastian got ready to leave last night was an unmitigated mess. Simply put, Eugene had become too clingy, and Sebastian did not do commitment. Once had been enough for him.

He shook his head. *What a day.* It had only just started, and he was already melancholy.

A footman raced by with a table, followed by another footman carrying a green tablecloth. They set up a table for baked gifts in the foyer, pushing it neatly against the wall and out of the way.

Damn, Sebastian had forgotten about the increase in visitors. The princes always had tons of callers after a ball, which required more security. He was going to need at least four men to come in and cover the two out sick.

Continuing toward the servants' stairwell, the only access to the basement, he contemplated a parting gift for Eugene. Perhaps a gold watch fob or—

"Milord?"

Oh, please don't let that milord be for me. Sebastian kept walking.

"Captain Wentworth. A word, please."

Blast. Stopping only a foot away from freedom, Sebastian gave the stairwell door a frown for good measure and turned. "Yes?"

Miller, the front entrance guard, stood wringing his hands. "There's a problem." He bit his bottom lip and darted a glance around the hallway.

Good galaxy. One would think Sebastian beat his guards, the way the man was acting. Sebastian prayed for patience. "Get on with it, Miller. What's the problem?"

"It's Prince Colton."

"What about him?" A lump formed in Sebastian's throat, and his stomach tied in knots. If anything happened to Colton—

"He's, er.... That is to say—I told him you said *no one* was allowed out without an escort." The guard swallowed hard.

"And?" Irritation replaced fear. Sebastian's head began to throb. He did not have time for any Townsend offspring theatrics. Especially Colton's.

"He said he didn't need an escort to ride on Townsend property and left."

"*Bugger*!" Sebastian clenched his teeth until his jaw ached. Colton thought he was above the rules, did he?

Miller's eyes widened, and a blush stained his cheeks.

Oops. He'd shouted the obscenity rather than thinking it. "Begging your pardon, Miller. Please carry on. I will locate Prince Colton." *And throttle him.* Sebastian changed directions. "Jeffers, have my horse saddled and brought around."

"Right away, Lord Wentworth," Jeffers answered promptly. "Is there anything else?"

"Yes. Are Hingham and Alcock on duty today?"

"No, my lord, they are not."

"Call them in. What other guards are off today?"

"Loring, Delafield, Clarke, and McGregor."

"Call in Loring and Clarke as well. Offer all four of the men double their hourly wages for today."

"Very well, my lord."

"One more thing, Jeffers. In what direction has Prince Colton ridden off in?" The front door opened as Sebastian reached it.

"To the north."

He never even broke stride as he cleared the threshold and made his way toward the stables.

Denny was just bringing Max around when Sebastian reached them.

Swinging up into the saddle, he mumbled a thank-you, then turned Max toward Wentworth Park. His earpiece would come in handy, but he wasn't going to risk Colton's safety to take time and go back for it.

Nearly ten minutes later, Sebastian topped the biggest hill—a mile and a half behind the castle—and found the disobedient brat. "Bloody hell." Sebastian closed his eyes for a second and tried to calm his racing heart. Colton was almost at Wentworth Park. Anything could've happened to him this far out.

Standing on the flat section of land that bordered the wood on the left, Colton hammered a stake into the ground and tied a white piece of cloth around it. He glanced up, spotting Sebastian. Completely ignoring him and without even a flicker of hesitation, Colton mounted Apollo, who had been grazing nearby.

This was the second time within the hour Colton had dismissed him, and Sebastian was beginning to think the incident outside the breakfast room wasn't a fluke. "Your Highness!"

As Sebastian drew to a halt, Colton turned toward him with a look of annoyance on his handsome face.

"What do you think you're doing?" Sebastian demanded.

"It's nothing for you to be concerned about. I'm not leaving the grounds." Colton heeled Apollo and began walking away. Something above his ear sparkled in the sunlight.

"Your safety is my—" Sebastian frowned. What was…? "Is that my earpiece?" He urged Max into stride next to Colton.

One of Colton's ebony brows rose in a perfect imitation of his sire. "You don't have to shout. I'm right beside you."

The superior expression irked Sebastian even further. Not only was Colton planning high-risk ventures and disobeying direct orders when it came to his safety, but now he was stealing? Who the hell was this nearly hostile man, and what had he done with the charming, smiling kid who hung on Sebastian's every word?

Taking a deep breath, Sebastian lowered his voice. "Answer my question."

"I need it to speak with Jeffers. We're taking measurements. Now what do you want, my lord?"

Sebastian gritted his teeth, leaned over in the saddle, and grabbed Apollo's bridle, making Colton pull back on the reins. "I'm out here because *you* disobeyed me." Once Apollo halted, Sebastian stopped Max. "*Did* the front door guard or *did he not* tell you I said *no one* was allowed out without an escort? And why did you think it was acceptable to filch my earpiece from my office?"

Colton sighed and rolled his eyes upward. "He did, but since Jeffers can see me—" He pointed to the com-con. "—and hear me, it doesn't signify. And I didn't *steal* your earpiece. I couldn't find my father's or Cony's, and I didn't think you were going to use yours today because you've been at the castle for over an hour now without retrieving it." Colton swatted at Sebastian's hand, making him release the bridle. "Now if you're finished—"

"I am *not* finished. Do you have any idea how dangerous it is for you to be out here by yourself?"

Colton opened his mouth to speak, but Sebastian cut him off.

"Do *not* give me that nonsense about Jeffers knowing where you are. No one could get to you in time to help you if you were in danger. You'll turn that horse around right now and head back to the castle."

"I'm not a child, and I don't need—"

"Now!" Sebastian's stomach rolled, and his ears rang. He hadn't felt this way since Aiden had been kidnapped last year. If the feeling was more intense this time, it could only be because he was now aware of their enemies.

Colton gaped at him for about two seconds before glaring. "Who do you think you're talking to?"

"Don't mess with me. I'm in charge of your safety, and your parents will stand behind me on this. Get your ars—self back to the castle immediately."

Screwing his face up in anger, Colton turned Apollo, clucked his tongue, and leaned over the horse's neck.

The stallion took off in a canter toward the castle stables.

Sebastian followed at a gallop until he caught up to Colton. He could be angry all he wanted as long as he listened.

When the horses were neck and neck, Sebastian slowed Max to match Apollo's gait. The wind whipped through his hair and over his face. Despite his mood, it actually felt great. The weather was beautiful for riding, and if he didn't have things to do, he'd love to stay out here all day.

Instead of detouring to the gate, Colton urged Apollo faster toward the fence. The way his trousers pulled tight over his arse as he rose in his stirrups to take the jump was quite fetching. As one, horse and rider cleared the obstacle with such grace it made the feat look effortless.

Pulling himself out of his musing, Sebastian put his heels to Max and sailed over a few seconds after Colton.

Colton could lose him if he wanted—Sebastian didn't delude himself about which of them was the better rider—but Colton kept pace with him. It was a pleasure to watch Colton ride. He had a magnificent seat and would've made a hell of a jockey if he wasn't so bloody big. Then again, his wide shoulders and lean hips were quite lovely. Much nicer to look at than a jockey's slender physique.

That definitely wasn't the form of a child. And the way he controlled his mount with such confidence.... Sebastian wanted to groan. This attraction he'd been fighting since Colton turned sixteen could amount to nothing. It was clearly time to find a new paramour. And that man could *not* be Colton Townsend.

As they slowed to a walk, Sebastian got his libido under control. He still needed to talk to Colton about locating a place for his stables, but Sebastian would find some time tomorrow to fit it in.

Denny jogged out of the stables.

Colton swung his leg over and dropped to the ground, handing the boy his reins. "Thank you, Denny."

"My pleasure, Your Highness."

Dismounting, Sebastian gave Denny his reins. "Thank you, Denny." Without waiting for a response, he followed. "Colton."

Colton stopped but did not turn.

"I want your word you will not go riding again without a guard."

With a dip of his head, Colton continued toward the castle.

A twitch started at the corner of Sebastian's right eye. "Turn around," he gritted out between clenched teeth. He was damned sick of this easy dismissal and near hostility.

With his hands balled into fists by his side, Colton swung to face him. Red tinged his cheeks. He stepped right up to Sebastian and stopped less than a foot away so they were eye to eye. When had he gotten so tall?

"What?" Colton demanded.

No one had challenged Sebastian in a long, long time. The action should inspire disdain, but it didn't. Before he'd given it thought, he had Colton by the face.

Prince Pain-in-the-Arse flinched but didn't back down. His sherry eyes blazed as his hands came up between them, seizing Sebastian's lapels.

Galaxy help me. Slamming his mouth down across Colton's pinched lips, Sebastian swept inside with his tongue.

The sweet taste of cinnamon buns and tea competed with a taste uniquely Colton. *Mmm….* Colton was so—not responding. It shouted inexperience and brought Sebastian to his senses, making him realize who he was mauling. He removed his hands from each side of Colton's face and began to step away.

Gripping his morning coat tighter, Colton jerked Sebastian forward and mashed their lips back together.

Sebastian froze.

Colton tentatively touched the tip of his tongue to Sebastian's lips. His hands unwound from the fabric and slid over Sebastian's shoulders, then back to Sebastian's chest.

The uncertainty made Sebastian smile. He opened his mouth and kissed back, letting his tongue tangle with Colton's. Sebastian's pulse pounded in his ears, drowning out everything but the sensual man in his arms. Taking Colton's hands, he placed them around his neck. He slid his arms around the slim waist, pulling them closer together until a nice, thick, hard cock pressed into his hip.

Shoving him, Colton stepped back so quickly he stumbled and nearly landed on his arse.

Bugger. Sebastian dropped his head into his hand, trying to get a grip on himself. He'd lost his bloody mind.

"Here." Colton jerked the earpiece out of his ear, flung it at Sebastian, and took off in a dead run toward the front of the castle.

Sebastian juggled the earpiece for several seconds before he caught it. "Colton, wait."

Colton disappeared around the corner of the gothic mansion.

Bloody hell and imploding planets. What have I done? Glancing back to make certain no one had seen the embrace, Sebastian put the communication device in his ear. Thankfully, Jeffers was silent. Had he not seen the kiss? Not likely, but Sebastian could hope.

He'd really messed up. Galaxy, his stomach hurt. Shame swamped him. One thing was for certain; he was going to have to assign someone else to guard Colton. Colton and his new guard could find several locations for Colton's stables, and Sebastian would ride out on his own and approve them. Yes, that would work.

CHAPTER THREE

"YOUR MAJESTY, Lord Wentworth is—"

"I see, Jeffers. Isn't it wonderful?" Steven beamed at the monitor displaying the front of the castle. Wentworth was kissing Colton. They were perfect for each other, but Steven had never dreamed Sebastian returned Colton's feelings until today. Steven doubted Sebastian even realized what he felt yet, but when Sebastian had complained about Colton ignoring him, Steven had known. It was going to be up to him to push them together and make Sebastian open his eyes. Kissing was a great start. Just look how tenderly Sebastian held Colton's face now. Resting his chin on his hand, Steven sighed.

"I beg your pardon, Your Majesty. Are you saying you do not want anyone to stop them?"

"I do not. From now on let them be. Treat them as you would Aiden and Nate or Raleigh and me. Oh, and this must stay our secret. Where's Raleigh?"

"Still in his meeting, Your Majesty."

"Good, good. Leave him be, Jeffers. That will be all."

Oh no, Wentworth broke the kiss before it really got started. Steven slumped back in his desk chair.

Colton grabbed Sebastian by the lapels and dragged him forward, planting a kiss right on his lips.

Yes! Steven shot forward again.

All Colton's longing came out in the embrace. It was wild and passionate. Wentworth wrapped his arms around Colton's waist.

Steven smiled so big his cheeks hurt, and he pumped his fist in the air. He couldn't have planned this better. Sebastian would take care of Colton and cherish him. He'd handle Colton's stubbornness without breaking his spirit. And Colton had been in love with Sebastian since the day Sebastian started working as head of security. It was quite unheard of for a titled gentleman to work, but with Wentworth's military record and a sterling recommendation from Admiral Jenkins, Steven had hired him. He'd never regretted the decision. The young man had needed something to do after the death of his husband. Over the years, it had become apparent the marriage had not been a happy one. And Wentworth deserved to be happy. Steven had no doubts whatsoever that his son would bring joy into the viscount's life.

Colton shoved Sebastian away and jogged toward the castle. The boy's impetuousness seemed to have diminished in recent years. He was much more responsible. *Blast it all.*

"Never fear, son. I'm going to help you." If anyone understood Colton's infatuation, it was Steven. He'd been the same way when he'd noticed Raleigh for the first time and had stopped at nothing until Raleigh was his. The infatuation hadn't let up yet. Raleigh was even more appealing with age and familiarity.

Humming, Steven pulled up the camera in Wentworth's office. Sebastian wasn't there yet, but Steven could judge Wentworth's response to that kiss better when he appeared.

Someone cleared their throat, jerking Steven out of his thoughts and making his heart stutter.

Raleigh's voice preceded him into the study. "Disregard, Jeffers. I've found him."

Steven tried to glare but doubted he was successful. There was no one he wanted to see more at the moment. "Don't sneak up on me, Raleigh. What're you doing lurking around corners?"

Cocking his head to the side, Raleigh squinted and pulled the door closed behind him. "Trying to figure out what you're up to." Arching a brow, he started around the desk.

Steven leaned back in his chair and crossed his hands over his stomach. Sometimes it was like Raleigh could read his mind. Steven smiled at his consort. "I was just thinking about you, actually."

"I'm not buying it. You were humming. You only hum when you're excelling at something or when you're pleased with yourself. Since I don't recall anything going on in the House of Lords, it must be something personal."

"It was. I told you I was thinking about you and the night we met. Other than that, I was merely looking over my correspondence." He glanced back at the monitor for a split second and nearly flinched. He was about to get caught spying on the soon-to-be couple. "Close the screen, Jeffers, and put the keyboard away."

"Ah-ha." Raleigh hurried around the desk. *Bloody hell.* "You can never keep eye contact when you lie."

He still couldn't? Steven frowned. He was going to have to work harder on that, then. He glanced at the screen again. On the camera, Sebastian had just sat in his desk chair. *Hurry, Jeffers.*

By the time, Raleigh made it to the other side, there was nothing on the screen. It folded into the desk, and the holo keyboard vanished. "Steven…."

Steven grinned up at him. "Yes, dearest?"

"What have you done?"

"I told you, I haven't done anything."

"Jeffers, bring the screen back up immediately."

"Raleigh, you're paranoid." Steven scooted back and pulled Raleigh into his lap. Raleigh's round behind nestled perfectly against Steven's groin. It was enough to bring the memory of this morning back to him. His and Raleigh's encounter had been nice before Colton had barged in with his plans for a racing stud. Sometimes having children was a nuisance. Even more of a reason to see them all happily settled.

The screen came back out of the desk as Steven wrapped his arms around Raleigh's waist. The smell of chocolate and mint flooded Steven's senses. Raleigh's skin appeared so smooth and biteable beneath his ear. Steven traced his tongue up the side of Raleigh's neck and found Raleigh's earlobe with his lips.

Raleigh shivered but wasn't deterred from his study of the screen. The man was like a dog with a bone when he'd made up his mind. He was right in this instance. Steven *was* matchmaking, but still the legendary persistence was annoying. Actually, Raleigh's penchant for always being right was just as vexing. Not that he wanted Raleigh to be anywhere else, but Steven couldn't get away with anything when he was around.

The monitor showed Sebastian leaning back in his chair with his hands over his face. The view changed abruptly to the boys' corridor. Trouble and Tarren were racing down the hall. What were they doing? They skidded to a halt beside Colton's door. The next camera shot showed

Colton walking up the stairs toward the hall that Trouble and Tarren had just sped down.

Raleigh pointed at the screen. "What is this? It's not correspondence."

"I was corresponding with Jeffers about camera angles."

Turning his head, Raleigh narrowed his eyes at Steven.

"What?"

"You're trying to tell me you were writing letters to Jeffers?"

If he told Raleigh what he was up to, Raleigh would object and then forbid him to continue. "I meant I was conversing with him."

Raleigh rolled his eyes upward. "If there was any justice in the world, you'd look like a mad scientist rather than a fallen angel."

Raleigh thought he looked like an angel? "I'm not doing anything. I was making certain the security system is running smoothly."

"One does not refer to *that* as correspondence." Raleigh's blasted brow arched.

Good galaxy, Steven's skin prickled under the scrutiny. "One does when one—"

Raleigh's other brow joined the first one.

"Stop it. I'm innocent, I tell you. I was in here daydreaming about you." Steven pulled him close until Raleigh's back rested against his chest. Breathing softly in Raleigh's ear, Steven whispered, "Be nice to me, Cony."

Raleigh sagged into his embrace, and his weight pressed against Steven's cock.

Gads, that felt nice. A tingle raced through Steven, traveling from his neck down to his toes. "How'd your meeting go?"

"It ran over."

"So I see. What do you have planned now? You don't have enough time to make it to your appointment at the haberdashers." He kissed Raleigh's neck.

"I love that you keep track of my appointments as well as your own." Raleigh dropped his head onto Steven's shoulder.

A chuckle escaped Steven. He'd learned a long time ago that Raleigh was a romantic whether he wanted to believe it or not. He kissed Raleigh's cheek. "Don't you always know where I am?"

"Yes. Or at least where you *should* be and what you *should* be doing."

Steven rolled his eyes, thankful his consort couldn't see it. That was not a line of thinking he wanted Raleigh following. It would lead right back to why he was watching Colton and Sebastian. "Since you know where I am, and I know where you are, what do you have planned now?"

"I don't have anything until Jeremy's fencing lesson this afternoon."

"I wonder what Trouble's argument to get out of the lesson will be this time."

"Mmmm…." Raleigh grinned and tilted his head, giving his husband better access. "I don't know. Last time he told me he preferred a knife to a sword, and it was much better because no one expected it."

The scamp had also snuck up on Raleigh and put a blade to his throat to prove his point. Raleigh had planted Jeremy on his arse and slapped him across the cheek with the flat side of his sword before Steven could yell at the boy. Jeremy definitely had Marcus's—his biological father's—ruthlessness.

"I'm betting on a fragger today. Let's hope he doesn't shoot me." Raleigh ran his palms over Steven's thighs.

His leg muscles jumped, and an appreciative sound rumbled out. "He'd better not." Sliding his hand down Raleigh's chest, Steven caressed his stomach for a few moments before drifting lower. "Get Rexley to take over for you today. Trouble wouldn't dare shoot Rexley. Then you can spend the rest of the day with me. We can finish what Colton interrupted this morning."

"What were you really doing when I came in?" Raleigh tried to sit up, but Steven caught him.

Groaning, Steven left one arm around Raleigh's chest and trailed the other back down. He fumbled with Raleigh's buttons as he kissed and nuzzled his way under Raleigh's cravat. "Are we back to that?"

"Yes."

Steven ceased working his hand inside the placket of Raleigh's trousers. "Colton went riding this morning without a guard."

After a few seconds, Raleigh stood up, turned, and sat on the edge of the desk facing Steven. "And? Stop hedging. Colton goes riding every day without a guard. Jeffers watches him. How's today different?"

"Wentworth said no one was allowed out without a guard."

"Like I said, Colton goes every day. This isn't news to Wentworth or anyone else."

"Exactly." Steven scooted his chair forward and placed his hands on Raleigh's knees. His gaze strayed toward Raleigh's groin before he made eye contact. Unfortunately he wasn't going to get ahold of that cock until he gave Raleigh an answer. "It's not safe. Besides, Colton was nearly at Wentworth Park, according to Jeffers."

"That isn't good, but it still doesn't explain your mood. Are you matchmaking again?"

Blast! "Moi?" Steven clutched his hand to his chest. "Don't be ridiculous, Co—"

"Don't you Cony me. You cease and desist right this instant. Those two would be a terrible match, and Colton doesn't need any encouragement in that direction. Galaxy knows he plagues Wentworth enough."

"I disagree. I think they'd be perfect together. And I think—"

"Steven Rexley Phillipe Edward Townsend."

"Did you just use my entire name?"

Raleigh's lip twitched. "I mean it. Whatever it is you have planned, you better unplan."

Dropping his hand behind his chair back, Steven crossed his fingers. "I haven't planned anything."

"Then don't. Wentworth has his hands full with the guards. He can't be Colton's personal escort. Besides, throwing him into Colton's company is a recipe for disaster. I like Wentworth as much as you do, but you know what his reputation is like. Why, just last week he was caught in a compromising position with Madison at the opera. And by Madison's consort, no less."

"Madison is a wanton. He'll fuck anything in trousers."

"Steven!"

"Well… it's true. And besides, Wentworth is the only one capable of keeping up with Colton on horseback." Steven's gaze drifted back down, and his hands returned to Raleigh's buttons. He needed to end this conversation.

Raleigh lifted his spouse's chin with his finger. "No one can get onto our property without Jeffers knowing."

One button came undone. "What about when he leaves our property?" Another button loosened.

"Then someone besides Wentworth will watch him. And I'm fairly certain Wentworth would prefer it that way as well." Raleigh batted at Steven's hand, trying to make his point. "Are you listening to me?"

Standing, Steven slipped his hand into Raleigh's trousers and pushed his smallclothes out of the way. "I always listen to you, love." He bussed Raleigh on the lips as he wrapped his hand firmly around Raleigh's cock.

"Steven—"

Steven seized his consort's mouth. With one hand squeezing Raleigh and the other firmly on the back of Raleigh's neck, Steven eased him back onto the desk.

"Umf." Raleigh tapped him on the arm, but Steven ignored him. Raleigh really did underestimate his tenacity sometimes. *Thank galaxy.*

Planting one knee on the desk, Steven levered himself next to Raleigh and leaned over him. His thumb brushed just under the crown of Raleigh's cock as the warmth of Raleigh's body seeped through Steven's clothing. Was there anything more wonderful than the feel of this man against him? If there was, Steven had never felt it.

"Ahh…."

Steven laved the inside of Raleigh's mouth and nibbled at his bottom lip until finally Raleigh wrapped his arms around Steven's neck.

Raleigh did some nibbling of his own. Thrusting his hips into Steven's hand, Raleigh trailed his lips over Steven's jaw and down his neck. Raleigh jerked the neckcloth loose and tossed it away, then grazed his teeth over Steven's skin. He fumbled with the placket on Steven's trousers and grabbed Steven's cock through his smallclothes.

"Ssss…." Steven never faltered in stroking Raleigh.

The dazed stare on Raleigh's face was a beautiful thing to behold. If his complete abandon didn't take Steven right over the edge of desire, his warm hand would. It had Steven's every nerve alive and sizzling with pleasure, and Raleigh hadn't even touched his bare skin.

"Steven," Raleigh mumbled against his neck. "Let's retire to the bedroom and finish this there." He managed to gain entrance into Steven's smallclothes and gripped a handful of cock.

Closing his eyes and trying to think of anything but his consort's ministrations, Steven arched his neck. "In a moment. We should finish this here and start all over upstairs." Oh yes, that sounded nice. It would more than make up for this morning's interruption. He squeezed his Cony's prick and—

A chuckle sounded at the door.

Steven froze.

Raleigh pulled his lips away from Steven's neck. "What—"

Dalton Fairfax, their only nephew, stood just inside the office. He wore his IN casual uniform and a smirk on his handsome face. Apparently he'd received their invitation to stay at the castle on his fortnight leave. Still smiling, he removed his cover, revealing sandy-blond hair, and dropped the hat to his side.

Raleigh turned his head, trying to see. "Bloody hell. Is that Ashbourne? All I can see is the lieutenant insignia on his coat."

"It's Lord Demon all right, and he has despicable timing." If Steven didn't adore the boy as much as Raleigh did, he'd throttle him.

Dalton chuckled. "And they say I'm insatiable."

Steven sighed. At least he'd derailed Raleigh's questioning.

LEANING AGAINST his closed bedroom door, Colton ran his fingers through his hair and let out the breath he'd been holding. What had just happened? He touched his lips. His mouth was tingly and swollen. Not to mention very warm and sensitive. *Dust.* He'd actually kissed Wentworth. No, Wentworth had kissed him.

Colton's stomach flip-flopped. He'd wanted that kind of attention from Wentworth for as long as he could remember, and now that it had happened, he had no idea how to feel about it.

He placed his quivering hand against his chest, and his heart thudded under his palm. Why now? Why after he'd given up hope of one day being with the man?

Blowing out a breath, he shoved away from the door and headed toward his bedroom window.

"Are you okay?"

"Ack." Colton jumped and whirled to face the intruder.

Trouble stood just inside the door connecting Colton's bedroom to his sitting room. Behind him, Colton's youngest brother, Tarren, sat forward on the loveseat, with his forearms resting on his knees. Both of them stared expectantly at Colton.

Heaving a sigh, Colton trudged to the sitting room. "I'm fine. Why wouldn't I be? What're the two of you doing in here?"

Trouble moved aside to let Colton pass, then planted himself on the loveseat next to Tarren. "I overheard Jeffers tell Steven you kissed Wentworth."

Splendid. Colton dropped to the damask chair opposite them, landing with a bounce. He was so dead.

"How was it?" Tarren asked with a grin. "Did the earth move? Did you feel as though your world was now complete? Like it was the moment you'd been born for?"

Groaning, Trouble shoved Tarren and looked back at Colton. "Steven told Jeffers to keep quiet and pretend it didn't happen. I'm guessing that means he isn't mad."

"He did what?" Why would Father do that? Why wouldn't he confront Colton? *Oh no.* "He must be waiting to tell Cony." Colton's head swam, and his chest constricted. *There goes opening a racing stud.* "Father and Cony are going to lock me up and throw away the key. I'll be confined to my room for the rest of my life all because of one lousy kiss."

"It was lousy?" Tarren frowned. "Gilbert Montrose said having someone's tongue in your mouth is kind of disgusting. He kissed Fielding, but Fielding is only in his first season. He probably didn't know how to kiss any more than Gilbert did. But Wentworth is an expert. Lord Tristian said Percy Edmonstone said when Wentworth kisses you it's like being struck by lightning and floating all at the same time." With a dreamy smile, Tarren sighed, flopped backward, and rolled his head toward the ceiling.

Trouble glared at Tarren. "Would you stop?"

"Whaaat?" Raising his hands, Tarren shrugged.

Glaring harder, Trouble growled, then returned his attention to Colton. "Forget being held prisoner, and forget—" He cut his gaze toward Tarren. "—Wentworth's apparent skill. I thought you gave up on Wentworth. What happened?"

"I did give up on him." Could Colton's life get any more confusing?

Tarren gasped. "But that's terrible. He's the love of your life."

Resting his elbows on his thighs, Trouble steepled his fingers. "Then why did you kiss him?"

"He kissed me." And it had stunned Colton so thoroughly he'd frozen. He'd made a complete ninny of himself. Wentworth probably thought he'd never been kissed before. Which couldn't be further from the truth. Colton had been kissed at least three times just last season.

You've never been kissed like that, you buffoon.

Tarren leaned forward again. "Did he wrap you in his arms and dip you backward? Did he use his tongue? Was it repulsive? How did—"

Colton and Trouble glowered at him. Tarren's sunny, fairy-tale outlook wasn't helping.

Tarren threw his hands up again and let them fall. "Very well. I'll be quiet."

Turning his attention back to Colton, Trouble cocked his head. "He actually initiated it? Why?"

"I wish I knew." Unable to bear the scrutiny, Colton stood. He still couldn't believe he'd kissed Wentworth. He reached toward his lips again but caught Trouble's gaze and dropped his hand. He'd practically thrown himself at Wentworth.

Colton paced to the end of the room. He hadn't given it much thought. When Wentworth had tried to end the kiss, Colton had just reacted. He'd waited forever for any intimacy with Wentworth, and he'd lost his head. Damn it. He didn't want to still be in love with the blasted man.

"What happened before he kissed you?"

"He lectured me about leaving the castle." Colton flicked open the curtains and leaned against the wall next to it. His stupid hands were still trembling. "He was trying to punish me." Staring out the window, not really seeing anything, he flattened his hands against the glass. "He wanted to scare me and get my attention."

"Are you sure?" Trouble leaned against the wall on the opposite side of the window. When had he moved?

Colton dropped his hands, turning to face Trouble. Why else would Wentworth suddenly show an interest in Colton? "It's the only thing that makes sense." It didn't help his ego any, but.... "It was just a way to show me the dangers awaiting me if I go out without a guard." He snorted and shook his head. The lesson had been splendidly successful because he would not disobey Wentworth again. That kiss had shown him all too well that he was way out of Wentworth's league. How did one kiss using their tongue? It certainly wasn't abhorrent, but was there a proper way?

Frowning, Trouble rested his head against the windowpane. His pale brows drew together as he stared at something below.

"It doesn't matter anyway. I don't want anything to do with him." Wentworth had not acted out of passion, and Colton was done setting himself up for heartache. And that's what hurt the most. He shouldn't still be this affected after the incident. It had shaken his resolve. "If Father doesn't skewer me with a sword, I'll count myself lucky to have escaped the king of rakes unscathed and go on with my life."

Trouble's eyes widened.

Colton stared at him, daring Trouble to contradict him. Thankfully he didn't. "Aren't you supposed to be fencing with Cony or something?"

Groaning, Trouble rolled his forehead against the glass, leaving a smudge. "I'm hiding out. I don't want to fence with him. He's driving me crazy. I swear the man is perfect at everything he does and makes sure I know it." He turned his head, looking Colton right in the eye. "He's better-looking, he's faster, he's stronger, he's—"

"Annoying." Colton nodded. Trouble was afraid of making a fool of himself in front of Cony. It had become apparent almost immediately how much Trouble respected Cony. "Yes, I know. My sire doesn't know how to fail. His shoes aren't going to be easy to fill, but—"

Trouble blanched.

Colton shrugged. "Look on the bright side. When you take over Regelence's military, you'll have more experience than Cony did when he first took it over."

Scrunching up his nose, Trouble blinked. "Huh?"

"It's one of Cony's duties as king-consort. Didn't you know?" Tarren joined them at the window.

Trouble shook his head. "I thought he didn't work."

"He doesn't. Being military advisor is more of a duty than a job," Tarren said.

The sitting room door opened. "Knock, knock."

Colton, Trouble, and Tarren turned from the window at the same time.

Speaking of military.... A sandy-blond head rounded the doorjamb, followed by the rest of Dalton Fairfax's lean frame encased in an IN uniform. "Can I come in?"

"Demon!" Tarren bounded across the room and launched himself at their cousin.

Dalton caught him, pounding him on the back. "'Ello, Terror."

"Who's that?" Trouble whispered.

Smiling, Colton grabbed Trouble's arm and dragged him forward. "Our favorite cousin."

"I'm your only cousin." Dalton hugged Colton and gave his attention to Trouble. "You must be Aiden's stepson." Dalton shook his head and grinned.

"Jeremy Hawkins." Trouble extended his hand to shake, but Dalton turned Trouble's hand palm down and kissed the back of it instead.

"Winstol."

Trouble groaned. "How'd you know about the blasted title?"

Releasing Trouble's hand, Dalton laughed. "Oh, you are a scamp. I know because Rexley has written me every week since I went into the IN."

"Rexley wrote about me?"

"Yes. Among other things, and I'm very happy to finally make your acquaintance." Dalton's eyes sparkled with good humor.

Sitting on the edge of the table, Colton explained, "Rexley has managed Ashbourne for the past two years, so he keeps in constant contact with Dalton."

Dalton's mouth dropped open. "You know about that?"

"Everyone knows about that." Tarren sat down on the sofa.

Trouble tugged at his cravat. "You have a title and an estate too?"

"Yes. Well, as Ravensburg's heir, it's a curtesy title, but he made me oversee management of Ashbourne, assuming I'd foul it up so he could teach me a lesson, but I showed him." With a grin, Dalton tossed his cover on the table beside Colton. "And Rexley would keep in touch with me even if he wasn't managing Ashbourne."

Trouble's eyes widened every time someone mentioned his fiancé. It made Colton feel warm inside. He didn't understand the relationship, because Rexley was Trouble's complete opposite, but it was endearing. Rexley deserved to have someone adore him.

All ears, Trouble sat next to Tarren and leaned forward.

Colton chuckled. He wasn't sure Dalton had really shown Ravensburg anything, since technically Rexley was the one managing Ashbourne, but he decided not to voice his opinion. "Rexley and Dalton have always been very close. Probably because they're only a few months apart in age." It was an even odder alliance than Trouble and Rexley. Dalton thrived on being scandalous.

"Wait." Trouble blinked. "I thought lords didn't serve in the military."

"Some do. But Dalton did it to irritate his father. Cony's brother is a real stuffed shirt," Tarren said.

Sighing, Dalton shook his head. "I didn't do it to tweak Ravensburg's nose. Well, not entirely. I've always wanted to be a Regelence Navy officer."

"Their uniforms are so romantic. In my favorite story, one of the heroes is a captain in the Regelence Navy. The other hero is the son of a viscount, and they meet on the street corner waiting for a hackney. It starts raining and—"

"When are you going into the Regelence Navy?" Colton asked Dalton.

Tarren kicked Colton in the shin. "I was talking."

Pain radiated up Colton's leg. "Ow. You were rambling about fake people as usual." He rubbed his calf and returned his attention to their cousin. Just wait until Tarren wasn't expecting it….

Dalton smirked and looked from Tarren to Colton. "After I return from leave, I report back to the IN base on Lerdra to start my specialized training. Then next year, I'll come back to the Regelence Navy base here in Classige and officially become a part of the Regelence Navy as RSR."

"So you'll be back home soon?" Tarren propped his feet on the table, next to Colton's hip, and laced his fingers behind his head.

Dalton nodded. "But for now, I have a whole fortnight in which I get to visit my family and hide from Ravensburg."

Ravensburg was a real bore, but he never came to town before Parliament started. "Ah, you haven't procured a town house yet." Colton shoved Tarren's feet.

They hit the floor with a thud, and Tarren sat up, glaring.

Dalton put his foot on the table next to Colton and rested his arms across his raised thigh. "No. I figured I'd wait till I come home for good, but while I'm here, I do want to look for a horse. Which is why I came looking for you, cousin."

"Wish I could have a town house of my own." Trouble pouted and hooked a finger in his cravat, pulling it out from his neck.

Dalton was unmarried and underage by Regelence law—he just turned twenty-one years old—but he did what he wanted regardless of the rules of propriety. Ravensburg couldn't control him, and Cony and Father didn't try… much. Nate, however, *could* keep Trouble in line, so he would not be getting a town house.

Colton leaned back on his hands and looked up at Dalton. "You cannot have my horse. Sorry."

Dalton's grin widened. "I want you to help me pick one. I heard from Gareth Fareweather that Rycroft will have a particularly fetching gelding up for auction at Tattersalls tomorrow. I'd appreciate your opinion."

How splendid was it that the whole family came to him on matters involving horses? It reaffirmed that he'd made the right career choice.

Colton smiled. "Wait. You know Gareth Fareweather?" Fareweather's father owned one of the best racing studs in Pruluce. Fareweather would be a wonderful source of information, and he knew everyone who was anyone in the racing world. This could be Colton's in. What if he could gain acceptance before he actually finished building his stables?

"Yes. Why?"

"You've got to introduce me to him."

Dalton's brow furrowed. "I'm not sure that's a good idea. He's not the sort you should be acquainted with."

Great. Now Dalton decided to have morals? A few months before Dalton joined the Navy, he had participated in a duel over a tryst with a married man.

"I'm acquainted with you."

"That's different. We're kin. Fareweather is a gambler, and he drinks entirely too much. I cannot in good conscience allow you to be in the company of a man of his ilk."

A smile tugged at Tarren's lips. "You could always teach us about men of that ilk."

Trouble waggled his eyebrows. "I'm in. I love learning about men of *that ilk*. The *Lady Anna* was full of them."

Dalton groaned. "No. All three of you need to stay away from men like that." He pointed at Trouble. "Not only would Rexley throttle me, but you've no need of the information because Rexley is most definitely not a rake." He gave Colton and Tarren a pointed look. "Uncle Raleigh and Uncle Steven would disown me." Dalton bobbed his head for emphasis to show he meant business.

Colton rolled his eyes at the perfidy of it all. "You've a warped sense of ethics, cousin. And if you want my help choosing a mount, you have to introduce me to Fareweather."

"Nice," Trouble mumbled. He coughed into his hand but couldn't disguise the mirth.

Dalton sighed. "I do admire a man willing to blackmail to get what he wants. Why's this so important to you?"

"I'm going to start a racing stud. I need connections."

"Uncle Raleigh and Uncle Steven are okay with this?"

Colton nodded. "They gave me their blessing this morning."

"Very well. I'll make the introductions at the ball tonight. But…." He straightened and held up a finger. "You must promise me not to be alone with Fareweather or any of his friends."

Colton did his best to rein in his excitement. "I promise."

"And you'll go with me to Tattersalls on the morrow," Dalton affirmed.

"I will."

"What if one of us needed to know about rakes?" Tarren smiled sweetly.

Standing, Dalton picked up his cover and looked from one to the other, then at Tarren. "How so?"

"If say"—Tarren cut his gaze to Colton and smiled bigger—"one of us was being pursued by a rakehell, would you give us lessons then?"

Oh grand. Seeing exactly where this was going, Colton glared at his younger brother. *Don't you dare say anything about that stupid kiss.* He kicked his sibling in the shin. "Oops. Foot slipped."

"Dust for brains." Tarren clutched his leg, pulling it up onto the sofa. "I just wanted to know for research."

"For what?" Trouble blurted. "Are you planning on being courted by a rogue?"

"Maybe." Rubbing his leg, Tarren pooched out his bottom lip.

Dalton held up his hands in surrender. "I'm not telling you anything." To Colton he said, "I'm going with all of you tonight to the Hamptons' ball. Fareweather should be there." Shaking his head and chuckling, Dalton left the room.

That had worked out splendidly, except…. Colton pointed at Tarren. "No telling about the kiss. It's over, and I want to forget it. It didn't mean anything."

"Or what?" Tarren dropped his foot to the floor.

Trouble came to his rescue. "Or he'll tell you brought another puppy into the house."

"That's no fair. I wasn't going to tell." Tarren crossed his arms over his chest. "Besides, are you sure he only kissed you to distract you? It doesn't sound like something he'd do. I read this romance last month where the hero had been pining away for the other hero for years, and one day—wham—he just kissed him, like—"

Groaning, Colton held up a hand. He'd thought they were past this. "Sebastian Hastings is not pining away for me. And romance novels are *not* real."

"Yes." Tarren held up a finger. "But what if…?"

Trouble scooted closer to the edge of the sofa until his knees were touching Colton's. "I hate to say this, but suppose Tarren is right? Maybe you shouldn't give up on Wentworth so fast."

Colton sputtered and clamped his mouth shut. It didn't matter. Any of it. He had his horses and his plans. If he never had Sebastian Hastings, well, he could live with that. And sooner or later, if he repeated it enough, his heart might start to believe it too.

Chapter Four

The Silver Swan gaming hell, downtown Classige, Pruluce

Bugger. He was late.

Sebastian snapped his pocket watch shut and crammed it back into the tiny pocket on his waistcoat. With any luck, Rourke would still be waiting for him. He was supposed to meet his friend at half past nine. It was already half past ten. He'd gotten caught up at the castle working on tomorrow's schedule. Today had started out badly and only gotten worse.

He glanced up at the gaming hell sign swinging back and forth on its chains as he walked past it. The Silver Swan was such an innocuous name for a place swarming in sin. No one would guess the debauchery going on inside the unobtrusive redbrick building. The place had a bit of everything.

Nodding to Billy, the doorman, Sebastian hurried up the stoop. The door opened, and the warm musty smell of bodies, whiskey, and cigar smoke drifted outside. A quiet hum of voices mixed with a melodious strain of some classical piece of music. Raucous laughter rang out. Ah, the scents and sounds of decadence. Sebastian smiled and stepped inside. Maybe all of today wouldn't be a bust.

The club was comfortable and elegant with jewel tones and dark woods, catering to the ton, high-ranking military officers, and the rich. There was gaming, drinking, and sex. The patrons consisted of men and women. Several of the club's courtesans mingled among the crowd, and upstairs, private rooms were available to let. This was a place where fortunes were won and lost, marriages made and dissolved, and alliances forged either over drinks or through blackmail. It was a place Sebastian felt at home in.

Taking a deep breath, he tilted his head side to side, exhaled, then unfisted his hands and relaxed his shoulders. He glanced toward the dealer-run gaming tables and recognized some of the players. A couple of seats stood empty at the hazard table, but he'd always preferred a quiet game among peers.

Sebastian caught a passing footman and ordered a drink, then headed toward the back of the club where the billiard tables were located. If Rourke was still here, he'd be in the back. That was where he and Sebastian went when they came to this particular haunt.

Leaving the carpeted area, he pushed aside heavy velvet curtains leading into the private section for members only.

The lights were dimmer, and the smoke hung in the air, giving it a sultry appeal. The sounds from the public room were muted, replaced with balls clacking together and more distinct voices rather than a continuous drone.

As he approached the back, something hit him in the thigh and thudded to the hardwood floor behind him. It hadn't hurt really, but he'd certainly felt it. Turning, Sebastian looked down.

A white cue ball rolled toward the dark green curtains he'd just come through.

He scooped up the ball and nearly landed on his arse when someone plowed him over. "Bloody he—" Sebastian's curse froze in his throat as he saw the imbecile who had bumped into him. Viscount Leith.

Their paths had not crossed much in the past twenty years, not since the day of Sebastian's mother's funeral. Even after all these years, the viscount rubbed Sebastian the wrong way.

"Beg your—" Leith looked up finally, laying eyes on Sebastian. His piercing midnight eyes widened. "Sebastian?" He touched his forehead for a brief moment and dropped his hand.

"Leith." Sebastian stepped around the viscount and rolled his head on his shoulders. He was not going to let that arse ruin his evening. He felt the weight of Leith's stare on his back, but Sebastian kept going. Their history didn't lend itself to politeness, or even acknowledgment, for that matter. Bugger, his heart felt as though it were going to pound out of his chest.

There were six tables from left to right, all surrounded by plush fabric sofas and winged chairs. And all occupied. The weight of Leith's stare pushed against his back, or so he imagined, but he would not turn to see if the man was still there.

Barnaby Plume, Leith's heir, stormed past Sebastian toward the curtain, but Sebastian didn't turn around.

A familiar, tall gangly man waved from the fourth table. "Oh, I say, sorry about the cue ball, Wentworth." Eastbrooke raised his cue stick upright and lifted his lips in a crooked smile. "Would you like to join us?"

Us consisted of Viscount Eastbrooke, the Earl of Ardingley, and Lord Thaddeus. Eastbrooke and Ardingley belonged to several of the same clubs as Sebastian. Lord Thaddeus Deveroux, the youngest son of the Duke of Moxborough, had partied with Sebastian on several occasions, and they'd sparred in the boxing ring once or twice. Deveroux was a nice fellow and a damned good boxer. They would not have been Sebastian's first choice of companions, but under the circumstances, he hurried to join them.

To the left of Eastbrooke, at the side pocket of the billiard table, two handsome half-dressed courtesans were trying to devour each other. One was blond and the other brunet. The blond held the brunet's leg hiked up on his hip and had a handful of hair. What a lovely picture they made.

Another dark-headed courtesan perched on Deveroux's lap. His hair was darker than the other brunet's, and he too was shirtless.

Sebastian tossed the ball to Eastbrooke. "I'm looking for Knighton. Have you seen him?" It was still odd to think of Rourke as Knighton. He'd only been the younger son of a duke when they were in the RSR together.

Deveroux trailed a hand over the backside of the man in his lap. "He was here earlier. Said something about a rout tonight."

Blast. It figured. Rourke had never been known for his patience.

"How do you know Leith?" Ardingley asked. "I didn't think you attended Parliament. With the exception of tonight, the House of Lords is the only place I've ever seen the man."

Damnation. Sebastian did not want to think about his past, much less discuss it. He shrugged. "I don't. My mother used to work for Leith." Sebastian barely contained a snort.

"Right, right. Forgot you were born a commoner." There was no censure in Ardingley's tone, only realization of a fact. He was a good sort.

Sebastian dipped his head in thanks.

"You missed the excitement. Leith just had it out with his son." Deveroux smirked. "Put on quite a show, they did."

"Sorry I missed it," Sebastian mumbled. Actually, he wished he'd missed *all* of it.

The two courtesans standing began to topple over onto the table, and Ardingley caught them. "None of that, now. It'll mess up the game." With a stick in one hand and the brunet's arm in the other, Ardingley chuckled.

"We're playing a game of distraction." Eastbrooke rounded the table. "Come join us."

Sebastian really should go, but what the hell. He needed to unwind after his encounter with the man who had put him on the streets. "Distraction?"

Deveroux chuckled. It was a lazy, silky sound that went perfectly with his dark good looks. "Let's show him," he whispered to the man on his lap.

The pretty brunet smiled and stood up.

To Ardingley, Deveroux said, "I believe it's your turn, old man."

Ardingley groaned and narrowed his eyes at the brunet. He trudged over to Eastbrooke and snatched the ball from him.

The brunet winked and glanced back at Deveroux.

Deveroux nodded. "Go ahead, Peregrine." He grinned at Wentworth. "Come have a seat. You'll like this game."

Sebastian sat next to Deveroux on the sofa, crossed one foot over his thigh, and sipped his brandy. There was only one party tonight, so he'd catch up with Rourke later.

"You two—Hector, Albie—come over here," Deveroux commanded of the other two courtesans.

Like obedient puppies, they bounded to the sofa. The brunet kneeled beside Deveroux and nuzzled the outside of his thigh. The blond stopped in front of Sebastian. "May I sit with you, my lord?"

Sebastian held out his hand toward the other side of the sofa.

The blond smiled and scooted in close to Sebastian's side. "I'm Hector." He trailed a finger down the front of Sebastian's cravat. Peering up from under the fall of bangs and ridiculously long lashes, Hector licked his lips. He was petite. What some would call boyish, but he appeared to be in his midtwenties. His straight wheat-colored hair fell over his eyes. The coy act worked with his size. It screamed *coddle me*. Maybe Sebastian was jaded, but his last three paramours had perfected that look.

Sebastian uncrossed his legs and pulled Hector closer.

Chuckling, Hector climbed onto Sebastian's lap. He continued to finger Sebastian's cravat and waistcoat. He fit nicely with his face on an even level with Sebastian's, but something was wrong. There was no frisson of excitement. No lust whatsoever.

"Wentworth, watch this." Eastbrooke came over and leaned against the side of the sofa with his stick out to his side. He dipped his head toward Ardingley. "A hundred pounds says you miss this shot."

As Hector blew in Sebastian's ear, he rubbed his palm softly over Sebastian's testicles.

Sebastian's shoulders tensed, and the same irritability he'd felt most of the day seeped back into him. He caught Hector's hand and moved it to his chest. "Watch."

"Oh, I know this game, my lord." Hector pouted. The simpering prickled at Sebastian. What was wrong with him? He had a handsome, experienced, and willing partner on his lap, but he wasn't the least bit interested.

Peregrine slinked around Ardingley, dragging his hands all over the earl. Peregrine was a beautiful man. He was tall, lean, and muscled. He wound himself around the earl like a vine and leaned against the table next to Ardingley. The black trousers pulled taut across his backside, emphasizing his thickly muscled legs and buttocks. He palmed his crotch and glanced up at Ardingley.

Sebastian stared, riveted. Why did this young man spark his interest when the willing, eager man on his lap did not?

Ardingley cleared his throat, blinked, and focused. "You're going to lose, Eastbrooke."

Purring, Peregrine unfastened his trousers and slid his hand inside. He tilted his head back and groaned as his hand moved up and down on his cock. When he turned his head toward the sofa, his gaze was unfocused.

Ardingley moaned.

Blinking, Peregrine seemed to snap out of his daze. The corner of his mouth twitched, and his eyes sparkled. The expression was familiar.

It made Sebastian ache. His stomach stirred with the first signs of arousal. Where had he seen that expression? He was certain he'd never met the young courtesan before, but—Sebastian gasped. Peregrine resembled Colton. Their size, frame, hairstyles, and coloring were similar.

Ignoring Hector's inquisitive glance, Sebastian closed his eyes. The image of Peregrine was replaced with Colton. Colton standing there stroking his cock with that same look of triumph. He'd seen it on the prince's face many times throughout the years. Sebastian's balls tightened, and his cock hardened. *Bloody hell.*

Crack.

Sebastian snapped his eyes open.

The earl straightened up from taking his shot. The ball dropped into the pocket, and he pointed his cue at Eastbrooke. "You owe me a hundred pounds."

"Take your next shot, Ardingley. If you make this one, I'll give you a hundred pounds too." Deveroux leaned forward and whispered something to the courtesan at his feet. "If you don't, you owe me the hundred you just won from Eastbrooke and another hundred on top of that."

"Deal." The earl hurried to line up his shot as Colton—no, not Colton, Peregrine—continued his slow seduction.

"Ah-ah. None of that. You know the rules. Go, Albie, tell Peregrine what I have in mind." Deveroux nudged the brown-headed man's shoulder.

Albie slinked across the floor and whispered something in Peregrine's ear.

A beatific smile lit Peregrine's face. His top lip curled higher on the left side. Without pulling away from Albie, Peregrine sat on the edge of the table. He looked just like Colton when he was about to get into mischief. Galaxy, when had Sebastian cataloged Colton's moods?

Sweat beaded on Sebastian's upper lip and forehead. Now that he'd realized the similarities between the prince and Peregrine, he couldn't unsee it. Galaxy be damned, he could not deny his overwhelming lust for Colton. He'd been attracted to him for some time, but that kiss this morning had intensified those feelings. Sebastian's pulse pounded in his ears.

Ardingley swallowed, making his Adam's apple bob.

"Please, my lord, may I open your pants?" Hector mumbled against Sebastian's neck.

Yes. Say yes, Sebastian. Maybe it would help get Colton out of his system. No, it wouldn't. He'd imagine it was Colton touching him. His chest tightened, making it hard to breathe. He had to get out of here.

"Not now." Smiling at Hector, Sebastian grabbed Hector's hand, kissed it, and brought it back up to his chest. He patted Hector's leg. "I have to go."

With a pout, Hector scooted off his lap.

As Sebastian stood, Peregrine opened the placket on his trousers, displaying his lovely prick, and Albie sank to his knees in front of Peregrine. Arching his back, Peregrine thrust his straining cock toward Albie. "Ooohhh…."

Albie licked his lips, opened his mouth, and leaned forward.

Sebastian's dick throbbed. Getting a piece of arse from some stranger wasn't going to cure his infatuation, and he certainly couldn't seduce Colton. But maybe if he concentrated on work…. He adjusted his dick discreetly. He needed to go locate Rourke and keep himself busy with finding new guards.

Burke House, the Earl of Hampton's residence in Classige, Pruluce

"THEN THE bloke disappeared into the stable with Dame de Pique's jockey." Lord Francis Rycroft waggled his bushy brown eyebrows. "By the time I got there, he had the jockey's whirligigs in his trap."

For the second time today, Colton was in *way* over his head. No way would he let on, though. His future in horse racing depended on it. These men were some of the racing world's elite. Dalton would just have to explain it all later. Colton glanced at his cousin.

Dalton wasn't even paying attention to the story. He stared off into space with a strange smirk on his face.

Colton rolled his eyes. Perhaps he'd read one of Tarren's silly romance novels. Better yet, he'd corner Aiden and question him about marital relations. Or were they even talking about marital relations? Wasn't a whirligig a type of carriage? Trap meant mouth. No, it couldn't be. A carriage wouldn't fit in one's mouth. Perhaps it was a trap like a snare, but that didn't make much sense either.

"Next thing I know he has his whole mitt inside the bloke's Roby Douglass." Lord Francis pushed his fist through his other hand.

"Nooo…." One of the guys—Edmund something or other—gasped. "Really?"

Lord Francis nodded. "I saw it with my own eyes."

Gareth Fareweather's mouth formed an O, then eased into a grin. "I would've *loved* to have seen that."

Who in the galaxy is this Roby Douglass fellow? Was that the name of the bloke Lord Francis met at the race? Colton wanted to ask, but something about how Lord Francis had worded his statement made him think better of it. Stars, he *had* to fit in with these guys. Copying the awed expressions of the men around him, he discreetly nudged Dalton with his elbow twice in quick succession.

Dalton never glanced away from whatever had so thoroughly captured his attention. Lifting his chin, he dipped his head like he was silently communicating with someone. Didn't he know how important this was?

Colton followed his cousin's gaze.

Across the ballroom, several of the wallflowers and chaperones clustered together. All but Colton's older brother Aiden conversed or stood around looking bored. Aiden lounged with his back propped against a pillar and his sketchscreen in hand. Apparently he'd given up all pretense of socializing. *I wonder if Nate or Cony have noticed him yet.*

"Who're you looking at?" Colton whispered.

"Pardon?" Dalton blinked at him.

"What's so interesting?" It wasn't Aiden. He was too engrossed in his sketch to notice Dalton's gestures. It couldn't be the wallflowers. They were a boring lot.

Raising his chin a little to indicate something across the room, Dalton grinned. "The admiral is taking champagne away from Trouble and his friend."

Trouble was pilfering drinks again? Colton spotted Trouble and Bannon about three yards from where Aiden stood. Still drawing, Aiden was oblivious to his stepson's antics. On the other side of the marble column, Nate shook his head at Trouble and Bannon.

Confiscating the champagne flutes from both of them, Nate dumped the contents into a potted plant situated in front of the column and stalked off.

A few feet away from Nate, Viscount-Consort Girton dipped his head toward the hallway repeatedly. He was trying to get someone's attention.

Colton jerked his gaze to Dalton.

Nodding, Dalton held up a finger close to his chest to indicate just a moment.

Across the room, Girton smiled.

Colton sighed. Girton was nearly old enough to be Dalton's father. Not to mention.... "Dalton, he's a married man."

"But I'm not." Dalton strode forward a few steps. Turning, he motioned with his hand toward the group of men standing around Colton. "Are you okay here?"

No. He had no idea what they were saying. It was like they were speaking a different language, but Colton nodded and waved his cousin away. Colton had more important things to do. Dalton had made the introductions, Colton could do the rest on his own. He'd never been an introvert like his brothers Payton and Aiden.

The first notes of a country dance started up, and a crowd swarmed to the dance floor, swallowing Dalton from view.

Edmund something or other raised his voice to be heard over the music. "I hear Viscount-Consort Leith is trying to acquire Heavenly Dream's colt."

"The Heavenly Dream who won the Daremere Classic this past year?" Colton asked.

Edmund nodded. "That's the one. I heard Mr. Inglish doesn't want to sell, but Viscount-Consort Leith won't take no for an answer. Rumor has it he's trying to acquire the horse for his son, Barnaby Plume. Plume's last horse, Weekday's Delight, was a resounding failure. He's trying to get back into the game, but no one will sell to him, so he has his sire doing his legwork."

"I heard Plume is overdrawn all over town, and the viscount has cut him off," Fareweather added.

"I heard that too," Edmund said.

"Can't say I blame Leith. Plume is a wastrel. Come to that, so is Leith's consort." Gareth Fareweather shrugged and turned toward Colton. "So, Ashbourne says you own Beaumont's Beauty's colt?"

Colton grinned. "I do, yes. Though he's no longer a colt. He's four summers. His name is Apollo."

"I wouldn't mind seeing him. Are you breeding him?" Lord Francis patted his chest, then glanced down, searching for something in his coat pocket. Assured whatever he was looking for was there, he dropped his hands to his side. He was the third son of the Marquess of Vale, who owned the last Devonshire Derby winner, so his interest in Apollo sparked Colton's excitement.

"I plan to. I've made an appointment with the Jockey Club for next week. I'm trying to get him a license. He's already in the breeding register. And I'm looking for an architect for my new stables." Colton even knew where he wanted to build his stables if Father and Cony would agree.

Fareweather snagged a glass of brandy from the tray of a passing footman. "The man who designed my father's stables is retired, but his daughter designed Roth's stables."

Bertram Nevil, the heir of the Earl of Wingate, otherwise known as Viscount Roth, nodded his agreement. "And did a damn fine job. I'll send her information to you if you like." Roth had gotten into racing only last season, but already one of his horses had won three of the minor races. Word had it that his stables were remarkable.

"Yes, thank you, that would be wonderful." Colton beamed. This was going rather splendidly. *Thank you, Dalton.*

"If you like, I can take you on a tour of my stables. Are you attending Tattersalls on the morrow? Perhaps afterward."

Colton smiled. "I am, yes. I'm going with Ashbourne. Maybe I can persuade him to make a detour after the auction."

"What say you all that we take a small break from the festivities?" Fareweather said. "I could use a smoke, and we can discuss the horses up for auction tomorrow. I've heard several rumors."

Edmund pressed something into Colton's hand. "Say you'll come outside with us, Prince Colton." He leaned closer, shielding his mouth with his hand. "I'm going to need help coaxing the list of horseflesh up for sale from Fareweather."

Glancing down at his hand, Colton bit back a groan when he saw the cheroot on his palm. *Cony will kill me.* Hiding the cheroot in his pocket, he noticed the others doing the same. "Do you think he knows something the rest of us don't?"

Edmund winked. "Probably. His father gets the best gossip where horses are concerned. Last year I was going to bid on Karmen, but Fareweather found out Mr. Harper was putting Summer's Breeze up on the auction block the very next week. Saved me a lot of blunt. No way would I have been able to afford both horses."

That was a bang-up tip. Summer's Breeze was hands down the better piece of horseflesh.

"Well, then. Let's all find ourselves a drink and meet outside. How about the lawn near the stables? In say…." Roth pulled out his pocket watch, studied it for a moment, and closed it. "Ten minutes?"

The men expressed their agreement and dispersed, leaving Colton standing on the side of the ballroom.

Drats. He could *not* go outside. On the other hand, he couldn't not go. He needed more than just Apollo if he was going to make it in the world of racing. He had a large allowance, but it wasn't infinite. Like with Edmund, a good tip could make a huge difference in his choices.

He needed a chaperone. Studying the room, he searched for someone suitable. His first choice, Dalton, was nowhere to been seen. He was probably in a dark corner with Girton.

Aiden waltzed with his consort. His arm was nearly looped around Nate's neck rather than resting on his shoulder. A piece of paper wouldn't fit between them.

Rexley—no, not Rexley. He'd never agree to them going outside. Nor would Cony or Father.

Where was Tarren? He was normally easy to spot. Socializing was his forte. He loved to talk. There he was, tucking something into the inside pocket of his evening coat. Probably his dance card. Slipping into a group of his friends, he began talking in his usual animated style, hands and all. Dragging him away would be no easy feat. That left….

Frowning, Trouble stood next to Rexley.

Colton sighed. How could he get Trouble's attention without Rexley seeing?

Rexley's lips moved, and Trouble laughed. A big belly laugh, causing several people to turn his way. Without glancing at Trouble,

Rexley smirked. When Trouble's mirth subsided, Rexley offered his arm. Taking it, Trouble allowed Rexley to sweep him away into the crowd of dancing couples.

Forget Trouble. He wasn't exactly a proper chaperone, anyway. Colton needed a blood relation or more than one friend to accompany him. Oh well, there was nothing for it.

Colton glanced over his shoulder to make certain neither of his parents were watching. They weren't. Strolling over to the end of the ballroom, he put his back toward the wall as though he was watching the dancing. He took one sidestep toward the veranda and then another. The breeze from outside made the hair on the back of his head flutter. So close....

He gave one more cursory look at the crowd—still no Father or Cony—and backed out the open ballroom doors.

CHAPTER FIVE

UNOBSERVED, SEBASTIAN leaned against the outside wall of Lord Hampton's study. Not only had he finally gotten his body under control and distracted himself from fantasies of a certain untouchable prince, he'd located his friend. Sebastian peered through the gauzy curtains and open french doors, trying not to laugh.

The Duke of Knighton was in the midst of a seduction. Sitting on the desk, Rourke leaned close to his prey's neck and removed the tumbler from his grasp. The move was so slick, it was captivating to watch. "Come now, Bernard, do you really want to spend the evening talking about the opera?" He set the glass on the desk next to an empty one.

Bernard? Sebastian squinted to get a closer look at Rourke's companion. Dark brown hair, pale skin, about five foot seven… Bernard Kearsey.

Bernard turned away from the fireplace as Rourke's lips landed on his jaw. Bernard's eyes fluttered closed, and a look of pure bliss crossed his face. "Your Grace." He asked breathlessly, "Wh-what else would we do?"

"I can think of several more interesting things to do." The duke began loosening Bernard's neckcloth.

Opening his eyes, Bernard clutched his cravat but didn't move away. "Your Grace?" His face turned a lovely shade of crimson. "Don't you want to talk about *I Puritani*?"

"No."

"No?"

Sebastian bit his lip. Everyone knew the duke kept a box at the theater, but Sebastian couldn't remember his friend ever actually watching an opera. The box was merely another trysting place.

With a chuckle, Rourke reeled Bernard in and nuzzled his Vandyke beard against Bernard's bare cheek. *Wicked bastard.*

"But, but… what if someone comes in?" Bernard shot a glance toward the closed study door. "I shouldn't be alone with you."

"Come now, Bernard. No one will know." The white neckcloth came free, and the duke kissed Bernard's neck.

"Your Grace, should you be doing that?"

"What?"

"Kissing my neck like that? It's not at all proper." Bernard slid away and plastered his back against the fireplace, bending forward awkwardly where the mantel touched his neck.

Oh dear, the debutant was either playing hard to get—which wasn't likely with the prospect of becoming a duke-consort if they were caught—or very naive. Sebastian decided to help the poor lad out. The young man was out of his league with a rake like Rourke.

Pushing gauzy curtains aside, Sebastian stepped inside. "I say, Rourke, how about sharing?"

"Sharing?" Bernard squeaked. "Sharing what?"

Rourke groaned. "Seb, your timing is deplorable."

Sebastian chuckled and propped his behind against the oak desk. "For you maybe, but for Bernard I'd say my timing is just about right."

Sighing, Rourke shook his head and stepped away from Bernard. He mumbled something that sounded like "Too much work anyway" and crossed to the sideboard. "I need a drink. Seb?"

"I'd love one. If I remember correctly, Hampton keeps some fine cognac in the cabinet under the scotch decanter." Sebastian tossed Bernard his cravat.

"Umm…." Bernard looked from one of them to the other. Almost belatedly, he bowed at Sebastian. "My lord."

Smiling, Sebastian bowed back. "Bernard, if I were you, I'd escape before your absence from the ballroom is noted."

The young lord's mouth dropped open, and he glanced at the study door. "Um, please excuse me, Your Grace? My lord?" He darted to the door, threw it open, and ran out.

Rourke brought Sebastian a snifter of brandy and closed the door before seating himself in the chair across from the desk. He propped his feet up on the ottoman. "Bloody hell, old man. I don't know whether to call you out or thank you." Sipping from his glass, he closed his eyes, seeming to savor it for a moment. "When did nineteen become so bloody young? I don't remember ever being that… that…." He waved his hand dismissively.

Tasting his own cognac, Sebastian shrugged. Colton was nineteen, and he didn't seem nearly as immature as Bernard. Sebastian took a sip. "Innocent?"

"Naive." Rourke stared down into his glass for several moments. "Where were you earlier? I gave up on you meeting me at the Silver Swan."

"Work. I didn't leave the castle until ten o'clock."

Looking up from his drink, Rourke grinned. "Don't you know we aristocrats are supposed to be living a life of leisure."

"I'm no aristocrat, and you know it." Sebastian set his glass down. "What was that all about anyway? I thought you preferred your lovers with a little more experience."

"I did. I do. Oh hell, I don't know. I'm bored out of my bloody mind. Do you ever get tired of the same old routine?"

Sebastian smiled. His life was anything but routine, but he understood what Rourke meant. Gambling, getting foxed, and chasing trousers was beginning to lose its appeal for Sebastian too. "At times."

"I miss the RSR."

Sebastian had only intended to ask Rourke if he knew if any of their old teammates were looking for work. Rourke certainly didn't need the money, but perhaps…. "Really?"

"Yes, really. To tell the truth, I'd sign back up if I had an heir other than my imbecile cousin. If I were killed in action, he'd run Knighton into the ground." Rourke had left the RSR to take over the responsibility of the dukedom when both his parents and his older brother died in a boating accident while on vacation off planet.

"Perhaps I have something to alleviate your boredom that isn't quite as dangerous as the RSR."

One obsidian brow shot up as Rourke took a drink and waited for an answer to his unasked question.

"I need more guards. I need men I can trust. Men with skills like ours, and I don't have time to train my guards that intensively."

"Doing what? Standing around the castle looking bored?"

"No, guarding the royal family, specifically the princes, on their daily outings. It would be a part-time job. Only during the day. And not every day. I intend to have the royal family make up a schedule and give me advance notice when they intend to leave the castle." Actually, he'd already made that demand, and so far only Raleigh, Steven, Rexley, and Aiden complied consistently.

Rourke tossed back the rest of his cognac, then dangled the tumbler from his fingers. "Isn't that rather like hiring a fox to watch a henhouse?"

Sebastian's reputation wasn't much better than Rourke's, and no one had a problem with him watching the princes. "Desperate circumstances call for desperate measures. Besides, if you so much as look at one of them the wrong way, I'll throttle you. Or are you looking to get leg shackled?"

Rourke gave a mock shudder. "Not particularly. But following their royal highnesses around town doesn't sound exciting. I suppose it would be a change of pace, but still… it sounds dull."

Snorting, Sebastian stood. "Trust me when I tell you it's never boring. Mischief follows them everywhere. Just keeping them from damaging themselves is a chore."

Rourke stood too and refilled his glass. "It can't be that bad."

Crossing to the open french doors, Sebastian leaned against the frame and gazed out at the night stars. "You'd be surprised, but suffice it to say it's a different adventure every outing." The curtains fluttered in the breeze and wrapped around Sebastian's legs. He batted the fabric, untangled it, and shoved it behind him.

"Let me think about it." Rourke joined him, leaning against the opposite doorjamb. "When do you need an answer?"

"You can let me know next week. Do you know where the rest of our team ended up? Last I heard from Julian, he was helping his father run the family shipping business. That was six months ago."

"I saw Julian a fortnight ago. He's still in the family business." Rourke held his glass down by his side and continued to stare outside.

"Ah." Sebastian followed his gaze up to the inky sky. He could remember nights just like this where it was only him and his team for miles around.

"I ran into Benny three months ago. He's working at a gaming hell as a bouncer. Not sure which one, though. I was rather foxed at the time. According to Benny, Seabrook married a lovely girl from Hillbourne, and they are expecting their first child in the spring."

The sound of rustling snagged Sebastian's attention away from the heavens and back to Regelence. A dark figure at the end of the veranda stepped up onto the stairs. He turned his head left, then right, before leaning against the railing and searching the grounds as though he were looking for something in the gardens. Probably a lover.

"Wonder who that is and whom he's meeting? Maybe we could persuade him to meet us instead."

Sebastian chuckled. "And they accuse me of having a one-track mind."

"You're the one who suggested sharing."

"I was only trying to scare Bernard away."

Rourke groaned. "I still don't know whether to thank you or throttle you for that."

"You should send me flowers and some cookies. Bernard is the son of the Marquess and Marquess-Consort of Halstead. His parents are aggressively looking for consorts for three of their five sons this season." Sebastian cocked his head, studying the silhouette—still looking at the garden—coming toward them on the veranda.

A set of stairs led down to the lawn about ten feet before the study door where Sebastian and Rourke stood. The man was nearly to the steps and hadn't noticed their presence. In shadow, he kept scanning the lawn. Sebastian couldn't make out his features, but he had wide shoulders and lean hips. He was fairly tall, at least six foot. He was definitely fair of form. "Bernard is one of those sons they wish to marry off."

"How in the galaxy do you know all that?"

Sebastian grinned. "Bernard is one of Prince Tarren's friends." What was the man pulling out of his coat pocket? He was getting closer now, walking with purpose. Sebastian glanced toward the area that had captured the man's attention. There was a group of lords just left of the gardens about fifteen yards away. He hadn't noticed them before and wouldn't have now except for the glow of cigars.

The shadowed man descended the steps before he reached the study. He retrieved whatever he'd been after in his pocket and carried it by his side. As he planted his foot on the immaculate lawn, the moonlight illuminated his handsome, very familiar profile.

"Bugger." Sebastian shoved away from the door and strode toward the steps.

BLAST, STARS, and damnation! Colton stiffened. If he wasn't so worried about the imminent confrontation, he might have blushed at the expletive.

But there was no mistaking the voice, and he wasn't lucky enough for Wentworth to let him pass on by. Colton turned, already knowing what he'd find.

Eyes narrowed and jaw clenched, Wentworth stormed down the steps.

Colton darted a glance toward the garden. He'd never make it. Wentworth was in top physical condition, and even though they were of a height, the viscount was lighter… quicker. Best to stand his ground.

"Don't even think about it." Grasping Colton's wrist, Wentworth tugged.

Colton drew back but could not break free. *Dust*, Wentworth was strong. "Galaxy, what is it with you manhandling me lately?" Colton snarled and dug in his heels.

"If you did what you were supposed to, I wouldn't have to manhandle you."

Someone chuckled. "Getting into the rough stuff these days, Seb?"

Jerking his attention toward the new voice, Colton lost his advantage, and Wentworth hauled him to the steps.

A tall man with black hair and a trim Vandyke beard leaned against the rail, watching them with a smirk. He was handsome in a sinister sort of way and looked vaguely familiar, but Colton couldn't place him. He'd also called Wentworth "Seb."

An ache bloomed to life in Colton's chest. Who was this man? He must be an intimate to have called Wentworth by his first name. No, not even his first name, a shortened version of it. A nickname. Colton swallowed the lump in his throat.

To keep from being dragged, Colton followed Wentworth onto the porch. "What exactly is it you think I'm supposed to be doing?" he ground out between gritted teeth.

"You're supposed to be inside. Chaperoned." Wentworth spun Colton around to face him so hard Colton's arm made a popping sound. A wince was the only recognition on Wentworth's part.

The popping hadn't hurt, but Colton rubbed his shoulder all the same. He glanced over at the man against the rail. Were he and Wentworth having an affair? He didn't seem Wentworth's type, but then again, from what Colton gathered, anything with two legs *not* named Colton Townsend was Wentworth's type. It cut him to the quick.

He should just let it drop and go back inside, but pride demanded he fight back.

"You. Are. Not. My. Keeper." He punctuated each word by jabbing at Wentworth.

Wentworth swiped the cheroot out of his hand.

Oops. Colton hadn't thought about what he was doing when he used it as a pointer. It hadn't registered that it was something he wasn't allowed to have.

"What in the—" Still holding the cigar up, Wentworth pinched the bridge of his nose. Lifting his head, he dropped his hand. His jaw relaxed, and when he spoke again, his voice was normal. Almost… resigned. "Colton…."

The tall man with the Vandyke snagged the cheroot from Wentworth's fingers.

Only propriety kept Colton from asking who the man was and more importantly how he knew Wentworth. Returning his attention to Wentworth, Colton sighed. "I don't need a chaperone. I'll be in a group."

An orange glow illuminated half of Wentworth's face. The light disappeared as quickly as it appeared, and the sweet smell of vanilla-flavored smoke perfumed the air.

Wentworth stared at his accomplice. "Do you mind?"

The man puffed on the cigar and pulled it from between his lips. "Not at all. Continue." The smirk and twinkle in his eye testified to his feigned ignorance. He offered the cheroot to Wentworth.

Growling, Wentworth shook his head.

Chuckling, Colton decided he liked this man. "It was *my* cheroot."

The man laughed. "Indeed it was. I beg your pardon, Your Highness." He held out the cheroot to Colton.

He had no idea how to smoke it, but—Colton reached out.

"I don't think so." Wentworth caught his hand.

The warmth of his grasp sent a thrill right through Colton. He glanced down at their entwined hands and back up to Wentworth's face.

The corner of Wentworth's lip twitched as he stared at the tobacco thief. "You're incorrigible, Rourke." Turning to Colton, he held out his other hand toward his companion. "Prince Colton Townsend, meet His Grace, the Duke of Knighton. Rourke is one of my dearest friends."

Colton's mood lightened further. They were only friends? It shouldn't matter, but now he liked Knighton even better.

Taking Colton's free hand, Knighton bowed over it. He pressed a kiss to the back of Colton's knuckles and winked up at him. "An honor, Your Highness."

Oh my. Smiling, Colton dipped his head. What a charming rogue. That explained why he seemed familiar. Since his first season, Colton had heard gossip about the Duke of Knighton. The duke had a worse reputation as a reprobate than Wentworth. "A pleasure to make your acquaintance, Your Grace."

Instead of letting go of his hand, Knighton steered him closer, making Wentworth relinquish his grasp. Holding up the cheroot once again, he asked, "Would you like this back? It's very good."

Colton chuckled at the playful gleam in Knighton's eyes.

Growling, Wentworth clamped a hand down on Colton's shoulder. He yanked him back, and Colton stumbled into him. "No, he does not. Knock it off."

Colton shivered at the feel of Wentworth's chest against his back and the soft breath near his ear. He couldn't help himself—he closed his eyes and leaned into the warm body behind him.

"Hmm…."

Wrenching his eyes open, Colton stepped away.

Knighton had his head cocked to the side, staring over Colton's shoulder. When he caught Colton's gaze, he smirked and winked.

Drats, what had he been thinking? Colton needed to meet Edmund, Roth, Mr. Fareweather, and Lord Francis. He'd wasted nearly ten minutes arguing with Wentworth. "It was nice meeting you, Your Grace, but I need to be going. I've got to meet—"

"No." Wentworth's voice was soft but firm.

The tone didn't bode well for Colton's plans, but he had to try. He turned to face his opponent. "But—"

Wentworth shook his head and glanced toward the carriage barn near where the men were gathered. "You cannot go out there. Group or no group, it's not proper. Your parents would have my head if I allowed it."

"Then go with me. You"—he glanced at Knighton for help—"and His Grace can accompany me." Not that he wanted Wentworth watching his every move, but Colton needed to go.

Knighton grinned. "Please, Your Highness, call me Rourke."

Wentworth groaned. It sounded rather harsh and unfriendly.

Ignoring him, Colton smiled. "Then you should call me Colton."

Rourke dipped his head in acknowledgment and focused on Wentworth. "Come on, Seb, let's accompany him to his friends. We'll act as his chaperones." He puffed his cheroot and offered Colton his arm.

Colton reached to take Knighton's arm, but Wentworth got there first. He snatched Colton's hand away. Placing it on his forearm, he turned toward Rourke. "*We* are not proper chaperones."

Colton's window of opportunity was slipping away. He had to make Wentworth understand how important this was. Maybe if he appealed to the horseman in him. "Gareth Fareweather has gossip about the stock up for auction at Tattersalls tomorrow. Please…."

Wentworth sighed. "You want to go out there because you might learn something about horses?"

"Yes." Why else would Colton want to go? "Last year Edmund got a good tip from Fareweather that allowed him to buy a better horse than he'd initially planned on."

"What if I send Knighton to charm your friends and get the information out of them? Would that be acceptable?"

Colton looked out at the glow of cigars. What would the group think if he didn't come? How would it appear if he sent someone else?

A finger traced down the center of Colton's forehead.

Startled out of his thoughts, he met Wentworth's gaze. Wentworth smiled at him. It was the most genuine smile Colton had seen from him in ages. Colton could almost fool himself into thinking Wentworth actually liked him.

"If you think any harder, you'll give yourself an apoplexy." He touched Colton's cheek before drawing his fingers away. "Please. If anyone can get information for you, it's Rourke. Let me take you back to the ballroom." His gaze swept over Colton's face, resting on his lips.

They stood there staring at each other, and a nervous twitter started in Colton's stomach. He could almost feel those hard, unyielding lips on his. The urgent press of Wentworth's tongue. This morning's folly came flooding back, but it no longer seemed like a joke or punishment.

A cloud of smoke surrounded them, giving the moment a surreal feel. Colton wanted a repeat of this morning more than he wanted his next breath.

Wentworth stepped closer.

"Ahem." Rourke took Colton's other arm. "Bad idea, Seb. If he's seen with you alone, his reputation will be in tatters. I'll accompany you both back to the ballroom, and then you can go seduce the gossip out of Colton's friends." He brought the cheroot up to his lips and puffed. "Colton and I will wait for you while we dance."

Running his hand through his hair, Wentworth groaned. "Right you are. We'll *both* escort him; then we will *both* go talk to Mr. Fareweather. There will be no dancing. I believe Colton said Roth was down there. Since you know Roth, you can handle the introductions." Wentworth began walking. "Colton, I like the spot you marked with the flag for your stables today. I think it will be an easy location to secure."

"You do?" Colton asked.

"I do." Wentworth droned on about how to protect the location and other various things about security.

Colton listened in a daze, surprised Wentworth approved, as they led him down the veranda toward the open french doors.

The music of a country dance grew louder. Even though both men walked at his side, Colton was only aware of Wentworth. How the viscount's trouser leg brushed his, how their steps matched. The muscles of his forearms were rock solid under Colton's palm. What did this new, gentler Wentworth mean? Would he have kissed Colton again if Rourke hadn't interrupted? Or had Colton merely appealed to Wentworth's love of horses?

His stomach tied in knots. He was losing sight of the goal in a hurry. The goal being the tip for the auction tomorrow, not Wentworth's attention. Maybe he'd go inside and plead a headache to Cony. He needed to sort out his thoughts.

"So, then. What time tomorrow morning shall I report for duty?" Rourke inquired.

Duty? Colton frowned. What were they talking about?

"Why do I have a feeling I'm going to regret inviting you to work for me?" Wentworth asked.

Rourke shrugged, and the smirk Colton was beginning to suspect was the duke being mischievous appeared. "I haven't the slightest idea what you mean, old man." To Colton he said, "Seb hired me to be a royal bodyguard." Snuffing his smoke out on the wall of the mansion, Rourke released Colton's arm. He bowed and put the cheroot in his coat pocket. "Good evening, Colton. Perhaps I'll accompany you to Tattersalls on the morrow."

Chapter Six

September 15, 4830: Townsend Castle

"Reporting for duty."

Good galaxy, could the man talk any louder? Sebastian tried to ignore the pounding in his head.

Rourke strolled into the castle, waving away Thomas, the underbutler, when he would've taken the duke's coat, hat, and calling card. The bastard looked right as rain. "What's wrong with you?"

"Other than the percussion section practicing in my head, you mean?" He and Rourke *both* drank entirely too much last night, but apparently Sebastian was the only one paying for it this morning.

Rourke's lips twitched. "It was the cheroots that did it. They keep you from realizing how much you've drunk. You need to smoke more."

"No, thank you." Sebastian had never been much of a smoker. It was rare he partook of cigars, never of pipes or cigarettes, and now he remembered why that was. "Do you recall all we learned last evening?"

After taking off his coat, Rourke laid it over his arm and removed his hat. "I believe so. What do you think Colton will find most interesting?"

"Probably the bit about the senior Mr. Fareweather selling one of his brood mares next week. Colton has a good stud but no mares with any racing pedigree I know of." Then again, Sebastian hadn't known Apollo had such impeccable bloodlines until yesterday.

Footsteps echoed in the entryway. "Oh, Sebastian, there you are."

Turning, Sebastian faced his king, who was coming down the stairs with his coat on, his hat under his arm, and gloves in his hand. "Good morning, Your Majesty."

Steven left the last step and joined them in the foyer. Pulling on his gloves, he stopped in front of Knighton.

Rourke bowed deeply. "Your Majesty."

Steven dipped his chin. "Knighton? What brings you here this morning?"

"Seb has offered me a job."

Steven looked at Sebastian, then back to Knighton. His eyes widened, and he nodded. "Oh yes. That's right. You were in the RSR with Sebastian before you inherited your title." Pulling on his last black glove, Steven smirked at Knighton. "You do realize it's not at all the thing for a man of your rank to work, don't you?"

Rourke beamed at the king. "Ah, but I prefer to set the trends rather than follow them."

"In other words, you do as you damn well please. A man after my own heart." Steven glanced around the hall. "Nice to have you with us, Knighton."

Thomas came rushing forward with Steven's walking stick. It was the mahogany one Sebastian had bought him for Christmas with a sword concealed within.

Putting his hat on his head, Steven took the cane from the assistant butler and returned his attention to the duke. "You'll do quite nicely, I should think. You're neither old nor fat."

"Steven." Sebastian chuckled, then wished he hadn't. *Oh my head.* He squeezed his temples with the thumb and middle finger of his right hand.

"What?" Steven asked with a straight face. "He's not. He's quite pleasant to look at." Adjusting his hat, he gave Sebastian one of those pointed looks that said Steven knew exactly what was what, but he was asking anyway. "What's wrong with your head?"

"He overindulged at the Hampton's ball."

Sebastian groaned. "Thank you, Lord Tattletale." He turned his attention back to Steven in time to catch his smirk. "I think it was the cigars actually."

Steven's smirk grew into a full-fledged smile. "Colton smelled like cigar smoke when he came to plead a headache last night. You wouldn't know anything about that, would you?" His smile had disappeared, but the faint laugh lines at the corner of his eyes remained.

"He went outside to talk to some of the racing set, and I intercepted him on the veranda." Sebastian held up a hand, hoping to forestall an explosion. "But he was only trying to learn some gossip for the auction today. Rourke and I sent him back inside and went in his stead. He was never in any danger." That was a matter of opinion. It had been sheer luck that Sebastian had run into Colton and steered him back to safety. But Sebastian didn't want to get him in trouble.

"Very well. As long as he was with you, I know he was in good hands. Did you get the gossip?" Steven asked.

"Is there any doubt? We were RSR." Huffing out a breath, Rourke managed to look almost bored. "Unfortunately, we didn't get to torture the info out of them. There's today, however. Who knows what needs may arise when I actually escort Prince Colton to Tattersalls."

Sebastian gritted his teeth, and a sharp stab of pain snaked up the right side of his face. Blasted hangover. He was not allowing Rourke near Colton. The flirting going on between them last night had set Sebastian on edge. Duke or not, Rourke was not good enough for Colton. "I'll talk to Colton today before I send—"

"Nonsense." Steven grabbed Knighton's arm and tugged him toward the door. "You can come with me to the haberdashers, and Sebastian will escort Colton and Dalton. You can tell me all about how you and Sebastian seduced the gossip out of those racing aficionados." As the front door opened for them, the sounds of more footsteps filled the vestibule.

"That isn't necessary. I can get—" Sebastian trailed off when it became apparent they were not listening to him. He didn't want to go to the auction.

Plopping his hat on his head, Rourke hurried into his coat. "Lead the way, Your Majesty." They stopped just outside the front entrance and stood silhouetted against the drizzly gray morning.

Leaning in to whisper something to Rourke, Steven waved.

Raising his hand, Sebastian strained to hear over the staccato of boots on the marble behind him.

Steven and Rourke glanced at him and continued to speak in undertones.

A lift pulled up, and the front door closed, blocking them from view. If Sebastian didn't know better, he'd swear they'd been talking about him. Turning toward the staircase, he rubbed his right temple. He was getting his wish to stay busy, but somehow he never imagined staying busy would include being Colton's personal bodyguard.

Last night at the Hampton's ball, Colton had shown Sebastian a side of himself that made him even more appealing. The complete abandon with which he pursued gaining a foothold in racing was tantalizing. He was finding his way in the world, calling his own shots despite the consequences. Not many men were so brave. Most followed others, letting popular opinion dictate their actions. In a way, Colton had always forged his own path, but last night something had changed. He'd displayed a maturity he hadn't had before. There'd been no childish tantrum when he hadn't gotten his way. Come to think on it, Colton *had* gotten his way, more or less. The information he sought had been obtained.

Side by side, Colton and Ashbourne descended the stairs. They were both dressed in black-caped greatcoats and black beaver hats. The two men topped six foot by a few inches and possessed lovely athletic physiques. But that was where the similarities ended. Not only were Colton's shoulders wider, but he was night to Ashbourne's day. Colton's dark hair and complexion were haunting and untouchable where Ashbourne's fairness was genial. Colton's eyes were half-mast this morning, lending the appearance of indolence. He looked… beddable.

"Good day, Wentworth." Placing his brass-handled cane on the floor in front of him, Ashbourne bobbed his head.

"Good day, Ashbourne."

The fresh scent of the outdoors that always clung to Colton teased Sebastian's nose as Colton drew abreast on the other side of Sebastian. "Morning, Wentworth."

Sebastian sighed. So much for his plan to fill Colton in and send him and Ashbourne on their way with two guards. "Thomas, please retrieve my coat, gloves, and hat. I'm accompanying Prince Colton and Ashbourne to Tattersalls."

STEVEN SAT down in the lift and considered Rourke, who'd settled into the seat opposite him. Steven was pretty sure he'd found himself a coconspirator, but he wasn't ready to confide in the man just yet.

"So… Sebastian is one of your best friends?" Steven put the walking stick between his feet and rested his hands on the handle.

Placing his hat on the seat next to him, Knighton smiled. "He is. We got our commissions at the same time and went into basic and RSR training together."

The lift door closed, and they started moving.

That hadn't been very revealing, and time was of the essence. Steven had truly planned to visit the haberdashers, but things had fallen into place too nicely. He'd been able to maneuver Sebastian and Colton together. Now he wanted to see if his scheming would pay off. How could he get the duke to reveal more? His efforts would be all for naught if Knighton blabbed to Wentworth. "Thank you for helping Sebastian corral Colton last night. The boy can be quite a handful, I'm afraid."

One side of Knighton's lip curled up, and his eyes narrowed. It was a sinister grin but filled with joy all the same. "It was no hardship. I rather enjoyed it."

Who would've thought a man so young would have laugh lines at the corners of his eyes? He was only in his late twenties.

"Oh?" Steven leaned forward.

"Mmm…." Knighton leaned back. The other side of his lip rose. He gazed out the window and began adjusting his coat.

Ooh, the rogue. He's playing me. Steven almost chuckled. Instead he whacked the man in the shin with his cane. "Give over, Knighton."

Knighton's grin remained in place. His dark eyes shone with good humor as he met Steven's stare. "Nice work back there. I was certain my offer to take Colton to the auction would've done the trick, but you played that quite well, Your Majesty."

"Oh, bah. Call me Steven. If you're going to be accompanying me now and again." Steven smiled. "Now talk."

Knighton chuckled. "Then please call me Rourke."

Rourke was Knighton's family name. "Not your first name?" His given name was Hugh, if Steven wasn't mistaken.

"I hate my first name."

Hugh wasn't a bad name, but whatever. When Steven tipped his chin in acceptance, Rourke continued.

"Last night I noticed Seb's obvious if reluctant affection for your son. He doesn't want to be attracted to Colton. He's fighting it. And

Colton—charming young man, your son—is quite smitten with Seb. I think they're perfect for each other, if you don't mind my saying."

Happiness bubbled up inside Steven. He smiled so big his cheeks hurt. "Can you keep a secret?"

"Of course I can. It was part of the job description being in the RSR." Rourke raised both brows. "Are we talking national security?"

"No. Life or death. If Raleigh finds out, he'll kill me."

"Then by all means my lips are sealed. I am sworn to protect my king, after all."

Steven bit back a laugh. "Good." Lifting his cane, Steven rapped on the ceiling and kept his eyes glued to the man across him. "To Tattersalls. Park a block away."

Rourke's lips twitched, but he said nothing.

"We're going on a spying mission. Because I happen to agree with you. Wentworth and Colton were meant to be together whether they realize it or not. May I count on your help to make them realize it?"

"Absolutely." Rourke stuck out his hand. When Steven shook it, he continued, "I owe it to Seb. He deserves to be happy, and I blame myself for not trying harder to talk him out of marrying the viscount."

Having known Sebastian for the past seven years, Steven had already surmised Sebastian and his former spouse had not been at all compatible.

Steven and Rourke continued to chat until the lift stopped and the doors opened. "We are at your destination, Your Majesty. The auction house is approximately one hundred and twenty-two point five meters to your right."

"Thank you. Wait for us here, and if anyone asks, we weren't here," Steven said.

"Very well, Your Majesty."

Grabbing his hat, Rourke exited the lift first. He stood, blocking Steven's way, looked around, then turned and extended a hand. "Steven." Somehow he seemed taller than before. Or maybe Steven just hadn't noticed it. Rourke was a big man, easily Nate's size.

"Thank you." Steven climbed down the steps. "Do you miss the service? What were you? A lieutenant?"

"Yes and yes. Seb was our team commander." Rourke kept stride beside Steven, scanning the area without being obvious. "RSR missions were pure hell at times, but damn, it was a rush. Gave a man a real sense of pride to know he survived it." There was a gleam in the duke's eye. "I was promoted to lieutenant commander and was in charge of the team after Seb left."

"You liked serving your planet." Steven had seen the same pride in many Regelence military men. It made him proud and humbled all at once. It was an amazing feeling to be a part of Regelence, to be able to keep this fine planet running smoothly and all of their heritage alive and flourishing.

Rourke nodded. "I would've stayed in the Regelence Navy if my family hadn't died. I loved being RSR."

"I'm sorry it happened. Your father was a good man. I could always count on him to back me." Knighton was an old title with a proud history. The Rourke family had always been supportive of the crown.

Thunder rumbled overhead, and the frigid wind whistled through the alleyway they passed.

Catching his hat so it wouldn't blow off, Steven tilted his head back to see the clouds. They were definitely darker than they had been when they'd left the castle. *Drats*. "I didn't think to bring an umbrella." He was so concerned with his hat that his cane slipped out of his fingers and clattered to the sidewalk. Before he could even turn, Rourke had bent to pick up the walking stick.

Steven waited, watching the duke. Goodness, he had a nice behind. Sebastian had taken it to heart when Steven told him he wanted a hunk.

Out of the corner of Steven's eye, something moved. He turned his head.

A man dressed in a brown morning coat and top hat came up behind them. The man met Steven's gaze and immediately detoured into an alley. The man must be meeting a lover. Or a prostitute.

"Here you go." Rourke held out the walking stick. A little more quietly he said, "He's been behind us since we left the lift. It could just be coincidence."

Steven blinked. Rourke already knew about the man? "I'm impressed. You're very good."

Rourke grinned. "It's my job. Besides, you don't leave the RSR without a healthy dose of caution and a smidgen of paranoia."

Steven chuckled. Raleigh, Nate, and Sebastian were like that as well. All three of them always seemed aware of their surroundings without even scanning around. At least, Steven didn't actually see them look. "I feel as though I've met the man, but I can't place him." Steven took the cane and pointed it toward the auction house. "Shall we?"

"After you. It may have been someone you've seen at a ball or somewhere. He's not behind us now." They walked another few yards, and Rourke stopped at the street corner. "How do you want to do this? We can't let them see us. If Seb finds out what we're plotting, he'll throttle me. And galaxy knows he has enough dirt on me to—ahem. Begging your pardon."

Steven chuckled. "Agreed. I'm sure he has dirt on me too, and I wouldn't put it past him to snitch on me to Raleigh if crossed. What gossip did you and Sebastian gain last night?"

"Not much. Sebastian seemed to think Colton would want to save his money until next week when the senior Mr. Fareweather has some brood mares for sale."

"In that case, let's go around back. Knowing Colton, if he's not buying, he'll be wandering the stables. Boy always has preferred horses to people."

They neared Tattersalls, and the first drops of rain began to fall. By the time they reached the stables, it was coming down in a steady sprinkle.

Just as Steven predicted, Colton and Wentworth were outside under the pavilion with the livestock. Colton walked the aisles looking at horses while Sebastian kept pace about three feet away from him. Ashbourne was nowhere in sight.

Rourke pulled Steven into an empty stall and put a finger to his lips. "We've got to be very careful or Seb will spot us. Follow my lead." Before Steven could even nod his agreement, Rourke situated Steven's hat down lower over his eyes, did the same with his own, and turned. Crouching, he peeked out the stall door and motioned for Steven to follow.

Steven crept out of the stall behind Rourke.

They pursued as Colton browsed and Sebastian stared out at the rain, pinching the bridge of his nose.

Bloody hell, they couldn't bond with that much distance between them. They weren't even speaking. Steven frowned. They were mostly alone, so why did Sebastian have to be so honorable? He was supposed to be a rake, *blast it*!

Rourke's back stiffened, and he ducked around a corner. Once there, he put his finger to his lips again and motioned for Steven to keep up.

Steven nodded and trailed Rourke around another corner. Where were they going? They were heading in the opposite direction from Colton and Sebastian. The hair on Steven's arms stood on end despite his heavy frock coat. Something wasn't right.

As they rounded the next stall, Rourke stopped. He held a hand out behind him.

Steven froze. They were now on the other side of the stall they'd started at, facing the opposite direction.

Rourke waved his hand forward and scuttled to the end of the aisle.

Steven tagged along close behind. At the duke's hand signal, Steven drew up next to Rourke and peeked around the wooden wall with him.

The same man who'd ducked into the alley stood in the middle of the stables gazing around like he was searching for something, or rather someone.

He was hunting for Steven and Rourke.

CHAPTER SEVEN

Tattersalls Auction House, downtown Classige, Pruluce

NO SOONER had Sebastian and Colton stepped out of the lift and under the covered area beside the auction building that housed the stables, than the rain started in earnest. The place smelled like damp hay. But as luck would have it, the storm meant fewer patrons, and the ones attending today—including Ashbourne—were already inside the auction building.

Having met up with a few of his Navy friends, the young earl had abandoned Sebastian and Colton as soon as Colton had given the nod of approval on the gelding Ashbourne wanted. He was supposed to be a sort of chaperone to Colton, and Colton to him, but in such a public setting, Sebastian wasn't too worried about it. Ashbourne's reputation was dubious anyway. Unmarried gentlemen *were* permitted to go unchaperoned with their friends, as long as they were in public view; it was perfectly acceptable. And even if it was a bit deserted, he and Colton were in public.

Passing the time, they browsed over the stock for sale. Up to this point the only outstanding mount they'd come across was the horse Ashbourne intended to bid on. The peace and quiet was doing wonders for Sebastian's headache, but it was playing tricks on his mind. He'd had that niggling at the back of his neck, the someone-is-watching-me feeling twice already, and no one was there when he investigated.

"Wentworth?"

This time when a chill tingled up Sebastian's back and uneasiness settled in his stomach, it was all Colton's doing. "Yes?" Almost afraid of what he'd find, he turned from watching the few stragglers outside in the rain.

Colton stared into a stall and removed his hat. "Hold this please." He offered the black top hat without looking away from the horse.

Taking the hat, Sebastian joined him at the door. "Why?"

"Because I don't like the way he's prancing about." Still, Colton did not turn.

Oh bugger. They were not supposed to touch merchandise without a trainer or owner present. "Colton—"

Before Sebastian could stop him, Colton opened the door and stepped in. Holding his hand out, he inched toward the stallion and crooned to him in an inflection much softer and deeper than his regular speaking voice. It warmed Sebastian from the inside out. What would it be like to have that voice whispering in his ear? The soft, warm breath caressing his cheek? It was the voice of a lover.

Damnation. There he went again, thinking things he ought not. He shook his head to clear it and wished he hadn't. The throbbing flared up with the motion. "What're you doing?"

The beautiful black horse danced out of reach, but his ears flew forward. Regarding Colton, the horse brought his front hooves in close to his back legs. His stance was awkward, and most of the weight rested on his back legs. Blue wraps covered his front fetlocks, and black boots covered his front hooves. Most trainers wrapped all four legs for traveling. Perhaps this horse had sustained an injury to his front legs.

"He won't stand still. Don't you find that unusual?" Colton stopped about a foot from the stallion. "Come now, sweets. I won't hurt you. I only want to have a look."

Sebastian glanced at the temporary placard on the side of the stall.

> *Razzle Dazzle is a five-year-old Plantation Walker. His gaits include: Flat Walk, Running Walk, Canter, Slow Gait, and Rack. Owned by Mr. Barnaby Plume.*

Great. Sebastian rubbed his temple. His headache had come back full-force.

The stallion nuzzled Colton's hand.

"Come on, Colton, get out of there. His legs aren't our concern. He's a walker. That's probably normal. They have an ambling gait. He's probably shifting about because of his training." If anyone saw them….

Sebastian glanced around. They were on a center aisle that formed an intersection. There was a gentleman at the end of the aisle and a stableboy around the corner.

"He shouldn't prance like this when he's in his stall, should you, boy. That's a good boy."

A tingle went down Sebastian's spine. Gads, that throaty murmur of Colton's was enough to make a man all liquid inside. It appeared to be working on the horse too. Despite his agitation, he reveled in Colton's attention. It *did* seem as if it hurt him to keep his weight on one foot for too long. Leave it to Colton to spot something like that.

The stallion let out a sharp exhale when Colton cupped his fetlock and pulled his foot up for inspection. He unfastened the leather boot and tossed it away. "Shhh.... It's all right, pretty." His mouth pinched, and his forehead wrinkled. He narrowed his eyes. "There's a nail in the hoof wall. He's not shod. And even if he were, it's way too high and tacked in from the wrong direction."

What? Sebastian leaned over the gate, trying to get a better look. "Why would someone do that?" It would be akin to someone driving a spike through the middle of one's thumbnail right into the thumb. *Ouch.*

Colton dropped the horse's foot back to the ground and patted him once more. "To make him lift his front legs higher. They usually go to more extremes to hide it, though." Crouching, he pushed down the wrap on the horse's fetlock. "I don't see any chemicals, but I'm no expert. To be honest, I've never even seen a Plantation Walker. I've only read about them." Walkers were not common on Regelence.

This was Plume's horse. *Like father, like son, apparently.* Who knew brutality could be a genetic trait? "I saw a couple about ten years ago. Wentworth took me to a horse show shortly after we married." There'd been a roan mare that had made a lasting impression on Sebastian. Her walking run hadn't been as pronounced as the other horses. She'd looked natural and elegant. The others had just seemed odd. "But I'm afraid I don't know much about them. Why would someone use chemicals on them?"

"For the same reason. It makes them sore, and they lift their legs, trying to keep weight off their feet for a longer period of time." Rising, Colton petted the stallion and glanced back at Sebastian. Colton's eyes drooped at the corners. His mouth pressed together in a thin line.

Sebastian understood the anger. He shared it. The haunted look made his gut clench, but this wasn't their horse.

Damnation, when had keeping Colton happy become so important? Last night, Sebastian had longed to erase Colton's agitation, and today was no different. The one thing they both agreed on consistently was horses. Sebastian understood Colton's desire to work with horses. It was something he'd always loved as well.

"Find a stableboy."

A rumble of thunder rattled the stables, and rain gave way to a sleeting downpour.

With a deep, vibrating snort, the horse sidestepped. He bumped into Colton and knocked him off-balance.

The tiny ice pellets created a roar under the tin-roofed pavilion, and the stallion whinnied.

"Whoa, boy." Colton caught himself on the wall.

Gasping, Sebastian unhooked the stall door. "Get out of there." He'd figure out what to do about the horse once his charge removed himself from harm's way. As he slid the door open, he offered his hand.

Colton righted himself and came within reach but focused on something past Sebastian. "You there. Boy." He crooked his finger. "Come here."

Sebastian glanced behind him.

The blond stableboy who'd been around the corner strolled their way, swinging a pail. "Aye, milord?"

"I'd like you to find me some nail pullers or pliers." Colton's regal tone brooked no argument, but the boy didn't react immediately.

He shifted his weight side to side and brought the pail in front of him, grabbing it with both hands. He bit his bottom lip and darted a glance to Sebastian. "Milord? This is Mr. Plume's horse."

"You heard His Highness. Off with you, and locate a veterinarian as well."

Eyes widening, the boy bowed to Colton. "Right away, Yer Highness." The bucket fell to the cement with a clang, and he took off. He stopped, turned back, and bowed toward Sebastian. "Milord." Then he ran around the corner.

Grinning, Sebastian caught Colton's arm when he would've returned to the stallion. "Guess he didn't recognize you at first."

Colton pressed his lips together again. "I want this horse."

Sebastian tugged. "Come on."

Losing his footing, Colton plowed right into Sebastian.

Sebastian wrapped his arms around him to keep him from bouncing off and nearly crushed the hat in his hand. The sound of the storm drowned out Colton's gasp, but the pretty heart-shaped mouth formed an O. Sebastian wanted to claim that mouth once more. To taste Colton's innocence and eagerness. Why couldn't he dislodge this man from his head lately?

As the warm, hard chest pressed against his own, a clap of thunder rumbled and footsteps echoed and grew louder. *Thank galaxy.* He set Colton away from him.

"Milord." The stableboy bowed and thrust out a pair of shoe pullers. "Will these work?"

"Yes, thank you. What's your name, child?" Sebastian asked.

"Jimmy, milord." Looking back and forth between Sebastian and Colton, the boy bowed.

"Thank you, Jimmy." Sebastian took the tool. "Now, go find a vet."

"Yes, milord." Jimmy bolted.

Colton snatched the pullers. "We also need to look at the other hoof. I suspect we'll find the same thing."

No doubt. Sebastian followed Colton inside and placed both their hats on the hooks used for tack. He wiggled his fingers. "Let me pull. You talk to him. He likes you. The sign says his name is Razzle Dazzle."

"Really?" Colton's face screwed up in disgust as he passed the pullers. "Why can't people just give horses normal names?" He brushed the back of his hand over the horse's nose. "Something unique without being silly?"

"You're asking me? According to Tarren, my horse shares a name with the great majority of horses in the romance genre."

Colton snorted. "Ignore Tarren. Maximilian is a good name." He paused long enough for Sebastian to retrieve the unbooted foot. "I'll call you Razz. Or do you like Dazz better, baby?" There was that sultry voice again. "Okay, Dazz it is."

If Colton kept it up, he was going to have more than just the horse wrapped around his finger. No, no, he would not. Sebastian would not allow him to have the upper hand. He'd vowed to protect Colton, not seduce him. Damn Colton anyway, why did he have to get older?

Sebastian brought Dazz's foot up between his legs and bent at the waist as he would while pulling a shoe or cleaning out hooves. His pants were going to get dirty. "The things I do to keep you happy."

Colton chuckled. It was a low, throaty sound a man could wallow in. "I was going to do the dirty work."

"I clean." The nail was far enough out of the hoof that the pullers fit around the head snuggly. Would bending the nail and using the leverage of the pullers to remove it hurt Dazz worse? A drop of perspiration dripped down the bridge of Sebastian's nose. Where was Jimmy with the vet? They always kept medical staff on call during an auction.

A loud crack of thunder rent the air as Sebastian tugged and pulled straight up. Dazz nickered and bobbed his head. He tried to move away.

Sebastian held his foot firm but lost his grip on the nail. He wasn't sure if he'd hurt the horse more or if the thunder had startled him.

"Shhh…. It's all right, Dazz. Wentworth is going to fix you right up. He knows what he's doing. Then we'll get you something for the pain."

The horse stilled.

Positioning the pullers again, Sebastian heaved upward. The nail came free and blood rushed to the surface of the hoof. *Bugger.* "We need a vet to clean the puncture wound and apply a clotting agent." He released Dazz's leg.

The horse pulled his head away from Colton and lipped his hoof. After a few moments, he raised his attention to Sebastian and whinnied.

Colton chuckled. "I think that was a thank-you."

"I believe it was." Petting Dazz's forehead, Sebastian smiled. "You're welcome, ole chap. With any luck we can get you doctored up soon and get something to help with the soreness." Moving to the opposite side, he set about removing the other boot. More effort was required to get the edges of the pullers under the nailhead, but when he did, the nail came out easier. He dropped Dazz's foot and patted his side. "There you go. Now if we can get the vet to look at you, you'll be good as new in no time."

"Thank you." Colton continued to hold the halter and run the back of his gloved hand over the side of Dazz's face. His long fingers caressed and soothed. The gentle drag was both smooth and constant. The action was mesmerizing. Sebastian would be willing to bet the touch felt as nice as it looked.

"You don't have to thank me." He hated to admit it, but he was having a good time. Horses never judged him and found him lacking. He'd always loved caring for horses, and in that regard Colton was a kindred spirit. They worked well together. "You know I'd never condone anything like this." His hand touched Colton's where it rested on Dazz's cheek. Sebastian caught Colton's fingers in his and squeezed. There was something so peaceful and yet alluring about watching Colton. Perhaps it was the simplicity of the moment. Contentment flooded Sebastian, making him grin.

Colton's gaze connected with his. They stood there staring at each other, understanding each other better than they ever had.

"Just what in the bloody hell do you think you're about? Remove your person from my stall."

Sebastian, Colton, and Dazz started at the outraged shout.

I should've known I wasn't lucky enough to escape a run-in with Plume. Sebastian rolled his shoulders and turned to face the man. He didn't know Plume, but he'd seen him around. They frequented some of the same haunts on occasion. "Mr. Plume."

"Wentworth." Barnaby Plume looked down his patrician nose at Sebastian. "To what do I owe the honor of you turning up in my stall?"

"I assure you, it's no honor. I ought to have you brought up on charges." Sebastian's headache insinuated itself behind his right eye, and the piercing pain made him catch his breath. He clenched his fist and stepped closer to Plume. "The treatment of this horse is deplorable and inexcusable."

Sneering, Plume wrenched the door open. "I've no quarrel with you. Remove yourself from my stall."

A tick developed in Sebastian's cheek. He ground his teeth to keep from shouting. "Oh, but I've a quarrel with *you*." He met Plume in the middle of the pen. When Sebastian stood chest to chest with the man, Sebastian grabbed him by his cravat.

Plume gasped and swung.

Ducking, Sebastian tightened his grip on the man's neckcloth and wrung a gurgle from him. Sebastian grinned at the sound.

"Sebastian. Let go." Colton's request was so soft it was barely audible. His gloved hand caressed Sebastian's sleeve. "Please."

Shoving Plume away, Sebastian unfurled his fist.

Plume collided with the wall, but Sebastian ignored him. Colton had called him Sebastian instead of Wentworth. It was a stupid thing to think at the moment, but it popped into Sebastian's head and would not subside. Their gazes locked. Once again they'd found common ground. This horse needed them.

Booming thunder broke the spell. The wind picked up, slicing rain onto the cement walkway under the pavilion.

"I want this horse." Situating himself at Sebastian's side, Colton confronted Plume.

Plume frowned and studied Colton up and down. He sneered and snarled his lip. "Your Highness. If you wish to purchase him, you can bid like everyone else."

The insult didn't faze Colton. He kept right on trying to stare Plume into the ground.

Sebastian, however, tensed, and heat suffused his neck. No one was allowed to disrespect Colton. Or any of the other Townsends, for that matter. "Pay your respects," Sebastian hissed through clenched teeth.

Fortunate for Plume, he understood the threat and bowed.

"Perhaps you're hard of hearing. I will be buying this horse. Name your price, or take what I give you," Colton said.

"You can't—" Plume sputtered and looked at Sebastian.

Sebastian stared back with a blank expression on his face.

"Seven and a half thousand pounds." Colton arched a brow, appearing more like royalty than Sebastian had ever seen him.

"I'd take him up on it if I were you," Sebastian suggested. As long as it wasn't directed at him, he rather enjoyed this haughty side of Colton.

"Are you threatening me?"

Sebastian just smiled. Let Plume make of it what he would.

"But the starting bid is going to be twenty thousand pounds. You can't do this to me." Plume glared and stepped forward.

Darting in front of Colton, Sebastian held his gloved hands up. "Move back."

"You, sir, are a bully." Plume tossed his head, flipping his overlong dark brown hair off his forehead. "I should expect no less of a lowborn—"

In one slick move, Colton advanced and punched Plume in the mouth. Plume's head flew back. He stumbled and fell on his arse outside the open stall door onto the wet pavement. Blood dripped from his split lip.

Damn, that was fast. Sebastian blinked.

Colton shook out his right hand. "Apologize."

"It's all right." A warm feeling spread throughout Sebastian, and the last of his anger melted away.

"No, it is not all right. He owes you an apology." Colton breathed deeply.

He was wrong. It was more than all right. No one had ever stood up for Sebastian that way. Not that he'd needed it, but still…. Tipping Colton's chin up, Sebastian nodded. "It's okay."

Dazz nickered behind them, and his uncovered hooves clicked against the floor.

Not only had Colton rescued an abused horse—a horse that would not further Colton's ambition of being a racehorse breeder—he'd stood up for Sebastian. The man was simply amazing.

Plume steadied himself on the wall, pulled out a handkerchief, and blotted at his lip.

"Ten thousand pounds will be sent to you for the horse by this evening," Sebastian said.

"Make it eighteen and you have a deal."

Colton's shoulders slumped.

Sebastian didn't let on that he noticed Colton's reaction. "Deal. Have him sent to the castle."

As Plume slinked away, Colton caught Sebastian's arm. "I can't afford that. My allowance is only five thousand pounds a quarter."

"I can afford it. You can pay the seven thousand pounds you originally offered, if it makes you feel better, and I'll pay the rest." Dazz could not be allowed to stay in Plume's custody, nor did Sebastian want to take a chance on a new owner making things right for the stallion.

Shaking his head, Colton threw up his hands and turned away. "That isn't right. You should have Dazz if you're paying the majority for him."

"If it makes you feel better, you can consider me a partner. I'll help you set up a stud. But you keep Dazz. He can be part of my buy-in."

Colton whipped around. His complexion had grown pasty. "I don't know if that's a good idea."

Neither did Sebastian, but it was too late to take it back now, and part of him didn't want to.

THE LETTERS and words all blurred together as Sebastian stared at the guard schedule displayed on his computer screen. This morning with Colton had not gone as he'd expected. He'd planned to distance himself from the prince, yet somehow he'd let his emotions get mixed in with the lust, and he'd become partners with Colton. He hated to admit it, but the prospect wasn't so bad. The thought of working with horses on a regular basis soothed something deep inside Sebastian, and his intuition told him it was a sound investment. He believed in Colton. With his tenacity, given a few years, Colton would be one of the leading names in the sport.

Leaning back in his chair, Sebastian closed his eyes. He was starting to see more than just a fetching form. Colton was as lovely inside as he was out. Oh, who was Sebastian jesting? He'd seen the man for his wonderful personality long before he'd noticed how stunning his face and body were. Sebastian propped his feet up on his desk and crossed his ankles. He'd still wanted Colton today, but he'd been able to control the all-consuming lust and concentrate on their friendship. Friendship? Yes, that was exactly what it was. Sebastian smiled. He could make this work.

"I'm glad you're comfortable. I've something to talk to you about." Raleigh lounged against the doorjamb with a grin.

Sebastian dropped his feet and stood. "Your Majesty."

Waving Sebastian to sit back down, Raleigh walked the rest of the way into the office and propped himself on the corner of the desk. "While I was in town this morning, I heard through the grapevine you bought Colton a horse and challenged a man to a duel over him. Another version had you stabbing another peer of the realm with a sword for kissing Colton in an abandoned stall, and proclaiming your undying love. Then there was my favorite, in which you both stole the horse and eloped." Raleigh's eyes practically danced with merriment.

Sebastian gaped. He didn't know whether to be appalled or amused.

Raleigh was obviously amused. "Since you and Colton are here, you didn't elope."

"Good galaxy, the things people do for entertainment. I didn't buy Colton a horse. I purchased the horse with him. And there was no invitation to a duel or any other violence committed. Unless you want to count Colton decking Plume." Sebastian grinned despite the situation.

Both of the king-consort's brows rose, but the mirth never left his eyes. "Colton assaulted someone?"

"Barnaby Plume, Viscount Leith's heir. The man had it coming. He was abusing a horse. Colton and I could not in good conscience allow the animal to remain in Plume's custody, and Colton couldn't afford the stallion on his own."

Chuckling, Raleigh stood. "I've no doubt the man probably deserved to be planted a facer. Colton isn't usually prone to violence. There'll be speculation on why Colton hit the man. No doubt the speculation will have to do with someone's honor, either his or yours, and him defending it. The rumors circulating already have the two of you engaged. I thought you should be aware, but you know how these things are. Given how wild and fantastical the stories are, I suspect things will blow over by tonight since clearly you're both still in town and haven't run off to get married."

Blast. Sebastian hadn't considered how the incident this afternoon might be seen, but Raleigh was likely correct. The ton had a short attention span, and surely no one would credit such asinine tales. "It couldn't be helped. As I said, the situation was dire, so Colton has agreed to take the money as a buy-in for his racing stud. We're going to be business partners. Nothing more."

"Is that a good idea?" Raleigh sat back down on the edge of the desk.

Sebastian had asked himself the same thing at least half a dozen times since he'd made the proposal. "I don't know, but I'm going to give it a chance."

"An unmarried man going into business with an older, widowed man? People will naturally assume Colton is your lover."

"I've no intention of announcing our business arrangement. I plan to stay a silent partner."

Raleigh watched him for several seconds.

Sebastian fought the desire to squirm under the scrutiny.

Finally, Raleigh stood again and nodded. "Very well. See to it that it remains a secret. I'll trust your judgment."

Sebastian stared at the door until the sound of Raleigh's footsteps disappeared. He grinned. He and Colton stealing a horse and eloping.... Chuckling, Sebastian shook his head and returned his attention to his computer screen. He still had a shortage of staff he had to remedy. The idiocy of the ton would have to wait.

"Jeffers, do you have an address for a Julian Towers? His family owns Towers Interplanetary, Inc." It was a long shot. Julian was working with his father, but who knew? Maybe like Rourke, Julian needed a change of pace.

"Yes, my lord. I have a listing. Would you like me to print it out for you, or would you prefer to view it onscreen?"

"Just print it out, Jeffers." Tonight he'd pay his old friend a visit. Sebastian went over tomorrow's schedule again. It appeared that tomorrow there were plenty of people to cover shifts.

"Seb, you won't believe the adventurous morning I had."

Holy meteor showers. The interruption had the same effect as a firecracker being thrown into barracks after lights-out. Sebastian hopped in his seat and glared at Rourke, who sauntered in and flopped down on the chair in front of Sebastian's desk. When his heart rate returned to normal, Sebastian asked, "How was your morning adventurous?"

Rourke looked around. "Do I get an office?"

"No."

"This place is rather bland. It could use some sprucing up."

The office was utilitarian. White walls, a metal desk, no windows, and a computer. "I don't spend much time in here. How did your outing go?"

Putting his feet on Sebastian's desk, Rourke interlaced his hands behind his head and reclined. "I was getting to that, but first...." One side of his mouth turned up, and his eyes twinkled with mischief. "I heard you and Colton are engaged."

Growling, Sebastian leaned back in his chair. "We are not. Good grief, the gossipmongers are working overtime today."

Rourke chuckled. "Oh well. It was amusing anyway."

"Give over. Why did you have an exciting morning?"

Clearing his throat, Rourke grew serious. "Steven and I were followed."

"I beg your pardon?"

Rourke nodded. "We were followed. Not to worry, though. He wasn't a professional. He clearly had no experience tailing someone, because he was blatantly obvious about it."

"Maybe he wanted you to know he was there."

"I don't think so. Steven and I gave him the slip quite easily. The poor man couldn't figure out what happened. He was definitely an amateur. Probably just someone who wanted a closer look at the king."

"Steven knew about it?"

Rourke dropped his feet from the desk with a thud and rested his hands on the arms of his chair. "Yes, and he doesn't want it mentioned to Raleigh yet."

"I really don't think that's possible. Aside from the fact Raleigh has an annoying tendency of knowing everything, he too could be in danger, as could the princes. And Raleigh is more than capable of helping guard our king. We cannot be too cautious. I've reason to be alarmed. Perhaps I should've told you before now, but—"

Rourke held up a hand. "I know all about the mess with the IN. Steven filled me in. And I assure you I am not taking this lightly, but my instincts say this was not the IN. Besides, Steven agreed to allow me to accompany him, Raleigh, and the princes to the ball this evening. I'll also be attending the musicale tomorrow night that they're going to."

Sebastian hadn't realized he'd tensed at the news until his jaw began to ache. He forced himself to relax. He trusted Rourke—the duke had excellent intuition—but Sebastian would feel much better if Raleigh knew about this. "I should send more guards with you tonight."

"No. I can handle this. Trust me."

It went against everything in Sebastian, but he trusted this man with his life as well as the life of their beloved king. "Very well, but if you see anything—anything at all—suspicious tonight, I will not only alert Raleigh, I will assign Steven four guards and an armed escort every time he so much as looks out a window."

"Fair enough." Rourke stood. "Steven has no more outings today, so if it's okay with you, I'm going to go get ready for this evening."

"Fine. Everyone else is back, and no one has informed me of any appointments. Go get ready. I'm searching for Julian tonight. If you need me, contact Christian McGregor here at the castle. He's in charge when I'm not here. He always knows where I am, but I'll be sure to check in with him every hour tonight. I'll drop by the ball after my errand."

"I wish you luck on your mission." Rourke turned to leave.

"Rourke."

"Yes?"

"There are fraggers and shoulder holsters in the supply closet right outside my office door. Take one of each with you." To Jeffers he added, "Jeffers, allow His Grace access to any of the weapons he chooses."

"Yes, my lord," Jeffers said.

Rourke grinned. "You're overreacting, but I'll take a pistol with me."

Sebastian sure hoped it was an overreaction. He had to have faith in Rourke, though. His teammate had never been wrong when it counted.

Sebastian shoved away from his desk and followed Rourke. *What a day.* A nap would really hit the spot, but there was no rest for the weary.

CHAPTER EIGHT

COLTON TOSSED the stick out into the gray drizzly afternoon and walked farther into the stables, away from the cold. At least it had stopped storming. He rubbed his arms up and down his shirtsleeves to rid himself of the chill from standing too close to the open door. Thank goodness the stables were heated. "So, Dazz, how do you like your new accommodations?"

The stallion's ears swiveled forward at the mention of his name.

Grinning, Colton rubbed his nose. Colton had been in here since he arrived home, and he was reluctant to leave, although Dazz seemed to be fitting in fine. The vet had given him a shot of painkiller, some nanomites to fight infection and heal the damage, and pronounced him good to go. With the exception of riding. Which Colton wouldn't have done anyway. Doc Jones wanted him to wait a couple of days and see how Dazz was doing.

The soft thudding of horse hooves reverberated outside, growing louder until Apollonia galloped into the stable heading right for him with the large stick in her mouth. If he didn't know her, she would've startled him. She was huge for only nine months old. Not something you'd want bearing down on you at such a speed. The filly dropped her stick at his feet and looked at him expectantly.

Colton picked up the stick, ambled to the doorway, and hurled the piece of sycamore out of the stables.

Apollonia turned slowly, then took off in a full gallop after her makeshift toy.

When Colton turned back to Dazz, Rexley was standing at the stall with a slight smirk on his face. He must have come in from the side door. "When did she start playing fetch?"

"The other day when I was brushing Apollo. She came and dropped a small branch over the stall door. When I tossed it out, she brought it back, so I started playing with her." He stopped in front of his oldest brother and reached a hand toward Dazz.

"You do realize she's a horse and not a dog, don't you?"

"Sure I do. I don't think she does, though." Colton chuckled. When she was around three months of age and venturing farther from her mother, she latched on to him. If he didn't let her out of her stall or wherever she was when he was outside, she got so riled up he was afraid she'd hurt herself trying to get to him. So he'd started letting her out. To this day, she followed him around like... well, like a puppy. "What're you doing out here?"

"I came to see you." The corner of Rexley's lip tipped up slightly. From Rexley it was a smile. A greeting.

Colton smiled in return. "You found me."

"So I did. How are you doing? Have you made any more plans for your racing stud?"

"I'm fine. And I talked to an architect a little over an hour ago. She said I'll be able to look at preliminary plans by the end of this week." The anticipation was going to kill him. "If I approve them, I'll have the final blueprints by early next week and should be able to break ground on the new stables and training facilities a fortnight from today." Colton bounced on his toes.

"Good. Have you decided on a location?"

"The west pasture. Halfway between the castle and Wentworth Park." It was the perfect spot. Far enough away from both homes to keep it from feeling crowded. "Wentworth approved of the location from a security standpoint."

"Ah. Speaking of Wentworth... I just got back from town and heard an interesting rumor."

Dazz head-butted Rexley's shoulder, jostling him until he was forced to catch his balance.

"Oh?"

"Yes. And I see there must be something to it, given this one's appearance." Rexley turned toward Dazz, patted his neck, and contemplated him. "I heard you and Wentworth assaulted some man and stole his horse."

Colton groaned. How had the rumors started? No one had been around to see. "They're saying we stole Dazz?" Colton scoffed.

"That's what I heard."

"That's preposterous."

The clip-clop of horse hooves echoed on the cement floor, and the scent of wet animal enveloped them. Colton wrinkled his nose. It must be sprinkling outside again. "That's not what happened at all. Dazz was being abused. Wentworth and I rescued him. The only connection between Wentworth and me is I had to take him as a partner in my racing stud because I didn't have enough money to buy Dazz on my own. If I had bought him outright, I wouldn't have enough for a down payment for my stables."

Rexley's eyes narrowed briefly, and his mouth pinched ever so slightly.

Shifting his weight, Colton glanced away and tried not to squirm.

"Are you sure that's a good idea?"

"I don't know, but I couldn't let Dazz stay with an abuser. It seemed like the only way at the time." He'd been pondering it all afternoon. While he knew there could never be a romantic relationship between him and the viscount, Wentworth's actions today reminded Colton why he'd always adored the man. It was going to be absolute torture having to deal with Wentworth on such a personal level and getting to see how honorable and kind he was on a daily basis, but Wentworth was wonderful with horses. And Colton had enjoyed himself. He'd found he actually liked Wentworth. They could be friends.

"Jeremy said you spotted Wentworth in a compromising position and decided you no longer want him. It's not true, is it?"

Blast it. Why had Trouble said that? Colton gritted his teeth. He didn't want pity. And that's exactly what he was getting. *Poor little Colton finally woke up and realized what an idiot he was.*

Rexley touched his arm. "He's worried about you, Colton. It's not like he's gossiping. He came to me upset the night you saw Wentworth with Eugene Collis. Jeremy was ready to run Wentworth through for hurting you, even if it was inadvertently." His hand slid down Colton's arm, and he pried Colton's fist open. He held Colton's hand for a moment. "I'm worried too. Let me be your partner? I have the money to buy Wentworth out. I rarely spend my allowance on anything but toys for Muffin, and I save way more than I spend."

Rexley was not a man who showed affection easily, and for him to make such an offer meant the world. It was like saying, *I love you, little brother*. Warmth blossomed in Colton's chest, and he surged forward and hugged his brother.

Rexley stiffened, and Colton thought he would not return the gesture, but then Rexley's arms wrapped around him. He rubbed Colton's back and moved away enough to make eye contact. "Let me help. Please."

"That you offered means everything to me, but I can't take advantage of you like that. You don't even like racing. Why would you want to be co-owner of a stud?" Besides… he could do this. He could be partners with Wentworth and friends with him without wasting away for love of the man.

"I don't *dislike* racing." Rexley cuffed him on the chin. "And I believe in you. This is something you love."

Colton blinked. How could he refuse? Yet how could he accept? It wasn't fair to do something like this without talking to Wentworth first, even though it was only a verbal agreement between them. Not to mention, he didn't want to use his brother to get him out of a situation he'd put himself into.

"Just say yes, little brother."

"But—"

"Say yes. Would you or would you not do the same for me?"

"Of course, but—" Was it fair to force Wentworth into contact with him? "I can't. It's not right to just oust Wentworth without talking to him." Even if it would make things more… comfortable.

"Then take me as a partner as well." Rexley held out his hand.

Arguing with himself for several more seconds, Colton stared at the elegant hand. How could he refuse? The more capital he had, the more chances of success.

"I'll make you loads of money." He shook on the deal.

"I'm counting on it. Now, tell me about Dazz's situation. How was he abused?"

Colton relaxed, feeling better than he had in a long time. "Mr. Plume, or someone who worked for him, had driven nails in Dazz's hoof walls. Wentworth and I more or less coerced him to sell Dazz to me. After I punched him."

"You punched him?" Rexley caressed Dazz's velvety nose.

"It felt wonderful."

"I'll bet. I've no tolerance for cruelty." Leaving one hand on the bridge of Dazz's nose, Rexley brushed a hank of mane out of Dazz's eyes with the other. "Where have I heard the name Plume before?"

Colton rubbed his new pet's neck. "Viscount Leith's heir."

A sorrel-colored head came up underneath Colton's arm and flipped it off of Dazz. Satisfied her human was now paying attention to her, Apollonia dropped the stick in her mouth.

Colton petted her and chucked her piece of wood toward the door.

She scuttled backward out from under his arm and took off after the stick.

Smirking, Rexley continued to pet Dazz. "Ah, yes. I knew the name sounded familiar." He turned to face Colton with a serious look on his face. "Plume has a reputation for not taking care of his animals."

"How do you know?" Colton studied his brother. Rexley didn't follow racing or any other sport.

"People talk. I listen." Rexley shrugged. "Lord Freeson had a run-in with Plume last year. Plume's an outsider in the racing circles, but he wants to make a name for himself. From what I've heard, I'm surprised he hasn't been blacklisted yet. He's vindictive and will do anything to get ahead or get back at someone he thinks has wronged him. Freeson took issue with how Plume was handling a horse, and Freeson's winning mare came up lame a week later. There was evidence the horse had been purposely injured, but not enough to pin it on Plume."

There wasn't much of a chance Plume could get on Townsend property without being caught, but the thought that Plume was known for his abuse made Colton's heart ache. At least he'd saved Dazz from the blackguard. "You learned all that from listening?"

Rexley nodded. "More or less. Plume asked Jeremy to dance last season, and Jeremy refused. Freeson overheard Jeremy tell me Plume made his skin crawl, and Freeson was all too willing to tell us his tale. He seemed quite genuine, so be careful and watch your back."

Apollonia came back and stopped in front of them.

Rexley held out his hand. "You're quite a handful, my lady. Which reminds me… it's Muffin's bath time." Apollonia nuzzled into Rexley's hand and gave him her toy. He tossed it and turned his attention back to Colton. "I'll get you a bank draft tomorrow morning. I need to get inside and find Muffin for Christy." He slapped Colton on the arm as he started past. "You okay?"

"I am now."

"Good."

Apollonia passed Rexley on her way back into the stables.

Chuckling, Colton grabbed her halter. "Come on, you little hellion. Let's get you brushed. I have a ball to get ready for." Maybe Wentworth would be there tonight. The bigger question was, did he want Wentworth to be there? And if so, what did he expect? He and Wentworth had definitely overcome a boundary today they'd not previously crossed. Only time would tell what it meant.

THINGS MUST not be going well for the family business if Julian was living in this neighborhood. Sebastian stepped around a squashed metal trash can, several torn boxes, and various trash. A lone streetlamp at the end of the block cast eerie shadows rather than brightening the corner. The other streetlights had long since burned out or been broken by street kids. The place reeked of despair.

No wonder lifts wouldn't come to this part of town. Sebastian had taken a lift to Pickett Street and had to walk the rest of the way. And it wasn't a pleasant jaunt. Today's rain and sleet had given way to frigid wind and a dusting of snow. A bit unusual for this time of year, but not completely unheard of; they'd been known to get snow anywhere from September to late March. He shivered, uncertain whether it was from the chill or the depressing surroundings.

As he walked down the filthy sidewalk, he was filled with a mixture of disgust and pity. Living in a neighborhood like this was a tough life. It made him appreciate the comforts of home. Not many men of his acquaintance would venture here, but Sebastian was no hypocrite. He was also no easy target for pickpockets, thugs, or thieves.

Even at this time of night, in this cold, there were signs of life. A cat—*or was that a big rat*—darted across the street into a hole in the foundation of a brick building. A wino slumped against the same building, talking to himself. At least Sebastian assumed he was mumbling to himself, since there was no one else near the man. Several yards in front of the man a door creaked open onto a stoop, and the yellow glow from inside flooded the street in a triangular pattern. A number four hung upside down over the doorway.

An old woman stepped outside with a broom. She swished the ragged bristles back and forth above the stoop. “Get, you! Scat, you dirty little bastard. Shoo. Stay off my porch.”

Until that moment Sebastian hadn’t seen the small figure curled into a ball. His gut clenched as the child unfurled himself and scrambled down the steps.

Sebastian would never understand how people threw their kids away. All children should have a nice warm bed and food in their bellies. Starvation was the worst sort of punishment. Even worse than being homeless. One never got used to the gnawing discomfort of hunger. You ate what you could to survive, but it was never enough. The hunger never seemed to vanish completely. Sometimes life sucked.

With a small shake of his head, he pushed away the memories trying to bombard him and continued down the street.

Soft sobs echoed behind him, along with the child’s shuffling feet. *Bloody hell.*

Sebastian kept walking. He was almost there. Ten was the address Jeffers gave him this afternoon. He’d see if Julian was there first, and if the boy was still here on his way back, he’d—

Sniffles joined the sobs.

Sebastian stopped. He closed his eyes for a moment, then turned around.

The little boy stood in the street, snow and vapor from his sobs swirling around him. As if sensing Sebastian’s attention, he turned his head. His grubby little face resembled a chimney sweep of old. No gloves graced his fingers, and his ratty coat was two sizes too small with holes in it.

Huffing out a breath, Sebastian walked toward the kid.

The boy’s eyes widened. “I din do nuffin, guv.” Backing away, he shook his head.

“Stop.”

The boy froze. Tears glistened on his face, streaking the caked-on dirt and leaving clean runnels.

“I swear it weren’t me, whatevah it was.”

“You aren’t in trouble.” Sebastian began removing his gloves. “How old are you?”

"Seven and ten summers."

Right.

Sebastian offered his gloves to the kid. "Try again. How old are you?"

Eyeing the gloves, the kid backed away. After a few seconds he answered softly, "Ten."

"What's your name?" Sebastian shook the leather at him. "Take these." When the boy snatched the gloves, Sebastian added, "And put them on."

"Me name's Digby." Digby stuffed his fingers into the gloves. He missed a hole and had to try again before getting them on correctly.

"Where are your parents?"

His forehead furrowed, and he eyed Sebastian warily. "Me mum's dead."

"Where's your father?"

"Ain't got one. Me mum didn' know who 'e was."

Which explained the reaction of the lady on the stoop. The boy really was a bastard. Sebastian's heart went out to him. Their society had no sympathy for kids born on the wrong side of the sheets. Bastards were shunned. It was better off to be orphaned than be a bastard. To be abandoned with your parentage unknown, like Lady Muffin, was preferable to being a child born out of wedlock. It had never made any sense to Sebastian. "You want a nice warm bed, hot food, and a job?"

Digby stepped back a few more steps. "I ain't no whore."

The fact the boy even knew such things existed broke Sebastian's heart. "I'm not looking for a whore. I assure you, you're way too young for my tastes."

"Then why would ye want me?" Digby glanced around, taking in his surroundings. He was about to bolt.

Sighing, Sebastian dug into his coat pocket. He pulled out a few pounds and his calling card. "If you change your mind, go to Wentworth Park and ask for Berkley. Tell him Sebastian sent you. I could use someone to help out in the kitchens." There was plenty of staff at Wentworth Park, but perhaps it would help persuade the kid to come work for him. It would get him out of the cold.

"Why would ye do this fer me?" Digby glanced down at the contents of Sebastian's hand and fumbled with the gloves.

"Someone helped me out once, and I want to return the favor."

Digby got one glove off and started on the other. “No ’fence, guv. But I don’t trust ye. I’m no whore.”

“Keep the gloves and take this. If you change your mind….”

Digby snatched the money and calling card. “I won’t.”

“Suit yourself.” Sebastian removed his scarf and tossed it at Digby. “Keep this too. Do what you will with the money.” He supposed he could alert the authorities and get the kid sent to a foundling home, but in Sebastian’s experience the kid was better off on the streets. Even the orphanages were tough on bastards. The foundling homes would boot out a bastard to make room for an orphan if need be.

With a sinking feeling in his gut, Sebastian turned and walked away. At least he’d tried. He couldn’t force the kid.

When he found Julian, he was going to deck him. What was he doing living in a place like this, anyway? Tension seeped into Sebastian’s shoulders and traveled up to his jaw. How dare the jackass not come to him for help. Julian always was a proud pillock.

In the alley to Sebastian’s left, four adolescent boys crowded around a trash-can fire. A fifth smaller boy sat huddled in a cardboard box rubbing his hands together. Within seconds the click-clack of footsteps followed Sebastian. *Dust.*

“Whoa there, toff. We’ll be having a word with ye.”

Bloody hell. He turned. He’d wanted to trounce someone, but not a group of kids.

Five boys no older than sixteen had made a half-circle behind him. They were a rough-looking lot, and all but one of them were as big as Sebastian. The one in the middle was shorter but much stouter than the rest. All of the boys appeared as though they could use a good scrubbing. The scent of smoke clung to them along with the stench of unwashed bodies. One boy had a bent pipe down by his side. Another one had a battered croquet mallet.

“I don’t want any trouble. I’m searching for a man named Julian Towers. Do any of you know where I can find him?”

Pounding feet and a flash of gray passed Sebastian. *Digby.* That probably didn’t speak well for Sebastian’s chances of getting out of this without hurting a few of these teens.

The group of four didn’t even glance at the child. Their gazes stayed on Sebastian. The boy on the left side of the middle held out his hand and smiled, showing off a broken front tooth. “What’s it to ye?”

His hair appeared a lighter shade of brown. Probably blond under all the dirt.

"Do you know where I can find him or don't you?" The anger at Digby's fate and poverty in general vanished, and calm took its place. Sebastian cataloged his surroundings.

The boy with the pipe, clearly the leader of the group, brought it up in front of him and smiled. "Ye can turn over yer blunt and valuables the easy way, or we can do it the hard way if ye like. 'Sup to you, chap."

So be it. Sebastian would not relinquish his purse to a bunch of thugs. Pickpocketing was one thing—it was a way of life for foundlings—but assault and robbery was another thing entirely. "You really don't want to do this."

"I think we do."

They rushed him all at once.

Sebastian deflected the first punch and followed up with a jab to the leader's lips, but missed a hook that caught him in the eye. He barely felt it as he caught the pipe and kneed the assailant in the groin. Ducking the mallet, he swept the boy's legs out from under him.

By the time he had the third boy down, the first was getting back up. As each one came at Sebastian, he easily dispatched them again. He had to hand it to them, for all their ineffectiveness, they were persistent. If they kept it up, they might just wear him down enough to get a blow in.

The boy with the broken front tooth let out a whistle, and four more hoodlums poured from the alleys on each side of Sebastian. Great. The boy with the wooden mallet swung at Sebastian again. Grabbing the striking end of the mallet, he turned, using the thug's momentum to dislodge his hold on his weapon. He smacked the kid in the rump with the handle and tossed the mallet away. He punched the next ruffian in the chin, and blood flew from his mouth.

The other five tried to flank him, but he moved with them, keeping them in front. Two of them came at him, but he kicked one in the ribs and punched the other in the gut.

A sharp pain exploded in his back, and the pipe clattered to the ground several feet in front of him. *Bugger that hurt.* Sebastian winced. He may have even grunted, but he didn't let down his guard. How had the little reprobate gotten behind him? He kicked back as the pipe thrower closed in on him.

Crack.

A wail rent the air.

Sebastian hadn't wanted to permanently damage any of them, only teach them a lesson, but he couldn't keep up this pace. He popped one of them in the chin and watched him hit the ground so hard he bounced.

"Hey!" The quick staccato of footsteps approached from behind.

Blast. Sebastian grabbed the kid closest to him and put him in a headlock, exerting just enough pressure to let the panic set in. He moved toward the nearest building, putting his back to it and opening up his field of view.

A big man came running down the street toward them, followed by a smaller boy. *Digby.*

The other thugs ran away, leaving Sebastian with the gagging, squirming kid in his hold.

What the— Sebastian squinted down the dimly lit street.

This man was not filthy like the others. He wore Hessian boots, buff trousers, a white shirt, and dark waistcoat, sans outerwear. His brown hair was a bit long for convention, and he held a saber in his right hand. He was also much bigger than the others.

Wonderful. Sebastian shoved the reprobate against his chest and dug down in his right boot for his knife. As Sebastian gripped the hilt of his weapon, a shadow loomed over him.

"Need some help, Commander?"

CHAPTER NINE

The Earl of Baxter's ball in Classige, Pruluce

SEBASTIAN'S LIFT pulled up to the Baxter town house and stopped. He was not at all fit to go to a ball. He should've gone in and freshened up when he'd dropped Digby off at Wentworth Park, but he hadn't wanted to waste any more time. He needed to check in on the Townsends to make certain Rourke had been correct and there really was nothing to the stalker situation he and Steven had found themselves in.

Bloody hell and imploding planets. His body ached. At least he'd found Julian, though. He desperately needed some elite guards, a few men who could take some of his burden because he couldn't be everywhere at once. His guards were good. He'd trained most of them personally—with the added help, he might have time to further their training—but they weren't special forces level yet, and with the things they might encounter having the IN as an enemy.... *Dust*, he didn't want to think about it.

He alighted from the coach and trudged up the front steps, ignoring the widened eyes of the doorman. Hmm... he must look worse than he thought. He'd already made certain he had no visible dirt or tears in his evening clothes. Therefore it must be his face. The skin under his left eye did feel rather puffy and tender. Oh well, nothing for it now. It wasn't like the ton would be surprised to see him looking less than appropriate. They thrived on his misadventures and sexual escapades.

The brightly lit mansion hummed with activity, although the foyer was clear except for a footman. The sugary smell of pipe tobacco billowed from the room on the right and loud music and the buzz of voices blared from the left. Handing off his coat to the footman, Sebastian headed left to the ballroom.

As he passed under the arched doorway into the ballroom, the butler said, “Lord Wentworth.”

Bugger. Baxter was one of those annoying gents who thought to have every guest announced, even after the ball had begun in earnest. As Sebastian expected, most of the crowd turned as one to gawk at him. He’d never get used to that.

Right away he spotted Rourke among the sea of faces. Not a difficult feat. Rourke was strategically in the best position to see all of the ballroom. He’d spotted Sebastian right away and gave a nod over the shoulder of a shorter man with whom he chatted.

Weaving through the crowd, Sebastian made his way to the duke. As he did so, Rourke extricated himself from the group he’d been in. Sebastian got two feet from him before the duke broke into a broad grin.

“Let me guess, instead of Julian, you found an irate cuckolded husband?”

“Very funny, smartarse. No. I found a group of street thugs, and Julian found me.”

“Was that before or after the thugs decided to use you as a punching bag?”

“During, actually.” Sebastian stepped up next to Rourke and turned to look out over the ballroom.

Rourke’s lip twitched. “I’m afraid I cannot claim to have had the excitement you’ve had tonight. I’m jealous.”

Sebastian snorted. “Don’t be. Somehow I don’t remember having the hell beat out of me hurting this bad.”

“Nothing a little brandy won’t cure. Perhaps a couple of cigars as well.”

“Bite your tongue.”

Rourke chuckled. “I haven’t seen our little friend. Nothing untoward has happened at all, unless you count Winstol tossing his dance card into the wall sconce over there.” He bobbed his head toward the right.

The front ballroom wall was pale yellow and lined with arched windows interspaced with fan-shaped, frosted-glass wall sconces. There was a dark rectangular shape silhouetted in the third from the right.

Sebastian grinned. Now that Aiden and Payton were married, it seemed Lord Trouble was taking up where they’d left off.

"Oh, and did I mention the rumors?"

"There are still rumors, even though Colton is here and obviously did not elope?"

"They've evolved to Colton stealing that horse."

"They've left me out of the rumors?"

"Not exactly. You aided and abetted. Oh, look over there." Rourke flipped his chin to their left. "It appears Lord Bannon is now looking to get rid of his dance card."

Standing next to Trouble, Lord Bannon had his dance card in his hand, searching left and right.

"Unbelievable. I can't fathom anyone stupid enough to believe Colton would do something so foolhardy."

"I'm not sure they actually do, but they're talking about it nonetheless." Rourke bumped him with his elbow. "Here goes. Did you see how Winstol nudged him?"

Sure enough, Bannon flung his dance card across the dance floor like one would skip rocks on a pond. It sailed across the wood floor, hit someone's foot, and bounced off, spinning in the opposite direction.

"Do you think it will get trampled on, or will someone find it and return—"

Mr. Potts, the portly middle-aged older son of Baron Henderson, stepped on the card. His arms flailed for at least five seconds, and then he grabbed the man next to him, and they both went down with a bounce. One of them let out a loud "Umph," and a cacophony of gasps and groans followed from onlookers. The next two men in line tripped over them, and all four ended up in a pile.

Rourke didn't even try to cover his laugh.

Lord Bannon and Trouble hightailed it out of the room as the music stopped and the rest of the dancers helped their fallen comrades from the floor.

Sebastian shook his head and coughed into his hand. He had to avert his gaze to keep it together.

"You were right. This job is not the least bit boring."

Finally the dance floor cleared, and the orchestra began playing a waltz. Steven and Raleigh were among the first couples to start the dance. Sebastian sought out the rest of the royal family but didn't get any further than Colton. He stood in front of a vase, contemplating it like it was a work of art. When did Colton take an interest in art? He was by himself. Was it because of the silly gossip? Usually there were several bucks vying for his attention.

Sebastian's chest tightened as he watched Colton. Colton should never be lonely, but perhaps it was to Sebastian's advantage. He started toward the prince.

"Where are you going?"

"To see if Colton would like to dance."

THANK GOODNESS horse theft was not a hanging offense in Regelence. As another group of peers passed Colton, the noise level decreased slightly. It was as if everyone held their breath. He bit his lip to keep from chuckling and studied the crowd. One man in particular kept watching him and turning back to his acquaintance. What a ridiculous notion that Colton could actually get away with such a thing. Prince or not, laws were laws.

Dalton sidled up next to him. "So…."

"I did not steal a horse."

"Okay, okay." Laughing, Dalton held up his hands. "I wasn't going to ask that. I wanted to see if you could identify someone for me."

"I can try."

Raising his chin a little to indicate something across the ballroom from them, Dalton asked, "Who's that talking to Trouble's friend?"

Colton spotted Bannon, looking quite petulant. Lord Redding, Bannon's older brother, was lecturing him. Redding shook his head and put his hands on his hips. "That's Viscount Redding, the future Duke of Eversleigh. Why?"

"What's his name? He's stunning."

Uh-oh. Colton jerked his attention back to Dalton. His gaze hadn't wavered from Redding. "You might as well forget it. He's nearly as stuffy as Rexley. He never ever steps out of line. His reputation is spotless." Colton understood Dalton's preoccupation, though. Redding was gorgeous. At nearly six foot, he was of average height for a Regelen. His build was athletic and toned, his features refined, his eyes big, his nose perfectly straight, and his jaw slightly squared. Bannon and Redding shared those incredible, vibrant, grass-green eyes. Bannon referred to them as Thompson green because they ran in the family. Their father also had them. But unlike his redheaded younger brother, Redding had rich brown hair.

"What's his given name?"

Colton sighed. "Blaise Thompson. But I'm telling you, you don't stand a chance. Even if you could get Redding to talk to you, you wouldn't get past Eversleigh."

"Hmm…." Dalton strode forward, then stopped. "Er… would you like to dance with me later?"

Colton fished his dance card out of his inside coat pocket and held it up. "Sure."

Someone touched his lower middle back and a shiver ran up his spine. Whoever it was stood very close behind him. It was intimate.

Dalton arched a brow, and a smirk eased onto his face.

A soft chuckle tickled Colton's ear and moved the hair at his temple. *Wentworth.* He knew that laugh as well as his own. Or maybe it was just the sixth sense he seemed to have where Wentworth was concerned.

Wentworth extracted the dance card from Colton's fingers and tossed it into the ugly purple urn to Colton's right. *Clink. Clink. Plunk.* "Now then, that will free you up to dance with me."

Turning his head, Colton came nose to nose with Wentworth, and a nervous flutter tickled his stomach. Wentworth was so close, it would take no effort to kiss him. And Colton wanted to.

As if reading his mind, Wentworth's gaze dropped to Colton's mouth.

Colton's lips tingled. Swallowing the lump in his throat, he licked his lips. The butterflies in his stomach increased, and warmth covered him from head to toe. The connection between them from this afternoon was still present. Maybe this afternoon wasn't a fluke.

"Good evening, Wentworth." Galaxy, was that his voice? It sounded much deeper and softer than normal.

"It is now," Wentworth whispered.

Colton studied him, trying to gauge his mood. But Wentworth appeared as he always did. Reading the man had never been easy. Colton turned to get a better look. *Dust*, he had such dark blue eyes and long las—"What happened to your eye?" A bruise marred his lovely face under his left eye. Within the beard shadow, a reddish scratch stretched from his earlobe to his nose, and his hair was a lot more windswept than normal.

Colton touched Wentworth's cheek just under his black eye. The thought of him hurt soured Colton's stomach. *I should've been there.* If he'd been with Wentworth—

What was he thinking? He couldn't follow Wentworth around. Still, guilt niggled at him. He had the insane urge to kiss the injuries better.

Dalton cleared his throat. "Good evening, Wentworth."

Colton jerked his hand away from Wentworth's cheek and stepped back. They were in a crowded ballroom with people who already thought them thieves. Impropriety was becoming a habit… again.

"Nice to see you too, Ashbourne." Wentworth bowed over Dalton's hand, bringing it to his lips. Wentworth's hands were ungloved and his knuckles were bruised. What in the world had happened to him?

"I trust that I leave my cousin in good hands, Wentworth?"

"You do indeed, Ashbourne." Straightening, Wentworth released Dalton.

Smirking, Dalton strolled off and Colton gave one last fervent hope he'd stay away from Blaise Thompson.

"How about that dance you promised me?" Wentworth winked at Colton.

"I—" He hadn't promised Wentworth a dance. "Sure." How many times had he wanted to do this? Dance with Wentworth?

Wentworth placed his hand on Colton's back again and led him to the edge of the dance floor.

Couples whirled about as the lights glistened off the crystal chandeliers, throwing sparkles around the room. It was magical. Colton inched his hand under his sleeve and pinched his arm. *Ow.*

Wentworth swept them into the crowd of dancers.

Caught off guard at the abruptness, Colton wobbled and squeezed Wentworth's shoulder. *One… two… three… one… two… three.* He stepped on Wentworth's foot. "Sorry," he mumbled.

"It's okay. I hope I didn't interrupt anything important. I needed to talk to you and thought it best if we didn't talk in front of others."

Colton's stomach sank a little. Wentworth wanted to talk to him? He supposed that explained Wentworth seeking him out. Colton met Wentworth's gaze. "You didn't interrupt. What happened to your face?"

"I was mistaken for a croquet ball."

Colton burst into laughter. "What?"

Wentworth grinned. Laugh lines appeared at the corners of his eyes. "You have a wonderful laugh."

"And you have an odd sense of humor. What really happened?"

"I ran into a gang of ruffians who thought to relieve me of my purse. They look much worse than I do."

Colton gasped. *A gang?* Good grief, he could have been killed. Bile rose up the back of his throat as the image of Wentworth lying in the street flashed into his head. "You should've just given them your money. Your life is worth much more than a few hundred pounds."

"Relax. I'm quite capable of defending myself. Besides, I had some help. One of my old teammates was there to back me up."

It was hard to reconcile Wentworth with a commando. He seemed too elegant and refined to have been involved in the RSR. What would Wentworth look like in uniform? He'd be dashing, but then he could probably wear anything and still turn heads. It was the man, not the clothes. Something about how he carried himself. His self-assured swagger.

As they turned, Colton caught a glimpse of some men on the edge of the dance floor pointing at them.

Wentworth must've seen them too, because he asked, "Has the gossip been too bad?"

Colton met Wentworth's gaze. "You've heard it, then?"

"Only secondhand."

"Rather silly tale, isn't it?" Colton smiled sweetly. He was having much too good a time to let the idiocy of the ton bother him.

"Extremely. But is that why you weren't dancing?" Wentworth gave him a soft smile that did wonderful things for his lips.

Colton shook his head.

For several long seconds, they held each other's gaze and moved as one. Pleasure shot through Colton, and his body coiled with excitement. The room and all the busybodies waiting for their next move faded into the background. He could not look away. He didn't want to.

Wentworth's eyes sparkled and with something in his gaze that Colton had seen before, but never directed at him. It was at once gratifying and terrifying. He'd wanted that admiration for so long, but now? He wasn't sure.

"Why have we never danced before?"

"You've never asked me."

"Stupid of me. You dance divinely."

"Thank you. So do you." Colton grinned. Caught up in the moment, he had not noticed their proximity to the edge of the ballroom until Wentworth whirled them out into the night air.

"Wentworth, where're we going?"

Wentworth tightened his grip on Colton's waist and dipped their hands down and back up, exaggerating their movements. "Sebastian. And we're going for some fresh air."

"Sebastian." Colton smiled bigger and followed Sebastian's lead. He couldn't believe this was happening. The cool air chilled and electrified him at the same time.

Their footsteps thudded softly on the wooden porch. The music and the quietness of the night filtered out the chatter from the ballroom. Together they danced, taking much grander steps than the crush inside allowed for. The moonlight gleamed off the snow, and the golden glow of candlelight in the lanterns lit their way. It was exhilarating… fun.

Sebastian seemed to feel it too. He threw his head back and laughed, letting the dance sweep him away.

When the music faded, the sound of applause followed, but they kept dancing. Sebastian pulled him closer until the heat of his body warmed Colton's front and there was barely space between them.

Lifting his head, Colton brushed his cheek with Sebastian's, his lips only a hairsbreadth away from Sebastian's. Colton's heart pounded as Sebastian turned his head and their lips met. Colton and Sebastian stopped moving.

Colton's toes curled in his shoes, and his cock began to fill. Had he wished this kiss into being?

Squeezing his hand, Sebastian deepened the kiss and leaned into Colton until their bodies touched. They fit so perfectly together, like they were meant to be. It was better than any fantasy.

Colton opened his lips, wanting more. And he got it. Sebastian nipped Colton's bottom lip and squeezed his arse.

Colton stiffened. Should he put a stop to this? He didn't want to, but he needed to.

Panting, Sebastian blinked as if coming out of a daze. "I'm sorry." He moved back so swiftly, the cold hit Colton where Sebastian's warm body had been and made him shiver.

"Come, let's get you back into the ballroom. I never should've brought you out here. I don't know what I was thinking." Sebastian took his arm and led him back inside.

Colton followed in a daze. What had just happened? How had things turned cold so quickly? Had he done something? Something other than kiss the man? *Blast.* Had he somehow coerced Sebastian into kissing him? He should've never accepted that dance.

IF ONE more person made so much as an innuendo about Colton stealing that blasted horse, Steven was going to come untethered. Of all the asinine rumors to pick up on. Why didn't they pick up on the eloping gossip?

He gazed out at the dance floor. Couples waltzed by, creating an intricate pattern. The whole crowd seemed to undulate together, forming one big rotating mass. Maybe he should find Raleigh and go waltz again. That might improve his mood. Or maybe a drink. Yes, that sounded just right.

He searched the throng for a footman. He spotted one, waved him down, and ordered himself a drink. Waiting on the liquor, he looked for the kids. He might as well be a responsible chaperone. Aiden usually loitered with the wallflowers and acted as chaperone, but he couldn't tell you what his brothers or stepson were doing at any given moment even if he was held at sword point. If he wasn't dancing with Nate, he was engrossed in a sketch.

Nate, however, usually knew where everyone was and what they were doing. But at the moment, Nate stood with his head next to Aiden's, looking at whatever Aiden was working on.

Rexley conversed with a group of peers by the punch table.

Trouble and Bannon Thompson leaned on a marble pillar gaping at something on the dance floor. Steven followed their gazes and spotted

Raleigh dancing with Tarren. Why was that gapeworthy? Raleigh usually danced with all of the boys within an evening.

Raleigh and Tarren whirled to the right, and in the spot they left, Colton and Sebastian walked arm in arm through the open terrace door. They'd been outside? Alone?

Steven grinned. Maybe tonight wasn't a total waste. Apparently, throwing them together this afternoon had been a splendid idea. How could he continue to keep them in each other's presence? Surely there were some errands he could have Colton run. And, of course, he needed someone to accompany Colton for safety's sake.

"Your drink, Your Majesty." The footman held out a tumbler.

"Thank you." Steven took the glass. When he looked back toward the side of the ballroom, Colton stood by himself.

"Steven, how are you this evening?" The Duke of Eversleigh stepped up beside him. He too stared out at the dance floor. "Is Wentworth courting Colton? I noticed them dancing together earlier."

"I can only hope. Wait. They danced together?"

"Yes. When you and Raleigh were dancing."

"Drats. I missed it."

Eversleigh chuckled. "Does Raleigh know you're matchmaking again?"

"I haven't a clue what you're blathering about, Eversleigh."

Eversleigh's chuckle morphed into a full-fledged laugh. "Your secret is safe with me." He was quiet for a few moments, then asked, "Steven, do you have a few moments? I need to discuss something with you." His face showed no hint of what he wanted to discuss, but Steven sensed whatever it was should be said in private.

Turning toward the ballroom entrance, Steven held out his arm, indicating Eversleigh should lead the way. "Let's borrow Baxter's library."

They made their way through the mass of bodies. At one point, Steven lost sight of Eversleigh but caught up to him again in the foyer.

When they reached the library, Eversleigh closed the door and ordered the computer butler out of the room. He flipped open the globe bar in the corner and poured himself a drink.

Steven took a seat by the fireplace and contemplated his friend. Warren Thompson was a solemn man in his early sixties. The duke was the Regelence IN council member. His grandfather and father held the position before him, but it was an appointed position, not an inherited one. It was a big responsibility, and the current Eversleigh excelled at the job. He was going to be difficult to replace when he decided to retire.

He sat next to Steven. "I'd offer you a cigar, but I know Raleigh would throttle us both."

"He's not as bad as he used to be. As long as I smoke the flavored ones, he doesn't mind. It's the smoke he dislikes, and those smell good. Or so he claims."

Eversleigh nodded. "Yes, Pierce prefers those as well. Personally, I don't have a preference." He crossed his ankles in front of him and leaned back. "The reason I wanted to talk to you is I've run into something that concerns me. It may be nothing, but—" He shook his head. "I don't know. It just seems odd to me, with all the things we've learned about the IN recently." He looked down at his drink and up at Steven again. "This requires a little backstory, if you will indulge me?"

Sipping from his drink, Steven motioned for the duke to continue.

"As you may know, Admiral Jenkins's wife is Regelen. He has a residence here in Classige and on the planet Delcorte. Since he's retired, I thought he might be a nice addition to my staff. Not to mention, I'd like to pick his brain and find out if he can enlighten us further on this predicament we find ourselves in with the IN."

"I think that's an excellent idea, but do be careful. Nate has the distinct impression the admiral knows more than he's told us, and he's not certain if he can trust him entirely. He hasn't been able to get ahold of him since he retired. Though I don't know how hard he's tried; he's been busy."

Eversleigh nodded. "Don't worry, I planned on feeling him out first and seeing what he'll tell me before I divulge too much. But I have a problem. I too have been trying to reach him with no luck. It's like he and his family have up and disappeared. They're not on Delcorte or here on Regelence. His son, Robert, who is an IN lieutenant, has gone AWOL. I think something has happened to them."

A sinking feeling gripped Steven. He downed the rest of his drink.

"No one seems to know their whereabouts." Warren sat forward, holding his drink between his open knees. "Isn't Wentworth kin to the admiral? Does he know anything?"

"No, Wentworth isn't actually kin to the admiral. The admiral bought Wentworth's commission into the IN, but I believe Sebastian still corresponds with Jenkins. I'll ask Sebastian tonight, but I'm certain if he knew anything, he'd have told me." Steven stood and stretched his back. He needed to visit the washroom. That scotch had gone right through him. "I wonder what information Jenkins had. Maybe we should find the last person he had contact with before he went missing." He turned toward the fire and rested his arm on the wall.

Joining him at the fireplace, Eversleigh set his empty glass on the mantel. "I've already got my staff trying to discover the last time they were seen. It makes me wonder, though. If he was in danger, why didn't he come to us for protection?"

That was a good question. Nate was convinced there was more behind the man's retirement than met the eye. "I don't know, my friend. I don't know." The happiness from seeing Colton with Wentworth had been replaced with an eerie feeling of impending doom. Chills skittered up his body and made the hair on his arms stand on end. What was the IN planning? How did the puzzle pieces fit together?

Steven and Warren left the library together, promising to meet up tomorrow after Steven spoke to Sebastian and Nate.

Heading toward the washroom, Steven let his mind wander. What did Jenkins know? So far they had stolen weapons, plans for an EMP superweapon, and an attempt to steal Regelence's procreation technology. How did all those things add up? Maybe Jenkins could tell them.

Steven rounded the corner into the hall of washrooms and searched for an open door. *Ah, there at the end.*

"What are you doing?"

Gasping, Steven slapped a hand to his chest. His heart pounded under his palm so hard it nearly beat out of his chest. "Damn it, Raleigh." He glared at his consort. "You scared the daylights out of me."

Raleigh frowned. "You've been gone for almost fifteen minutes. I was worried. Where have you been?"

To tell or not to tell? Steven's bladder decided for him. He really had to go. Grabbing Raleigh by the hand, Steven tugged him inside the washroom and locked the door. "I think the IN has murdered Admiral Jenkins and his family."

Chapter Ten

SEBASTIAN WAS beginning to think he was a prime candidate for Bedlam. His brain was scrambled. Confusion didn't come close to describing what he felt. Had it only been a day ago he'd decided staying away from Colton was his best course of action? Now, he wanted to spend every waking moment in Colton's presence.

He'd gone to the ball tonight to check in on Rourke and make certain nothing untoward had occurred. He should've left immediately after he'd ascertained everything was fine, but he'd seen Colton standing on the edge of the ballroom. Before he'd even made the conscious decision, he was across the room, drawn like steel to a magnet. He'd wanted to dance with Colton. It was as simple as that. He'd wanted to hold him close.

Galaxy give me strength. Colton was quickly becoming an addiction.

Laying his head on the back of the chair, Sebastian stretched his legs out in front of him and closed his eyes. He ran his hands down his face, and a muscle pinched in his back. It was like being raked with shards of glass. He'd forgotten all about the blasted street fight he'd gotten into searching for Julian. Damn, it had been a long day.

Nate came into the study and crossed to the sideboard. "What happened to you?" He picked up two glasses and poured scotch in them.

"Ran into a band of hoodlums while looking for a friend of mine."

Pausing, Nate turned his head. His eyebrows shot up as he studied Sebastian. He shook his head and went back to pouring. After stoppering the decanter, he picked up the glasses and crossed the room. "You look like you could use one." He handed a glass to Sebastian and sat on the chair next to him.

"Thank you." Scotch was not his preferred drink, but it was bound to help with the pain. He sipped. "Any idea why we're here?"

"Not a clue. In the lift on the way home, Steven told me he was calling a meeting and wanted me present."

Aiden came into the room, making a beeline for his consort. He kissed Nate on the cheek, and they stared at each other for a few seconds. Aiden's hand lingered on his consort's shoulder. The admiral laid his free hand on top of Aiden's and squeezed. It was intimate and improper, but it was also beautiful. They made a striking couple. Aiden was elegant and lovely while Nate was big and handsome in a masculine way.

Sebastian couldn't look away. What must it be like to have a relationship like that? Giles would never have shown such affection in front of others. All the Townsends, thus far, had found love matches.

Stealing his consort's drink, Aiden sat on the loveseat opposite them. He drank as he glanced at Sebastian. His eyes widened, and he removed the glass from his lips. "What happened to you?"

"He got into a gang fight." After removing a cigar and cutter from his coat pocket, Nate snipped the end.

"A gang fight?" Aiden blinked. "I don't suppose you lopped anyone's head off, did you?"

Groaning, Nate dropped his head into his hand, but he was smiling.

Sebastian's mouth gaped open. Only a Townsend would ask such a question. "No. Why do you ask?"

"He's painting a war scene." Lifting his head, Nate went to the sideboard and dug a lighter out of the drawer. Lighting his cigar, he sat next to Aiden. He patted Aiden's leg, leaving his hand there, and reclaimed his drink.

"Getting the blood splatter right is giving me a devil of a time. Where are Father and Cony? I thought this was an important meeting. Any idea what it's about?" Aiden toed off his right shoe and tucked his foot under his leg, angling his body toward Nate. Resting his right arm on the back of the sofa, he absently played with the admiral's neck.

"We were just discussing that when you came in." Sliding his hand farther up Aiden's thigh, Nate took a drink of scotch. Holding the cigar in the same hand, he gave the glass back to Aiden, who sipped from it. "Surely if it were very important, they'd be here already."

"One would think." Sebastian smiled. The ton was full of couples who barely tolerated one another. It was refreshing to see a couple so in love. Men did not share their drinks with one another. It just wasn't done. It spoke of the devotion and intimacy between the two men. Would Colton be that affectionate with his consort? A knot formed in Sebastian's stomach. The idea of Colton married and sharing things with another man did not sit well with him. He had no claim on Colton, yet something inside him screamed out Colton was his.

"Ah good, you're all here." Steven came into the room with Raleigh on his heels.

"Jeffers, stop all recording and leave the room." Raleigh closed the door behind him and sat next to Steven on the desk.

"Yes, Your Majesty," the butler answered.

Laying his hand on Raleigh's thigh, Steven cocked his head and studied his son. "Aiden, what're you doing in here? Not that I care, but…."

"Saving Nate the trouble of having to repeat everything."

Slipping his hand on top of the one Steven had on his thigh, Raleigh wound his fingers with Steven's. Did he even notice he did it? They, too, always seemed to be touching each other in little ways. Sebastian was certain they did most of it unconsciously.

Raleigh grinned. "Aiden, Nate doesn't tell you everything."

The admiral thought about it for a second. "Actually, I do. Anything of importance, anyway."

Aiden beamed at him.

Sebastian chuckled. If he married Colton, would they share all their secrets?

Where had that come from? He'd sworn off marriage after Giles died. He had no need to marry again. It didn't matter to him if the Wentworth title was passed on or not. It wasn't his family name. The title and estate could revert back to the crown for all he cared.

"Okay, fair enough. We can use the extra brain pow—good galaxy. What happened to your face?" Raleigh gaped. "Do you need an ice pack?"

"I'm fine." Sebastian waved the questions away. He was getting tired of explaining it, but it warmed his heart that they cared. "I ran into some delinquents when I went to find one of my old teammates. They decided they needed my money and belongings more than I did. I begged to differ."

"Did you find your teammate?" Aiden wanted to know.

"I did. He starts work tomorrow. His name is Julian Towers. That's one more guard who can accompany all of you on your outings. I prefer you take Knighton, Julian, or myself rather than the other guards." He looked at Nate. "I wish you would reconsider having an armed escort to the base every morning."

Nate puffed on his cigar. "It's only a mile away."

Sebastian sighed but didn't say anything. It wouldn't do any good. The man had made up his mind, and he was as hardheaded as the rest of the family.

It got quiet for several seconds, and then Steven cleared his throat. "Eversleigh, as you know, is our permanent IN council member. He's been trying to track Admiral Jenkins down for the past two months with no luck. He's not on Delcorte or here on Regelence. As far as we know, those are his only two residences."

Nate gasped.

Aiden whispered, "Oh no."

Sebastian sat, too stunned to do anything.

Looking at Sebastian, Steven asked, "Do you know of any other places he and his family might be?"

Sebastian shook his head. "The last time I talked to him was after the ceremony where he retired and named Nate his successor." Surely Carl was all right. He had to be.

"Why would Wentworth know where the admiral lived?" Aiden's brow furrowed.

"Jenkins was his mentor," Nate said.

Actually, he was more like a savior. If it wasn't for Carl, Sebastian would probably be dead by now. "He's the one who got me into the IN. His wife is from Regelence. I met him when I was sixteen, and he was on leave. He was able to get special permission for me to join the IN at sixteen." *Please be all right, Carl.* To Steven he asked, "I take it you have not located Betty either?"

"I didn't know his wife was from here." Aiden leaned forward slightly.

"Yes, his son was born here. Robert is just a couple of years younger than me." Sebastian said.

"Why didn't I know this?" Putting his feet on the floor, Aiden leaned forward more.

"I don't know." Sebastian gulped some of his drink.

"Hmm… come to think on it… I have seen the admiral at balls before," Aiden said.

"Aiden, do you mind?" Raleigh arched a brow.

Aiden's shoulders drooped. "Sorry, Cony."

With a smirk at his son, Steven continued. "I also heard that Carl's son, Robert, went AWOL. Nate, can you check that out?"

"I'll check it out first thing in the morning." Nate set his cigar in the ashtray next to him and retrieved his drink from Aiden. Peering down at the liquid, he shook his head. "I sensed something was wrong. I should've offered him protection. I should've confronted him about it."

Sebastian's thoughts exactly. He too should have asked after Carl. His stomach was queasy.

"There is no use beating ourselves up over it. Let's just find them." Raleigh stood and stretched his arms over his head. "He obviously knows something. When we do find him, we'll see to it he and his family are protected. Now, unless anyone else has something to add, I'm going to bed."

"Me too." Nate stood and offered his hand to Aiden.

After putting his shoe back on, Aiden accepted the assistance and stood. "Good night, everyone." Still hand in hand, Aiden and Nate left the study.

Raleigh stepped up between Steven's legs. He touched Steven's cheek, then dropped his hand. "Are you coming?"

Steven lifted Raleigh's hand to his lips and kissed it. "In a moment." The romantic gesture made Sebastian's mind wander once again to Colton. He was so passionate and vibrant. No doubt he'd throw himself into a relationship with as much ardor as his parents did.

"Don't stay up too late. You aren't going to find him tonight." Raleigh dipped his head at Sebastian. "Good night, Wentworth. Go put some ice on your face." He closed the door on his way out.

Steven stared at the closed door with a soft smile on his face, but he looked a million miles away.

Sebastian downed the rest of his drink and set it aside. He leaned forward, resting his elbows on his knees. "Do you think he's dead?"

"I hope not. But yes, that's my fear."

Sebastian's pulse skipped a beat, and a wave of dizziness swamped him. Sadness nearly choked him. He owed Carl so much.

"Don't beat yourself up over it. Like Raleigh said, we aren't going to find him tonight." Steven gave him a sad smile. "While I've got you here… I wanted to ask you about something else."

"Anything."

"I saw you and Colton tonight. The two of you look good together."

Sebastian fought to show no outward sign of surprise. "He looked lonely when I went to check in with Rourke, and he wasn't dancing, so I asked him to dance."

"Then I take it you've heard the rumors about you and Colton?"

"Not personally, but I know people are speculating Colton and I stole the horse."

"That's not all."

"Yes, yes, the elopement rumor. I've heard about that one too."

"How about the one claiming the two of you are lovers?"

A sinking feeling settled into Sebastian's gut. "No, I hadn't heard that one."

"What do you intend to do?"

Sebastian sat back and rested his hands on his thighs. What could he do? "The rumors will die down." Perhaps his dancing with Colton tonight would help. Surely no one would think he'd flaunt their relationship in front of Colton's parents. Or given Sebastian's reputation, maybe they *would* think that. Sebastian cringed.

"And what if they can't be quashed?"

Taking a deep breath, Sebastian closed his eyes. He'd do anything to protect Colton. "Then Colton and I will get married." He waited for the panic to come, but it didn't.

THE WIND caught the door, throwing it and Colton against the side of the stable with a bang. "Bloody hell." The icy breeze buffeted his face as he struggled against the weather. *Brrr*.... The chill cut right through his clothes; it was freezing out here. Perhaps he should have gotten his coat, but he hadn't expected the change in weather. His hands were frozen. It was amazing they hadn't cracked and fallen off.

Fighting with the door, Colton was determined to win. He dug his heels in and heaved. At that precise moment the current of air faded, and the door slammed shut with a resounding boom. He landed on his arse inside the stable.

The horses shuffled their feet and snorted. One of them kicked a wall. Apollonia nickered, already fussing to be let out. The wind whistled outside, but the crisp, clean scent of hay and oats surrounded him. He loved that smell.

Teeth chattering, Colton lay on his back in the middle aisle with his lungs burning. He'd planned to check on the horses, but he hadn't known he was going to get a workout. What a picture he probably made. Now his appearance was as ruffled as his emotions.

Tonight, he'd not only danced with Wentworth, but kissed him. Obviously, Wentworth had not been as thrilled by the kiss as Colton, so why had Wentworth done it? Why had he even danced with Colton? Colton groaned. Since the man was now his business partner, he couldn't ignore him—not like he was doing a good job of that anyway—but he had to keep things professional between them. And for galaxy's sakes, he had to stop kissing the blasted man.

Trying to catch his breath, he stared up at the haylofts on each side of the peaked roof and groaned. What was he going to do with Wentworth?

Apollonia nickered again, louder this time.

"Hush, Apollonia." Sitting up, Colton rubbed his arms and pushed to his feet.

Apollonia danced in place inside her stall.

His lip twitched. "Okay already." On the way by, he petted her mother, who had stuck her head out of her stall. "Good evening, Belle." Moving to the next stall over, he unlatched Apollonia's door and pointed his finger at her. "You can have out of your enclosure, but we aren't going outside."

She hurried into the center aisle and turned back to him, nudging his arm and flipping it up with her nose.

His hand landed on her head, making him chuckle. "Okay, pretty girl." He rubbed her neck. The red chestnut coat appeared even darker in the dim overhead lights. Resting his head on her shoulder, he put his arm around her neck and the other on her back. He was still chilled, but her warmth and the heat in the barn seeped into him. "Maybe Wentworth's libido got carried away, and I was in the right place at the wrong time. Or is that the wrong place at the right time?" None of it had felt wrong.

Even now his lips tingled, and he fancied he could feel Wentworth's lips pressed to his. Or maybe they were just cold.

Apollonia leaned against him.

"Ack." Colton shuffled around to keep from being knocked over and shoved against her side. "Stand up, you dolt."

She turned her head to look at him as if to say, *You started it; I was only cuddling.*

Colton patted her side once more for good measure. "You have not developed the fine art of listening like your father."

Apollo, who was next door to Apollonia, lifted his head. Some hay hung out of his mouth as he chewed. Flicking his tail, he looked at Colton. How many times had he come out in the middle of the night to brush and talk to Apollo over the years? Too many to count. "Hi, boy. How're you this evening? Let me check on Dazz and see how he's settling in; then I'll come brush you." Colton rubbed the velvety nose and started down the aisle.

Halfway there, the stable door opened and a chill whipped down Colton's back. Wrapping his arms around himself, he turned to face his intruder.

With his frock coat flapping in the wind, Wentworth struggled to close the door.

That familiar tingle Colton got whenever Wentworth was near niggled at him. He hadn't thought to see Wentworth again so soon. Maybe it was too soon. Colton had no idea where things stood between them.

The door finally slammed shut, and the roar of the air rushing inside converted to a howl outside. Wentworth glanced around. When his gaze landed on Colton, he grinned. "I wondered if you'd be out here." Wentworth's shoulders sagged more than normal, and his black eye was darker than it had been at the ball.

"What're you doing here?"

"Max is here." Wentworth gestured to the back of the stable.

Colton glanced over his shoulder. Sure enough, Max was in a stall at the back. "Oh. I was checking on Dazz."

"How is he do—" Something jangled as Wentworth strode forward. He stopped in front of an open enclosure. "Give me that." The deep dulcet tone was like wrapping up in a blanket.

Glancing around, Colton realized Apollonia was not in the center aisle anymore. *Oh no.*

Wentworth disappeared into the empty stall. "No. Bad."

The jingle sounded again, and Apollonia snorted. Her hooves clicked a few times in rapid succession on the cement floor. What was she into now?

Amused, Colton walked over to investigate.

She held the end of an old leather harness clenched between her teeth. Wentworth gripped the other end. "Gimme this. You don't need it." A tug-of-war ensued, and Wentworth's boots slid on the concrete floor. Little by little she tugged him right into the pen with her.

Stifling a laugh, Colton grabbed the harness and added his strength to Wentworth's side. "Apollonia." He *tsk*ed. "Drop it."

She turned her head slightly, eyeing him.

"Why is she out of her stall?" Wentworth shook the ends of the halter, trying to loosen her grip.

"Because she wanted out." Colton tapped her cheek. "Just what do you think you're going to do with this, young lady?"

Wentworth groaned. "That's the problem. You try to reason with her, and you think everything she does is funny. Training her is going to be pure hell because she runs right over y—*ahh*!"

Apollonia had let go.

Colton and Wentworth went down in a tangle of arms, legs, and frock coat. Colton's back hit the cement, and the air whooshed from his lungs. His head hit something soft. Gasping for breath and not getting any, Colton tried to grab his chest but Wentworth's weight on top of him made that impossible.

"Ow. My back. Are you okay?" With his coat over his face, Wentworth eased off Colton and fell to his side, leaving his arm under Colton's head. He jerked the heavy fabric down with a grin. "Colton?" The grin faded.

Colton shook his head, still unable to breathe from having the air knocked out of him. He needed air. Now. He had to breathe. He couldn't.... *Air*.

"Shh.... Relax. Calm down. Listen to me." A featherlight touch brushed Colton's cheek. "Calm down and take a deep, slow breath."

Staring into the blue depths of Wentworth's midnight eyes, Colton willed himself to relax. The pain in his chest eased little by little, and air filtered back into his lungs. Closing his eyes, he inhaled several times before the burning let up entirely. "Dust, I hate that. I haven't done that since I was a kid, when Aiden shoved me off a swing and I landed on my back."

Now that his lungs were functioning properly, he was cold. Why couldn't he have landed in one of the occupied pens where there was hay? He opened his eyes and was caught by Wentworth's gaze. His breathing ceased normal activity for an entirely different reason.

Wentworth's hand still rested on Colton's cheek. His dark hair lay over his forehead in disarray, and his face was flush with exertion. Sebastian's blue eyes appeared deeper than normal. A man could get lost in those eyes. Bedroom eyes, Colton had once heard them called. It was fitting. The slightly lowered lids hinted at naughty secrets. They gave Wentworth a wicked gleam.

Wentworth traced Colton's lips, and his gaze followed his movement.

Oh galaxy, he's going to kiss me. Colton wanted to taste those lips again. For years, he'd fantasized about that mouth on him…. He now knew reality was even better than the fantasy.

"Wentworth." The whispered word sounded needy.

"Sebastian." Sebastian pulled Colton's bottom lip down with his finger.

"Sebastian," Colton whispered and closed his eyes.

The soft press of lips against his wrung a moan from Colton. Or was that a sob? Sebastian's tongue eased inside, tracing Colton's lips. The sweet caress warmed Colton inside and out. It was like being surrounded by the glow of a fire on a blustery night. He was no longer cold. Contentment and excitement warred within him. His cock began to stir. His abdomen and legs tensed. He was wary of the attention, yet he craved it.

Sebastian moved closer, settling his leg over Colton's body until they touched head to toe. He took his time, caressing Colton's mouth. It was as if he were trying to learn every crease and hollow.

Their breathing, the shuffle of horse feet and the whistling wind became secondary to the sound of blood rushing through Colton's ears. The scent of cedar and an earthy spice he'd always associated with this man teased him. The tender caress of Sebastian's lips on his crowded out every other feeling.

Wrapping his arms around Sebastian's back, Colton returned the kiss. His erection under the weight of Sebastian's thigh would've embarrassed him if he hadn't been aware of the equally hard cock against his hip.

Breaking their kiss, Sebastian stared down at Colton. "Say it again."

Colton's lips were so sensitive he swore he could feel the air hitting them. "Say what?" He touched the beloved face, feeling the stubble under his fingers. He didn't want this to end… ever. If that made him a ninny, well, then, he was a hopeless ninny.

Sebastian caught Colton's hand, dragged it to his lips, and placed a kiss in the center of the palm. "My name."

"Sebastian."

"Mmm…." Sebastian released Colton's hand and tugged at Colton's neckcloth. "I hate you calling me Wentworth all the time." He freed the ends of the cravat and traced a fingertip down Colton's neck. When Colton swallowed hard, Sebastian grinned. He unbuttoned Colton's waistcoat and spread it open to reveal his shirt. "We shouldn't do this." Sebastian rested his hand on Colton's chest. "Damn me, but I can't help myself." Cupping Colton's cheek, he brushed a quick press of his lips against Colton's.

"Why *are* you doing this?" Colton swallowed, and it was like glass going down his throat. "I gave up on you. Why now?" Sebastian's hand stroked his stomach, but Colton didn't take his eyes off Sebastian's face.

"I can't get you out of my mind. I—" Sebastian closed his eyes briefly and shook his head before meeting Colton's gaze again. "Tell me to stop."

Colton's chest ached. He refused to get his hopes up, but he wanted this. Wanted Sebastian…. Colton had no interest in marriage these days, but he had an interest in this. Maybe this would even get Wentworth out of his system once and for all. He lifted his head off Sebastian's arm and poured every ounce of yearning into a kiss.

Moaning, Sebastian returned the passion. He tangled his tongue with Colton's as his bare hand touched Colton's chest.

The sounds of their wet, smacking kiss made Colton's cock jerk and his testicles draw tighter. He lifted up against Sebastian's thigh, and pleasure shot through him, making him itch with need. He wanted so much more, but he didn't know how to ask for it or if he should.

Sebastian sucked Colton's bottom lip. He nipped his jaw and trailed kisses down Colton's throat, sending shivers up his neck. Colton's arms broke out in goose bumps. It tickled and felt divine all at once. He tangled his fingers in Sebastian's thick hair, unwilling to relinquish him. For years, he'd longed to touch this man, feel him.

Moving his leg, Sebastian pressed his palm against Colton's cock and licked a line up his neck.

Oh my galaxy. Gasping, Colton tightened his grip in Sebastian's hair. He stared up at the ceiling, unsure what to do. He wavered between shock and melting into the floor. He'd always belittled the men Sebastian had liaisons with for being wantons, and he was no better.

Sebastian sucked on Colton's earlobe and began rubbing his hand up and down the rigid length of Colton's prick. Colton wanted his trousers off… now. Gritting his teeth, he arched into the touch.

"If you pull on my hair any harder, it's liable to come out." Sebastian chuckled in his ear and nipped his earlobe.

"Oh." Turning his head, Colton met Sebastian's gaze. He slid his hands down to Sebastian's back, which was still covered by his overcoat. "Sorry."

In answer, Sebastian gave him a soft peck on the lips, then went back to his neck.

The friction against Colton's cock was too much and not enough. He should stop this, he didn't want Sebastian to think him easy, but—Colton contracted his abdomen muscles, trying not to come. Was he supposed to come? Was he not supposed to? Was there a proper etiquette? *Oh dust.* A shudder shot through him, and he squeezed his eyes shut.

Sebastian sucked at his neck so strongly it almost hurt, but it did nothing to douse Colton's pleasure. Still rubbing, Sebastian pressed down harder with his hand. "Let go, sweeting."

The low breathy rumble in Colton's ear was too much. Every muscle in his body tensed, pleasure exploded inside him, and he came. Colton swore he saw stars. His head was spinning, but he could no longer feel his other body parts. It was a catharsis that had been building for years. He hugged Sebastian to him, not wanting the moment to end.

A groan broke the spell. "Cut it out." Sebastian raised his head, leaving a cold spot where he'd been.

Colton blinked open his eyes.

Apollonia stood over them, nibbling at Sebastian's hair.

Sebastian's gaze locked with his, his lips twitching, and merriment shone in his eyes.

Trying to hold back his laughter, Colton pressed his lips tight together.

Sebastian wasn't as successful. His shoulders began to shake. He bussed Colton on the lips. "Your horse is eating my hair."

COLTON SNUCK back into the castle as Sebastian was saddling Max. He made it all the way to his room before it occurred to him Jeffers had been quiet during the encounter with Sebastian. "Jeffers?"

"Yes, Your Highness?"

Colton winced. Any moment now someone was going to burst through the door and ground him for the rest of his life. He couldn't believe no one had done so already. How'd he forgotten about *the spy*? Not just him, but Sebastian, too, had forgotten about Jeffers. "Jeffers? Do you think we can keep this incident between us?"

"What incident do you speak of, Prince Colton?"

Pausing in the act of shucking off his soggy trousers, Colton stared at the ceiling. It wasn't as if he could see Jeffers, but…. Maybe he should just keep his mouth closed. Jeffers didn't have video in the stables. He only had audio and heat sensors outside the castle. Had Sebastian turned Jeffers off? No, Sebastian was more strict about security than even Cony. Maybe Sebastian bypassed Jeffers in the stables? "Jeffers? Will there be anyone coming to my room?"

"Not that I am aware of, Your Highness. Do you wish me to call someone?"

"No!" If he got away with this, he was never going to do anything like it again. He had no idea what he'd been thinking. More to the point, he hadn't been thinking.

This path only led to heartache. Realizing he and Sebastian would never be anything to each other had hurt the first time. It would be so much worse now. He had to stop this craziness. He would not be a paramour to any man. Not even Sebastian Hastings.

Colton kicked his pants aside. "Shower one hundred and four degrees Fahrenheit." He'd talk to Sebastian about Jeffers's absence in the barn tomorrow. He could surely think up some reason to go to Sebastian's office in the morning. They were business partners after all. Colton stepped into the shower. And business partners were all they could ever be.

Chapter Eleven

September 16, 4830: The Thompson Family Musicale at Thompson House, the Duke of Eversleigh's town house in Classige, Pruluce

MAYBE HE'D developed leprosy and hadn't realized it. It would figure, the way Colton's day was going. Last night was a mistake, and today was a travesty.

Colton sighed. Wentworth had been running errands instead of overseeing day-to-day security operations at the castle, and Colton hadn't been able to ask him about Jeffers. Oh who was he kidding? He wanted to see Wentworth. He wanted to know if Wentworth was going to treat him differently after last night, and that made him furious with himself. He didn't want to care, because it didn't change anything.

A couple of men walked by on their way out of the ballroom, and they both turned to look back at him.

When was the entertainment going to start? He didn't envy Bannon having to play his violin in front of people, but at least it would take some of the focus off Colton for a bit. The rumors should've died down by now, but apparently they'd gotten worse.

He'd only been here for half an hour and no fewer than six people had whispered behind their hands while looking at him. Lord Vale even gave him the cut direct. No one else had seen it, but still.... It took every ounce of restraint Colton had to resist getting in the man's face and forcing acknowledgment. The worst thing about this whole escapade was people wanted him to know they were talking about him.

Two more men passed him, craning their necks.

If Colton wasn't mistaken, one of those men was Mr. Potts, who had been involved in a scandal just last season. Potts had reputedly been caught taking Lord Higginbotton's favorite jeweled snuff box. Hypocrites, every last one of them.

"Having fun, Your Highness? I do hope you're happy with your purchase. Was Razzle Dazzle worth what you paid?" The contemptuous tone skittered down Colton's spine like nails on a chalkboard.

Swiveling around, he came face-to-face with Dazz's former owner. With as much scorn as he could muster, he said, "Plume." He itched to wrap his fingers around Plume's neck but settled for a warning. "If you so much as touch *my* horse—"

A blur of dark blue fabric and auburn hair jumped between them.

Blinking, Colton wobbled backward. Where had Bannon come from?

Plume laughed and walked away. Gads, even his laughter sounded vile.

Colton gritted his teeth and glared at Plume over Bannon's head. He could not remember having this strong a dislike for another person before.

Bannon sighed. "As much as I'd love to help you pummel that jackanapes, it will only make the rumors worse."

Chuckling, Aiden came up beside them. "You should've let him get in one good lick. Although if you did somehow or other, it would be my fault. So maybe it's for the best, because I can practically hear the lecture."

"I wasn't going to hit him… again. Give me *some* credit." It sure would be nice to hold him and let Dazz kick him, though.

Over the cacophony of voices, pianoforte keys jingled and a violin whined. The musicale was to take place in the music room across the hall. Colton sought Bannon's gaze. "Aren't you supposed to be warming up?"

Groaning, Bannon snarled. His shoulders sank, and he huffed out a breath, making his auburn bangs flutter. "My parents hate me. They know I'm not a musician, but every year they force me to play with my brother and my cousins. I'm an artist, damn it."

Aiden's eyes sparkled with mirth. "I told him I'd sneak him out of here."

A man across the room pointed at them, and his friend knocked his arm down. Colton gritted his teeth and tried to ignore them.

"It won't work. My parents are expecting it because of last year." Bannon's bottom lip pooched out. "We would've gotten away with it if you"—Bannon leveled a stare at Aiden—"hadn't stepped on the hem of my dress, tripped me, and slowed us down."

"His dress?" Colton's eyes widened.

"Rupert and I disguised him as a scullery maid."

Colton grinned. He vaguely remembered Cony fussing about Aiden's involvement at the time.

Was that Lord Dunsford staring at him from behind that potted plant?

Bannon rolled his eyes and shoved Colton's shoulder. "Leave off, Colton. I see you smirking. It was a good plan."

"A scullery maid? Didn't you think people would wonder why Aiden and Rupert were hanging around a scullery maid?" Colton frowned. That was definitely Dunsford. "Why not a butler or a footman?"

"I don't know. A maid seemed like a good idea at the time. Oh well. At least I won't be entirely alone in my misery this year. My father is planning on asking Tarren to sing a few songs."

Aiden smiled. "I'd like to say I feel sorry for the brat, but anyone with a voice like Tarren's owes it to the galaxy to use it. I can't believe he hates singing so badly."

"I won't argue he has a gorgeous voice, but at least he's normal. My brother and cousins actually like performing." Bannon scoffed. "Can you believe that?"

Two more men walked by, not so discreetly watching Colton. The two men actually turned their heads to look over their shoulders at him as they passed. *Unbelievable.*

Colton snapped. He couldn't take any more. Why was such an asinine rumor still making the rounds? If they wanted something to talk about, he'd give them something to talk about. Leaning around Aiden, Colton glowered at the lords and stuck up his middle finger.

"Stop that." Aiden slapped his hand down. "Are you insane? You'll get us both into hot water. I can't believe Trouble taught you that."

Colton shrugged. "They won't know what it means, anyway. It's an IN thing. Besides, they deserve it. They're fueling the fire. I'm tired of everyone staring at me and whispering. They don't even have the bollocks to accuse me of theft to my face."

"What did that hand signal mean?" Bannon whispered.

Ignoring Bannon, Aiden said, “I don’t think they’re still talking about your horse. I think Plume is spreading new rumors, but no one is stupid enough to repeat them in my hearing.”

“He had to be the source of the first gossip too. As far as I know, he was the only one around when Wentworth and I helped Dazz. He’s trying to get even with me for punching him and making him sell to me.”

Bannon growled and stomped his foot. “I’ve got to go, but I want to know what that hand signal meant, when I get done with this stupid concert.”

Waving him off, Aiden scanned the ballroom. “I’ll tell you later.”

Colton fluttered his fingers at Bannon. “Break a leg or whatever it is they say.”

What tales could Plume be spreading around? Colton searched the crowd for Plume. Was the dastardly man even now telling people falsehoods? Darn it, he couldn’t see over the heads of the men in front of them. “Blast, I’m not tall enough.”

Aiden snorted. “At least you’re not the shortest man in the family.”

“Neither are you. Payton is.”

“Are you sure?” Aiden bounced on his toes, trying to see over the crowd.

“Yes.”

Aiden beamed at him. “I’m not the shortest?”

Colton shook his head. He wasn’t sure what Aiden was so pleased about. He was only a couple inches taller than Payton. Which still made him pretty short. In truth, Aiden actually looked shorter unless he and Pay were side by side because Aiden’s shoulders were wider. Payton had more of a slim, sleek look, but no way was Colton going to dash Aiden’s happiness and tell him that.

Dalton strolled up to them with a tumbler full of an amber-colored liquid. No doubt something he shouldn’t be drinking. “Who’re the two of you looking for?”

“Plume,” Aiden answered at the same time as Colton. They glanced at each other and shared a smile.

Dalton swirled his drink before taking a sip. He too began searching the crowd. “Barnaby Plume? He’s an arsehead. Why do you want him?”

“We don’t want him. We’re trying to see what he’s up to. Does this mean you haven’t heard the rumors?” Colton asked.

“What rumors?”

"Where have you been? I hate society, and I've heard the rumors." Aiden stopped a passing footman and grabbed a drink from his tray.

Dalton shrugged. "Not all of us have a gorgeous husband to, er… entertain us. Some of us have to actually seek out our amusements, if you know what I mean."

Aiden offered his drink to Colton. "Here, take this. You've earned it."

"In other words, he's been hanging out in brothels and gaming hells rather than soirées." Colton took the glass and sniffed. Alcohol of some sort. What the heck? He *had* earned it. What was the worst that could happen? He'd get called on the carpet by Cony. He'd been called on the carpet before.

He swigged back the drink. *Dust.* It sucked the air right out of him and stung his insides all the way down to his stomach. An uncontrollable round of coughing racked his body, and tears streamed from his eyes. Good galaxy, he was going to die.

Dalton began pounding him on the back.

Aiden grabbed the glass. "Cripes. You weren't supposed to try and down it in one gulp."

Now he tells me. Colton tried to inhale deeply. Several moments passed, but his hacking subsided into wheezing. When he was able to breathe normally, he glared at his brother.

Ignoring the glare, Aiden gripped Colton's arm and started walking. "Come on, everyone is going into the music room to find seats."

Dalton grasped Colton's other arm and leaned around him to talk to Aiden. "I still can't believe you married Captain Hawk."

"Admiral," Aiden corrected.

Dalton went on like Aiden hadn't spoken. "The man is a legend. Half the soldiers I know are in love with Hawk."

"Too bad." Aiden smiled at Dalton and drank from the tumbler. "They can't have him." Unlooping his arm, Aiden handed Colton the glass again. "Here, take another drink. A sip this time, not a gulp."

Colton swallowed another drink, and Aiden explained the events surrounding the gossip to Dalton. By the time Aiden got to the part about Plume seeking Colton out tonight, Colton was seeing blurry figures rather than actual people. *Whoa, was the room moving?*

Dalton's arm tensed under Colton's hand. "I'll see if I can learn what rumors are going around. I've a good mind to call Plume out."

Blah blah blah. Colton ignored the conversation and stifled a chuckle. He shouldn't think *blah blah blah* when his family was trying to come to his aid, but he couldn't seem to help it. Colton hiccupped and slapped a hand over his mouth. For some reason that was hilarious. His hand did nothing to hold back the laughter. Hiccupping again made the giggles increase. His limbs were loose and heavy… floppy.

He needed another one of those coughing drinks. One more drink, and he wouldn't care about anything. No wonder Trouble was always trying to pilfer strong spirits.

"Give me some more of the coughing drink." Colton snatched the drink from Aiden's hand and swigged. It stole his breath, but he didn't cough this time.

Why were Aiden and Dalton staring at him? He glanced behind him. Just a plant. *Hmm….* When had they made it to the music room?

"What?" He hiccupped again and smiled.

Dalton frowned, snatched the drink away from Colton and handed it back to Aiden. "Look what you started. I can't believe you gave him that. You could've at least waited until dinner, so he'd have something in his stomach."

"It was just a little scotch. I had no idea it would affect him like this," Aiden said.

A lord—he *had* to be a lord because he had a pompous air—gawked at them. Oh, so did the man beside him. And the one over there by the marble column.

Should Colton glare back or wave? *Hiccup.* He was in much too good a mood to give in to rudeness, so he waved.

Aiden jerked Colton's hand down. "Cut it out."

Colton tugged at his cravat. The room was getting hotter.

"Maybe we should go look for some coffee," Dalton suggested.

Across from them, Roth, Lord Francis, and Mr. Fareweather entered the music room.

Waving, Colton smiled. His head swam, making him a little dizzy.

Lord Roth looked his direction and turned away, giving him the cut direct. Lord Francis did the same. Mr. Fareweather lifted his hand, but before he got it past his waist his smile faded, and he glanced back at his friends. He followed the other two men but spared Colton a backward glance.

Colton's stomach dropped and flopped like his other limbs. This rained meteors.

"Let's get a seat. Maybe sitting down for a bit will clear his head. Just help me hide him from Father and Cony. Dinner is right after the performance. We'll get him some coffee then." Aiden led Colton toward a row of seats a few aisles back from where the pianoforte, a harp, and some chairs with smaller instruments on them were set up.

Hiccup. Head still spinning, Colton scooted sideways through the narrow line of chairs with Aiden in front of him and Dalton behind him. Dalton only had to steady him once.

As they took their seats in the middle of the row, someone behind them spoke Colton's name. He listened intently but only made out whispers after his name, not actual words. Maybe the lack of clarity was because his head was so foggy. As they sat, he glanced at Dalton to ask if he'd heard.

Dalton stared straight ahead with a goofy grin on his face. It was doubtful he'd heard anything the way he seemed mesmerized.

Following his gaze, Colton found Blaise Thompson setting his sheet music on the piano.

Colton leaned close to Aiden and lost his balance. "Whoops."

Aiden pushed him back in his seat.

Hiccup. "Can you make out what the men behind us are saying?"

"No. I only caught your name." Aiden dragged his attention away from where the musicians were setting up. "But I found the jackass." He tilted his head in a jerky manner toward the front of the room.

Plume stood in the front row. With a smirk, he held up a champagne flute in a mock toast. Downing the liquid in the glass, he gave Colton his back and sat.

A chill went through Colton.

Nate slid into the chair next to Aiden. Resting his hand on Aiden's thigh, Nate leaned forward to catch Colton's gaze. His jaw was tense and his brows lowered. "You've apparently become Wentworth's paramour."

AS SOON as Sebastian walked in the front door of Townsend Castle, Thomas handed him a note. "Lord Wentworth, Jeffers has received a message for you from the duke."

Sebastian unfolded the paper, and fear clawed at his gut as he read the typed words.

Your presence is required at Thompson House posthaste. There is a problem with Colton. He needs you.

A problem with Colton? Every possible scenario flashed through Sebastian's mind, and they were all bad. Had Colton been injured? Kidnapped? Killed? *Oh galaxy no.*

Pain twisted in his gut as he turned and headed back out the front door. "Jeffers, have the lift return immediately."

A cold blast of air hit him in the face as he strode down the front steps. Gads, not only was he still holding the note, his hands shook. He stuffed the note into the breast pocket of his evening coat, but there was nothing he could do about the quivering. What if he never saw Colton again? What if—

The lift pulled up, and Sebastian jumped in. "To the Duke of Eversleigh's town house." The coach was dimly lit, but Sebastian pulled out his pocket watch. Hoping to borrow some light from the streetlamps, he held it up toward the window. What time was it? How long had the note been waiting for him? Sebastian stuffed his watch back into his waistcoat pocket. He had no idea when Rourke had sent the note and couldn't see the blasted watch anyway. His skin crawled with nervous energy. If this bloody lift didn't hurry…. "Faster. This is an emergency."

The lift sped up marginally.

"Bugger." Sebastian closed his eyes, fisted his hands, and clenched his jaw. He opened his eyes. This was still faster than walking. If only he'd ridden Max this evening. He'd taken a lift to investigate Admiral Jenkins's town house and gotten nowhere. He now had even more questions and no answers.

After what seemed like forever, the lift slowed. Outside the window, the Duke of Eversleigh's town house glowed with life.

Sebastian jumped to his feet and swayed as the lift stopped suddenly. The door opened, and the sense of calm he'd always gotten before going into battle claimed him.

The street was deserted, yet the house held a warmth. The atmosphere was tranquil. Normal. The night was cool but refreshing. A nice hum came from inside the mansion. Death and injury had a way of seeping into the air, and there was no evidence of it here. No screams, no frantic pace, no emergency lifts, nothing.

Feeling much more in control, Sebastian ascended the steps. It would be nice to know what he was walking into. When he saw Rourke, he was going to instruct him on how to send a proper message.

The foyer was empty except for a doorman. Music floated in from the open music room doors. The place was packed. Everyone was enjoying the show.

Scanning through the crowd, Sebastian searched for Colton. He found Knighton first. The duke sat several inches above everyone else. The admiral was easy to spot since he was also taller than most. Aiden sat next to him. On Aiden's other side was a dark-headed man and then Ashbourne. Colton must be there somewhere.

By his second survey of the music room, Sebastian's uneasiness was beginning to return. He'd located all the Townsend offspring except Colton. He returned his attention to the man between Aiden and Ashbourne. That had to be Colton.

The music came to an end, and the audience broke out into applause. As he clapped, the ebony-haired man turned his head slightly. It was just enough to show off the high cheekbones and a stubborn chin. *Colton.*

Sebastian frowned. Why had he dismissed Colton at first? Colton's shoulders didn't look as wide as they normally appeared. Nor did he seem as tall. Colton was slouching. Something was definitely wrong. Maybe it was from the hours on horseback or from his upbringing, but Colton always held himself upright. Some would call the posture arrogant, but it wasn't. He had an innate self-confidence.

Careful not to draw attention to himself, Sebastian eased away from the door and sought out the doorman. He offered the man a hundred pounds for his silence about Sebastian's presence and asked for paper and pen. When the man returned, he'd jot a quick note and have the man deliver it to Colton.

"Sebastian?"

Turning, Sebastian came face-to-face with Steven. "Your Majesty."

"I'm glad you're here. Come with me." Making an about-face, Steven walked away.

Combined with Colton's slouching, Steven's pace didn't give Sebastian a warm, fuzzy feeling. Sebastian hurried to catch up. "I got a note from Knighton saying Colton needed me. What's going on?" He jogged to keep up. The unease he'd had in the lift came back full-force.

Steven went into Eversleigh's parlor and closed the door as soon as Sebastian cleared it. The room was empty and mostly quiet. Music could still be heard, but it was muted. Steven walked to the fireplace and faced him. "The rumors have gotten worse. Now the predominant one is that you and Colton are lovers, rather than the two of you stealing the horse."

"Bugger." Heat suffused Sebastian's face and neck. His muscles bunched and the same fierce protectiveness he experienced before rose in him. "Are people shunning him?"

"Yes." Steven didn't sit down as Sebastian expected but paced back and forth in front of the fireplace. "Oh don't get me wrong, they aren't stupid enough to talk about him in my and Raleigh's presence. But I've seen several peers watching Colton and whispering when they don't realize I'm looking."

The thought of Colton being treated so unfairly made Sebastian sick to his stomach. How had things spiraled out of control so quickly? True, he hadn't done much to quash the tales, but even still, he'd done nothing to encourage them. He could only think of one way out of this. One way to protect Colton.

The muscles in Sebastian's throat constricted, and his palms began to sweat. He didn't know if he could do it. Old self-doubts gnawed at him. Could Colton live with him? The *real* him? Could Colton deal with Sebastian's past? Giles couldn't.

Sebastian would just have to keep Colton from learning the truth. What mattered was protecting Colton. A little voice niggled at the back of his mind telling him not to jest with himself, he wanted Colton, but he ignored it. It didn't signify. His wants and needs didn't play into this. If they did, he wouldn't be about to do what he was about to do.

Sebastian composed himself. "I don't think there's any stopping these rumors now. Steven, with your permission I'd like to ask Colton to marry me." *No turning back now.*

Steven strode forward with his hand extended. "My boy…." When Sebastian grabbed his hand, Steven pulled him into a hug and pounded him on the back. "Not only do you have my permission and gratitude, but you've made me very happy. I'd welcome you to the family, but you've been part of our family for years."

A burning sensation started in Sebastian's chest. He hugged Steven back, feeling like a fraud. "I'll take care of him and protect him with my life."

"You always have." Steven let go of him. He cocked his head to the side as if he were listening to something.

The sounds of footsteps and people talking had replaced the music.

"Sounds like it's time for dinner." Steven patted Sebastian's back and strolled to the door. His step seemed a little bouncier than usual. "Why don't you go find Colton and join us in the dining room? Eversleigh will not have a problem with you joining us." He opened the door and held out his arm as if to say after you. Yes, he was definitely happy about this arrangement.

Sebastian smiled even though it felt as if a heavy weight had been dropped on his chest. He still had to ask Colton for his hand in marriage. What if Colton said no? Sebastian's lungs constricted.

Oblivious to Sebastian's unease, Steven slapped him on the back again and strolled into the crowd coming out of the music room.

Sebastian turned the opposite way, swimming upstream against the throng for only a moment before people began stepping out of his way. He became cognizant of the stares and whispers. The hairs on the back of his neck stood up. The smell of sweat, cologne, and liquor stung his nose, and the press of bodies closed in on him. Even though he couldn't see it and knew it was his imagination, the weight of the stares pressed against his back, propelling him forward at a pace above his normal walk. Was this what Colton had dealt with all night?

"Seb." Rourke stood right outside of the music room door. "You got my message?"

"Yes. And I just spoke with Steven. Where's Colton?" Sebastian stopped beside Rourke.

Several heads whipped back around as his gaze landed on them. "Good galaxy. Have they nothing better to do with their time?"

One corner of Rourke's lips turned up. "No. They live for this sort of thing. And to answer your question, Colton went out the other door." He hitched his thumb over his shoulder in the direction of the music room. "Toward the washrooms with Aiden and the admiral."

Inside the music room, past the rows of chairs, another door stood open. People milled about like a flock of sheep in the hallway beyond.

"Thank you." Sebastian started into the room but stopped. "We need to discuss your missive writing."

Rourke chuckled. "There isn't a thing wrong with my missive writing. It got you here, didn't it?"

He supposed it did. Growling, Sebastian continued through the room and into the hall. Only a few of the washroom doors were closed. Everyone seemed to be leaving and going to the other end of the passage, Colton included. With his shoulders slightly slumped, he walked between Aiden and Nate.

Sebastian frowned and hurried to catch up. "Your Highness."

Aiden and Colton both turned.

As soon as Colton's gaze met Sebastian's, Colton smiled. The genuine response went right to Sebastian's head. He returned the smile, feeling much more in control.

"Good evening, Wentworth," Colton said as Sebastian drew near.

"Hello, yourself." He took Colton's hand and brought it to his lips, ignoring Aiden's grumble. Sebastian found that despite his reluctance at marriage, he wanted to kiss Colton. If they'd been alone, he would've done just that. Did Colton still have a mark on his neck from last night? *Dust*, he had to stop thinking like that.

Nate stepped closer to his consort and rested his hand on the middle of Aiden's back. "I trust you'll be escorting him to dinner?"

Sebastian nodded. "I will."

Glancing around, Aiden put his hand to the side of his mouth and practically hissed, "There are already rumors."

Sebastian had always respected the Townsends and their loyalty to one another, but it still caught him off guard from time to time. Taking Aiden's hand, he bowed over it. "I know. I've come to help dispel those rumors."

"We'll save you both a seat." Nate steered his consort around.

"But…." Aiden glanced up at his husband with a frown.

Nate didn't relent. He kept moving Aiden forward. "Behave yourself."

Colton shook his head. "Nate is forever having to tell him to behave. You'd think by now he would've learned it's a wasted effort." He wobbled a bit and threw his hands out to his sides.

Sebastian grabbed his arm. "Are you okay?"

"Yes, just a little floppy." His eyes were darker than normal. No, wait… they weren't darker, they were dilated.

Sebastian leaned close and sniffed. "Are you foxed?"

"I wouldn't say foxed, exactly. I only had two." Colton held up two fingers and grinned. "And I think it's wearing off."

"Why in the galaxy are you drinking?"

Colton shrugged and teetered to the side.

Sebastian caught him again, put Colton's hand on his arm, and started them walking. What else could go wrong tonight? It was definitely a night of surprises.

"Thank you."

"You're welcome."

They passed a group of four lords loitering outside the dining room, and Sebastian tipped his head to them. Let them say something with him here. He had no qualms about fighting duels.

They all returned his gesture and resumed their conversation.

"Plume is spreading a rumor that I'm your latest paramour." A blush washed over Colton's face. "I guess it's sort of true after last night."

"Yes, well, about that. I want to ask you something." *Here goes nothing.* He opened his mouth, but before he could speak, another voice broke in.

"And here is the happy couple now."

To their right lay the dining room. How had they gotten this far this fast? There were at least thirty tables full of people, and they were all staring. A round of applause and well wishes poured from the room.

Steven held up his glass from where he stood next to the Duke of Eversleigh at the head of the main table. "To Colton and Wentworth."

Blast. Sebastian's stomach plummeted to his feet. Surely Steven hadn't announced their engagement before Sebastian could even ask Colton.

"The wedding will be held tomorrow at Townsend Castle. It's a private affair, but rest assured there will be a ball to celebrate."

Yes, that was exactly what he'd done.

Colton squeezed Sebastian's hand to the point of pain.

Bloody hell.

NO DOUBT about it, tonight he'd be sleeping on the sofa in his suite's sitting room. Steven pinched the bridge of his nose. He felt a headache coming on. One could argue it was of his own making, but that didn't make it any less irritating… it made it more so. He'd done the right thing; he was sure of it. Colton and Sebastian were so obviously made for each other, but how could he convince Raleigh of that?

"Damn it, Steven. Are you listening to me?"

No. So do be quiet. Steven didn't dare say it aloud. A night on the sofa he could handle. A whole week? Not so much. He dropped his hand and looked up at his consort. Was it his imagination or did Eversleigh's library chairs seem lower to the ground than most chairs? Raleigh seemed impossibly imposing. He hadn't grown taller since he was nineteen, so it had to be his glowering.

Steven sighed. In for a penny… in for a pound. "I did the right thing, Raleigh. Sebastian asked me for permission to marry Colton when he learned about the rumors."

"Did you see *your* son's face? Unless I miss my guess and completely misread his actions, Sebastian didn't even have time to ask Colton before you announced their engagement." Raleigh made a sound halfway between a groan and a hiss, threw his hands up, and paced toward the other end of the library.

Steven didn't miss the emphasis on the word *your* in Raleigh's question. The emphasis had the desired effect. Colton's smile *had* been forced, and Sebastian's hand had turned white where Colton was squeezing it. A weight settled into Steven's stomach. He glanced down at his boots and the blue Persian rug. He should have handled it differently, but he was still convinced it was for the best.

A door clicked open, drawing his attention.

Raleigh stood in front of the open glass door leading outside to a rose garden on the side of the house. He stared out into the night. The gentle breeze ruffled his black hair, but his jaw was tight. His back moved with a deep breath, and when he spoke his voice was soft. Resigned. "I told you not to meddle."

"You told me they'd be horrible together."

Raleigh whirled around, and his hands flew to his hips. "Because I didn't want you meddling. They're perfect for each other, and anyone with a set of eyes can see it. But you weren't supposed to interfere. And don't think I don't know about you telling Jeffers to keep their meetings secret from me."

Steven's eyes widened. He opened his mouth to speak and slammed it back shut. Raleigh knew about that? Wait. Raleigh thought Colton and Sebastian belonged together? "You were trying to maneuver me?"

Crossing to stand in front of Steven, Raleigh sighed and ran a hand through his hair. "Don't act so affronted. I've been getting you to do what I want for years. Only this time you botched things up because you didn't listen. So stop your whining and help me figure out how to fix this mess you've made. Because Colton won't marry if he truly does not want to, and I will not try to make him." Squatting, Raleigh put his hands on Steven's knees and met his gaze. "You know how I feel about forced marriages. Would you condemn our children to marriages like both of our parents had? I thought we broke that cycle."

They had. Steven cupped Raleigh's cheek. Galaxy, he loved this man. He wanted their children to have what they had… have. Couldn't Raleigh understand that? This *was* that match for Colton; Steven would bet his right hand on it. And that was his favorite hand. Heck, he'd even throw in a leg.

Leaning into the touch, Raleigh closed his eyes. "Your parents were too busy carrying on their cozy little foursome with Marcus's parents to make you too miserable, but mine…." Raleigh opened his eyes. His gaze bore into Steven's. "My parents spent their entire marriage trying to destroy each other and me and my brother in the process."

"Your brother is an arse." As far as Steven was concerned, the only good thing Barclay Fairfax had done in his entire life was to father Dalton. Ashbourne was a good kid—wild and scandalous as the day was long, but a decent young man.

Raleigh nodded. "How do you think he got that way? He learned from our sire." Barclay always was Raleigh's sire's favorite.

Steven wrapped his arms around his consort, forcing him to abandon his crouch and drop to his knees. When Raleigh rested his chin against Steven's shoulder and hugged him back, Steven kissed his ear. "The reason you've given is exactly why I want Colton and Sebastian together. They *will* make each other happy. So why is this a bad thing?"

"This is something they have to discover for themselves. Didn't you learn anything from watching Aiden and Nate muddle through? It's our job to give them a push now and again but not make the decision for them."

Rubbing his back, Steven smiled. "Wentworth is beginning to realize what he feels for Colton. I'm sure of it."

"Exactly. They *were* getting there all by themselves."

"So how do we give Colton the time he needs? How do we make him understand this is right for him?"

Raleigh pulled back and kissed Steven's lips in a quick smack. It wasn't near long enough. "We let it soak into his thick skull tonight and take him aside before the wedding tomorrow morning. Then we'll tell him he doesn't have to marry."

He brushed his lips across Raleigh's. Raleigh was spot-on about Colton. He was stubborn, but Raleigh had overlooked something. Colton was nearly as prideful as he was hardheaded. And that, more than the stubbornness, concerned Steven.

Raleigh arched a brow. Was there anything more sensual than that blasted eyebrow? "You think that'll work?"

"It has to." If it didn't, it would be his fault.

With a hand on the back of his neck, Raleigh pulled him down until their foreheads touched. "I love you. I want to suffocate you in your sleep with your pillow sometimes, but I love you."

Steven chuckled and nipped Raleigh's full bottom lip. "I love you too, Cony." Running his fingers through the back of the thick black hair, Steven urged Raleigh forward. "Please don't murder me in my sleep." Their lips met.

Raleigh's arms slid to Steven's back, rubbing, as Raleigh slipped his tongue into Steven's mouth. Steven tilted his head, deepening the kiss.

Moving to pull Raleigh into his lap, something distracted Steven out of their embrace. He couldn't put his finger on what it was. An odd sense of… being watched. Or maybe it was leaves blowing into the library via the door. He glanced at said leaves.

A shadow passed over them. His gaze shot upward. Something moved into the darkness of the garden. Steven jumped to his feet and a groan sounded, followed by muttering.

Raleigh fell on his arse on the floor.

"Sorry, Cony, I thought—" He stepped over his consort. The uneasiness persisted. His skin was ice cold, and seconds ago he'd been hot and bothered.

As he drew near the door, the rose arbor and trellis of climbing bushes came into view. A lone lamp in the center stood sentinel over the small garden.

A figure emerged at the far edge of the lawn.

"Stop." Steven bounded out the door and across the yard. Dodging a rose tree, he ran under the covered arches and past the birdbath.

Raleigh was right behind him. Blast, the man was quick.

The gate leading out to Ketterstone Street slammed shut.

"Damnation." Steven stopped.

The wind rustled the plants and the moon illuminated the garden, but it was otherwise quiet. No running footsteps. Where had the man gone? Standing at the gate, Steven searched the street.

A few people milled about. It was a fashionable part of town and across from Regelence Park. Lifts passed by. There was one on the corner. Its door hissed shut, and it pulled away from the curb. A man with brown hair stuck his head out the window, saw Steven, and ducked back inside. It was *him*. Steven was sure of it.

Raleigh touched Steven's shoulder. His breath made a visible fog in the cool night air. "What's going on?"

"That's the man."

"What man? What're you talking about?"

Steven turned to face his husband. "The man who followed Knighton and me at the auction the other day." As soon as the words left his mouth, he realized his mistake.

Raleigh's cheek began to twitch. "Why am I just hearing about this, and why were you at the auction?"

Damn. Steven was back to sleeping on the sofa. *Not much to lose at this point.* He sighed and confessed the whole story. "You know if I thought it was important, I would've told you immediately."

"Your idea and my idea of important vary widely." Raleigh's tick finally ceased, but he still glared. "You will not leave the castle without me by your side until we find this man and figure out what he wants. Let's go find Knighton and tell him about this. Now, is there anything else you need to confess?"

Was there? Steven rolled his eyes upward. There was the— No, Raleigh had found out about that. Maybe the— No, Raleigh had uncovered that. Oooh. No. Raleigh knew about that too.

Steven shook his head. "No." He always told Raleigh eventually. Steven's ability to keep secrets from the man was nonexistent.

Smiling, Raleigh shook his head, looped his arm through Steven's, and led him back to the house. "What am I going to do with you?"

"Oh, I can think of several things." Steven shivered with excitement.

Raleigh chuckled. "Later, dear. Later."

Chapter Twelve

He should have his head examined.

Sebastian glanced up at the stained-glass window of the Regelence coat of arms above the entrance to Townsend Castle. What he was looking for he had no idea. Divine intervention, maybe? He wasn't going to get it, that was for certain.

Something cold and wet landed on his cheek. He brushed it away and glanced at his hand. Huh. It was snowing again. It floated around him, dancing on the air before drifting gracefully to the ground. As a boy, it was one of his worst enemies and claimed several of his friends, but now it seemed almost magical. Yet another thing that made tonight feel like a dream. When had his perspective changed so much?

The front door opened, wrecking the serenity. Frisk, one of the guards, poked his head out. Odd, considering the guards only stood by the door during daylight. During the night, when the castle was on lockdown, they stayed in the basement and helped monitor the grounds from cameras. "My lord? Are you coming in?"

Nodding, Sebastian reluctantly went inside. "Where's Thomas?"

"He had to um—that's to say… he's… uh… indisposed, Captain. May I take your coat?"

It was strange to think of Thomas as, well, human. He seemed such an extension of Jeffers. Thomas was always where you needed him. Not that Sebastian needed him now.

"Sure." Sebastian removed his gloves, hat, and coat.

"Sebastian?" Steven came out of the study, straightening his cravat. Stray locks fell over his eyes and stood out at odd angles around his head.

"Steven, I came to see Colton." Sebastian's hands had been cold, but now that he was inside and facing Steven, his palms were a bit sweaty. Sebastian fought the urge to wipe them on his trousers and swallowed hard. What if Steven denied his request? *Bugger.* "I was not able to gain Colton's agreement before you made the announcement this evening. And dinner was so hectic with all the well-wishers, I didn't get a chance to speak to him before we left the musicale. I can't in good conscience go through with the ceremony until I speak to him."

"I know. I'm very sorry, Sebastian. I should've waited. Raleigh and I talked to him before he went up to bed. I told him to sleep on it and make his final decision tomorrow."

Sebastian's stomach churned. He had to talk to Colton tonight. It wouldn't wait until tomorrow. He opened his mouth to tell Steven so but was interrupted.

"What if he refuses to marry you?" The question came from inside the study. "The scandal will be worse, but we will not force him." Raleigh stepped up behind Steven. His hair also stuck out on one side, his cravat was askew and his waistcoat misbuttoned. Raleigh was never this unkempt. At least someone was having a good time tonight.

Steven said, "I won't make him go through with it."

And there it was, all out on the table. Though his stomach cramped at the potential loss, Sebastian's esteem of both men went up even further. Most men of their ilk would not hesitate to force their child's acquiescence in this situation. The truth of it was while he wanted Colton, he didn't want someone who didn't want him in return. He was certain they could have a good life together, but if Colton was dead set against the wedding, their life would be a living hell.

"Nor would I want you to. If we cannot come to an agreement, I'll let Colton break the engagement. That way the fault lies with me. But I hope he will agree."

"He's already in his room for the night." Raleigh rested his hand on Steven's shoulder and faced him. "As an engaged couple, a few minutes alone would be acceptable, wouldn't you say?"

Steven smirked at his consort. "Absolutely." He began to nudge Raleigh back into the study, but his smirk faded and he stopped. "With all the excitement this evening and my jumping the gun, I forgot to ask you.... Did you find anything at Jenkins's place?"

Jenkins. Sebastian closed his eyes for a second. Bloody hell, he'd forgotten all about Jenkins and what he'd learned tonight. "The place was ransacked, and the computer butler had been taken. Someone definitely went there looking for something. There's no way of knowing if they found it until we locate someone familiar with the house. According to neighborhood gossip, the Jenkinses had only six servants. I've got men questioning neighboring servants, and I'm trying to track down Betty's family. She has a couple of sisters who live on Regelence."

Steven nodded. "Good idea. Nate is still following up on Jenkins's son. There was something funny regarding his going AWOL."

"I figured as much. I'm thinking of sending Julian to Delcorte to check on the residence there."

"Good idea. We'll talk about this more later. Right now.... You know where Colton's room is, Sebastian. I trust you will put considerable effort into persuading him." The door closed. A loud thud and some laughter followed.

The Townsends' eccentricities never ceased to amaze him. Sebastian stood there stunned for several seconds. Had they just given him permission to seduce Colton? Surely not.

Actually… he was pretty certain they had. He smiled and headed up the stairs.

HE SHOULD be happy—this was what he'd always wanted—so why wasn't he? Colton tossed his toothbrush back into the vanity drawer and closed it. He stared down at the running water. To marry or not to marry? He had until tomorrow morning to decide.

"Water fifty degrees." Cupping his hands under the faucet, Colton bent over and splashed water on his face. "Brrr." That was colder than he'd thought it'd be, but it didn't clear his head any. "Water off." The faucet cut off, and he grabbed the towel he'd laid out. He dabbed the rivulets of water off his face, neck and chest, then tossed the towel on the counter.

Bracing his hands on the vanity, Colton stared in the mirror at the bruise on his neck. He'd noticed it this morning. It had taken him several minutes to realize what it was and how it had gotten there. A love mark, he'd heard it called. Thank goodness his cravat covered it. The rumors by themselves were bad enough. If anyone saw the evidence.... Running his fingers over the dark spot, he sighed.

Last night when Sebastian put it there had been amazing. Funny, as much as he'd been castigating himself for his weakness, Colton had never considered it meant he was compromised. He hadn't considered that until everyone thought he and Sebastian were lovers. Colton snarled at the mirror. And wasn't that ironic? Because there was no way anyone could know about what happened in the stable. His parents didn't even know. It was all speculation based on Plume's big mouth.

Shoving away from the counter, he headed to his bedroom. "Lights out." The light from the fireplace in his room, glowing through the open doorway, guided him out of the dressing room.

Perhaps he should've taken Rexley and Aiden up on their offer to talk instead of pretending everything was fine. They were probably in bed by now. It would be afternoon on Englor. Maybe Payton—no. Colton stepped off the cold dressing room tile onto the plush sapphire carpet of his bedroom. His bare feet sank into the pile, and he glanced down at his toes, wiggling them. Should he put stockings, boots, shirt, and coat back on and go to the stables? He could get on Apollo and just keep riding. *And what? Leave my family? Leave Apollonia? Leave... the future he was beginning to build?*

Snorting, Colton sauntered to his bedroom window. He pushed back the curtains. *Huh, it's snowing again.* He grinned. He'd imagined marrying Sebastian for years. And this wasn't like he'd anticipated. He'd never considered it might snow. In his fantasies, it had always been warm and sunny. Nothing would be like he'd imagined. There would be no pristine white wedding clothes, nor an open landau coach with four white horses to take him and Father to the cathedral. And none of those things seemed important. Now the only thing that really mattered was whether Wentworth was being forced to marry him.

Father had sworn Sebastian had talked to him before he'd made the announcement. But why? Why would Sebastian want to marry him? Was it because of the speculation on their relationship? Of course it must be. Sebastian was an honorable man. He'd feel obligated to offer for Colton's hand.

Someone knocked on the door, startling Colton out of his thoughts.

If it was Father and Cony again, Colton wasn't sure he wanted to be interrupted. "Come in." *Please be one of my brothers... but not Tarren.* Tarren was way too romantic to be practical about this, and if Colton was having visitors, he needed someone he could talk to rationally.

The door clicked open, then shut.

Resting his head on the glass, Colton looked toward Wentworth Park. Funny, he'd just been wanting someone to talk to, and now he had someone, he wished they'd go away. Maybe if he didn't look at them, they would.

No such luck. There was no sound, but suddenly the heat of another body came close, standing directly behind him. He looked down.

Two shiny black boots bracketed his foot. Something, *a finger*, traced down the middle of his bare back along his spine.

Colton shivered.

"Stunning."

Sebastian.

A pair of warm hands touched Colton's back and glided to his shoulders. "Absolutely stunning."

Colton spun around.

Sebastian's gaze wandered over Colton's nude torso, down his trousers to his feet and back up. A slow smile lit his face. "You're even more lovely than I'd imagined." He dragged his fingers over Colton's pectoral muscle and to the center of his chest.

Too surprised by Sebastian's presence to react, Colton watched the caress all the way to the waistband of his trousers. *Dust*, he was nearly naked. He crossed his arms over his chest. "What're you doing here?"

Curling his fingers into the waistband, Sebastian pulled Colton close until they were nose to nose. Sebastian brushed a kiss over Colton's lips. The warm breath mingled with Colton's as Sebastian whispered, "I had to talk to you."

The firelight cast him in shadow, making him seem bigger somehow. His gentleness was mesmerizing, the way he watched everywhere he touched. Colton could almost believe they had some sort of a relationsh—

His parents would be barging in at any minute. Colton leaned around him to see the door.

Chuckling, Sebastian drew him upright and bussed his nose. "I have permission to be up here." He cupped Colton's cheek, sliding his thumb across Colton's bottom lip.

Colton closed his eyes and leaned into the touch. He should be talking, asking about the wedding and trying to get an idea how Sebastian felt, but he didn't want to move. No. He had to. His future depended on it. He stepped out of reach. "I can't think with you touching me like that."

"Fair enough." Sebastian was quiet for several seconds as he glanced around the room. Finally, he met Colton's gaze again. "I'm sorry about this evening. Your father got ahead of me. I should've talked to you before I talked to him."

"Then you did ask him? He didn't force you into it?" Colton paced around his bed and Sebastian, going to stand in front of the fire. He should put a dressing gown on. He rubbed his arms.

"You should know me well enough to know no one forces me to do anything. I asked him, and he was quite pleased by the idea of us marrying." Sebastian spoke from close behind, then touched Colton's back again. "Will you marry me?"

And there it was. The question. Colton put his hand over Sebastian's where it had come to rest on his shoulder. "I didn't know there was a choice at this point."

"There is always a choice." Sebastian kissed Colton's knuckles. "And I'm giving it to you. If you want to back out, I'll take the blame. I'll let *you* jilt me."

Shaking his head, Colton stared at the red-gold flames. The heat of the fire warmed his outside, but inside he was cold. He had some pride, damn it. "I wouldn't do that to you. This mess is all my fault. I should've gotten out of that stall when you told me to. This whole thing has just been blown out of proportion and—" He dropped his hand and turned around.

"And what?" Sebastian captured Colton's hands, holding them. He caressed the tops of Colton's knuckles with his thumbs.

"I don't want you to marry me out of pity or some misplaced sense of duty. I can handle the scandal, but I can't handle your resentment for the rest of my life." He had to have something, anything, a glimmer of hope that they could one day be more to each other. He couldn't marry to save his own reputation. He wouldn't.

"And in the meantime you suffer for it."

"So?"

Sebastian lowered his left hand and wrapped it around the back of Colton's head. He pressed his forehead to Colton's. "I know what that militant look is all about, but you're wrong." He gripped Colton's hand

and mashed it against his erection. "Does this feel like pity? Did it feel like pity last night?"

Colton gasped, his gaze fell to his hand, and he shook his head. Last night was—

He sighed.

"Marry me. You'll be able to open your stables without scandal. Your business will suffer if you don't, and you know it. Eventually, people will have to be somewhat cordial because you are a prince and they don't want to risk making our king too mad, but they don't have to do business with you."

That was true. With this scandal, any hope of having a successful racing stud was dashed, but if he married Sebastian….

Removing his hand from Sebastian's cock, Colton blinked up at him. "What would you get out of the marriage?"

Touching the mark he'd made on Colton's neck last night, Sebastian smiled and met Colton's gaze. "You." His voice was soft, his eyes sparkling in the firelight. For a brief moment, Colton thought he saw something in Sebastian's eyes. Tenderness and… something.

Sebastian rested his cheek against Colton's and wrapped his arms around him. "Think about it. We have things in common. We're already business partners. We get along well. It's more than a lot of people have."

That *something* in Sebastian's gaze did funny things to Colton. Did it make him weak to want to give in? He closed his eyes and hugged Sebastian back.

September 17, 4830: Townsend Castle

COLTON GLANCED up from reading the stable blueprints on his com-pad and met his valet's gaze. "Did you say something, Everett?"

Everett gave Colton's cravat one last tug and pointed at the mirror. "Take a look. You cut a dashing figure."

Turning toward the vanity mirror, Colton frowned. He appeared the same as always. The lavender waistcoat wasn't to his taste—he preferred bolder colors—but it would go nicely with his charcoal-colored morning coat and light gray trousers. "Thank you, Everett. As always, you've done an exceptional job. I had completely forgotten I'd ordered this waistcoat."

"I thought it quite appropriate for a wedding, milord. If you don't need anything else, I'll start packing."

"Yes, yes that's fine, Everett." Colton went back to his plans. He wished Everett hadn't mentioned the *W* word. Colton was trying his best not to think about the wedding. If he did, he was going to be a nervous wreck. He'd thought of little else last night after Sebastian had left. What if Sebastian didn't show this morning? What if he realized his folly? What if the ring Colton ordered didn't get here in time? Did they need a license?

Grrr. He was doing it again. Back to the plans. *Concentrate on the plans, Colton.* He focused on the blueprints. The breeding pen needed to be a bit bigger in his opinion, but the addition of a room above the birthing stall was brillia—

Why was Everett packing? "What did you say?"

Everett's voice grew louder. "What was that, milord?"

"Packing? What are you packing?" Colton glanced up.

"Your things of course."

"Whatever for?"

"Oh dear." Everett frowned and exited the closet. He was only four years older than Colton, but at the moment he looked much older. He crossed his hands in front of him. "I wonder where your parents are. They haven't come up to see you this morning, have they? Not to worry, milord. It's just prewedding jitters. Everyone has them. I'm sure your parents will be up to have a talk with you."

Waving his valet off, Colton pursed his lips. He hadn't even considered he'd be living somewhere else after tonight. How had he forgotten that detail? Colton got up and went into his bedroom. He tossed his com-pad on the bed and wandered over to his thinking spot. Just as he pulled the curtains back, his bedroom door opened.

"Good morning." Rexley closed the door behind him. "Is it still snowing?" He wore black pinstripe trousers and a white shirt and cravat. His waistcoat was burgundy, and he was without a morning coat. He was dressed as he was every morning, but something about his demeanor declared this morning different. Or maybe it was only Colton's imagination running away with him again.

Colton let the curtain fall closed, trying to ignore the queasiness in his belly. "It appears to have stopped for the time being. Have you been downstairs yet?"

"Yes, why?" Rexley perched on the edge of the bed. "What's wrong?"

"Nothing. I was just wondering if Wentworth has shown up yet. I—oh, never mind."

Rexley got up and crossed the room to stand in front of Colton. He put his hand on Colton's shoulder and squeezed gently. "Nervous?"

"No."

Rexley arched a brow.

Colton sighed. "Yes. And then Everett reminded me I would be living at Wentworth Park and made it even worse. Do you suppose Father and Cony will mind if I keep my room? Do you think I need to move my new stables now that I won't be living here?"

"Of course not. You picked a great spot for the stud. Halfway between here and Wentworth Park. And I am certain you'll still have a room in the castle. Although I suspect they'll give you a larger one since you'll be married." Rexley was right. Payton didn't live here anymore, but he still had a room of his own. Or rather he *and Simon* had a room. It was down the hall from Aiden and Nate's suites. "Relax."

Colton covered his face with his hands. He was overreact—

"Don't"—Rexley grabbed his wrists—"run your fingers through your hair. Everett will be devastated if you ruin his handiwork."

Colton laughed. It was hair, for goodness' sake. Could it really be messed up? The stiffness left his shoulders. He'd needed that.

Rexley let go and smirked. "Perhaps I'm a bit nervous for you. Are you sure this is what you want?"

"It's not the love story I conjured in my mind all these years, but we like each other well enough, I suppose. We'll have a comfortable marriage." He knew Sebastian lusted after him, but after last night, he was certain Sebastian also liked him. While he would've rather they waited to see if their feelings grew, Sebastian seemed pretty adamant this was a good thing. Colton had hope. He could make this work.

Rexley frowned.

"Come, let me show you something." Colton looped his arm around his older brother's shoulders and led him to the bed. He picked up his com-pad and handed it to Rexley.

"Is this your stables?" Rexley used his finger to move the blueprints, looking at all sides and skimming down to the front and back elevations.

Colton leaned into his brother so he could see the screen too. "Olympian Stables. What do you think, partner?"

"Olympian because Apollo is the name of a Greek god?"

"You hate it."

"Not at all. I love it, and I think it's fitting. Apollo's been the inspiration for this whole thing, so I think it's only right to honor him. I know you'll do good things with this. I'm looking forward to going with you to races and auctions." He smiled.

"I'd like that." Colton smiled back.

"I can watch the master at work." Grinning, Rexley glanced back at the screen. "This looks amazing."

"Master? I don't know about that. I'll be learning the business as I go."

"Yes, but you know and love horses. You're going to do just fine. And I'll handle the money part if you like."

"I definitely like the sound of that."

The door clicked open.

Aiden bustled in, wagging a large sketchbook with him. He smiled at Colton. "Good morning." After closing the door, he crossed the room and set the book on the bed. "Is this the stables?"

"Yes," Colton and Rexley answered together.

"Nice. Has Cony been in to see you yet?"

Weird. Everett had suggested his parents would be coming to see him this morning too. "No. I wasn't aware I was expecting him. Do you know something I don't?"

Aiden shrugged. "I just assumed he'd come to have *the talk.*"

Rexley snorted. "I can only imagine Cony's slant on things. I bet by the time he's finished, you won't have a clue whether he's discussing the weather, the latest opera, or a life-threatening medical condition."

Colton burst out laughing.

Aiden grinned. "Pretty much. Can you imagine Father's version of things?"

"No." Rexley thought about it for a moment. "I think Father's accounting would be more confusing than Cony's."

"Which is why I'm here. I thought he needed more info than *watch your teeth and use lube*."

Letting the screen fall on the bed, Rexley dropped his head into his hand. His shoulders began shaking. "Did Cony actually say that to you?"

"Oh yes. Needless to say I had no idea what he meant."

Colton tried not to blush, but he wasn't sure how effective he was. "Um, while I'm touched you've decided to spare me from Cony, I don't need *the talk*. I *am* opening a racing stud, remember? I know what sex is."

"Yes, but it's different. People aren't like horses. So I brought my sketchbook to show you some pictures." Aiden picked up the pad he'd brought in with him.

"And that's my cue to leave. Have a nice chat, gentlemen." Rexley dipped his head and started for the door.

Rolling his eyes, Aiden grinned. "I doubt I could show Colton anything you don't already know."

Stopping, Rexley raised an eyebrow in a perfect imitation of their sire.

A secretive smile curved Aiden's lips, and he winked at Colton. "He has quite an impressive collection of *etchings* stashed in a secret file on Jeffers."

Colton's gaze shot to Rexley. *Rexley? Really?* Rexley never did anything wrong.

Rexley still had a raised eyebrow, but there was no other outward reaction to Aiden's pronouncement. "I will see you both downstairs." To Colton he said, "The stables are going to be first-rate." With that he left and closed the door behind him.

"Did he blush at all?" Aiden asked.

"Not that I noticed." Their brother was impossible to read when he did not want to be read. "He has pornography on Jeffers?"

"Oh yes. I'm certain it's his." Aiden flipped the cover over on the sketchbook.

"How?"

"Because it's not mine, yours, Tarren's, or Trouble's. If they were Nate's, he would've shown them to me. If Payton left it here, none of us would be able to access it. And Cony and Father have no need to hide such things; they would just password protect it. We aren't allowed in their private files."

Well, well, Rexley was human after all. Who would've thought their stuffy older brother would have such things? "How did you find them?"

"Quite by accident. I was looking through art files." Aiden sat on the end of the bed and set the sketchpad on his lap. "Now." He wrinkled his face up. "How do I do this?"

Colton shrugged. "I have no idea, but I'm telling you there's no point. I know about sexual intercourse." Unless, of course, they were going to discuss whirligigs and traps. He still had no idea how those things pertained to marital relations, but.... No, on second thought, he did not want to discuss physical intimacy with his parents or his brothers. He'd read all about it back when he was around thirteen, and he'd first heard the term rakehell in conjunction with Sebastian. Since then Colton had some experience thanks to Sebastian. Granted, it wasn't much, but Sebastian had taught Colton that he was more than willing to try out the rest.

Aiden turned the page, and all reluctance fled.

The charcoal drawing was as beautiful as all of Aiden's work. His talent really was amazing. But what held Colton so captivated was the subject matter. A penis with a ring through the head and coming out of the slit. Not only had he never even heard of such a thing, the anatomy itself was impressive.

Colton flopped down on the bed next to Aiden. "What's that?" Colton had never been so appreciative of Aiden's ability to produce photorealism.

Aiden glanced down at the sketch, and a blush spread up his face. "Oh." He hurried and flipped the page. "Forget you saw that one."

"Why? Go back. That was—" What? Lovely didn't seem like the correct word. Although it was indeed lovely. "Oooh...." The next sketch was even lovelier. Way more graphic, but tastefully done. It was erotic and artistic and.... "Whoa."

The artwork depicted a man's hand and—*oh dear*. Colton blinked. Yes, that was a finger in the man's arsehole. "When did you start drawing erotic art?"

Aiden shrugged. "I just dabble. I only use paper, though. Because this is not something I want in Jeffers's memory."

"I'd say that's a good idea."

Aiden flipped the page.

The next sketch contained two entwined bodies. No faces. One figure bent at the waist, or maybe the man was on all fours. Only the torso with an inch or two of thigh showed below the arse. It was a three-quarter view. The other body was bent over the first with just the head of his penis inside the other man's arse. His hand gripped the other man's arsecheek, holding it open. It was a big masculine hand with a vaguely familiar gold band. *Hmmm….* The detail was spectacular. For all the explicitness of the sketch, he could not help but appreciate the artistic skill and composition. But he'd never seen anything so graphic in his life.

Heat raced up his neck and down his back. He'd read about doing *it*, even overheard conversations about *it*, but seeing *it* was something entirely different. He'd be lying if he said it wasn't arousing as well. Colton cleared his throat. He wanted to see more, yet at the same time he did *not* want to get hard in his brother's presence. "Does it hurt?"

Shaking his head, Aiden prepared to turn the page again. "No, it's just odd at first. After you get used to—"

"Oh my stars!"

"Ah!" Colton and Aiden both jumped. The sketchbook slid off Aiden's lap and onto the floor with a splat. Colton and Aiden whirled around as one to face their intruder.

Cony stood at the side of the bed, one hand on the post, the other at the base of his neck.

"Umm…." Colton stood up. He knew he was blushing to the roots of his hair. One glance at Aiden confirmed he was as well. "Cony, we…. Um…."

Aiden picked up the sketchbook, closed it, and faced their sire. "No offense, Cony, but your prewedding-night talk was not helpful, so I thought I'd…." He shrugged.

The urge to point at Aiden and blame him was strong, but Colton resisted. "Aiden's sketches are quite beautiful, don't you think?" *Oh, wonderful. Shoot me now.* He couldn't believe that had come out of his mouth.

Cony's lip twitched.

"After looking at those, I think your talk with Aiden about lube seems like good advice." *Guh! Someone shut me up, please.* Colton groaned and dropped his head in his hand.

Aiden stepped back away from Cony, inching himself next to Colton. "Say something, Cony?"

"Well, then. I guess this concludes our talk. Any questions?" He didn't wait for an answer. He turned toward the door. "Good. I'll see you both downstairs in five minutes." Twisting the knob, he said, "The sketch *was* beautifully done, Aiden." He quit the room.

Colton looked at Aiden.

Aiden looked at him.

They burst out laughing.

The door opened again, and they slammed their mouths shut.

Nate stuck his head in. "What did the two of you do to Raleigh? He was blushing and didn't even look at me when I told him good morning."

Aiden fell against the bedpost and slid to the floor, chortling.

Joining his brother, Colton missed the post and dropped to the bed.

CHAPTER THIRTEEN

Evans Jewelry Store, downtown Classige, Pruluce

"THIS IS it." Sebastian held the ring up toward the light one last time. The sapphires sparkled, and the platinum shone so bright it was blinding. It was big and masculine yet elegant. Colton was going to love it. The horseshoe shape was perfect, and blue was his favorite color. Sebastian had expected to come get a simple wedding band, but instead he'd found this ring. It was as though it were made just for Colton. "Wrap it up. I'll take it." Sebastian handed the ring back to the jeweler. Today was going to be a good day.

"Very well, milord. Good choice," the jeweler commented.

Rourke leaned against the glass display case and crossed his arms over his chest. "What's wrong with a signet ring as a wedding band? Most men give their consorts a signet ring to celebrate their new title." He frowned and glanced down at Sebastian's hand. "Speaking of…. Why don't you wear one? I know at one time you and Hastings both had one. It was *your* wedding ring."

Sebastian shrugged. "I've no idea where it is." Furthermore, he didn't care. He used the Royal Guards seal when he needed one to seal the wax on his formal correspondence. "You know I could care less about the viscountcy."

"Right." Rourke held up his hand and admired his gold signet ring, with his crest cut into a square emerald. The Duke of Knighton's crest held a shield with a knight's helmet, lance, and some vines twined around the letter *R* for the last name Rourke. But along with the Knighton crest, which was on all the members of the Rourke family's rings, it contained a dagger at the bottom of the shield, Rourke's own unique emblem he was given at birth. "I wish I had my parents' and brother's rings." They'd been lost at sea with the bodies.

Sebastian didn't know what to say. What was it like to have such a long and proud heritage? Rourke got melancholy when his family was mentioned. Fortunately the jeweler came back with the boxed ring, sparing Sebastian.

"Here you are, milord." The jeweler handed Sebastian the open box. "I'll charge your account?"

"Yes, please." Sebastian closed the box and tossed it to Rourke. "You'll do the honor of being my best man again, I assume?"

Rourke caught the box and stuffed it in his coat pocket. "I wouldn't have it any other way."

Sebastian opened the door and held it for Rourke. He followed the duke outside, and they headed toward the public stables where they'd left their horses.

It was a nice day. The snow had let up, and even though the cold lingered, the sun was shining and the streets were full. The smell of fresh cinnamon and buttercream drifted past them, along with a hawker's call of "Fresh cinnamon buns, bagels, and tarts."

Today was the big day. It was an impossibility to be as ignorantly happy as he'd been on his first wedding day, but he *was* pleased. He'd come a long way from the idiotic twenty-two-year-old he'd been then and had a much healthier sense of reality instead of a fairy-tale vision. He wasn't looking for love in this marriage, but he was certain he'd be happy.

"You look deep in thought." Rourke contemplated him. "Nervous?"

"No."

Watching where he was going once again, Rourke said, "I seem to remember you being a wreck the last time."

Who wouldn't have been? "Get married in Regelence Royal Cathedral in front of four hundred people and see if you don't have a slight attack of anxiety."

"No, thank you. Frankly, I'm wondering if it would really be so bad to let my cousin inherit the title." Rourke shuddered.

Chuckling, Sebastian shook his head. "You've no intention of allowing your cousin to inherit Knighton, and you know it."

Rourke sighed and waved his hand. "Doesn't matter. We're discussing you. Are you happy?"

"Oddly, I am. I hadn't planned to marry again, but I rather like Colton."

Rourke smirked. "If I didn't know you were completely serious, I would laugh. But since you are, I'll just say good. I am quite certain you did not *like* Wentworth. Lusted after, admired, even envied, but you didn't like him. But then, he was not a likable fellow in my opinion."

No, he hadn't been. Too bad it had taken Sebastian a while to realize that. "Is this where you say I tried to tell you…?"

"No, this is where I say I approve of your choice this time around. So go on a wedding trip, enjoy yourself, and leave everything here to me."

If only it were that simple. "I cannot leave until Jenkins is found." Not to mention, Colton would probably balk at the idea. He was about to break ground with the stables.

"I was afraid you were going to say that. At least take a day or two off. I can handle things at the castle."

He supposed he could take a day. Yes, a day with nothing but Colton to do sounded rather nice. He squinted against the glare of the sun. A soft breeze caught his hair, tickling his ear. Perhaps that was a good omen. It had been storming the last time he'd gotten married.

They passed three parked lifts and a vendor selling oranges. As they walked into the stables, Sebastian revised his opinion on what kind of day it was going to be.

Barnaby Plume came out of the stall next to Max. He caught sight of Sebastian and snarled. "Well, well, aren't the reprobates up early this morning. Just headed home from carousing?" He leaned his arm against the stall and turned to face Sebastian and Rourke.

"Sod off, Plume." Rourke sneered as he retrieved his horse.

Plume smiled. "How very rude, Your Grace. Been taking lessons from Wentworth and his little prince?" The words *Wentworth* and *prince* might as well have been synonymous with *pond scum* the way Plume said them.

Heat suffused Sebastian's face and neck, but he refused to take the bait. He unhooked the rope closing off the stall he'd let for Max.

Max ambled out toward him.

"You know, I was talking to my sire yesterday evening and—hmm…." Plume tapped his chin and glanced at the ceiling. "Now where was I going with that? Oh yes…." One side of Plume's mouth lifted. "Keep tight rein on your prince or you may both suffer an even bigger scandal."

A pain lodged in Sebastian's throat, making it impossible to swallow. He kept from gasping but just barely. There was something about the twinkle in Plume's eye. *He knows.* Why else would he mention his sire? Leo Plume, Viscount-Consort Leith, despised Sebastian. It was a threat. It had to be. A wave of dizziness overcame Sebastian as he took Max's reins and tossed them over Max's head.

Sebastian hoisted himself into the saddle, striving for an outer calm he wasn't close to feeling at the moment. Reining Max into Plume, Sebastian sat up tall in the saddle. With any luck Max would blow snot on the weasel.

When Max crowded Plume against the next stall, Plume blanched and tensed up.

Sebastian leaned over to see around Max's head. "Don't threaten me, Plume. You may not like what you get in return."

Rourke rode up beside him and stopped.

Sebastian glanced at him, then forward. "*Kch, kch.*" He nudged Max's flanks.

"Ow. Oh. Ow. Bloody hell. My foot." Plume hopped and reached for his foot.

Smiling, Sebastian petted Max.

As they cleared the stable, Rourke looked back over his shoulder. "Did that sniveling arsehead just threaten you and Colton?"

"Apparently." And it scared the hell out of Sebastian. A physical attack he could handle, but having his past laid bare? It terrified him. He forced himself to relax his grip on the reins and unclenched his jaw. Plume's family had as much to lose as Sebastian did by unburying the past.

"I say we kill him."

Startled, Sebastian glanced at his friend.

Rourke's expression was blank, no-nonsense, the look in his eyes steady and pointed. He was completely serious.

It was why the man was his best friend. Rourke didn't ask what it was about—it didn't matter—but he was willing to kill to protect people he cared about.

Sebastian grinned and some of his tension dissolved. "I don't think the authorities will like that. He hasn't done anything but run his mouth."

And Sebastian was fairly certain Plume wouldn't cut off his nose to spite his face. Plume would keep his silence.

"As an elite Royal Guard and captain of the Royal Guards, I believe that makes *us* the authorities."

Sebastian laughed. "So we are. Do you think it's an abuse of power?"

"Not if no one knows we did it."

And they were good enough to make certain no one did. They'd done it more than once in their time in the RSR. In and out like ghosts.

"I doubt he has the balls to try anything else." At least Sebastian hoped.

They rode on for several minutes talking about nothing in particular. By the time they arrived at the castle, most of Sebastian's good mood was restored, even if a bit of uneasiness lingered.

A few horses milled about close to the castle. Colton's spoiled-rotten filly was among them. The grooms must be cleaning stalls. As he and Rourke drew closer, she caught sight of Sebastian and loped toward them through the snow. She truly was a beauty.

"I have to thank you, by the way," Rourke said.

"For what?"

"I rather enjoy working again."

Apollonia drew up beside Sebastian and began snuffling at his arm. Max for the most part ignored her. However, she gave Sebastian no choice but to acknowledge her.

Sebastian petted Apollonia. What if…? He chuckled. That was brilliant. "Brat, you just gave me the most excellent idea."

"What?" Rourke looked at him.

"I was talking to the horse."

"Um… okay?"

"Yes. More than okay. Come on." Sebastian heeled Max's flanks, and they took off in a run. He had plans to make. Plans that would make Colton happy.

"ARE YOU ready?"

Colton turned from his intense study of the canopy over his bed to find his father standing at his door. He was more than ready. He'd been lying here with his legs dangling off the foot of the bed since Aiden left some ten minutes ago. It wasn't long really, but having only his thoughts for company was not a good thing. Every disastrous wedding scenario imaginable had played out in his head.

Colton rose from the bed, grabbed his morning coat, and met Father at the door. "I'm ready. The priest is here?"

"Yes." Father offered his arm as Colton closed the door.

"Who else is here?" He took his father's arm and followed down the hall.

"Knighton and Mr. Towers. Towers is one of Sebastian's ex-RSR teammates and our newest bodyguard." Father stared at him with an odd look on his face. "I know I asked you last night, but are you sure you want to do this?" He stopped them and turned to face Colton fully. He buttoned Colton's morning coat and adjusted his cravat.

Colton leaned forward and kissed his father on the cheek. He actually had to bend down a little. He was taller than his father now, but only by a few inches. "Yes."

Father wrapped his arms around Colton and hugged him tight, squeezing him almost to the point of pain. "I'd never want you to marry if you weren't certain. I'm sorry if I pressured you by making that announcement. I just—" He pulled back, clasping Colton's biceps and meeting his gaze. "I thought I was helping. He's what you always wanted, and I wanted to make you happy. But your expression when I announced the wedding—" He shook his head. "Are you certain, son? If not, I'll go downstairs right now and call this whole thing off. We'll deal with the fallout. I don't want you to worry about that. I don't want that to be the reason you're going through with this. What I want from you is to know if this is truly what you want and if you're going to be happy. If it's not, it needs to be stopped."

Colton's vision blurred as tears welled in his eyes. He looked up, trying to get his emotions under control. "I don't want it stopped, Father." He took a deep breath and glanced back down at his parent. Something in Father's gaze, so full of love, made Colton wistful… sad. He missed those days when he'd sit on Father's lap as he worked, or when he'd snuggle with Cony in front of the fire while Father read to them. How many times had his father and his sire carried him to bed after he'd fallen asleep somewhere in the castle playing with his brothers?

Colton hadn't thought of those things in years, but suddenly he couldn't help but mourn the loss of those much simpler days. "I never considered how hard it'd be to leave all of you. Do you know, I was okay this morning until Everett reminded me I'd no longer be living here? After he mentioned packing my things, I got a stomachache. It didn't let up until Rexley and Aiden came to see me. It's still not gone entirely."

"I always jest about your Cony wanting all of you kids and me trying to talk him out of it, but you do know that's not true, don't you? We *both* wanted all of you, and it's something we've never regretted regardless how we tease." Tears welled in Father's eyes, and he too had to look up to stop them from flowing. "I love you, Colton. As much as I want you boys to be happy, I hate you not being here with me. I can't tell you how happy I was to gain Nate and Jeremy rather than lose Aiden. It nearly killed me to let Payton go back to Englor. At least I know you're going to be near, and I'll see you often. Talking to Payton every other night on televid just isn't the same." A tear dripped down his cheek, and he dashed it away with a chuckle. "As long as I live, you'll *always* have a place here. If you ever need me—"

"I know where you are." Colton smiled and hugged his father to keep from crying. "You know if you ever need me, I'm here for you too."

Father laughed. "Indeed I do. Come, let's go get you married. I rather like Sebastian."

"I rather like him too." His father's acceptance and love made Colton feel much better.

They made it to the main staircase, and Father said, "Maybe you'll even take pity on me and give me a grandchild I can see every day. Galaxy knows Aiden and Nate aren't in any hurry."

A knot formed in Colton's stomach. So much for his bellyache going away. "You're *not* helping my nerves." He hadn't even thought about kids. He had his hands full with Apollonia. Did Sebastian want kids? He'd never had any with his first husband. Of course he must want them at some point. He needed an heir. "I'll make you a deal. Lay off me about grandchildren for a couple of years, and I'll help you guilt Aiden into having one." Not really. Even though he was fairly certain Nate was ready and even wanted another child, Aiden most definitely did not. Colton would never pressure his brother over something so serious, and apparently his brother-in-law felt the same way, because he always put a stop to any talk of procreating where Aiden was concerned. At least in Aiden's presence.

"Deal. Tell me… what did you and Aiden do to your Cony?"

Colton wasn't sure what made him do it. Maybe it was revenge for his father making him miss his childhood and nearly reducing him to tears, but—"Aiden decided to talk to me about sex. Only he didn't want to actually talk, so he showed me some sketches. They were quite beautiful. You know how incredibly talented Aiden is." He cleared his throat, trying not to smirk. "The piece Cony saw was of two men. One had only the head of his—"

"Never mind! I get the idea."

"But, Father, I haven't finished telling you about the sketch. The one man was bent over the other's back slightly and his pe—"

"Colton Edward Townsend." Father slapped a hand over Colton's mouth.

Colton tried to hold back his laughter, he really did, but the only thing it accomplished was to make his shoulders shake and his eyes water.

"Shame on you both." Father's lips twitched. "No wonder your Cony looked as though he'd seen a ghost."

Wiping away tears of mirth, Colton composed himself. He wondered if he could commission Aiden to paint him a piece like the ones he'd seen. The shock value alone would be well worth the cost. "Oh, but that wasn't the best part. I suspect Cony's reaction was due to the noticeable depiction of Nate's wedding band on the hand gripping the other man's arse."

Father groaned, and his cheeks blazed as bright as Cony's had. "You're an evil, evil child." The humor in his voice made it crack a bit. "You best be glad you're going to Wentworth Park tonight else I'd ground you for the rest of your life for putting that image in my head."

Leaning his head against his father's, Colton laughed louder while his father mumbled about bratty children and having nightmares of his children doing such intimate things.

As they made their way to the foyer, Sebastian stepped out of the parlor.

The laughter froze in Colton's throat.

Sebastian was so handsome it took Colton's breath away. He wore black trousers and a black morning coat. His waistcoat was silver. His sable hair was windblown as usual, but he was freshly shaven. And he had the most beautiful smile on his face Colton had ever seen. The smile even made his eyes sparkle. Sebastian almost never showed that much joy. His normal look was one of boredom. *He's really here. He does want to marry me.*

Sebastian met them at the foot of the stairs and offered his arm to Colton. "What's so funny?"

"It's nothing. I'll tell you later." Or maybe not. Such a conversation with Sebastian would be embarrassing. Heat rose up Colton's neck. Tonight he'd be expected to actually do the thing he didn't want to describe. The prospect both embarrassed and excited him. His hand shook as he set it on Sebastian's forearm.

Cony strode out of the parlor and to Colton. Cony looked Colton up and down and kissed his forehead. There was no trace of the blush that had stained Cony's cheeks earlier. "You look very handsome."

"Thank you, Cony."

Sebastian placed his hand on top of Colton's where it rested on his arm. He turned to Colton as Cony went to Father's side and began whispering. Cony was probably asking if Colton wanted to go through with the wedding.

Sebastian asked, "Is everything okay?"

"Yes." It was now. Colton smiled. Sebastian had shown up. And until he'd noticed Colton's tremors, he'd seemed happy. What more could Colton have asked for?

"Well, then, come along. I have a surprise for you. Everyone thinks I've lost my mind."

They thought Sebastian crazy for marrying Colton? It was like a knife through the heart. Did Sebastian agree? Was he having doubts? Reluctantly, Colton allowed Sebastian to lead him into the parlor.

Colton greeted the priest in a daze. He glanced around the room, spotting his family minus Payton and Simon, who were on Englor. Rourke and a man Colton had never seen before stood in the parlor too. The new man was about Colton's height—six foot two—with brown hair and a friendly smile—he must be Mr. Towers. The priest was the same one who'd presided over Aiden's wedding. He was tall and thin with a hawklike nose, silver hair, and side whiskers. He always looked mean until he smiled. Fortunately, he almost always smiled. He was a nice man.

"Have the two of you chosen your witnesses?" Father Adams asked.

Witnesses? Colton didn't even know if the wedding band he'd ordered this morning was here. *Oh no.* What if it was the wrong size? He had no idea what size ring Sebastian wore.

"Yes. Rourke will stand up with me." Sebastian smiled at Colton. "Who'd you choose?"

Was Rourke one of the people who thought Sebastian was insane for marrying him? Colton wouldn't have thought so, but.... Colton glanced at the duke. He stood conversing with Mr. Towers, Aiden, and Nate.

"Colton?" Sebastian frowned.

"I don't know. I didn't think to ask anyone." He raised his brows at his family, hoping one of them would agree.

"Me. I'll do it." Muffin ran forward, her pretty pink ruffled dress rustling with her movement. "I'll be Colton's best man."

Everyone chuckled.

Rexley put his hand on her shoulder. "How about we both stand up with Colton? Colton, is that all right with you?"

He wanted to say thank you and tell his brother and niece it would be an honor, but all he could do was nod.

"Good. If everyone will indulge me… please follow me. And before any of you give me that look again, I am aware you all think I'm a candidate for Bedlam." Sebastian turned and guided them out of the parlor.

No one had disputed the fact they thought Sebastian crazy. Colton's heart beat so rapidly his temples throbbed. He glanced up at Sebastian to ask him if he felt as his friends did, but Thomas was handing out coats to everyone. "What's going on?"

Rexley sidled up beside him, holding Muffin's hand in one of his and Trouble's in the other. "I've got the ring you ordered in my pocket. I meant to give it to you upstairs, but I forgot."

"Thank you." Colton shrugged into his coat and took Sebastian's arm again. He must've gripped Sebastian's arm harder than he thought, because Sebastian looked down at him.

"If you don't want to have the ceremony in the stables, we don't have to. I just thought you'd like that. I don't care if everyone else thinks it's odd, but if it bothers you, we'll conduct the ceremony in the parlor."

Colton stared at him in shock. The pressure in his chest loosened, and once again he found himself laughing. This was going to be the perfect wedding after all.

WHOEVER INVENTED morning coats should be drawn and quartered. Sebastian could only catch glimpses of Colton's delectable arse as he climbed the stairs. Silly tails hid entirely too much, and what was the point of walking behind someone if you couldn't watch their arse? Assuming they had a nice arse of course. He would not want to be stuck behind, say… Lord Filbert. That man had the bottom the size of a—suffice it to say his arse was rather large.

"Which door?" Colton asked as he stepped onto the landing. The breathless excitement was enchanting.

"Third left." Sebastian vaguely remembered his first tour of Wentworth Park. If recollection served, he too had been enraptured. Unfortunately the demands of marriage had quickly overpowered the thrill of the estate.

He should show Colton their sitting room first, which was the fourth door, but Sebastian was done with the tour. He'd waited long enough. He'd gotten married in a stable, with Colton's pesky little filly trying to nibble on the sleeve of his morning coat, and Muffin asking Rexley every two minutes—until she got sidetracked by the horses—if she could hand Colton the ring. Even Payton and his consort Simon had joined them via televid. The atmosphere had been relaxed, fun, probably a bit improper, and definitely in poor taste in the eyes of society, but it had been absolutely perfect. And now? The part of the day he'd been waiting for.

Colton opened the door and stepped in.

"Welcome to your new room." Sebastian closed the door behind him.

The fire in the fireplace glowed throughout the room. It made the place cozy and romantic.

"I love it." Colton walked past the big cherrywood sleigh bed, dragging his hand along the midnight-blue duvet, and stopped at the window. He brushed the heavy curtains aside, letting the remaining sunlight flood the room.

Throwing up his hand to shield his eyes, Sebastian blinked against the glare. It took several moments for his eyes to adjust.

The setting sun radiated across Colton's high cheekbones and strong chin. *Stunning.* The utter stillness shouted his self-control and confidence. He had such a proud, regal bearing. Perhaps because he resembled their king. Standing there, he could've been a classical statue: beautiful, graceful, but strong and unyielding. Sebastian had always thought of Colton as untouchable, but now he made Sebastian ache in all the right places.

He'd been half-hard since they'd started their tour over an hour ago. Sebastian's footsteps thumped on the dark wood floor, then muffled on the rug as he moved behind Colton. "The back of the house has a better view."

"This is the opposite view I've had most of my life."

Sebastian wrapped his arms around Colton's waist and inhaled deeply. He smelled of fresh, clean air and evergreens. He was the same height as Sebastian, which made it easy to look over his shoulder. His height would also come in handy for other things too. Other things Sebastian intended to do shortly.

"Is that a good thing?" Sebastian rested his chin next to Colton's ear.

Colton stiffened. "It's just an observation."

A frisson of unease trickled through Sebastian. He'd never seduced an innocent before. Should he let go? Before he could decide, Colton sighed and slouched into him. *Thank galaxy.* Sebastian picked at Colton's cravat, loosening it along the strong jawline. Such a tempting neck. "Are you nervous?"

Colton shook his head and rested it back on Sebastian's shoulder. "Well, perhaps a little."

Was that a freckle just below his ear? Untying the neckcloth, Sebastian gave in to temptation and closed his mouth over the long tendon in Colton's neck. He grazed the skin with his teeth as he tugged the cravat off and dropped it to the floor.

Colton shivered against him and let out a soft, guttural moan.

The sound vibrated through Sebastian. He slid his hands inside Colton's coat and along the taut muscles of Colton's abdomen covered by his waistcoat. Sebastian unfastened one button of the waistcoat, then another.

Canting his hips back, Colton nestled himself against Sebastian's groin, pressing into Sebastian's erection. Oh *yesss*….

Humming his approval, Sebastian pushed forward. The pressure on his cock sent a thrill of excitement through him. It seemed like forever he'd been waiting for this. Had it only been the other night he'd had Colton restless in his arms and straining for release? Sebastian slipped both the coat and waistcoat off, moving back enough to let the clothes fall between them.

Colton touched his thigh, tentatively at first, and dragged his hand up to Sebastian's erection.

Sebastian bit back a groan at the pleasure. Like a magnetic force was at play, he ran his fingers up to Colton's shoulders. He tugged the ties holding his shirt closed and revealed the reddish, purple bruise. *My mark.* Sebastian's cock bucked against Colton's hand.

Sebastian licked a line down Colton's neck and bit his shoulder. *Dust*, he had to get this man naked. He wanted to see more of what he'd seen last night. Fumbling with Colton's shirt, Sebastian untucked it from his pants.

Colton gripped Sebastian's arms and turned his head slightly. His sweet, warm breath fanned across Sebastian's face. "It's still daylight."

"Yes, it is." Grinning, Sebastian kissed Colton's jaw right below his ear, and Colton's racing pulse thrummed against his lips. Sebastian kissed him again and rubbed his hands up and down Colton's arms, trying to soothe and comfort. "Is that a problem?"

Colton shook his head, dislodging Sebastian's attempt at nuzzling. "No." He faced Sebastian and tugged at Sebastian's morning coat, shoving it off his shoulders. "You have too many clothes on."

"So do you." Sebastian got his arms free of his coat and started on his cravat. It came off in no time, and he tore at his waistcoat. A button sailed across the room, landing on the wood floor and rolling under the bed.

"Yes." Colton nodded and hastily undressed. He jerked his shirt over his head. He was even lovelier than last night. Once again the firelight added a rosy glow to his skin and shadowed his muscles. His lean body flexed with his every breath as he stood there watching Sebastian watch him. Down the center of Colton's chest was the faintest line of dark hair that grew darker and thicker until it disappeared beneath the waistband of his trousers.

Colton tugged Sebastian's shirt over his head.

After that, clothes flew in every direction. Sebastian pulled off one boot and tossed it over his shoulder. Something crashed behind him, but he didn't care. He removed the other and gave it the same treatment. Once his stockings were off, he helped Colton. "Sit down."

Dropping to the edge of the bed, Colton grabbed one boot and Sebastian pried off the other. The stockings came next, thrown somewhere behind him. They froze, both in only their trousers, staring at each other, Colton on the bed, Sebastian kneeling in front of him.

With a trembling hand Colton touched Sebastian's cheek and leaned forward. The caress trickled along Sebastian's jaw, over his chin and back up again. With his eyes half-mast, Colton followed his gaze with his fingers.

Closing his eyes, Sebastian turned his face into Colton's palm and kissed the center. Sebastian couldn't remember ever being touched like this. He should move them along, get things back on track, but he couldn't tear himself away from the sensation. Gads, where had his self-control gone? He was much more accomplished than this at seduction. He always took charge and gave his partners what they wanted. So why wasn't he now? What was different?

"I've wanted to touch you for so long. I can't believe I finally get to." Colton's voice was barely above a whisper, but it was the tone more than the words that went straight to Sebastian's head.

Sebastian wasn't used to being worshipped this way. It was uncomfortable and addicting all at the same time.

Colton tilted his head. A soft smile played over his lips.

"You may touch me any time you want. Any way you want." Sebastian blinked and stared into sherry-colored eyes. Eyes he could gladly drown in. "But first…." Dropping back on his haunches, he unbuttoned Colton's trousers. "Let's get these off."

Colton stood, and Sebastian eased his trousers and smallclothes over his hips. Sebastian inched the fabric down over sharp hipbones and a defined lower abdomen that made a perfect V where it angled down to his groin. And his cock…. Slightly curved toward his belly, it was a thing of beauty. His thighs were all hard muscle and thick.

Sebastian dragged the trousers down until Colton could step free of them. The statue analogy had been right on the mark, because Colton was a work of art.

"Exquisite." With one hand Sebastian drew the back of his knuckles up the velvety ridge of Colton's erection and cupped his testicles with the other. Colton's legs trembled and his cock flexed. "Absolutely exquisite."

Colton's hands clenched at his sides, and his stomach rose with a shuddered breath. Sebastian wanted nothing more than to take the head of his cock into his mouth and see if it tasted as good as it looked, but if he did, he didn't know if he'd be able to stop. Instead, he wrapped his hand around the hard flesh and got to his feet.

Colton looped his arms around Sebastian's neck. "I'm glad you think so." The flirt nipped his chin and thrust into Sebastian's hand. The smooth glide of warm skin pushed through his grip. "Your turn." Colton slipped his hand down Sebastian's shoulder and his arm to wind their fingers together. He backpedaled to the bed, taking Sebastian along with him. Colton crawled onto the mattress and scooted backward onto his knees, giving Sebastian no choice but to follow. When Sebastian's knees hit the edge, Colton stopped. As he reached for the falls on Sebastian's trousers, a flash of uncertainty crossed Colton's face, and he swallowed hard.

The mix between virgin and seducer was extremely enticing. Sebastian wasn't sure what he'd expected of an innocent, but this wasn't it. Of course he should have because Colton never did anything by half measures. He'd always had a passionate nature. He was going to be a natural at this.

Sebastian brushed Colton's hands aside and unfastened himself. "Remember what I said."

Colton stared up at him.

Sebastian's heart raced. *Oh, those eyes.* They drew him in and held him captive.

Shaking his head slowly, Colton whispered, "I don't want to muck this up."

"You can't possibly muck this up. Do whatever feels right. As I said before, you may do *anything* you like. I'm at your mercy." And Sebastian couldn't think of anywhere he wanted to be more at the moment. He shucked off his trousers and his smallclothes.

Colton gasped, the look of wonder on his face laced with desire.

Sebastian smiled. He was used to the surprise. He was not a small man by anyone's measure. Some of his partners in the past had been reluctant to continue after seeing how well-endowed he truly was.

Colton, however, didn't seem to have any reservations. He wrapped a hand around Sebastian's cock. A wicked gleam lit his eyes, and he tugged, leading Sebastian by his dick. "Come here."

With pleasure. Sebastian's patience came to an end. He had to do some touching of his own. Climbing onto the bed, he faced Colton. Their mouths met as he took Colton in hand. Together they fumbled and stroked until they ended up with Sebastian sitting on the bed and Colton straddling his legs.

Nipping his chin again, Colton soothed it with a quick peck. A soft smile flitted across his face, and he planted his hands in the middle of Sebastian's chest and shoved.

Sebastian fell on his back with a bounce.

"I always knew you'd be this beautiful." Colton explored Sebastian's chest, working down his stomach and back up.

Not only did the way he rubbed over Sebastian's skin feel wonderful, but the sheer enjoyment on Colton's face was mesmerizing.

Colton paused in his slow, mind-numbing caresses, fell to Sebastian's side, and propped himself on his elbow. "Tell me how to make you feel good. I'm not entirely certain I know what to do, but I take direction well, and I want to please you." His gaze strayed to Sebastian's lips, and he toyed with the ends of Sebastian's hair along the side of his neck. It tickled but was also relaxing. It made Sebastian want to close his eyes and bask in the pleasure.

"You? Take direction well?" Sebastian chuckled. "You most certainly do not. You absolutely hate being told what to do."

"I'll make an exception this once."

Where had that deep gravelly voice come from? Sebastian gave thanks he was lying down at the moment, because he was certain he'd melt into a boneless puddle otherwise. First, Colton had defended him at the auction and now this. No one had ever asked him what he wanted. Instead they informed him what they liked. "Everything about you pleases me."

"Good." Colton pressed his hand against the side of Sebastian's head, bringing him forward, and covered his mouth with his. He probed with his tongue momentarily before sliding down his body, kissing his way lower and lower.

Sebastian hissed at the feel of warm lips tickling his stomach. He knew exactly where this was headed and wanted the same thing himself. "Colton, turn around."

A pair of languid eyes peered up at him from above his lower stomach. Colton's lips were already red and swollen. He was the very picture of debauchery. He widened his eyes as what Sebastian wanted dawned on him. He turned himself around as Sebastian rolled to his side.

Gripping the narrow hips, Sebastian pulled them forward until the tip of Colton's dick touched his lips. He stuck out his tongue, and warm heat closed around the head of his cock. He froze when all he wanted to do was grab the back of Colton's head and surge forward. "Bloody hell."

Colton half moaned, half chuckled, sending vibrations up the length of Sebastian's cock. He released Sebastian only to take him in his mouth again. Several times Colton repeated the action.

Lost in a haze of pleasure, Sebastian squeezed Colton's arse and dragged him forward. He sucked Colton between his lips and slid the heated flesh all the way to the back of his throat, showing Colton by example what to do. The salty-sweet taste of precome infused his mouth and made him want more.

The slow, teasing kiss on his own cock continued. Colton didn't manage to go more than halfway, but he was a quick study and used his hand to compensate.

Sebastian's testicles drew up more, and his cock throbbed. Fingernails raked over his arsecheeks, making him sensitive to the air. Had anything ever felt so good? A finger teased his crease, slowly working its way toward his arsehole.

Sebastian closed his eyes in bliss. *Dust*, he loved a finger up the arse while being blown. *Please*, he silently pleaded.

The tickling caress continued for several seconds, just grazing the place he wanted it most, and disappeared entirely. More precome flitted across his tongue, and then the finger was back, slick now, pushing inside him. Sebastian groaned around Colton's cock.

Sebastian pushed back on the questing digit, wondering how much more he could take. Just the idea of what Colton was doing had him ready to blow. Sebastian released the lovely dick from his mouth and panted. He couldn't even speak, it felt so good. This was his seduction. He was supposed to be sweeping his new consort off his feet, and here he was reduced to gasps and grunts.

Colton kissed his cock, swiping the top of his tongue across the tip, and sat up, his finger still in Sebastian's arse. He too was breathing hard. A nice pink flush had washed up around his shoulders and chest. His hair was in disarray, his beautiful eyes dazed. He sat there for several seconds, his chest muscles flexing with every breath. A line of perspiration trickled down the center of Colton's chest, and Sebastian wanted to catch it on his tongue. He moved to do just that, but Colton shoved Sebastian onto his back and pushed his legs apart with his free hand. Colton's finger sank deeper only to pull back and plunge in again, his attention glued to his actions.

A moan forced its way out of Sebastian's throat as he clenched his arse. He needed to take charge. To get up and make love to his consort. Colton deserved to be worshipped and coddled.

Sebastian stared at Colton's mesmerized profile and reveled in the attention he bestowed. What was the matter with him? Good heavens, he had not bottomed in years. It was just expected that he'd take charge. His reputation was no exaggeration. He was an accomplished lover and good at seduction. He was in his element controlling how things went, and at the moment he wanted nothing more than for Colton to fuck him senseless. What was wrong with him?

"Tell me what to do," Colton whispered and ran his free hand over Sebastian's lower abdomen. He bent and placed a kiss below Sebastian's navel, raking his fingers through the dark hair above Sebastian's cock. "I don't know what you expect of me." Tilting his head, Colton rested his cheek against Sebastian's hip, but his attention never strayed from Sebastian's face.

The pressure in his arse increased, and he realized Colton had added another finger. Sebastian touched Colton's cheek. He couldn't not. Why had it taken him so long to realize what a gem he had? He'd worked so hard to escape Colton's attentions, and for the life of him he could not come up with one good reason as to why. "You're doing wonderfully, sweeting. All I want is for you to be you." Because that was enough. It was more than he'd ever had. "What do *you* want?"

Bloody hell, Colton was so beautiful he almost hurt one's eyes. That must be why Sebastian's eyes were watery. Sebastian blinked and continued to stroke Colton's cheek. It was smooth and soft. The image of Colton when he was determined to have his way, with his set jaw and determined brow, flashed into Sebastian's head, and he grinned. How could something hard and unyielding be soft?

"I want…." The rosy flush on Colton's chest spread up to his cheeks even as he continued to finger Sebastian's arse.

Now he's blushing? Sebastian chuckled and crooked his finger. "Come here." It was time he wrested control back. Time to become the seducer instead of the seduced.

Removing his hand, Colton crawled forward in a move that would make a practiced courtesan envious.

Sebastian growled and bit down on Colton's shoulder when it came into reach.

Colton shivered against him. The sound ripped from him was the sexiest thing Sebastian had ever heard. He had to have Colton. Now. Rolling to his side and taking Colton with him, Sebastian held his hand under the discreet lube dispenser on the side of the headboard. Once he had a decent amount of the warmed substance in his hand, he wrapped it around Colton's cock.

Colton's caressing hands and innocent kisses on his neck and chest ceased. He arched into Sebastian's hand and threw his head back. The tendons in his neck strained, and his Adam's apple bobbed. His skin glistened.

Sebastian's sweet, innocent, provocative consort needed no further assistance. Colton rolled them back to their original position and spread Sebastian's legs. He gathered some of the lube from Sebastian's hand and rubbed it on Sebastian. Seizing his cock from Sebastian's grasp, Colton pressed the head against Sebastian and sank slowly inside.

With a gasp and wide eyes, Colton braced himself with his hands on each side of Sebastian's chest. "Sebastian?" His voice came out in a strangled murmur.

Sebastian moaned and fought letting his eyes roll back in his head. Bloody hell, it felt better than he'd remembered. Sex toys were no substitute for a flesh-and-blood man. Bringing his knees up, Sebastian cupped the gorgeous face looking down at him in awe, and dragged Colton forward for a kiss. The movement sent Colton's cock deeper inside him, and they both cried out. "Move, sweeting."

"Like this?" Colton bucked forward, keeping his upper body off Sebastian's.

Sebastian longed to pull that lovely firm chest against his own, but he rued messing up the delicious angle of penetration. "Just like that." His stomach quivered, and his cock ached for stimulation. He pushed into Colton's every thrust, hurrying him up a bit.

In no time, Colton had a nice rhythm, driving them both toward climax. The sounds leaking from his mouth were nearly as exciting as the movement of his hips.

Sebastian wanted to see Colton. Watch him. Memorize the way he looked in this exact moment.

Colton's thrusts sped up and faltered. "I—I—oh dust." He froze, his pelvis mashing into Sebastian's arse, cried out, and came. Colton's eyes snapped shut. The muscles in his shoulders and stomach strained. Even with his face contorted in ecstasy he was beautiful.

Sebastian's muscles clenched, and heat rose up his body. The pressure and passion built. He gripped his own cock and began stroking, racing for completion.

Colton collapsed over him for a moment, panting, sweat dripping down his temples onto Sebastian's neck. Abruptly, he scooted down the bed. His cock came free with a gush of semen.

Shoving Sebastian's hand away, Colton grabbed Sebastian's cock. Instead of stroking like Sebastian expected, Colton took the head into his mouth and used his hand as he had earlier. It was awkward and nowhere near as good as Sebastian's own hand, but it didn't seem to matter.

Sebastian's vision whited out. Every sensation coalesced in his testicles and exploded forth. He vaguely registered the sound of gagging. When his mind finally caught up with his body and the last remnants of pleasure trickled to a stop, he realized he had his hands buried in Colton's hair. "Bugger." He opened his palms and jerked them up. "Colton? Are you all right?"

With watery eyes, Colton gave him a crooked smile. A smear of semen dabbed his chin. Clearing his throat, he nodded. He lay down and rested his head against Sebastian's hip, his nose and chin nearly touching Sebastian's spent cock, and closed his eyes. The soft smile never left his face.

A strange ache started in Sebastian's chest as he brushed the hair off his new consort's forehead with an unsteady hand. What in the galaxy just happened? He'd never experienced anything like that before. Deep down he'd known Colton would be this passionate, but Sebastian had never imagined Colton would take command of the situation and grab hold with both hands. Their first time together exceeded Sebastian's preconceived notions, but it also confused him.

Sebastian had lost all sense of control. His stomach grew queasy. This marriage was supposed to have been a way to save Colton, but Sebastian suddenly felt as if he was the one who needed saving.

CHAPTER FOURTEEN

September 18, 4830: Townsend Castle

"FATHER? YOU wanted to see me?" Rexley stepped inside the study door. Not a hair was out of place, as usual. The tan trousers and maroon morning coat emphasized his broad shoulders and long legs.

Steven smiled. Everyone said Rexley looked like him, but Steven disagreed. Rexley was a much better-looking version of him. And thank galaxy he'd gotten his Cony's height. Colton was the tallest of the boys, but Rexley was only about an inch shorter.

"Yes. Yes. Please come in. Do you have a free moment?"

"For you? Absolutely. I was just about to have money transferred to Colton's account so we can break ground early next week, but it can wait a few hours." Rexley strode forward, grabbing a chair on his way and situating it in front of the desk. A wrinkle creased his brow as he took a seat. "Is this about Ashbourne?"

Steven chuckled. He'd known Rexley had taken over his cousin's estate from the beginning. His chest swelled with pride at the skill with which Rexley had taken the estate that was merely breaking even and made it prosper. His son was a brilliant man. "No. But I know, as everyone else does, that you took over management of Ashbourne for Dalton. Does Dalton realize how wealthy you've made him?"

Rexley shrugged one shoulder. "I've sent him reports. He should have some idea if he bothered to look over them. Which he probably hasn't. When he returns home permanently next year, I shall take him to task over it."

No doubt he would too. Steven winced just thinking about it. Rexley had an intimidating stare. It was never what Rexley said but rather how he said it and the look on his face when he did so. Steven loved taking Rexley to meetings with him and watching even the oldest, most outspoken lords squirm under his icy regard when they spoke out of turn. He'd make a wonderful king one day.

"How is the Winstol estate business coming along? I understand you took over management for Aiden and Nate." Steven drummed his fingers on the desk.

"It's going."

"Uh-oh. Did the manager I appointed not do a good job?"

"The manager did fine. He just continued with what the last marquess did. Marcus really was brilliant. Much more intelligent than his father, I might add. He made a lot of improvements, but in the fourteen years or so he's been gone, there've been vast improvements in farming techniques." Rexley rested his elbows on the arms of the chair, steepled his fingers together, and sighed. "My biggest issue at the moment, however, is pinning Jeremy down to go over things with me. He needs to learn how to run the estate, but every time I mention working on it, he blanches and remembers something he has to do."

Steven chuckled.

Rexley's lips twitched.

"Speaking of Trouble…. Jeffers, have you informed Lord Winstol we're waiting on him?"

"I have, Your Majesty. He is on his way," the butler answered.

"Jeremy is joining us?" Rexley pinned Steven with that blasted stare of his.

Steven would not squirm. "Yes. What I've got to say involves him as well."

A rapid slapping noise echoed in the foyer.

They both turned to look at the door.

The flapping grew louder until Trouble appeared at the door. His cheeks were flushed, his platinum curls tousled, his cravat crooked and on his feet were a pair of white bunny slippers. In one hand he held a rapier and in the other his blue morning coat.

Steven bit his lip to keep from laughing at the picture he made. Trouble had grown a good three inches in the last several months, and his face had taken on more maturity. He was becoming more handsome than cute, but he was still adorable. With his personality he could be no less.

"You wanted to see me?" Trouble huffed out a breath. "I got here as fast as I could."

"I can see that." Steven motioned to the door, still fighting his mirth. "Shut the door and come take a seat."

Trouble put his coat over the other arm and closed the door.

"Jeremy, where are your boots?" Rexley asked, coming to his feet and meeting Trouble halfway.

"I couldn't find my black ones, and the brown ones pinch my toes."

Rexley straightened Trouble's cravat, took the morning coat from him, and held it open.

Trouble turned and put one arm in, switched his foil into the other hand, and stuck the other arm through the sleeve before facing Rexley.

"How in the world were you fencing in those?" Rexley pointed to Trouble's feet and buttoned the coat. He brushed off the shoulders, stepped back, and gave an approving nod. They really did complement each other.

"Not very well. I kept tripping."

The scene was so domestic it made Steven's nerves ease a bit. He sensed victory. He'd been right in calling this little conference. He cleared his throat. "Well, then. Trouble, grab a chair."

Rexley relieved Trouble of his weapon and laid it on the loveseat as Trouble gripped the back of the other chair and began dragging it across the floor with a horrendous screech.

Steven cringed.

Wincing, Rexley retrieved the chair from Trouble, picked it up, and set it next to his.

Trouble shrugged. "Oops. Sorry." Taking a seat, he fumbled with his cravat.

"Go on, Father. What did you wish to speak to us about?" Without looking, Rexley caught Trouble's hand, pulled it away from his cravat, placed it on the arm of the chair, and patted it.

Oh yes, this was going to go just the way Steven wanted it to. Raleigh would praise him for his noble deed, and everything would continue as planned. Steven grinned. He loved it when a plan came together. "Boys, I've found a way to break the betrothal contract."

"No!" Trouble bolted from his seat and shook his head.

Frowning, Rexley reached forward and caught Trouble's hand. He tugged until Trouble sat back down, but Rexley didn't let go. "I appreciate your effort, Father, but it's not necessary. The betrothal stands."

Elation filled Steven. It was like a giant weight had been lifted off his shoulders. He gave in to his smile. "Good, good. If you are certa—"

"Yes." Trouble leaned over and gave Rexley a quick peck on the lips.

When Trouble moved to sit back in his chair, Rexley caught his chin. He tilted his head and pressed his lips to Trouble's.

Moaning, Trouble opened his mouth.

Rexley took complete advantage and deepened the kiss.

Steven swore he saw tongue. His mouth dropped open, but he couldn't force a single sound out. *This cannot be happening.* With him sitting right there… watching…. Bloody hell…. *Dust*, that was one heck of a kiss.

Wrapping an arm around Trouble's back, Rexley pulled him into his lap, and Trouble made a whimpering sound.

"Steven!"

Startled, Steven jerked his gaze to the door.

"Boys. Stop that this instant." Raleigh strode forward.

Nate came in right behind him. "Jeremy Hawkins."

Trouble stayed exactly where he was, gazing into Rexley's eyes. "Whaaat…?" He turned his head toward the door, spotted Nate, and bounded off Rexley's lap.

"Why are you yelling at me?" Steven returned his consort's thunderous expression.

Rexley sat in the chair, looking bored as if nothing had happened.

Trouble stood in between Rexley and Steven's desk. His arms were crossed in front of him, his back unnaturally straight.

"Why were you just sitting there?" Planting his hands on the desk, Raleigh glowered at him.

"I was in shock."

"Jeremy—" Nate started.

"That was all Rexley's doing," Steven explained. Trouble was… well, always in trouble. Steven couldn't help but want to defend the kid. He was a good boy. Just a little on the energetic side. He was no worse than Tarren. Okay, maybe a bit more sneaky about his mischief, but not a lot. Trouble certainly didn't deserve to get in trouble over this. Who could blame the kid? Apparently, Rexley knew exactly what he was doing, and poor Trouble hadn't stood a chance.

Raleigh spun around, hands on his hips, and stared at Rexley.

Rexley stared right back, and then his eyebrow went up.

Oh bother. Steven bit his lip, waiting for the explosion. Raleigh was going to kill the boy, and then they'd have to demand Payton come home and learn Rexley's duties.

For several moments, Raleigh and Rexley faced each other.

Trouble backed up until he bumped into the desk.

Nate, still glowering at Trouble, pointed to the door. "We'll talk about this later."

Finally, Raleigh turned back to Steven. A slow smile crept onto his face. "Rexley, we will discuss this later. Boys, you're dismissed."

Standing, Steven prepared to make his getaway with the kids.

"Not you." Raleigh pointed at the chair. "Sit." He was still grinning. That had to be a good sign.

The rapid, slapping sound that had preceded Trouble's entrance grew distant, and Steven glanced around his consort to see Rexley slowly swagger out the door. Trouble was nowhere in sight.

Raleigh flopped down in the chair Rexley had vacated and started laughing.

"I'm sorry." Nate's lips twitched, and he sat in Trouble's chair. "I'll talk to him."

Steven chuckled and shook his head at his consort, who was now red-faced. Galaxy, Raleigh was beautiful when he laughed. "Really. Rexley started that."

Closing his eyes, Nate grinned. He glanced over his shoulder and stretched his long legs out in front of him. "Other than Rexley acting un-Rexley-like and Jeremy being Jeremy, what did we miss?"

"I told them I'd found a way to break the betrothal and was told rather forcibly the contract was not to be broken."

"Excellent." Raleigh glanced at Nate.

"I agree," Nate said. "That's the best news I've had all day."

Speaking of news…. "Did you find out anything about Jenkins's son?" Steven asked Nate.

Nate sighed. "One of the reports said Robert had just gotten back from visiting his parents here on Regelence, but from what you learned from Eversleigh, the admiral has been missing for nearly two months. I know it's been at least that long since I last got a hold of him."

"Sebastian checked at the Jenkins's residence two days ago. The place had been ransacked like someone was trying to find something, and the butler has been taken, his hard drive missing. Sebastian plans on sending one of his new men to Delcorte to check on the admiral's other residence, and he's searching for the servants and Betty's family to see if they know anything." Steven looked from Nate to Raleigh. Both wore grim expressions.

Standing, Nate stretched. "I can check into those things. Sebastian and Colton deserve at least a little bit of a honeymoon."

Steven nodded. "I agree. Talk to Knighton. He's taking over for Sebastian for a day or two. He'll know where Sebastian has searched so far."

"I'm going to do that now. I'm not working today." Nate left the room with a "Good day" to both Raleigh and Steven.

After a few moments, Raleigh stood up and leaned over the desk. He kissed Steven on the lips and said, "I'm proud of you for talking to Rexley and Jeremy."

"I have a confession to make."

"Oh?"

"I wouldn't have done it if I wasn't pretty certain they would want to remain engaged."

Raleigh kissed him again. "That's okay. You still gave them the choice. And for what it's worth, I think things will work out with Colton and Sebastian too."

Yes. Now, if he could just find someone for Tarren….

Regelence Park in Classige, Pruluce

STANDING IN his stirrups, Colton swept his frock coat out from under him and glanced at Sebastian as they rode through the front gate of Regelence Park. It'd been ages since he'd ridden in the park.

Sebastian grinned. "Are you having fun?" His eyes sparkled, and Colton had to resist the insane urge to laugh for the sheer enjoyment of the moment. That look, the pleasure in it, was directed at him.

"I am. Are you?" Colton tipped his hat to Bernard Kearsey and his older brother Walter, who were on horseback right inside the gate.

"I'm having more fun watching you than actually riding." Sebastian's voice lowered an octave below normal, and he winked.

Colton's cock noticed the sultry sound and decided to remind him of last night. Just in case he'd forgotten… which he hadn't.

"Ah, sweeting, what a fetching blush." Sebastian got Max as close to Apollo as he could without crushing his and Colton's legs and reached for Colton's face.

Colton tilted forward until Sebastian's hand made contact. He closed his eyes and reveled in the warm caress on his cool cheek. Perhaps they should go home. Their horses drew apart, and Colton jerked upright to keep from losing his balance.

"Okay?"

"Yes." The sensation of being watched niggled at the back of Colton's neck. He spotted the source at once. Inside the open landaus, chaises, and phaetons lined up on the carriage drive, several heads craned in their direction. The queue of carriages stretched outside the gate to where the trees obscured the inside of the park. Even pedestrians strolled through the snow-covered grounds. As was their habit, the haute ton had come to see and be seen. A nosey and vain lot they were. Not even weather could stop them. It was cold, and the sky was growing darker by the moment. It would snow again soon.

"Which way do you want to go? By the lake or by the trees?"

Pointing toward the lake, Colton urged Apollo into a trot. The trail around the trees was the place to see and be seen. It ran parallel to the carriage drive, but Colton had grown rather tired of the constant attention lately. And the lake route was much less crowded. A better place to let Apollo stretch his legs.

Sebastian heeled Max and clucked his tongue. "Come on, Max, let's give them a run for their money."

As soon as Sebastian and Max passed Colton, he gave chase.

They were neck and neck until Sebastian had to rein in to pass some slower equestrians.

Colton cut him off. "I think not."

Sebastian grinned and went to the outside. His hat caught the wind and would've flown off if he hadn't grabbed it. He drew abreast of Colton, and they rode side by side.

It was exhilarating despite the icy wind whipping their faces. The sense of freedom strummed through Colton's veins like a shot of adrenaline.

They rounded the corner together with neither of them trying to take the lead.

Colton's smile grew larger until he threw his head back and laughed. He reined in and slowed to a walk. "I love riding fast."

Sebastian and Max matched pace with Apollo. "So do I."

Within seconds they'd left the other equestrians behind.

Reining to a stop, Sebastian smiled at him. "Come here."

Colton drew Apollo close. "Here?"

"Closer." Sebastian leaned toward Colton.

Colton did the same. Their lips met and tongues clashed. Colton shivered and tilted his head to get a better angle. His cock, already stiff from the excitement of their race and Sebastian's vicinity, grew even harder.

Pulling back, he stared at Sebastian, and Colton's smile melted into a grin. The first flurries of the day trickled down around them, painting his cheeks with icy pinpoints of snow. A white speck caught on his lashes, and he blinked it away. Moments passed, the horses shifted under them, the snow danced around them, but still Colton held his husband's gaze. Colton's whole body warmed from the inside out. The nip in the air became nonexistent. How could something as innocent as a smile fulfill him so thoroughly? But it wasn't only the smile. He'd never tire of staring into those blue eyes. They were ever-changing, yet constant and steady like the man himself.

"Oh, the two of you are ready for another scandal, I see," sneered a familiar voice.

The spell was broken, replaced by fury. Colton wheeled Apollo around toward Plume. He'd had quite enough of this jackanapes. "If you have something to say to me, I suggest you grow some bollocks and come say it to my face. I assure you, I've no qualms about planting you another facer."

Drawing abreast, Sebastian gripped Colton's arm. "Let it go. He's only trying to rile us."

What? Surely Sebastian was not going to let Plume get away with talking to them like that. Colton gaped at him. Where was his fearless bodyguard who closed down even the slightest threat?

"Ignore him." Sebastian's head lowered, and his eyes flared. A twitch started at the corner of his eye. He gripped Colton's reins and turned Max, making Apollo follow, and faced them away from Plume.

The anger at Plume melted into confusion. Sighing, Colton nodded. He supposed Sebastian was correct. One could not argue with oneself. If he ignored Plume, eventually the arsehead would go away.

The clip-clop of horse hooves danced by, along with Plume's maniacal laughter.

"Ho there." Several someones trotted up behind them. Out of the corner of Colton's eye, the posting movement of a rider came to a halt, and bridles jangled.

"Good morning, Your Highness. Wentworth. Hold up."

Colton sat up straighter and raised his chin a notch. The anger and confusion mingled together again, and his jaw tightened. What did they want?

Lord Francis Rycroft sidled up to Colton's right on his palomino. His cheeks were rosy and chapped from the cold. He wore a flaxen-colored coat that blended in perfectly with his horse's mane. "I just wanted to say I'm sorry for the other night. There were so many rumors flying around and…." He glanced down, and the rosy hue on his cheeks deepened. "Please say you'll accept my apologies, Your Highness."

Sebastian closed his eyes briefly. When he opened them, he frowned and looked at Lord Francis and his friends, then back to Colton. The fearless, no-nonsense bodyguard was back. Sebastian opened his mouth to say something, but Colton gave a shake of his head. He didn't want to get into how the group had shunned him right now.

Colton's posture eased a little, and he dipped his head. "All is forgiven. Your confusion was understandable under the circumstances."

"Colton, you are too kind. We *all* owe you an apology." Lord Roth pulled his horse to a stop next to Sebastian. "We also owe you congratulations on your marriage."

Lord Francis, Mr. Gareth Fareweather, and Edmund Smithe offered their felicitations in chorus as Mr. Fareweather and Mr. Smithe positioned their mounts in front of Colton and Sebastian as well.

Colton studied them all, trying not to glower.

"Thank you. I'm a lucky man. His Highness finally put me out of my misery and accepted." Sebastian smiled at their audience.

Colton gasped. Sebastian was making their marriage sound like a love match rather than a consequence of scandal. If only it were true.

Colton beamed at him. "After all, a man can only take a certain amount of hounding." He winked at Sebastian. "Although I dare say you withstood it well for many years, Wentworth."

Sebastian erupted into laughter along with Fareweather and the others.

A couple of riders squeezed to the side of the trail to pass them.

"Is this the famous Apollo?" Mr. Smithe asked, steering his bay horse around to make room for passersby. He was the only one of them bareheaded.

"This is he." Colton leaned forward and patted Apollo on the neck. Pride filled him, making him finally relax a little. There was nothing quite like talk of one of his babies to put him at ease.

"Beautiful conformation," Gareth said.

Lord Francis turned his attention to Max while the others fawned over Apollo. "I say, Wentworth, your horse is quite fetching as well. Don't see many true solid blacks."

"I'd never part with him." Sebastian petted Max's neck as he snuffled and nuzzled his nose against Lord Francis's horse. Max was a beauty, but he was not in the same class as Apollo. Apollo's musculature was impressive even by racehorse standards. He looked as fast as he was. And in a dead run, he was even more of an impressive sight.

The men discussed business for several minutes, asking about Colton's stables and appointments with the racing commissioner and Jockey Club. Perhaps he should give them another chance.

Colton told them how he'd arranged a meeting for Apollo to be licensed and how Rexley was handling the builders for the stables and corrals. They all seemed genuinely excited for him.

"Colton, I know it's short notice and you've just married and all, but my father has arranged a private race for several of the owners tomorrow. Would you be interested in joining us? Perhaps you can show us what this beauty"—Mr. Fareweather dipped his head to indicate Apollo—"is capable of. I'll be riding my father's newest stud, Great Escape."

The others nodded their approval.

Roth said, "I'll be riding my Georgie here." He rubbed the chestnut's shoulder. His ears swiveling, Roth's horse perked up at the mention of his name.

Colton widened his eyes and nodded. He stopped midnod, glanced at Sebastian and raised his brows. "Well, Captain?" he asked, making it clear he was asking a professional opinion. *Please let Sebastian understand how important this could be to my career.*

Sebastian turned his attention to the other men. "Has the event been publicized?"

Gareth shook his head. "No, my lord. It's invitation only."

Sebastian smiled. "I trust His Highness's security team will have full access to the facility."

Colton bit his bottom lip. His eyes squinted slightly in merriment. Sensing victory, he gave in to a smile. Would whooping and hollering be inappropriate?

"Yes, of course," Gareth assured him. "My father will have servants who can help out as well. So what say you, Colton? Will you come?"

Sebastian and Colton answered together, "Yes."

The men made their excuses and rode off with reassurances they'd see Colton tomorrow.

Colton waved, feeling good down to his toes. This was the break he needed.

Nudging Max into a walk, Sebastian asked, "What did they do?"

"They cut me at the Thompson musicale."

Sebastian growled and tightened his grip on the reins.

"It's understandable. They'd only just met me two days prior."

"That's not the point. Anyone can see you are an honorable man. And none of them have pristine reputations."

"But they're all of age. I am not, and how can anyone possibly deduce my honor on such short acquaintance? Besides, I need the connections, and I think it says a lot about them that they acknowledged their behavior."

"You're too gracious."

Gracious, but not stupid. Colton caught his gaze. "Not really. They'll have to gain my trust. I might have forgiven, but I'll never forget."

Sebastian laughed and accidentally pulled back on the reins, drawing Max to a standstill once again. The merry sound filled Colton with warmth.

The snow came down in earnest now. Visibility was fading fast. If not for the voices in the distance and the clatter of carriage wheels, Colton would've thought them alone.

Colton stopped Apollo. "Thank you."

Sebastian leaned forward, wrapped his hand around the back of Colton's neck, and kissed him. "Let's go home."

CHAPTER FIFTEEN

Wentworth Park, Viscount and Viscount-Consort Wentworth's residence, in Classige, Pruluce

"YES." *VICTORY is mine.*

Panting, Colton stopped in the open door of the bedroom. His mad dash from the stables to the house and up the stairs had left him winded. He hated to lose at anything. He threw his hands in the air. "I wi—Oof." Sebastian hit his back with so much force it propelled him across the room. Colton landed flat on his stomach on the bed with a bounce and Sebastian next to him.

Laughing, Sebastian propped himself on his elbow and rested his head on his hand. "It's a tie." The smile his mirth had morphed into was pure joy.

"It was not. Clearly I won." Colton rolled to his side. Happiness bubbled up within him. The past couple of days he'd seen a side of Sebastian he'd never seen before. When Colton had tossed his coat, hat, and gloves at a baffled servant and darted up the stairs, he hadn't expected Sebastian to give chase.

"You cheated. Besides, you said the first one to the bed, not the bedroom. Therefore it's a tie." Sebastian brushed back the hair that had fallen into Colton's eyes. The feel of cool fingers left a tingling warmth in their wake. For all the casualness of the touch, it was intimate.

"I didn't cheat."

Sebastian gave him a pointed look that lacked severity.

"I improvised."

"Declaring the race after you'd already started and before I had my coat off is not improvising; it's cheating. Pray tell, out of curiosity, what does the winner get?"

"You." Colton dragged a finger over the Osbaldiston knot of Sebastian's cravat.

"I'll concede you may have won."

Colton chuckled. "I thought I cheated."

Sebastian shook his head. "A very genius improvisation." He crooked his finger. "Come and collect your prize."

Colton hooked his finger in the knot and loosened it. Unwinding the cravat, he met Sebastian's gaze. "I have to unwrap my prize." He tossed the white cotton aside. He leaned in and flicked his tongue across the salty skin.

"Oh no. You won. You shouldn't have to do anything. I'll unwrap your prize." Sebastian pressed Colton's shoulders into the mattress and straddled his hips. Sebastian pulled off his coat and waistcoat. He lifted the lawn shirt over his head and dropped it over the edge of the bed. The sunlight coming in from the parted curtains highlighted his magnificent chest. Sleekly toned with only a bit of hair. The tops of his hipbones jutted out and narrowed into a V down to his groin.

Colton had heard Sebastian claim he was out of shape once. If this was out of shape, he'd have loved to see what Sebastian looked like when he was in the RSR. It didn't seem possible to look any better than he did now. "You have your prize, but what else do you want?" Sebastian asked.

"I want you in me." Colton ran his hands down Sebastian's chest to his stomach, exploring each hill and valley. The skin rippled under his fingers, and Sebastian tipped his head backward with a soft hum.

"Then you shall have me." He flexed his shoulders and peered down at Colton through his hair, his midnight eyes half-lidded. He quivered once more and pressed his hands on top of Colton's. "Let me do everything." Sebastian diverted Colton's questing hands and began to work on Colton's cravat. Once he got it off, he held each end of the cloth in front of him. "Should I tie your hands together?"

A shiver rippled through Colton, but he shook his head. If he had his hands tied, he couldn't use them. Of course, that was the purpose. In some ways the thought thrilled him, but in others he didn't like the idea of being at anyone's mercy. Even Sebastian's.

Working on the buttons of Colton's coat, Sebastian grinned. "Another time, then." He unfastened the waistcoat and untied the shirt. "Up." He scooted back on Colton's thighs and helped Colton sit. The garments on Colton's upper body joined Sebastian's on the floor. Once his chest was bare, Sebastian urged him onto his back again. "You're amazing, sweeting." He swirled his finger around Colton's nipple.

Goose bumps rose on Colton's skin, and he wiggled, trying to shrug off the touch.

"Oh ho ho. Someone's ticklish." Sebastian dug his fingers into Colton's armpits.

Laughing and bucking, Colton tried to dislodge Sebastian. "St… st… stop it." Colton laughed until his lungs burned. He twisted to the side and pulled his arms into his chest, trying to block Sebastian's efforts, but Sebastian stayed with him. It was maddening but exhilarating. Colton's cock hardened even as he strained to catch his breath.

Finally, Sebastian let up. He too was laughing. He dropped his hands on the mattress beside Colton's head, and the humor faded. His eyes dilated and he dipped down, brushing his lips across Colton's.

Seized by the intensity, Colton returned the kiss. He wrapped his arms around Sebastian's back and let the passion bleed into him. The only thing that came close to this mind-numbing, tingling pleasure was being on horseback. It was like running through a meadow with the wind in his face, whipping through his hair. Colton rubbed Sebastian's back and savored his lips. He'd never get enough of this man.

Sebastian sat up. He slid backward off Colton, put his feet on the ground, but kept his chest so close the heat of his body seeped into Colton. He kissed his way down Colton's stomach.

Colton tensed but held the gaze. He was thoroughly captured and could not look away if his life depended on it. His body liked the proximity of Sebastian's mouth. He arched his back slightly.

Burrowing his chin against Colton's erection, Sebastian unhooked the falls of his consort's trousers.

Colton hissed at the pressure. His testicles drew closer, and his thigh muscles tightened. The look Sebastian bestowed on him as he dragged the fabric off Colton's hips intensified everything. Sebastian's lips caressed every inch of skin the trousers and smallclothes revealed as they were removed.

After freeing Colton's cock, Sebastian left a wet trail all the way to the tip with his tongue. He pulled the trousers down to Colton's ankles. Grabbing the heel of Colton's boot, Sebastian tugged. It came off, and he repeated the process with the other until Colton lay completely naked. Sebastian toed off his own boots and shucked off his trousers before returning to the bed with his erection bobbing free.

Struck again by the size of him, Colton reached for him only to have Sebastian bat his hand away.

Grabbing Colton's ankles, Sebastian put his knee on the bed. "Move back a little and put your knees up for me."

Colton moved until his head was at the headboard, and was rewarded for it by a kiss to his inner thigh.

Climbing onto the mattress, Sebastian lay on his stomach between Colton's open legs. Colton's position made him vulnerable, and self-consciousness reared its head.

Sebastian chuckled. "Relax." He flicked his tongue across Colton's testicles.

"Oh dust."

Doing it again, Sebastian gripped Colton's cock. He squeezed and pumped while his mouth went to work down below. He laved and sucked. The feeling was amazing. It almost tickled, but not quite. Not enough to make Colton laugh or move away. He wanted to move closer. To hold Sebastian's head there. Shutting his eyes, Colton luxuriated in the new sensations, but too soon the caress ended.

Sebastian crawled up Colton's body and captured his lips. The salty taste of Sebastian's tongue and the way he rolled Colton to the side and moved against him made Colton's breath quicken. Sebastian gripped Colton's arsecheeks and rocked. Their cocks slid together as their tongues did, adding just enough pressure. Spots of moisture squished between them but did nothing to make them slide together easier. Sebastian's fingertips traced the crease of Colton's arse.

Colton didn't recall Sebastian getting lube, but the ease with which his fingers glided said he had. He brushed across Colton's hole once, then returned to push against it. He pressed a digit inside Colton's arse a little before retreating and plunging in again.

Stiffening, Colton broke their kiss.

"Shh…." Sebastian scooted down, eye level with Colton's cock, and covered it with his mouth.

"Ahh…." The pressure of Sebastian's invading finger and the intense pleasure of Colton's cock down Sebastian's throat shocked him. It ratcheted up the intensity. With each thrust of his finger, Sebastian plunged down on Colton's cock, taking it to the back of his throat. He continued the assault until Colton thought his body would fly apart.

When the pleasure was too much, Sebastian added another finger.

Colton balanced on the hard edge of gratification and not-quite pain. No, definitely not pain, but pressure. It was maddening and exhilarating. Every time he thought he could go no further, Sebastian added another finger. Scissoring them, thrusting them in and out.

Colton shoved forward into Sebastian's mouth and back on his fingers. He'd lost count of how many fingers were in him. The intensity swept him away, until he was one big ball of sensation, his testicles so tight and his buttocks so tense. Galaxy, he was going to lose his mind.

Releasing him, Sebastian panted.

A loud groan of frustration escaped Colton. He too began to pant, so close to release he ached. He was ready to beg and plead.

Resting his face against Colton's hip, Sebastian continued to finger his arsehole. "I'm going to fuck you, sweeting. Any objections?" He kissed Colton's oversensitive skin, and his hot breath fanned over the area.

Colton shook his head. He didn't care what Sebastian did as long as he did it soon. His legs trembled. The hand he petted Sebastian's head with shook.

The bed dipped and swayed as Sebastian got to his knees.

Colton groaned at the loss of Sebastian's fingers. His body all but shouted *come back*, as his arsehole clenched and unclenched.

From the headboard dispenser Sebastian collected a glob of lube in his hand and wrapped it around his dick. As he stroked, his head lolled backward and the tendons in his neck strained. His body quaked. He was mesmerizing. Beautiful. He let go of his cock and got more lube. Tapping Colton's hip, Sebastian situated himself between Colton's legs.

"Raise your knees for me again." His voice rumbled much lower than normal.

Colton lifted his knees and gripped his cock. He caressed it, needing the sensation.

Sebastian bent between Colton's outspread legs and propped himself over Colton on one arm. Staring into Colton's eyes, Sebastian pushed the tip of his cock slowly in.

The intrusion bordered on discomfort, but it soothed a deep-down ache at the same time. The sting and the pleasure coalesced together. By the time Sebastian began to move, Colton couldn't catch his breath. He continued to pump his cock. The friction took his mind away from the awkwardness of penetration and kept him on the knife's edge of climax. Over and over the sensations climbed and ebbed.

Sweat beaded on Sebastian's forehead and upper lip. He dropped his head to Colton's chest and kissed, impeding the movement of Colton's hand. Sebastian's hips met Colton's arse as Sebastian ground into him. He whispered encouragement, how good it felt, how long he'd waited for Colton. The ecstasy built and built. There was no pain now. Only bliss.

With his eyes squeezed shut, Sebastian reared up.

Together like this, Colton could almost believe Sebastian loved him. Colton would cherish this always, but it made him want more. He wanted to win Sebastian's love. And he would… there was simply no other choice.

With one final thrust, Sebastian groaned and froze. The strain on his face was both horrible and lovely.

As Colton watched his consort's face contort in cataclysmic delight, his own orgasm descended upon him. Semen ran over his hand and splashed his stomach. He cried out as wave after wave of pleasure bombarded him, until there was nothing left but the heavy-limbed, contented afterglow.

Sebastian moved to lie next to him. He tangled his fingers in Colton's and squeezed. "What is it about you that makes me lose every ounce of finesse I've ever had?" he gasped out.

"I'm just irresistible I guess." Colton grinned and turned his head to meet Sebastian's gaze.

Laughing, Sebastian rolled to his side. "You are that, scamp."

Sebastian sat up, kissed Colton, and slid off the bed. The way he moved was so fluid and graceful. The view wasn't bad either.

Wait. What was that? Colton sat up. Below Sebastian's right arsecheek about four inches down was a mark.

"Do you have any plans for this evening?" Sebastian started to turn, but Colton stopped him.

Ignoring the semen dripping down his groin, Colton bent closer.

"What are you doing?" Sebastian peered over his shoulder, trying to turn.

It was a birthmark. Not just any birthmark, but a Regelence birthmark. In the shape of a rose. Colton let go of his consort and lifted his right arm to compare. Yes, the marks were identical. Why was it on Sebastian's thigh?

"What? Why are you frowning?"

"I thought you were conceived naturally."

"What?"

Colton pointed. "You have a Regelence birthmark."

"It's not a Regelence birthmark. I *was* conceived and born naturally. I had a mother."

"But it's the same exact shape as mine. It's just in the wrong spot."

"Which is why it's *not* a Regelence birthmark. It's a weird coincidence. Now then… what plans do you have for tonight? I got a message from Rourke before we went riding, and he has a lead on the whereabouts of one of our old team members."

How had Sebastian gotten a birthmark in the shape of a rose? Colton stood and walked around behind Sebastian, or tried to. Sebastian caught his arm.

Sebastian's jaw tightened, and he sighed. "Colton, it's not a Regelence birthmark."

It was. But how? He'd known Sebastian had a mother. His story was a bit of a fairy tale. He was baseborn, but due to his record in the military, he'd gained the attention of Giles Hastings. It wasn't unheard of, because military men were well admired in their society. Sebastian's rank alone had made him eligible to a peer of the realm.

Sebastian tipped Colton's chin up and kissed him. "You're dripping on the floor."

Colton glanced at his body. Semen ran down his legs, headed for his ankles.

"Blast." He jogged to the washroom.

GOOD GALAXY, of late his thoughts resembled a parliamentary debate—loud, busy, and only a step above Bedlam. Sebastian ran a hand down his face and leaned back on the sofa. Then again, some of the chaos could be contributed to his current surroundings. A gaming hell was no place to sort one's thoughts out, but home was even worse at the moment. Because Colton was there, and Colton—lovely as he might be—was a distraction.

Something poked Sebastian in the chest.

Sebastian glanced down. A round blue chalk mark marred his gray waistcoat. Frowning, he raised his head. It was like waking from a dream. Cigar and pipe smoke hung heavy in the air, and the sound of pool balls clacking together melded with voices and laughter. When had Rourke gotten so close? Had Rourke asked him something?

Rourke stood a couple of feet away with a smirk on his face and a pool stick in his hand. "If you are going to sit there and brood, you might as well go home."

"Not sure why he's here anyway. If I had Colton to play with, I wouldn't be here." Julian leaned over the table and took a shot. Balls clacked and scattered, but none dropped into pockets. "Bloody hell. I'm awful at this tonight. I think I need another pint." He strolled around the table, leaned on it in front of Sebastian, and looked at Rourke. "A fight?"

"Nah." Rourke shook his head. "He's proving a point."

Sebastian groaned and rolled his eyes. "You're both bottleheads."

They ignored him. "What point?" Julian asked.

"That he can still do what he wants and won't answer to anyone, even a consort." Rourke turned toward the table and studied the balls. "That's my guess, anyway."

"Your guess is wrong," Sebastian mumbled. *Cripes*, they were busybodies. "I just needed some space."

Rourke leaned over the table but glanced at Sebastian. "After only one day of marriage?" He took his shot, and the six ball zoomed to the right side pocket and fell in.

"Bloody hell!" Julian shoved his stick at Sebastian. "Hold this damn thing." He strode off toward the front of the gaming hell.

Rourke chuckled. "Bring me a pint too." He smirked at Sebastian. "Seriously, why are you here? I could've offered Benny the job just as easily as you could." And point in fact, he had. Rourke had seen Benny at the door—Benny guarded the front door of this particular gaming hell—invited him to join them on his break and offered him a job, which Benny accepted, all before Sebastian had arrived.

Sebastian shrugged and grabbed the pool stick with both hands, put it between his feet, and rested the weight of his upper body on it. He should be on his way home, but he was a bloody coward. Not only did Colton ask too many questions—*damn that stupid birthmark anyway. No one else had ever paid it much attention*—but Sebastian found himself wanting to spend every waking moment with Colton, and that was unacceptable. He sighed. "I needed some time alone to think."

"What's to think about? He's not like Giles, you know."

Sebastian suppressed a wince. Leave it to Rourke to pick up on what Sebastian himself hadn't wanted to voice even in his head. "I know that." He did, and it scared him witless. Colton was everything Giles wanted to be but never quite measured up to. Colton was the real deal. What you saw was what you got. He was honest, loyal, sophisticated, handsome, cultured…. Giles would've hated Colton. His jealousy would've gotten the better of him. Sebastian grinned, then sobered.

The sinuses in his forehead clogged up, and his palms grew damp. He hated feeling out of control. He hadn't felt this way since he was ten… when his whole life had turned upside down.

"Seb?" Rourke crouched in front of him and shook his shoulder. "Are you sure you're feeling all right?"

"Yeah. Sure."

Rourke raised his brows as if to say *yeah right.*

"We didn't quarrel."

Rourke nodded, but his narrowed eyes said he didn't believe it. He sat on the sofa next to Sebastian. He too gripped his pool stick with both hands and used it to slouch. "You're terrible company tonight."

"Thank you."

"You're welcome."

Sebastian rolled his eyes and leaned back in his seat. He set the stick aside, balancing it against the arm of the sofa.

"With you in this mood, I see why Colton kicked you out of the house." Rourke smirked, seemingly on the verge of laughter.

Sebastian glared. "He didn't kick me out."

"Ah, so you ran. I hate to be the one to break it to you, but it's too late to run."

"What in the devil are you blathering about?"

"You're trying to escape, and it won't do you any good. You, my friend, are in love. And—" Rourke gave a mock shudder. "—much as I pity you for it, I'm happy for you. Now go home."

A pain started behind Sebastian's right eye. Was Rourke correct? Was that why he was here? Was he running? Colton could become his entire life if Sebastian would let him. Giles's betrayal had hurt, but going through the same thing with Colton would destroy Sebastian. Oh, bloody hell. He *was* already in love with Colton. When had it happened? Panic tried to take hold of Sebastian, but he wrestled it under control.

Rourke, the smug bastard, beamed at him. "Better you than me." At least someone found this situation amusing.

"Hold your tongue. I cannot wait until you fall in love. I hope he's as annoying as you are."

Rourke laughed. "It will never happen. I plan to choose a consort based on intellect, not emotion. But that's neither here nor there. We were discussing your marriage, and for the record, I think you've done well this time around."

"Done well at what?" Julian stopped in front of them with two ales.

"Marriage," Rourke answered and reached for one of the glasses.

"Oh yes. I think Colton was a much better choice for you."

"Thanks for getting me one," Sebastian grumbled. He didn't want to talk about this anymore. It made his stomach unstable. Just because he loved Colton didn't change anything. It only made Sebastian's resolve stronger. Sebastian had to keep his head. He could never reveal the things to Colton that he had to Giles. Sebastian couldn't take the chance.

"I did get you one, smartarse." Julian looked over his shoulder. "I met someone at the bar and invited him to join us." He grinned, leaving no doubt as to what Julian hoped would be the outcome of his invitation.

Sebastian leaned to the side to see whom Julian referred to.

Eugene Collis, Sebastian's ex-paramour, came ambling up with two glasses in his hands and a big cheery smile on his face. *Wonderful. Just wonderful.*

Rourke whacked Julian in the legs with his cue. He whispered, "Why did you invite him to join us?"

"Ow." Julian rubbed his shin with the heel of his other foot. "Because he said he knew Seb. Why are you assaulting me?" he whispered back.

"Sebastian." Eugene slinked right up in front of Sebastian, handed him his drink, and sat so close his body was plastered to Sebastian's side.

Sebastian scooted over. "Good evening, Eugene. How have you been?"

"Missing you." Eugene pouted and fluttered his eyelashes. "Have you missed me?"

Oh good galaxy. Sebastian drank his beer. He couldn't answer that. To say no was rude. Saying yes would invite Eugene's attention, which Sebastian did not want.

"Oh." Julian's eyes widened. "Eugene, have you met His Grace the Duke of Knighton?"

"I have." Eugene gasped and hopped to his feet, spilling a bit of his beer in the process. He bowed at Rourke. "A pleasure to see you again, Your Grace." His voice dripped with flirtation. Good, let him paw Rourke.

"The pleasure is mine, Mr. Collis." Rourke stood, lifted Eugene's hand, and kissed it. "Would you like to join us in a game?"

"I'd love to."

Rourke reeled Eugene in by the hand he still held. Rourke whispered something in Eugene's ear, and Eugene let out a squeal. Rourke led him to the sofa and patted his leg. "Come. You can take turns sitting on mine and Julian's lap while the other takes his turn at the table."

Bless Rourke. *I hope he gets a piece of arse tonight.* More than likely he and Julian both would. In the past, Sebastian, Rourke, and Julian had been known to share. But no more. This wasn't helping, and Eugene's presence complicated matters in ways Sebastian didn't need.

Sebastian took another drink, set it on the table, and stood. He was going home to his consort, where he should've stayed. It was where he wanted to be. Did that mean he was doomed? Probably. Sighing, Sebastian picked up his evening coat off the back of the sofa and put it on. "Gentlemen, I'll bid you good night. I've a gorgeous consort to get home to."

"You're leaving?" Eugene looked up from tracing patterns on Rourke's facial hair with a pout.

"I am. Good night." Sebastian gave Julian and Rourke a smile. "I'll see you both tomorrow. Have a good evening, and thank you for finding Benny."

BY THE time Sebastian crawled into bed, Colton was sound asleep.

Sebastian kissed Colton on the lips and rolled him to his side. Spooning in behind him, Sebastian breathed in the fresh outdoor scent that always clung to Colton.

Colton slept on.

The urge to wake him and tell him everything was strong. Colton would stand by him. Sebastian was sure of it. But then… he'd been certain Giles would too.

Chapter Sixteen

September 19, 4830: Townsend Castle

"Hello there, boy." Colton patted Dazz's nose. "How're you this morning?"

From inside the stables, Apollonia whined.

"Hush, young lady. You cannot go this time," Colton shouted and returned his attention to Dazz. "What do you say, boy? Is your foot better? Want to give me a ride to the track?"

Dazz snuffled a bit, butting his head against Colton's hand when he stopped petting.

Colton chuckled. "Good. We'll just wait for Sebastian and Julian to join us, and we'll be off. Shall we ride in the meantime?"

Colton put his foot in the stirrup, gripped Dazz's neck, and swung himself up onto the saddle without fuss. Leaning forward, he clucked his tongue.

Dazz started walking with a gait so smooth he practically glided.

Julian rode up next to Colton on a brown thoroughbred. "I'm thoroughly impressed."

"I am too. I swear he's floating."

"Then have him float that way." Julian pointed at the front gate.

As they rounded the end of the stables, Sebastian and Max came into view. Sebastian had a big smile on his face.

Colton's insides fluttered, and he smiled back. "Look." Colton held an arm out to his side. "Isn't he marvelous?"

"Yes, he is." Sebastian's gaze traveled along Colton's body, not Dazz's. His expression was blatantly sexual. Glancing at the horse finally, Sebastian moved where he could see Dazz from the side. "I think I got a bargain for what I paid, and I shall be eternally grateful to Dazz."

Heat rose to Colton's cold cheeks as they drew abreast of Sebastian, and he fell in on Colton's other side. "You mean *for* Dazz."

Sebastian just smiled. Turning to Julian, he tossed him something.

Julian caught the black box and looked at it.

"You're in charge of recording the race for the other Townsends to watch later." Sebastian met Colton's gaze. "It was the only way I could talk your family into not coming with us, sweeting. In the future, I'll have to have more advance notice of races so I can prepare a security detail for a bigger group."

Julian cleared his throat. "I hate to change the subject, but why do they call you Lord Calamity? Should I worry about you falling off your horse during the race?"

Colton bit his lip to keep from laughing. "No. Horseback riding is the one thing I do well. You know our nicknames already?"

"Oh yes, a couple of the guards took great pride in telling me yesterday afternoon."

Sebastian leaned forward in the saddle to peer past Colton. "He's Lord Calamity because he's always breaking things. When he was twelve, I think he managed to destroy every vase on the first floor of the castle."

They rode out the front gate, and it closed behind them.

"Not every vase," Colton protested. He couldn't believe Sebastian actually knew about what he'd done all those years ago. Sebastian had just started working at the castle. "I'd try so hard to stay away from the breakables, but they jumped out in front of me. I'm not so bad anymore. Except perhaps windows, but I'm only averaging a window a year nowadays. I've gotten much better."

Turning onto the main road into town, Julian laughed so loud he drew gazes from passersby.

"Come to think on it… I haven't broken a window this year." It must be a new record.

"Oh good. Try to do it when I'm on duty," Julian said.

Colton tried to look serious, but he failed miserably. "Who says I'm going to break one? Maybe I've totally weaned myself off windows."

Sebastian snorted. "Now you have two households worth of windows to choose from."

"If you do, the staff will have to come up with a new name for you." Julian didn't have even a hint of a smile.

"You say that like it's a bad thing." Colton rolled his eyes. "Like you two weren't mischievous at twelve. I bet both of you ran your parents ragged."

"No." Sebastian sat stiff in the saddle, looking left and right. Was he expecting trouble, or was it something else?

Unease moved through Colton. Sebastian had never mentioned his parents, only that he had a mother. "Did your mother not have any nicknames for you?"

Sebastian shrugged. "My mother wasn't around when I was twelve. She died when I was ten."

"Oh." The air whooshed right out of Colton's lungs. "I'm sorry, I didn't know. You've never said." He frowned. He felt stupid for not knowing anything about his husband's family. He'd guessed Sebastian's parents were deceased, but he hadn't realized Sebastian's mother had died when Sebastian was so young.

"He doesn't talk about his family. Never has," Julian said.

"What about your father?" Colton asked Sebastian.

Sebastian's jaw hardened. "I don't—I lost him the same time I lost my mother."

"I'm sorry."

Sebastian patted his leg. "I'm not. We're here. Let's go find Apollo and Brooks."

Fareweather Track, on the grounds of the Fareweather Stables, in Classige, Pruluce

Cecilia Brooks grabbed Colton's hands in her dainty white-gloved ones to keep him from wringing them. "Relax. I think Apollo is going to amaze everyone. And I also think I may have found us a mare."

"Really? Where? Who?"

She chuckled and caught Colton's hands again. "You're making Dazz nervous." She let go. Her hunter-green pelisse swirled around Colton's legs as she turned slightly. Absently, she stroked Dazz's nose over the hitching post.

Colton glanced at the stallion. His ears were back, his gaze darting here and there. Colton petted him. "Sorry, boy."

Brooks tipped her head to the right, gesturing toward the barn where a boy walked a beautiful dark bay mare with a red winter blanket on her back. "I'm going to watch her in the race, but I have a feeling about her." Brooks grinned, showing off the charming dimples in her cheeks. "She's two years old. Rumor has it her owner, Mr. Clamtin, is looking to sell." A breeze blew some of the strawberry-blonde hair that had escaped Brooks's chignon.

The mare nudged her groom, placing her forehead in the middle of his back, making him go faster.

Colton chuckled. "She's impatient."

Brooks nodded. "She'll fit right in with Apollo and Apollonia. The mare has attitude, but she seemed likable when I petted her. Her name is Tresham's Thunderstorm, but the groom calls her Stormy."

"What are the two of you looking at?" Rourke sauntered up, patted Dazz on the neck, and stared off in the direction of the mare. "Seb said to tell you he'd be back over here before the race started. Star dust, he is lovely, isn't he?"

Behind Rourke, Max gripped his reins with his teeth and tried to yank them free of the hitching post.

Brooks curtsied. "Good morning, Your Grace."

"Good morning, Rourke." Colton tugged the leather from Max's mouth. "That horse is a she," Colton answered. "Where've you been?"

"I've been here the whole time. Within three yards of you since Seb and Julian went to scope things out. I was just looking around, watching people. You really are nervous, aren't you? And I was talking about the young man who the horse is bossing around, not the horse."

Brooks cocked her head slightly. "He's a little young for my tastes, but he's good with Stormy."

"He's too…." *What?* The petite brunet was a nice-looking young man, cute in a Tarren or Trouble kind of way—which probably meant he was as obnoxious as both of them too—but not someone Colton would normally look twice at. "The jockey is too slim and small. And yes, I'm nervous."

"I like slim and small. Why would I want a big ox like me?"

"I agree with Colton. I prefer my men larger." Brooks turned back to Colton. "I've got to go saddle Apollo for you shortly. But now, I'm going to go mingle with the other trainers and see if I can learn any good gossip. I'll be back to help you get ready before the race. Stop fretting. Olympian Stables is going to be a household name before we even open." She bounded off toward the track in a flurry of green velvet and pink muslin.

"You know she's right. Already I've heard talk. People have taken note of Apollo. And Dazz, for that matter. You might want to consider selling Plantation Walkers too. I'd buy one. I rode one once on a mission in Glaudia and even loaded down with my pack and weapons, that horse was a smooth ride. Had to fight the rest of the guys off. They all ended up with quarter horses." Rourke shrugged. "The guide they sent with us was a pretty good ride too."

Colton groaned and tried not to blush, but that was one of the things he liked about Rourke. He didn't censor himself around Colton like everyone else did. He treated Colton as an equal. "I thought Sebastian didn't know much about Plantation Walkers."

"It was after Seb left." Rourke sighed. "I miss the old days."

"What was it like? In the RSR, I mean?" Colton searched the crowd for Sebastian and noticed the track was completely clear of snow. Goodness, Fareweather's employees were efficient.

The duke brushed his knuckles over Max's nose. "It was exciting. Freeing. And quite an experience for a gently raised guy like myself. A culture shock at first, but once I got used to it, I had a hard time leaving it."

"I can see where it would be an adjustment. Were you the only lord out of the group?"

"Yes. Julian comes from a wealthy family, but he was not brought up with the strictures you and I were. Out of all the guys, I probably had the hardest time adjusting. Hell, just sleeping in a room with other men was scandalous in the extreme, not to mention showering with them and dressing in front of them." He clasped a hand to his chest and smirked. "Shocking." Dropping his hand, he chuckled. "They used to make fun of me."

Colton smiled, starting to relax a bit. "Even Sebastian?"

"Good grief, yes. Seb thought it hilarious to try and make me blush. He actually dragged me to a brothel on my twentieth birthday. After that…." Rourke got one of those odd smiles and a faraway look. He shook his head and glanced back at Colton. "After that, I embraced the life of a soldier and learned rather quickly ton soirées were the best places to pick up men." He ran his hand over his beard. "Or maybe Seb is the one who figured that out. On leave, I used to drag him to balls with me. He and Julian were the only ones who talked like we do and felt comfortable mingling with our crowd. Probably because they'd both had private tutors growing up."

Sebastian had had a tutor? Yet something else Colton hadn't known about his husband. It made sense, Colton supposed, because Sebastian had always talked like an educated man. Colton couldn't remember him ever being awkward around society, so he had never thought to question it. But he'd been under the impression Sebastian had been from a poorer family. He had hinted that the old admiral had bought him a commission. Star dust, was Sebastian ever going to open up to him? How could he win Sebastian's love if they didn't know each other?

Fareweather stood nearby, checking his horse's hooves. He spotted Colton and waved.

Colton returned the gesture and turned back to Rourke. Perhaps he could get some information out of the duke. Rourke seemed to know Sebastian better than anyone. "Then Sebastian had been to ton events before he went into the RSR?"

"I don't know. Between you and me, sometimes over the years, I wished I hadn't taken him with me because he met Wentworth at a ball I took him to." Rourke shook his head. "I regretted introducing them for a long time."

"Why? I thought his and Hastings's marriage was a love match." The mystery around Sebastian just kept growing. Granted, Colton had been young then, but he'd been under the impression Sebastian had left the Navy to marry Hastings.

"I think Seb cared for him at first, but it didn't take him long to figure out he was nothing more than a plaything to Giles."

"Colton." Gareth Fareweather sauntered up to him. "The race is about to start. Come take a look at my father's newest stud."

Blast Gareth's timing. Colton wanted to learn more about his husband. He smiled at Fareweather and said, "I'd love to. I'm to meet my trainer in the stables shortly." He glanced back at Rourke. "Your Grace?"

"Go ahead. Just stay within my sight. And if I don't talk to you before the race… good luck."

"Thank you. You'll tell Sebastian where I am?"

Rourke dipped his head.

As Colton walked with Fareweather, a group of loud, laughing men passed them. Normally, Colton would've ignored them, but he heard

Sebastian's name. Colton lengthened his stride to keep pace with the group, but no matter how he tried, he couldn't hear their conversation.

"Are there any jockeys racing?" Colton asked.

"No. No jockeys allowed in this race. This is for fun and for the owners and trainers to test out new stock. We do this every other month or so."

Well, that was one less thing to worry about. He wouldn't be riding against professional jockeys. Colton heard Sebastian's name again. He wanted to know what those men were talking about.

The group stopped and huddled together, still talking.

Fareweather pointed at something in front of them. "That's Helford's newest mare. She's a beauty, isn't she?"

As they passed the group of men, one of them said, "Wentworth and his companions gave him a grand ole time, from what I heard."

Gave who a good time? A queasiness tickled Colton's stomach and tried to climb up his throat. Sebastian *had* been out last evening. Not long, of course, but then Colton had learned firsthand that a tumble didn't necessarily have to take that long. Who had Sebastian been with? He'd said it was to locate another of his ex-teammates.

"Colton?" Fareweather turned toward him, and Colton realized he'd stopped.

"Oh sorry. Yes, she is beautiful."

The revelers whispered as Colton started walking again. They never even looked at him. One of them pointed to something. "Look. He's talking to Wentworth now."

Colton's pulse began to race. His throat clogged up, and he followed the man's finger.

By the stables, Sebastian stood talking to none other than the man Colton had seen him with at the Marquess of Crestview's ball, Eugene Collis.

"I'M IN a real hurry, Eugene." Sebastian headed to the stables. Colton should probably be there with Apollo by now.

Eugene jogged to catch up to him. He was dressed smartly in black Hessians, beige trousers, and a dark green morning coat. His wavy blond hair was tamed by a black top hat. The chilly air added pink to his freckled cheeks. "Quite all right. I won't slow you down. I'll follow you." Eugene reached for Sebastian's arm.

Sebastian sidestepped out of range.

Eugene blanched. "Sorry. It's a habit. I meant no disrespect to Prince Colton or you."

If Sebastian hadn't known what a spectacular actor Eugene was, Sebastian might have believed the embarrassment.

"My lord, I wanted to apologize for last night. I came on awfully strong. And…. Knighton says you married Prince Colton out of affection, not to save his reputation." Eugene's big green eyes widened, begging Sebastian to contradict the information.

Sebastian just nodded.

"I suppose I was jealous. Do you think you can forgive me? I really do wish you happy."

Stunned, Sebastian headed toward the barn where Apollo waited. He wasn't certain what to say. He'd never expected this. He wasn't even certain it was real. Eugene could very well be scheming something.

"Thank you." Sebastian stopped at the door, not wanting Eugene to follow him inside.

Sticking his hand out, Eugene gave him a sheepish grin. "No hard feelings?"

"No hard feelings." Sebastian shook his hand.

Eugene glanced at the door and at his feet before looking back at Sebastian. "Well, then, I guess I'll just get going. I need to get back to my friends, and I don't want your consort to see me talking to you." He started to leave but hesitated. "Sebastian?"

"Yes?"

"If you ever get bored with your prince…." Eugene shrugged one shoulder. "You know where to find me, yes?"

So that's what this was about. "Yes, Eugene, I know where to find you, but I won't get bored."

Waving his fingers, Eugene disappeared into the crowd, headed for the stands.

What an odd encounter. Shaking his head, Sebastian entered the stables.

"Hello, Apollo." Sebastian unlatched the stall door and went inside.

Apollo neighed in greeting and nudged Sebastian's chest with his nose.

Sebastian pulled his watch out and opened it. Fifteen minutes till start. Where was Colton?

Apollo snatched the watch out of his hand, flipped his head up as though he were trying to eat it, then dropped it.

"Not what you expected?" Chuckling, Sebastian bent to pick up his pocket watch. "Be still, ole chap. No stepping on my hand with those monstrous feet of yours, okay?" He gripped the watch with one hand and used his other to steady himself on Apollo's front leg.

Apollo never even acknowledged he was being used as a support.

"Such a good boy, even if you did try to eat my watch." Sebastian rocked back on his heels and pushed to his feet. *Wait. What was that?* Stuffing his pocket watch back in his waistcoat pocket, he moved to Apollo's side and crouched down again.

Sebastian leaned closer and ran his finger under the girth of Apollo's saddle. The strap was frayed on the edges. There was a thin channel on the underside of the leather. The inside had been cut almost all the way through. He unhooked the girth and pulled it away from Apollo to inspect it. The surgical incision could only have been man-made.

Sebastian gnashed his teeth together. The slightest pressure would snap the cinch. If the culprit would've taken the time to clean the edges better instead of leaving shavings of leather clinging to it, Sebastian would've missed it. Icy tendrils of sensation snaked down his back. Someone was trying to hurt Colton. If Sebastian hadn't seen this, it would have broken during the race. Galaxy, he couldn't breathe.

Why hadn't he stationed someone with Apollo? He'd made certain there were no easy hiding spots for snipers, he'd made certain Colton was always watched, but he had not even considered someone tampering with the saddle and trying to hurt Colton that way. Dizziness made Sebastian's head swim. He rested his forehead against the saddle.

"Lord Wentworth?"

Sebastian turned his head but left his face against the cool leather saddle. This race meant a lot to Colton. The image of his expression when Fareweather had invited him to this race popped into Sebastian's head. Sebastian should take Colton home right this instant.

"My lord?" Brooks opened the gate and cocked her head. Her forehead wrinkled. "Is everything all right?"

"Brooks, go get the girth off of Max's saddle and bring it here." He should have his head examined. Every protective instinct in him screamed this was a bad idea, but he'd be damned if he'd disappoint Colton since Sebastian's logic said the damage had already been found. He'd already determined the grounds safe.

Sebastian unhooked the girth from the other side of the saddle and tossed it to her.

"I just saddled him about ten minutes ago. What's wrong?" Brooks fingered the old girth. Her brow wrinkled, and she gasped. "This was cut."

Sebastian was certain she had nothing to do with the cut. He'd known her since she was a young teen and started work at Townsend Castle as a groom. "Yes. When you go get my cinch, make certain Colton doesn't see you do it. Tell Knighton and Julian to keep quiet about it. Also, bring the duke with you and tell Julian to watch the horses and Colton carefully."

She nodded, laid the damaged girth over the gate, and jogged out of the building.

As Sebastian walked around Apollo, the stallion turned his head to follow Sebastian's progress.

Sebastian ran his fingers over the white star on Apollo's forehead. "Too bad you can't talk." Pulling the saddle and saddle pad off, he checked them both for more tampering or anything that would pain Apollo. Satisfied neither item had been damaged, Sebastian laid them over the wall.

"Here's the girth." Out of breath, Brooks stopped at the gate.

"Good, check it well and put it on the wall with the saddle." Sebastian grabbed Apollo's right front hoof and rested it on his knee.

Rourke stopped next to Brooks, looking like a giant in comparison. "What's going on?"

"I found that." Sebastian bobbed his head toward the girth that lay over the gate.

Rourke picked up the strap and examined it. "I'll go talk to Fareweather and see if there are any cameras in this area. Even a heat signature might give us a clue as to the size and shape of the perpetrator." He strode off, carrying the girth with him. Turning around, he came back with a scowl on his face. "Are you letting him race?"

"What do you think?" Sebastian valued his friend's opinion on security matters over anyone else.

The duke didn't say anything for several moments, then nodded as though he'd come to a conclusion. "I think it's safe. I suspect whoever did this thought this would do the trick. Even still, I think we should keep him away from people. I've already told Julian to bring him back to where we're camped out and watch him closely."

"I don't think we should let Colton race." The worry in Brooks's voice came through loud and clear.

"We caught it. Just help us keep an eye out. I agree with Knighton; I don't look for anything else to happen today," Sebastian said.

She sighed but didn't argue. As Rourke left, she opened the gate. "Do you see anything? Do you need a pick? Who would do this?" Her skirts swished about Sebastian's legs as she glanced over his shoulder.

"I don't see anything. This hoof is clean."

"I cleaned them before we left." She leaned in close. "I did not see that cut when I saddled him. It had to be made after I put it on him. Someone came in here and tampered with it."

"Yes." He dropped Apollo's foot and patted Brooks's shoulder. "The next time we will bring a groom to stay with our horses at all times." Maybe he could have Digby trained to work in the stables. Since the boy started working at Wentworth Park the morning after Sebastian had met him and offered him a job, he'd shown an interest in the horses.

She nodded. "I agree. We need to hire grooms and run a thorough background check on them. I should've thought of something like this. Racing is a big business, and it can get cutthroat. I just never imagined anyone would want to hurt Colton." She petted Apollo's neck and walked around to the other side of him. "I've got this hoof." She lifted Apollo's front foot, messed with it for a minute, and dropped it. "Check his back one."

Sebastian checked out his last hoof and set it down. "Brooks?"

"Yes, my lord?" She ran her hands over Apollo's stomach, looking at him rather than Sebastian.

"You're certain Colton didn't see you take the cinch from my saddle?"

"I'm positive. He was talking to the younger Mr. Fareweather and some of his friends."

"Good. I need you to keep this between us for now. Just me, you, Julian, and Knighton."

"I agree. It would only worry Colton, and he's already nervous." She pulled the saddle pad off the wall and placed it on Apollo's back.

Sebastian did likewise with the saddle, and together they saddled the stallion, checking every piece.

"I don't like it, though. This is scary stuff." She bit her bottom lip and idly twined and untwined her fingers in Apollo's mane.

"We're going to get to the bottom of it. I promise you, I'd never let Colton go through with this if I thought he was in danger." He patted her shoulder. "Try not to worry."

"I'll try. Will you give me a boost? I'll ride him to Colton and make certain we didn't miss anything. This way I can see if he's acting like himself." She led Apollo out of the stall.

"Good idea. You know him better than I do." Sebastian gripped her waist and hefted her onto the horse's back. She weighed next to nothing.

"Thank you." She hooked one small boot heel in the stirrup and sat sideways in the saddle.

Sebastian handed her Apollo's reins and steered Apollo out of the stables.

Even riding sidesaddle in a saddle not meant for riding sideways, Brooks had a nice seat. She was easily as good a rider as Colton, maybe better considering she was riding in an awkward position. She may be a trainer and stable master but she'd make a heck of a jockey, and her size was a bonus. She probably didn't weigh much over six stone.

Sebastian watched Apollo and Brooks stroll around the barn, then went in search of his spouse.

He found Colton waiting at the hitching post where Max, Dazz, and Julian's and Rourke's horses were tethered. Rourke and Julian stood around him, and Colton laughed at something one of the men said. It was a deep belly laugh that made his eyes practically disappear and tugged at Sebastian's heart. It also assured Sebastian that he'd made the right decision. No way could he ruin Colton's day when he was fairly certain the attack was over. Whoever cut that strap had meant for it to come off during the race. Fear cut through Sebastian sharper than the cold wind. He kept an eye out as he walked toward Colton. Max's saddle, minus the girth, sat unfastened on Max's back and none of the men seemed to have noticed.

Colton spotted him first and waved.

Rourke and Julian glanced over their shoulders.

As Sebastian waved back, Brooks came up beside him. "He's acting fine. I even had to keep him from running. He's raring to go."

"Good."

SEBASTIAN HAD the best vantage place in the small stands, he had two trained ex–special forces soldiers playing lookout along with him, but he was still nervous.

With her hands primly in her lap, Brooks sat in front of them, and she too seemed to be studying the crowd.

"Splash of Spirit isn't racing," she called over her shoulder.

"Is that a good thing?" Julian asked.

She shrugged. "I don't know. It will make Colton feel better, but to be honest I think Apollo would beat him. I've no doubt he's going to win this race. Apollo does twelve furlongs in under one minute forty-nine consistently. We've clocked Apollo at seventy-nine point five kilometers an hour. Granted, that's with me on his back, and Colton weighs a good six stone more than I do, but I expect him to come in somewhere around one minute fifty-six seconds even with the extra weight."

Rourke let out a long whistle.

Julian's eyes widened. "Damn." He slapped a hand over his mouth. "Begging your pardon, ma'am."

Dumbfounded, Sebastian couldn't say anything. He'd had no idea Apollo was *that* fast. *Holy meteor dust.* Why hadn't Colton raced him sooner? Most racehorses started racing about two years of age; Apollo was already four.

Brooks chuckled. "Don't apologize. *Damn* is quite fitting. Apollo's speed is impressive. He won't do eighty kilometers for the entire race, but I'm fairly certain he'd do it down the stretch with a lighter rider on his back."

Before Sebastian could even digest that info, the gunshot sounded. Reflexively, he reached for his weapon. *Bugger.* It was just a starter pistol. Since Rourke had spotted someone following him and Steven, Sebastian had taken to carrying a fragger in a shoulder holster whenever he was anywhere with the royal family, including his consort. Could the saddle incident be related to the guy spying on Steven?

The horses were off. Colton and Apollo were in the third spot.

Brooks jumped to her feet.

Rourke clapped his gloved hands. "Go."

Sebastian bit down on the insides of his cheeks. He alternated between watching the crowd, the other side of the track, and Colton.

"Why isn't he winning? I thought you said he was fast?" Julian held the camera in front of him. "Go, Colton."

"It's okay. Colton's holding him back." Brooks cupped her hands to her chin. Her lips tightened, and she bounced on her toes. "If it were up to Apollo, he'd try to run full out. This way he won't tire before the final stretch."

Sebastian pulled his eyes away from Colton and back to the crowd. He was here as bodyguard first, husband second, and silent partner in Olympian Stables third.

The small crowd was on their feet, cheering and yelling. There were a few women but mostly men. Several of the faces were familiar, and Sebastian looked for anyone acting out of place.

Rourke, Julian, and Brooks grew louder, pulling Sebastian's attention back to the race. Colton and Apollo were in the lead by a good half body length and gaining. The wind whipped through Colton's hair and Apollo's mane. Colton's cheeks flushed red in the chilly air, and even from here Sebastian could make out Colton's grin. Sebastian's chest swelled with pride.

"Yes!" Brooks jumped up and down.

The stands vibrated under their feet with all the stomping.

Apollo crossed the finish line a whole horse length in front of the second-place winner. The crowd undulated with motion, everyone screaming and clapping.

Sebastian smiled so big his cheeks hurt. As Colton slowed Apollo and headed toward the side gate of the track, something caught Sebastian's eye.

Off to the side, next to the kids who were playing, stood a man with his back ramrod straight. He'd drawn Sebastian's gaze because he was not cheering like everyone else.

Who are you? Sebastian glanced around to see if anyone else had noticed the man.

Rourke caught Sebastian's gaze and dipped his chin. He started down the stands toward the man.

As if the man sensed their attention, he turned and looked up. The side of his mouth lifted in a sneer.

"Bloody hell."

It was Barnaby Plume.

Chapter Seventeen

THEY'D DONE it. They'd really done it. He and Apollo had won. Already people were begging for Apollo's offspring. But some of Colton's excitement was dimmed by the chance Sebastian might still be keeping that light-trousers Eugene Collis as his paramour.

If Colton hadn't known they'd been lovers in the past and seen them talking today, he might've discounted it. But he couldn't erase the uncertainty from his mind. It gnawed at his heart and ego. Sometimes he could almost think Sebastian cared for him, and other times, like now, gaining Sebastian's love seemed hopeless. First, there was the Regelence birthmark on his thigh, then his upbringing, and now this. How many other things was Sebastian hiding from him? How could Colton get Sebastian to open up?

"I thought we'd celebrate your victory."

Colton turned.

Sebastian walked into the study with a bottle, two glasses, and a corkscrew. "We needed something special to toast your win." He held up the bottle. "A thirty-six-year-old Bordeaux, reputed to be the best." He grinned. "And it better be, for the price."

So that's where he'd gone, to get wine. Colton breathed a sigh of relief, but what came out of his mouth was "Is Eugene Collis still your lover?"

Sebastian froze.

Biting his lip, Colton sat in the chair in front of the fireplace. He wasn't sure he wanted the answer to his question, but he wouldn't take it back. He'd never been one to shy away from speaking his mind, and he wouldn't do so now. The fact that a lot of husbands kept lovers, and he and Sebastian didn't have a prior arrangement that they wouldn't, did not lend him comfort. Colton wanted a marriage like his parents. Maybe he wanted too much.

"You saw me talking to him."

Colton nodded.

"I'm sorry, Colton. I tried to avoid him, but he followed me." Sebastian crossed to the mantel and set the bottle, corkscrew, and glasses on it. He stepped in front of Colton and extended a hand. The wedding band on his finger glimmered in the firelight. His hand was steady as though he had nothing to hide.

At first Colton just stared into Sebastian's dark blue eyes. "I saw you two together in Crestview's garden the night of the ball." Reluctantly, Colton took Sebastian's hand and waited for the bad news to come.

Groaning, Sebastian pulled Colton to his feet. Sebastian cupped Colton's jaw, ran his thumb over Colton's cheek, and smiled softly. "Eugene has not been my lover since that night. I broke things off with him the next day." Sebastian's gaze drifted to Colton's lips. "The day I first kissed you. I haven't been able to get you out of my head since then." He feathered a kiss across Colton's lips. "Last night when I went to find Benny with Rourke and Julian, Eugene was there and came on rather strong. I rebuffed him. This morning, Eugene sought me out to apologize. That was all there was to it. I've no interest in Eugene Collis or any other paramour. I've got something much better right here." Sebastian's steady gaze gave no doubts to what that something was.

Colton wrapped his hands around the back of Sebastian's neck and pulled him in for a kiss. Sweeping his tongue inside his consort's mouth, Colton poured every ounce of feeling into the kiss.

The fire crackled and painted the room in a warm glow. The dark curtains blocked out all other light. There was nothing but the two of them. No race, no paramour, no castle security, or missing admiral… just them.

"You can trust me, love," Sebastian whispered against his lips. "I don't want anyone else. There will be no more paramours."

Colton melted. This was more than he'd hoped for. He was making progress. One secret at a time. Sebastian may not be willing to open up about his childhood and upbringing yet, but at least he was willing to commit to their relationship. It was a start.

Colton's mind quickly went to lust. Maybe it was the idea of eventually gaining Sebastian's love. Whatever it was, need burned inside Colton. His cock filled. He wanted Sebastian now. Colton fumbled with the falls on Sebastian's trousers until he got them open and shoved down the linen blocking his view.

Sebastian chuckled. “In a hurry, sweeting?” He cupped Colton through his pants.

Ah. Bucking into Sebastian’s hand, Colton gripped the lovely dick in front of him. It wasn’t hard yet but well on its way. He wanted it in his mouth. Could practically imagine the velvety softness against his lips. Tearing off his cravat, he got to his knees. He wanted to explore. To be inside Sebastian again. Colton wanted… everything. “Lie down.”

“Oh. Feeling rather dominant today, are you?” Sinking to his knees in front of the fireplace, Sebastian smirked at Colton.

He supposed he was. He had this overwhelming desire to claim and conquer. It must be leftover adrenaline from the race and his suspicions about Eugene Collis coursing through his veins.

“Does it bother you?” he asked.

“Not one bit.” Sebastian lay down on his side and propped his head on his hand. His cock was hard now. The way he lay there so casually with everything covered but his privates was exhilarating. It sent Colton’s adrenaline rush a bit higher and made Colton’s cock harder. Colton had to touch some more. Stake his claim.

Gripping Sebastian’s dick, Colton stroked how he himself liked. He loved the feel of Sebastian in his hand. So thick. It was strange feeling the sensations in his hand rather than his cock. Colton could practically feel what Sebastian was feeling.

Sebastian groaned and closed his eyes. Colton loved how Sebastian not only let Colton do as he wished but reveled in it.

He eased onto his side with his feet toward Sebastian’s head and closed his lips over the tip of Sebastian’s cock.

A shudder undulated through Sebastian’s body. “Oh galaxy, that feels wonderful.”

Using his hand as he had the first time he’d done this, Colton pleasured his consort. He wanted Sebastian to come before Colton took him. Colton wanted him squirming with desire, as he always seemed to make Colton do.

A caress brushed across his crotch. Just the barest touch. His breeches sawed against his erection a few times, and then cool air touched him. Colton glanced down as Sebastian pulled Colton’s prick through the hole in his smallclothes. *Oh galaxy, yes. Please.*

Even though Colton wanted it, expected it even, there were no words for the ecstasy that slithered through him as Sebastian sucked

Colton's cock. Anticipation of the next caress sizzled in Colton's belly. If Colton didn't concentrate on something else, he'd never make himself last until he was inside his consort's amazing arse.

Focusing on fulfilling his husband, Colton tightened his grip on each upstroke when his mouth held only the head. He gathered more and more saliva, easing his hand's way. Except…. *Stupid shirt.* The billowy sleeve kept getting in the way, absorbing the moisture where it touched. He sat up, dispatched his waistcoat and shirt. Resuming his position, he took Sebastian in hand again. A tiny bead of precome seeped from the slit, beckoning Colton to continue.

Swiping his tongue across the tip, he gently squeezed Sebastian's testicles.

Sebastian moaned around Colton's cock, gripped Colton's hip, and held him steady. Sebastian set to work at the same time Colton did. Together they licked, sucked, and caressed each other.

It wasn't long until Colton had Sebastian pulsing his hips back and forth. Colton had already learned Sebastian's signs. He was close. Colton felt the thread of tension flow through Sebastian's body. His thrusts became smaller, choppier. Sebastian worked his mouth and hand harder, quicker, with more pressure.

Colton tapped Sebastian on the hip but didn't release his cock. *Wait. Stop. Please. I don't want to*—Come filled his mouth and his own climax neared. He jerked his hips backward, trying to get away from the intense pleasure, but it was too late. He'd passed the point of no return. As Sebastian's legs relaxed and his movements became less forceful, he grabbed Colton's cock.

Colton came, moaning around his husband's dick.

Sebastian's hand slid over him and milked him dry.

Colton collapsed, letting go of Sebastian. Colton wrapped his arm around Sebastian's thigh and rested his head against Sebastian's trouser-covered hip. Mashing his cheek against the warm, wet column of flesh he'd just released, Colton sighed.

A tongue swiped over the head of his cock and a chuckle drifted down to him. Sebastian patted Colton's bottom and sat up.

Blinking his eyes open, Colton yawned. "That wasn't exactly what I planned but it was rather—" He burst into laughter.

Sebastian's dark blue waistcoat was no longer pristine. A glob of semen ran down the right side. There was a wet spot on his shirt as well.

"Oh. I'm so sorry. I tried to warn you."

Sebastian chuckled and pushed himself to his feet. "Think nothing of it. Why don't you get dressed while I go clean up, and we'll uncork the wine. We still have to celebrate."

Rolling to his back, Colton stretched his arms over his head.

"Mmm…. We'll try that again after we've had some wine." Sebastian's gaze skimmed Colton's chest as Sebastian tucked himself back in his trousers. He stood there several seconds just looking his fill, with a twinkle in his eye and a grin on his face.

Colton smiled and pushed himself onto his elbows. His whole body flushed, and his cock tried to perk up again but couldn't quite manage. Mentally, though, he was raring to go another round. He was quickly becoming addicted to this kind of attention. Perhaps he was easy after all. Who knew?

"Tempting as you are, you'll have to wait a bit." Sebastian held out his hand.

Taking the assist, Colton stood. He nuzzled his face into the crook of Sebastian's neck, cursing the cravat but enjoying the scent all the same.

Sebastian lifted Colton's chin and stared at him for several long seconds. His gaze touched everywhere. Sebastian kissed Colton on the lips. "I'll be right back."

"I'll be right here. Waiting."

As Sebastian used the tiny washroom attached to his study, Colton pulled his shirt over his head and tied the laces at the throat. There was no hope for his cravat, so he tossed it on the chair along with his morning coat and waistcoat. It was not unheard of for men to walk around in shirtsleeves in their own homes, especially when no unmarried men or ladies were present. He tucked in his shirt and fastened the falls on his trousers. Just as he stuck his foot in his boot, Berkley spoke.

"Your Highness, one of the Royal Guards is here with a message for Lord Wentworth. Shall I send him in?"

"Yes, Berkley, send him in." Colton hurried into his other boot. Goodness, he was too sated to move that fast. It made his head spin.

The door opened and one of the guards, Peterson, walked in. He wore plain clothes instead of his uniform. He bowed to Colton. "Your Highness."

"Hello, Peterson."

Peterson smiled and glanced around the room. "I've a reply to a message the captain asked me to deliver. Is he available?" In his hand, he held a vellum note folded over with a purple wax seal.

Colton held out his hand. "I'll see that he gets it."

Peterson hesitated and his forehead wrinkled.

Stepping forward, Colton chuckled. "Really, Peterson, I'm quite trustworthy. I've no intention of harming the royal family. You can trust me. I'll see to it that Wentworth gets it immediately."

"Right you are, Your Highness." Peterson grinned and handed the card to Colton. "The captain is expecting that." He bowed and took his leave.

The door closed and Colton shook his head, giving in to another chuckle. Really, did Peterson think Colton couldn't be trusted with royal secrets? Flipping the card over, he headed to the desk. He didn't recognize the seal. *Hmm....* He squished the card to form an oval without busting the seal. He held it up to the light. There was only a short sentence written in an elegant scrawl.

I'll meet you in the alley beside Gunter's on Dublin Lane tomorrow at eleven in the morning.

No signature.

Colton let the note card go back to its normal shape and studied the purple seal again. It had only a peacock. No coat of arms. No initials.

Tossing the card on Sebastian's desk, Colton turned toward the fireplace. Who was that from? *Eugene?* Colton groaned, went to the mantel, and retrieved the wine and glasses. He was being silly. Sebastian had told him nothing existed between him and Eugene, and Colton believed him.

Still, a little seed of doubt tried to wiggle its way into his head. He glanced back at the desk. The note lay there like an elephant in the room. Should he ask Sebastian what it was about?

Colton shook off his unease and peeled the foil off the top of the wine's cork. Using the corkscrew, Colton popped the top on the wine.

He had two victories to celebrate. One, his winning the race. Two, he'd made a step in the right direction with his husband. They were getting closer, he was sure of it.

Arms wrapped around his waist as he poured the first glass.

Sebastian nipped his earlobe. "Pour me one too, sweeting."

"Mmmm…." Colton snuggled back into the embrace. Yes, he'd definitely made headway with Sebastian today. The note was probably in regards to Admiral Jenkins. Colton was going to trust his husband, and maybe his husband would trust him in return.

Dogwood House, Viscount Leith's residence, in Classige, Pruluce

THE ICY wind whipped through the alley next to Dogwood House, the Viscount of Leith's town house, cutting right through the black fatigues Sebastian wore. He hefted himself over the stone wall and onto the viscount's side lawn. Backing into the English ivy along the wall, he surveyed the place from his hiding spot.

It had been years since he'd seen the place, and there was a weird nostalgia in seeing it now. As a boy, he'd always loved the surrounding dogwoods from which the house got its name. In spring their white flowers looked like tufts of cotton candy. Now with winter approaching, they were bare, giving the yard a sinister appeal and lots of eerie shadows to hide in. It still smelled of pollen and fresh dirt, though he was certain it was his imagination. Who could smell those things under a blanket of snow?

In his pocket Sebastian fingered the device that made him invisible to the house computer. He had a mission to accomplish and not much time. He didn't want to chance Colton waking and finding him gone.

The information Rourke had collected this afternoon placed Plume's bedroom as the third balcony on the right at the back of the house.

Using the rain gutter, Sebastian climbed to the terrace, and pulled himself up and over the railing. After taking the computerized lock pick from his belt, he opened the door and entered Plume's room.

It was dark, but he'd always had good night vision. He closed the door behind him and studied the room. It looked like most other young buck's—large canopy bed with curtains, a couple of chairs, a dressing table, and an escritoire with a com-pad on top.

Situating himself next to the door, Sebastian waited. It had been oh three hundred hours when he'd left Colton in bed sound asleep, exhausted from too much wine and hard lovemaking. Plume should be back any time now according to the intel Rourke and Julian had collected this afternoon. Plume didn't use a valet to undress, no worries there, and he never brought men home. He kept a paramour in a nice little house on Broad Street whom he visited on Tuesdays, Thursdays, and Saturdays. Today was Monday.

Sebastian didn't want to be here, but Plume had left him with no choice. He'd tried to harm Colton, which put Sebastian between a rock and a hard place. Threats were one thing, but the cut girth had been another entirely. Sebastian didn't want to chance Plume disclosing what he knew about Sebastian, but the threat to Colton's life couldn't be ignored. If Sebastian had to lose Colton, it would be because Colton didn't want to be with him, not because Colton was dead.

Sebastian would use any means to assure Colton's safety. Including erasing the threat permanently. It wouldn't be the first time he'd killed someone, and it probably wouldn't be the last.

Outside, the wind blew, rattling the windows. A creak sounded in the corridor. Sebastian extracted his knife from its sheath and lowered it to his side. The old house had the same feel as it did when he'd lived here. Upstairs in the servants' quarters you could hear everything. Sounds and smells seemed to seep through the walls and bare floors.

On missions he never used to mind the waiting, but now he wanted to be back home with Colton, snuggled up in bed. Rourke had offered to do this, but Sebastian had to do it himself. He wanted Plume to fear *him*.

The doorknob rattled and turned. The door opened and closed. Plume stopped inside the door and began stripping off his evening coat. He tossed it on the end of the bed and unfastened his waistcoat. It too landed on the bed along with his cravat. He reached for his cuffs, and Sebastian made his move.

Slapping a hand over Plume's mouth, Sebastian touched the tip of the knife to Plume's throat and whispered in his ear, "Not a sound or I'll slit your throat before you get it all out. Do you understand?"

Plume tensed and clutched Sebastian's forearm. Plume's head bobbed frantically, and he swallowed hard.

"Listen and listen carefully because I will not say this again. Next time I'll simply kill you. And I think I've aptly demonstrated I can do so easily, and you'll never know what happened."

A slight tremor shook Plume.

"Stay away from Colton. Don't even speak his name. If he happens down the same sidewalk as you, you best cross the street. If he attends a ball you're at, you'll leave. If any rumors circulate about him, or me—anything that could harm him—you'll never see it coming. Is that clear?"

Plume nodded.

"Good."

September 20, 4830: Downtown Classige, Pruluce

"ARE YOU excited?"

Colton couldn't contain his smile. Glancing over at Rexley, he held up his finger and thumb an inch apart. He had Apollo licensed and Apollonia listed in the breeding resister. Of course he was excited. Apollonia didn't even try to eat the swab when they did her DNA testing.

Too bad Sebastian had had an appointment this morning. He hadn't told Colton what it was, like Colton had hoped he would, but he hadn't acted like it was a big deal.

They turned on Griff Street toward the middle of downtown. The toy shop Muffin wanted to go to was a few miles from the Jockey Club headquarters where they'd met with the race commissioner.

Rexley chuckled. "Now are you going to find a jockey for him?"

"I need to, yes. I really should be riding Dazz instead of him, but I cannot give him up to racing entirely. He'd be miserable." And so would Colton. "I've been thinking. Last night Wentworth came up with an idea. He suggested getting Brooks to jockey. I'd considered it briefly myself yesterday when thinking about her weight in comparison to mine. What do you think?"

"I wanna be Apollo's jockey. I'm little." Muffin, who was sitting astride Belle in front of Rexley, beamed at Colton.

Rexley ignored her. "I think the idea has merit. Have you talked to Brooks about it?"

Muffin leaned to the side, making Rexley have to grip her waist, and glanced back to where Apollonia was tethered to Apollo's saddle by her halter. "Why can't I ride Nia now?" She'd been fussing about having to ride with Rexley since they left the commissioner's office some thirty minutes ago.

"Apollonia hasn't been taught to wear a saddle yet. She's still a bit too young," Colton tried to reason. To Rexley he said, "Not yet. I intend to speak to Brooks when we return."

Muffin groaned. "I can ride her without a saddle. You ride Apollo like that sometimes."

"Colton is an experienced rider. You're a beginner."

"Bollocks." Muffin folded her arms over her chest and huffed out a breath.

Colton bit his lip to keep from laughing.

"Melanie Pricilla Townsend." Rexley caught her chin and forced her to look at him. "Where did you hear that?"

"Jeremy."

Rexley's lip twitched. "Do not say that again. I'll have a word with Jeremy when we return." He released Muffin's face and rolled his eyes after she turned back to the front.

"I won't say it anymore, but can I please be a jockey?" She wrung her hands together and fluttered her lashes. "I'd be really good at it."

Hmmm....

Rexley raised both his brows, lowered his chin, and peered up at Colton. "No."

"She's a good little rider, and with some work—"

Muffin clapped her hands and bounced in the saddle. "Yay!"

Rexley sighed. "I'm not going to win this, am I?"

"No reason we cannot train her to be a jockey if she wants to. There's nothing saying we have to put her in races. She may not even be small enough when she's actually old enough to race." Colton shrugged but he suspected she would be plenty small enough since she'd always been small for her age. Regardless, she'd be an asset if she stuck with it. She could help with training. "If she really wants to learn, I'm willing to teach her. Just imagine if Father and Cony had refused to let me learn to ride when I first showed an interest. I was much younger than the rest of you and younger than she is now."

"Fine. You may teach her, but only after her studies are finished."

"Yes." She clapped again and did a little side-to-side thing with her head, making her red curls sway. "Can we go home and practice now?"

"I thought you wanted to go to the toy shop?" Rexley smirked.

"Oh right."

Rexley glanced at Colton. "Are you sure you don't mind going to the shop with us?"

"Not at all." He'd needed Belle present for Apollonia's DNA test. Accompanying his brother and niece on an unexpected trip to get toys after the test was a small price to pay, even if it was way across town. Oh, who was he kidding? He'd jumped at the chance to come to this part of town, knowing Sebastian would be having his meeting nearby.

They passed Dublin Lane, and Colton craned his head to see down it. Was Sebastian there now? Waiting? Blast it all. He'd promised himself he was not going to worry about what his consort was doing, but his stomach almost ached with the doubt. What if Sebastian was meeting Eugene?

"So tell me, how did it feel to win that race yesterday? The video was splendid. I wish I could've been there in person." Rexley steered Belle down the next street over from Dublin Lane, Dyson Street, toward the toy shop.

"It was fantastic." It made Colton wish he was a lot smaller so he could race professionally.

They reached the toy shop and pulled their horses to a stop. He was so close to Gunter's. It was only a block up and a street over. Maybe he'd just take a peek to reassure himself. Colton glanced back at their new guard, Benny, and one of the old guards. He seemed nice enough, but he was not as friendly as Knighton or Julian. Still, he was a friend of Sebastian's. "I think I'm going to stay out here and wait for them."

Benny frowned. "Begging yer pardon, Yer Highness, but wouldna ya rather go inside? I'll accompany all of ya, and Loring here can watch the horses." He and Loring got off their horses and pulled the reins forward.

"No thanks. Go ahead and go with Rexley and Muffin. I'll stay here with Loring and help him with the horses." Apollonia was already getting restless. He tugged her tow rope until she sidled up next to her father. Colton rubbed her ears and smiled at Sebastian's old teammate.

Poor Benny's expression was pained, but before he could argue, Rexley came to the rescue. "It's quite all right. We won't be long. You can wait inside the door so you are able to keep an eye on us and Colton. I'm sure Wentworth wouldn't mind." Rexley handed Muffin to Loring and dismounted. Rexley winked at Colton and caught Muffin's hand. "Come along," he said to Benny and strolled to the shop door.

Benny grimaced and glanced at the uniformed guard. They did a silent-communication thing with their eyes, and Benny followed Rexley and Muffin.

Colton would've laughed if he didn't think it would get back to Sebastian. No one argued with Rexley. Well, no one not related to him, anyway. Although Colton suspected Rourke would've vetoed them. Julian would've charmed them into doing his bidding, but poor Benny was outmaneuvered. Learning that enemy combatants were no match for the royal family must not be easy to digest, because the man looked as though he were stricken with indigestion.

Loring, who'd been on staff for several years, chuckled. "You do know, my lord, that he's going to report back to your consort, don't you?"

Apollonia nipped at Colton's thigh.

Colton tapped her on the nose. "Quite all right, Loring. I like you too well to leave you out here alone with my little hoyden here."

"Thank you." Loring blanched. "I hadn't thought of that."

Colton threw his leg over Apollo's head and slid out of the saddle. He landed in between father and daughter, handed Apollo's reins to Loring, and unhooked Apollonia's rope from Apollo's saddle. "I'm going to walk Apollonia to the end of the block to that alley up there"—Colton pointed his finger—"and back."

Leading Apollonia behind him, Colton started to walk.

"Your Highness?" Loring cleared his throat. "Is that a good idea?"

"I won't be out of your sight, Loring." Colton walked down the street next to the sidewalk. Gunter's backed up to the building on the next corner.

A man and a woman drove by in a curricle. Couples strolled arm in arm along the sidewalk on Dyson Street. Colton tugged his hat down lower over his eyes to block the sun. It was bright out today and only forty-two degrees. A wonderful day for a stroll. *Yeah, right.* He really didn't believe Sebastian was engaging in an illicit encounter, so it wasn't spying, was it? It probably *was* something to do with the admiral. And if it were dangerous, Sebastian would have taken backup, right?

A lift turned down the alley in front of Colton. Apollonia stepped on the back of Colton's boots, making him stumble.

"Knock it off, pest. We're not going to go any faster than we already are."

She blew out her mouth at him.

He tugged Apollonia up onto the sidewalk. "Beg your pardon." Colton nodded at a nanny pushing a buggy. A group of men dodged Apollonia's swinging tail. "Excuse us."

Someone called out a rude comment about horses on sidewalks, but Colton ignored it. He got to the corner and peeked around it.

Apollonia peered over his shoulder.

Sebastian was not in the alley, but there was a man standing in the alleyway with one hand on his hip. He gestured wildly with the other, obviously talking to someone, but the other person stood behind the building.

The man Colton could see was in profile. He had a classically handsome face. He even looked familiar, but Colton couldn't place him. He definitely wasn't Eugene Collis. But his expensive many-caped greatcoat and gray beaver hat screamed peer.

Colton huffed out a breath of relief. He'd known it wasn't Eugene, and it certainly didn't look to be romantic in nature.

Sebastian came into view. Even from here, Colton could see the anger in his expression.

Apollonia whinnied.

"Shh…." Colton turned and pushed at her chest, making her move back. *Interesting.* The lift had a crest with a peacock on it. The peacock's tail was fanned out, and it had a snake clutched in its talons. So the seal on the letter had been a variation of this man's crest.

Apollonia whinnied again, and horse slobber landed on the sidewalk by Colton's feet. *Guh.* He shoved her back.

From the far end of the alley came an answering whinny.

Colton froze with his hands on Apollonia's chest. He turned back to the lane. A black horse stood near the entryway at the other end. Blast. Max had noticed them.

Colton gasped and ducked back around the wall. He took another quick peek. Sebastian hadn't seen him. No matter. When Colton got home, he was going to confess and beg his consort's forgiveness. He was also going to find out what all of that was about.

"Colton?"

Colton met Rexley's gaze. "All done?"

"Yes. She bought another toy horse." He grinned. "She's going to drive you insane about training her." He started walking back to the horses, their guards, and Muffin, who was already seated on Belle with her toy horse in hand.

Colton led Apollonia back to the others. “Rexley, whose crest has a peacock with a snake hanging from its right foot?”

Rexley pursed his lips.

They both mounted their horses in silence and turned homeward bound. Colton fastened Apollonia back to Apollo’s saddle, and Rexley situated Muffin in front of him.

“Look, Colton.” Muffin held up her toy. “She looks like Nia. That’s what I’m going to name her.”

Frowning, Rexley said, “I believe the crest belongs to Viscount Leith, Barnaby Plume’s father.”

Chapter Eighteen

SEBASTIAN HATED to admit it, but Aaron Plume was a handsome man. He was tall and fit. His hair appeared to still be mostly black under his brown top hat. The viscount was about ten years older than King Steven and King-Consort Raleigh.

Leith's face was characteristically blank as he approached Sebastian. It had always been difficult to read him. If he'd been into gambling, he would've made a fortune with a poker face like his.

Gads, he was too close. Sebastian backed up and leaned on the wall of the building. "So nice of you to make it on time."

Leith's lip twitched. "Still quick-tempered, I see. I do beg your pardon, Sebastian. My tardiness couldn't be helped. I had an appointment. I'd tell you it's nice to see you and congratulations on your marriage, but I know you don't give a damn what I think, so to what do I owe this honor?"

Sebastian snorted. He didn't believe for one minute Leith wanted to see his face again. "I called you here to tell you that you'd better get a handle on your son, or I will do it for you. And I seriously doubt you'd like that. Your dear consort, Leo, would have an apoplexy, and we can't have that now, can we?"

At the mention of Leo, Leith snarled, and he got a tick in his right cheek. "What is Barnaby doing now? Does he owe you money too?"

Sebastian narrowed his eyes. He'd expected Leith to counteract by blaming Sebastian. "You cannot be serious? For a man so concerned about appearances, I'd think you'd have a better idea of what your heir is up to."

"Barnaby is a grown man and I refuse to clean up his messes any longer, so whatever he's done—"

"Perhaps I *should* take this up with your consort. I'm quite certain he's concerned. He wouldn't want *me* dealing with Barnaby."

Again, a muscle in Leith's cheek jumped when Sebastian mentioned the viscount-consort. *Interesting.* Then again, maybe not. Leith and Leo quarreled constantly, even coming to blows a time or two, or at least they had.

Leith sighed. "What's going on, Sebastian? Enough of this cryptic bullshit."

Unbelievable. He really did not know what his son was doing. Apparently the rumors of him devoting all his time to Parliament and getting new laws passed were true. "He's the reason for my hasty marriage, for starters."

"Are you referring to that nonsense about the horse?" Leith shook his head. "Only you would complain about marrying a prince. Barnaby did you a favor. Prince Colton is a much better match for you than that first pompous popinjay you married." Leith was as big, if not bigger, a pompous arse than Giles was.

Sebastian closed his eyes and counted to three. He would not plant the viscount on his arrogant, presumptuous arse. Sebastian opened his eyes and glanced out at the street. He could not bear to see that smug, disapproving face. "My marriage is none of your business, but you'd better make your son your business because he's tormenting my consort. Yesterday at the races, he cut the girth on Colton's saddle. Fortunately I saw it before Colton rode. And the day before my wedding, he threatened to make my past public knowledge."

Leith gasped. "Are you certain? How could he? He doesn't know anything about you. He was a toddler when you left Dogwood House."

"Left Dogwood House? Left?" Sebastian made eye contact again. He'd been thrown out in the dead of winter with only a coat. He hadn't been allowed to take any of his belongings or even the money he'd earned working in the stables after his mother's death, but he wasn't going to argue semantics. He was here to get results, not rehash the past. "What happened in the past is in the past. I want it to stay that way. I paid your son a visit last night, but let me relay the same message to you just to make certain we understand each another. If he even thinks about harming Colton again, you won't have to worry about him blowing through his allowance and disgracing the family name. And furthermore, I'll have you brought up on charges of treason for knowingly letting it happen. Is that understood?"

Leith stepped closer, getting into Sebastian's face. Leith's dark blue eyes blazed. "Don't threaten me, boy." He jabbed Sebastian in the chest with his finger. "You forget who you're talking to."

Sebastian grabbed Leith's hand and twisted it. "It's not a threat. It's a promise."

Someone gasped.

A man said, "Oh dear."

They'd gained the attention of several passersby on Dublin Lane. A lady in a blue bonnet openly stared at them as the man next to her ushered her along. *Blast.*

Releasing Leith, Sebastian stepped back. "See to it you handle your heir and there won't be a problem." Bloody hell, he was so overheated a drop of sweat dripped off his forehead. Why did he still let this man get to him after all these years? "I don't think you want our names linked together any more than I do, and that may very well happen if your son keeps pushing."

"I'll take care of Barnaby. And I suspect Leo is involved in this too." Leith's jaw hardened. "Now explain to me what you meant. Did you or did you not run away from Dogwood House?"

"Why don't you ask Leo about that too while you're at it."

"We aren't done with this discussion, Sebastian. I was so distraught over your mother's death, and I didn't realize for several days that you were gone."

"I suppose you didn't realize Leo put me to work in the stables either?"

"What?" If Leith were acting, he was a damned fine thespian. His face actually paled.

Could he really not know? Had Leith been so caught up in himself that he'd been oblivious? He had spent most of the time between Mother's death and Sebastian leaving, in the bottom of a bottle, but how could he not know? The fact that he didn't spoke volumes on the importance of Sebastian in his life… didn't it?

"I'm going to have it out with Leo, and then we are going to talk. We have postponed this discussion for long enough, and I am done with allowing you your space. I've given you plenty of time, years in fact, to get over this… whatever this is. No more." The statement was more of a command than a suggestion. Leith gave Sebastian a hard glare, turned, and walked back to his lift like he didn't have a care in the world.

Sebastian's mind reeled, and his emotions weren't much better. He took stock of them and easily recognized rage, shock, disappointment, and… hope? No, it was definitely fury he felt. He ran his hand through his hair and was surprised to see it wasn't quite steady. "Bugger." He'd meant to keep his cool and not let their past get between them. Worst of all, he hated letting Leith have enough power over him to induce him to anger after all these years. Oh well, if it kept Colton safe…. Colton was a lot more important than Sebastian's pride.

COLTON UNBUCKLED the last cinch fastener on the left side and went around to Apollo's right. He couldn't get what he'd seen off his mind. It had plagued him all the way home.

Maybe Sebastian's meeting with Leith had something to do with the admiral being missing. *Oh star dust*, he didn't know, and his brain hurt from trying to figure it out. At least Sebastian hadn't been meeting a paramour, right?

Colton sighed and turned his attention back to Apollo. He supposed he should stop mulling it over for now.

Frowning at the brown leather strap, he unhooked the last buckle from the billet. This wasn't his girth strap. This girth had elastic only at one end; his had it at both. Also the stitching on the leather was black, not white. He turned it over. *Hmm….* The groom must have grabbed the wrong one when he'd saddled Apollo this morning.

Colton shrugged it off and laid the strap over his shoulder as he removed the saddle and the saddle pad. He patted Apollo's back. "How does it feel to be licensed by the Jockey Club?"

Apollo swiveled his ears back but continued to chew on the hay he'd gotten out of the hayrack on his stall wall.

Colton grinned. "I'll take that as you could care less." He gathered the saddle, pad, and girth. He bumped into Apollonia right outside the stall. "Hello, girl." Nudging her out of the way, he headed to the tack room.

He half expected her to follow, but she didn't. She was too busy exploring her surroundings. He'd taken her back to Townsend Castle to be with her mom, but she'd kicked up such a fuss at being left that he'd brought her back here. She was no longer nursing, but Colton was reluctant to remove her from her mother overnight. This afternoon was a trial. If she did okay, he'd let her stay the night. He and Sebastian were riding over to the castle to go in the lift with his family to the ball tonight, so if he needed to, he could take her back then.

He pushed the tack room door open with his foot and put Apollo's saddle and pad away.

His girth wasn't on any of the pegs. *Hmmm*.... He was stumbling upon one mystery after another today.

A shadow loomed over him, and the little bit of brightness in the tack room dimmed.

"Apollonia, get out of my light." He hung the girth on the hook above his saddle.

"I'm not *that* big. And I certainly hope I'm not *that* much of a pest."

Colton froze. Excitement vacillated with trepidation, but excitement won out. Patience. He had to have patience. "Sebastian." Smiling, he turned toward his consort.

Sebastian stepped into the room and opened his arms. "How did it go? Is he officially a racehorse?"

"He is. And my baby is now listed in the breeding register, so when the time comes, she too can be licensed." Colton rested his forearms on Sebastian's shoulders and gave him a quick kiss. "How about you? Did you get your errand taken care of?" He couldn't possibly put any more suggestion into his tone without sounding suspicious. Hopefully Sebastian would take the hint and confess why he'd met with Viscount Leith. Even if he did without Colton having to ask, a confession was in order. Shame at having spied on his consort tried to creep in.

"Yes," he whispered against Colton's lips. Sinking his tongue into Colton's mouth, Sebastian palmed Colton's cock.

Star dust, the pressure on his cock felt good. So good in fact, Colton hardened under Sebastian's hand. Wrapping his arms around his consort's neck, Colton brought him closer. He thrust his hips forward a little for encouragement.

Chuckling, Sebastian removed his hand and leaned back. "Haven't you had enough with last night and this morning?"

"Well, apparently not, and I'm not the one who decided to fondle me, so maybe you should ask yourself that question." Colton stuck his tongue out.

"Do that again," Sebastian growled only inches from Colton's face.

A sizzle went through Colton. "What? This?" He stuck his tongue out again.

Putting his hands on Colton's shoulders and rubbing his thumbs along Colton's neck, Sebastian closed his lips around Colton's tongue.

A shiver went through Colton. *Good galaxy*, who knew caresses on the neck could be so erotic?

"Mmm…." He opened his mouth.

Sebastian ravished him with a slow, sensual assault. No wonder he was infamous for his sexual escapades. What he could do with a kiss alone devastated the senses.

Colton's toes curled. The soft glide along Colton's lips and tongue sent his mind reeling. His testicles drew taut. They were alone in the tack room. The stables too, for that matter. Would it be bad form to push down on Sebastian's shoulders? That mouth had done wicked things to Colton this morning. Or perhaps he should be the one to drop to his knees. That sounded good too.

With a sigh, Sebastian pulled back. When Colton didn't immediately let go, Sebastian grabbed Colton's wrists and unwound them from his neck. Sebastian held them, running his thumbs over Colton's knuckles. "Let's go inside. We can't do this in here, sweeting."

"Why can't we?" Goodness, Colton's voice had squeaked. "Does Berkley have camera functions in here?"

Sebastian smirked. "For one thing, this room is too small. And the grooms are liable to come in any moment. And no, Berkley does not have cameras in here. Only audio. He has most of the same capabilities as Jeffers, except his range. His range over the grounds isn't as great as Jeffers's." He kissed each of Colton's hands on the knuckles. "Are you done in here?"

"I need to take Apollo's bridle off."

Sebastian backed through the door, still holding Colton's hands. "Let's do that so we can go upstairs. Oof." Sebastian ran into Apollonia.

Colton chuckled. "Speaking of Apollo's tack… I can't find my cinch." Had Sebastian just winced? "What?"

"I didn't want to tell you yesterday, but…." Sebastian turned and shoved at Apollonia's side. "Go get Apollo settled, and we'll talk." Sebastian's voice was clipped.

Uh-oh. An itching sensation started along Colton's shoulders. Something was up. Something Colton probably wasn't going to like, although he couldn't imagine what. Had someone stolen his cinch? Cinches weren't expensive, but the gall.... Did they think it would keep him from racing?

Apollonia moved out of their way but turned to stare at them. As Sebastian walked past her, she swiveled her ears toward her rump and backed up.

Colton reached out to soothe her. "Shh...."

She raised her head, her eyes wide, then finally sniffed and nuzzled into his hand.

"That's my girl. Shhh...." Colton gave her one last reassuring pat and went to her father's stall.

Waiting on Colton, Sebastian had leaned against the wall outside Apollo's enclosure. His brows lowered and his mouth tightened, but he was slouched rather than rigid.

"Come on, tell me what's going on." Colton's erection had taken a hike, and in its place his ire was rising.

"Yesterday before the race, I went to Apollo's pen first to see if you were there." It *had* been a little odd that he'd come out with Brooks.

"And?" Colton unfastened the cheek strap and pulled the bridle over Apollo's ears.

"While I was in there with Apollo, I noticed your girth had been cut."

Dropping the bridle by his side, Colton turned to face his consort. "Someone cut the girth on Apollo's saddle?" Why would someone do that?

Jaw tense, Sebastian nodded once. "It was cut so that a little pressure, probably during the race, would've snapped it in half."

Whoa. The bridle hit against the wall as Colton leaned on it. Someone wanted to hurt him. *Why?*

Sebastian touched his cheek. When had he come inside the stall? "It's okay. I had everything under control. If I'd thought there was the slightest chance something else would happen, that you were in more danger, I'd have never let you race."

Colton shook his head. "I just don't know why someone would do that. Do you think it's related to Aiden and Trouble being kidnapped? Or the admiral missing? Could it be the IN behind it?"

"It was Plume. He was there and seemed irritated when you won the race without incident."

That son of a whoremonger. Gritting his teeth, Colton stormed past Sebastian and into the tack room. He hung the hackamore on the peg with the girth and slammed the door. He was going to get even with Plume if it was the last thing he did. Colton should've pummeled Plume the other day in the park. If he—

Blast. That's why Sebastian had met with Leith.

Butterflies swarmed in Colton's stomach. He should be ashamed of himself. He'd spied on his husband, and the whole time Sebastian had been trying to protect him. His consort had been looking out for him. *Guh. I'm a ninny.* A nontrusting, stupid ninny who needed to beg his consort's forgiveness.

"Colton?"

"What?" he snapped. Great. Now, he was taking out his frustration at himself on Sebastian. "Why didn't you tell me this when it happened?"

"I didn't want you to worry." Sebastian closed Apollo's door.

Better to get the truth out in the open. "Is this why you met with Leith today?"

SEBASTIAN WHIRLED around and narrowed his eyes to slits. *Oh galaxy.* Colton knew. The gate swung open and hit him in the behind because he hadn't locked it. "What did you say?" Surely he'd heard wrong. Colton couldn't possibly know. Sebastian balled his hands into fists as his stomach clenched painfully.

"I asked if that's why you met with Leith." Colton hesitated for a second and continued forward. "I'm sorry. I know I shouldn't have, but I went to the toy store with Muffin and Rexley after my meeting with the commissioner because it was near where the note asked you to meet…." He shrugged. "It's not a good excuse. There isn't one for what I did."

"You were spying on me." The accusation in Sebastian's voice came out loud and clear. His face was cold and tingly. Colton had seen him with Leith. What if Colton put the pieces together? What if he found out?

Colton nodded.

How in the world had he found out about the meeting? Unless—

"You read that note yesterday," Sebastian accused. Colton didn't trust him.

Stopping halfway to Sebastian, Colton studied his feet. "I thought it might be a paramour you were meeting with."

Already it was starting. Just as it had with Giles. "After I told you I had no paramour?" Sebastian's voice climbed, and he struggled to rein his temper back in.

Colton nodded. "I'm sorry, but you're so secretive sometimes. You won't talk about your family or your life before the Navy. And your birthmark.... There has to be an explanation for the mark on your leg other than coincidence."

Sebastian's worst fears were coming true. Bugger, what was he going to do? Colton was getting way too close. Galaxy help Sebastian, he was in love with Colton and too selfish to let him go. "Just because I married you, doesn't mean I have to tell you everything. You don't own me."

Colton took a step back, his eyes wide. When he spoke, his voice was soft, hurt. "I don't want to own you. I want honesty."

Oh bloody hell, not only had Colton spied on him, but Colton had put himself in danger to do so. Sebastian's heart pounded so hard his chest ached. The pit of his stomach churned. If he held his hands up, no doubt they'd quake. "Where were your guards when you were busy playing detective? No, never mind. I can guess. They have a lot to answer for." Sebastian turned on his heel and strode toward the stable door. He had to get away. He needed time. He needed space.

"Wait! Where are you going?"

He should answer. He didn't want to worry his consort, but Sebastian didn't glance back. Maybe being left, even if it wasn't permanent, would make Colton think. Then again, maybe it was Sebastian who needed to think. At least Colton had told him what he'd done, and he seemed truly regretful. How big a heel did that make Sebastian that he wanted his consort to be as miserable as he was at the moment?

He was mad and scared and… maybe he should be honest with his consort.

Chapter Nineteen

Blackwell House, the Earl of Tarnwell's residence in Classige, Pruluce

COLTON STARED at the cornice around the Earl of Tarnwell's ballroom without really seeing it. He'd messed up in an epic way. The plan was to get Sebastian to fall hopelessly in love with him, but instead Colton had alienated his consort and destroyed his trust. Against all his wishes, it appeared as though he was going to have to settle for a typical ton marriage. He just didn't see any other choice, because Sebastian did not want to open up to him. How could they possibly have a real marriage, a marriage like his parents had, under the circumstances? They couldn't. *Dust*, the thought made his heart hurt.

"Is the wall particularly interesting this evening?" Aiden cocked his head slightly and stared up at the cornice.

"Don't start." Colton was not in the mood, and smartarse remarks from his brother weren't going to improve his disposition. Aiden couldn't understand. He had a husband who adored him.

"No fewer than three people have tried to get your attention in the last thirty minutes." Aiden looped his arm through Colton's and started walking. "Come along. You can be antisocial outside as well as you can in here." They skirted the dance floor and headed for the garden door next to the orchestra. Without breaking stride, Aiden motioned at someone to their left.

"What if I don't want to go outside?" Colton asked, though he didn't care where he went. One place was as good as another.

Footfalls hurried behind them, and Colton's other arm was snagged. "Did you find out what's eating him?" Nate asked Aiden over Colton's head.

Aiden shook his head. "Not yet."

Colton groaned. "Not only are you forcing me to be social, but now the two of you intend to grill me, don't you?"

"Talking to your family isn't being social," Aiden grumbled. "We don't count because you're supposed to talk to us whether you want to or not."

Nate shrugged and looked across him to Aiden. "What are your intentions? Do we need to interrogate him?"

"Absolutely." Aiden tugged to the right.

Nate tugged to the left. "This way." To Colton, Nate said, "To answer your question, yes. We intend to grill you."

Aiden groaned. "Why that way? I wanna go to the fountain."

"It's too cold out here to be by the overspray." Nate steered them toward the small garden.

"What if I don't want to go *anywhere* with the two of you?" Colton asked.

"Too bad," they answered in unison.

They passed under a rose trellis and out onto the lawn, just beyond the scope of the veranda torches, before Colton's brother and brother-in-law released him.

The garden was small and simple, really more of a lawn, but beautiful and serene since they were the only ones out here at the moment. Probably because unlike a lot of the other gardens, this one had no secluded trysting spots, or perhaps it was because it was chillier than it had been the last several days. The fountain trickled off to their right. All along the stone wall that concealed the alley behind the town house, evergreen plants glistened with a little dusting of ice. The grass was completely covered in snow. It, too, sparkled in the moonlight, now starting to diminish behind the increasing clouds. Snowfall once again appeared imminent. Things seemed so desolate and… alone out here. It fit Colton's mood perfectly.

Aiden shivered and hugged his arms to his chest. "What gives? You've been unusually quiet all evening. You didn't even pick at Tarren in the lift on the way over here, and he was really asking for it too with his comment about dogs being smarter than horses."

Colton frowned. "He said that?"

Aiden looked at Nate as if to say, *Are you hearing this?*

Nate stepped behind Aiden and began rubbing Aiden's arms. "I think it was Tarren's way of trying to find out if you're okay. When you didn't react, we all realized you aren't, and we're worried about you." He lowered his mouth to Aiden's ear. "Still cold?"

A stab of jealousy pierced Colton. The two of them were so perfect together. *They* had a marriage like Father and Cony.

Shaking his head, Aiden relaxed into Nate and leaned on him. “According to servant gossip, Wentworth came by the castle earlier. He called one of the guards and the new bodyguard, Benny, into his office. Stayed for about fifteen minutes and left. Didn’t Benny accompany you, Rexley, and Muffin this morning? What’s going on?”

Good galaxy, was anything a secret? Apparently not in the Townsend household. Colton groaned. He supposed he might as well tell them. The state of his marriage was going to become obvious eventually. “After my meeting with the race commissioner, I went to—” Colton winced. Put into words, it sounded really bad. “I spied on Sebastian.”

Nate’s eyebrows rose.

“Doing what exactly? And why did you find it necessary to do that?” Aiden’s nose wrinkled.

“I thought he might have a paramour, and I read a missive he got at Wentworth Park yesterday. I couldn’t tell who it was from, but I sort of manipulated things where Rexley, Muffin, and I would be in that area at the time of the meeting by suggesting Muffin’s favorite toy shop. It wasn’t a romantic meeting.” He didn’t feel right telling them who the meeting was with—Sebastian seemed really agitated that even Colton knew—so Colton rushed on, hoping they’d let that piece of information pass. “I apologized. I was wrong, and I feel terrible.”

“I swear. Every one of you Townsends has enough curiosity and sneakiness for three men,” Nate grumbled and ran a finger along the edge of Aiden’s cravat.

Aiden grinned and turned his face up to Nate. “I haven’t the slightest idea what you mean.”

“Of course you don’t.” Nate’s shoulders shook, but his laughter was silent.

Glancing back at Colton, Aiden frowned. “What’s the problem if you apologized?”

“He didn’t accept my apology. He stormed off.” Colton’s gorge rose. What if Sebastian never forgave him? He’d tried to convince himself he didn’t love Sebastian once. Maybe he could do so again.

Nate gave Colton a sad smile. “He’ll come around. He’s not going to stay mad forever, and just because he’s angry doesn’t mean he doesn’t care.”

That was the crux of the problem. Colton wasn’t sure Sebastian did care. Oh, sure, he cared a little or he wouldn’t have married Colton, but Sebastian didn’t have any deep abiding love. Not like Colton did.

"What'd you just think?" Aiden asked. "You looked so sad."

Colton glanced up at his brother. "I was thinking Sebastian doesn't care for me. I guess I'm foolish because I always assumed I'd have a relationship like Father and Cony. Like you two." He shrugged. "It's okay. I'm going to be so busy with the stables that I don't really have time for all that anyway." Right? Oh bloody hell, he was going to have to come to terms with his future.

"Stuff and nonsense," Aiden protested. "And you don't sound the least bit convincing."

"I think you're wrong, Colton." Nate slid his arm around Aiden's middle and pulled him closer. "And if Sebastian doesn't care, he doesn't know what he's missing."

"I'll tell him," Aiden growled.

"Stand down, killer. Beating the man to a bloody pulp isn't going to help this situation any." Nate met Colton's gaze. "You need to go talk to him. Give him time to calm down and tell him why you did what you did. And I don't mean this whole jealousy thing. It stems from something much deeper than that. Sometimes you have to make yourself vulnerable to get what you want."

But what if Sebastian didn't love him? What if Sebastian didn't even want to stay married? A pang of fear hit Colton. A numbness settled over him. "You make it sound so easy. It's not." Could it be? He wanted— Colton shook his head. "You're a romantic, Nate."

"I've never claimed otherwise." Nate chuckled. "And it *is* that easy. I speak from experience when I tell you it's worth the risk."

Aiden glanced up at his consort with an adoring expression. "So much for pride?"

Nate nodded. "Exactly."

Maybe— Something cold touched Colton's wrist. He glanced down and noticed the drop of water. He raised his head. Snowflakes fluttered around them. It was mystical. He watched the flurries for several moments, and it occurred to him what he needed to do.

"Thanks." Colton hugged them both and jogged into the town house. He had to get back to Wentworth Park and wait for Sebastian.

"WAS THAT Colton?" Steven glanced over his shoulder. His children had lost their minds. Colton walked right past him like he wasn't there, even after he'd tried to hail him, and now—He faced Aiden and Nate again. "What are you two doing out here in the snow?"

They stepped up onto the veranda, and Nate brushed the dusting of white off his arms. "Yes, that was Colton. And we were—"

"Wait." Steven held up a hand. "Does it have anything to do with why Colton was in such a hurry to get away from the two of you? Never mind. I'm not sure I want to know." Steven helped sweep off the back of Aiden's black evening coat. The snow was really coming down.

Craning his neck over his shoulder, Aiden gaped at him. "Exactly what do you think we were doing, Father?"

"I thought we already established that I don't want to know. Do either of you know what's wrong with Colton? Did he give an explanation as to why Wentworth didn't accompany us as planned?"

Nate leaned against the railing. "Just a difference of opinion. I suspect they'll work it out. Unless I miss my guess, Colton is headed back to Wentworth Park now."

"Rourke will take him. Rourke's been shadowing Colton all night. Sadly, I don't think Colton has even noticed." Aiden gripped the rail and hopped up to sit on it next to where Nate stood.

Steven glanced out at the garden. Rather plain compared to most, but quite pretty. The snow, too, was a sight to behold. It brought back happy memories. He and Raleigh used to have snowball fights every winter when they first married. Oh how he wanted that sort of fun, loving relationship for his boys. He hoped Aiden and Nate were correct about Colton and Sebastian working things out. "I hate to see them fighting already. They haven't even been married a week. Perhaps I should send them on a wedding trip." That might be just the thing to push them closer together.

"Wentworth won't go. Not right now while things are so…." Aiden waved his hand, trying to find the word. "You know how seriously he takes guarding all of us."

"He'd have a problem with us being out here, no doubt," Nate agreed. "Although I daresay I'm quite capable of taking care of us," he grumbled.

The music blared for a moment, then silenced. Footsteps clicked across the porch, coming closer.

Nate grinned and rolled his eyes upward.

Aiden sighed and whispered, "We're in trouble now."

Turning around was not necessary because Steven knew without a doubt who had joined them. And Aiden was right; they were about to get a lecture.

"Would you like to explain to me why the three of you are out here in the cold? Without a guard, I might add." Raleigh set his hand on Steven's shoulder to get his attention. Which was ridiculous since he had Steven's undivided attention the moment he'd opened the door.

"We were talking to Colton." Nate perched himself on the rail he'd been leaning against.

"Yes, well, Colton has gone home, and Knighton has accompanied him." Raleigh slid his hand casually down Steven's back, raising goose bumps, before he settled it at Steven's waist.

"Ah, so His Grace tattled on us," Steven grumbled. He was going to have to have a word with Rourke about that.

Raleigh rubbed soft, sensual circles on Steven's back, contradicting the annoyed tone in his words. "Yes, he did. He's an excellent bodyguard, and furthermore…."

Steven grinned and tuned the sermon out. It was quite easy to do with Raleigh so near. Steven may have even leaned closer. The slight hint of cedar, bergamot, and mint in Raleigh's soap teased Steven's senses. *Mmmm….* Perhaps they should all take Colton's lead and retire back to the castle.

The low dulcet tones of Raleigh's voice made Steven's heart race. He closed his eyes for a moment, then stared out into the garden. It was so quiet, like they were the only people in the city tonight. But they weren't….

An odd sense assailed Steven. They were no longer alone here in the garden. He peered around, wondering where the strange feeling came from. He tuned Raleigh out completely and closed his eyes. There was a crack, like the break of a stick, and a crunch of snow. Steven snapped his eyes open.

At the far corner of the garden a man strolled toward the house. He seemed oblivious to them. Why wasn't he dressed in evening finery? *Oh!* It was him. The man who'd been spying on him.

In his peripheral vision, Steven caught Nate staring at him.

Abruptly, Nate turned and searched the area, spotting the man too.

"Ho there!" Lifting his arm to flag the man down, Steven hurried to the steps.

Aiden and Raleigh, who'd been conversing, quieted.

Nate stood, reaching inside his evening coat.

The man, now close enough the light from the veranda touched his face, froze. His eyes widened, and he took off toward the back of the garden and the brick wall with his frock coat flapping behind him.

"Bloody hell." Steven leaped down the stairs and gave chase. His boots sank in the snow with a crunch.

The man vaulted the wall in one smooth, graceful leap. His feet hit the ground on the other side with a slapping sound, and the staccato of footfalls followed.

"Steven!" Raleigh yelled.

No way was Steven stopping. It was time to get some answers, damn it.

Only seconds behind the man, Steven jumped and gripped the top of the wall. He heaved himself up and caught a brick with the toe of his left boot. He used the foothold to propel himself over the wall and hit the ground running.

The peeping Tom turned the corner, and Steven pushed himself faster.

The loud rattle of metal clanked and echoed through the passageway.

A garbage can rolled in front of Steven. A couple of rats scattered across the way. The rancid odor of rotten food permeated the air.

The man looked back over his shoulder.

Shouting came from behind Steven, but he ignored it. He could not lose the man this time. Steven jumped the overturned can but slipped on some of the garbage and had to throw his arms out and slow down to regain his balance. *Damn it!* Catching his footing, he rounded the corner in pursuit.

The lane was empty. *Dust*, navigating around that trash can had cost him precious time. Where the hell had the man gone? Steven slowed again and listened.

The pounding of feet on pavement came from behind him and… to his left.

Ignoring the burning in his lungs, he took off again down the left alleyway. He ran to the end of the lane where it opened up on to Grosvenor Street and looked both ways.

To the right, the street was practically empty, only a lone lift at the end. To the left, streetlamps illuminated the fluttering snow. At the edge of the streetlamps' light, a silhouette disappeared.

"Stop." Raleigh grabbed Steven's arm. "Steven, we can't catch him now. Stop." Raleigh breathed heavily.

Reluctantly, Steven gave in as he watched the figure emerge in the next lamp glow some twenty yards away. He inhaled deeply, fogging the air around them.

Footfalls pounded behind them, and Aiden zipped past them.

Nate drew to a stop next to them. He dropped his hands on his knees. One hand held a fragger.

"Aiden!" Raleigh shouted.

Aiden continued to follow the man at breakneck speed. He'd gained ground and was closing in on him. In another few moments, he could probably catch him. And then what?

An icy chill swept over Steven's body, and it had nothing to do with the weather. What if the man hurt Aiden? *Oh no.* The man was much bigger than Aiden. "Aiden, stop!"

Raleigh dashed after their son only a split second before Steven.

Nate was right with them.

"Aiden," Steven yelled, but it came out as a hoarse cry. He didn't have enough lung capacity to yell and run at the same time. He stopped and cupped his hands over his mouth. "Aiden."

Still Aiden ran. He was close to the man now.

Raleigh was too far behind to be of assistance if Aiden should catch the man.

"Freeze!" Nate's voice boomed beside Steven.

Aiden skidded to a halt, whirling to face them. He put his hands on his hips.

Steven strode forward. The terror that had gripped him slowly began to recede. His chest hurt, but his child was no longer in danger. *Thank galaxy.*

Raleigh stopped next to Aiden. Something shiny gleamed in the hand he held by his side. His boot knife.

Aiden's posture shouted irritation, but Raleigh grabbed him by the shoulders and shook him, then hugged him. No doubt the lecture would start in a moment. And if Raleigh didn't give it, Steven would. The boy had scared ten years off his life with that stunt.

Putting a hand to his burning chest, Steven tried to slow his breathing. To Nate, who was walking beside him, Steven said, "That's the man who's been following me. Now that he knows I'm not going to take being spied on, we may never know who he is or what he wants."

"I know him," Nate croaked out. "That was Lieutenant Robert Jenkins. Admiral Jenkins's son."

Chapter Twenty

Wentworth Park's stables

HE'D DONE a lot of thinking in the last few hours, and he'd made some decisions. Unfortunately, putting them into practice was easier said than done; he was procrastinating. Sebastian was hanging out in the barn with the horses instead of going inside and seeing his consort.

Cowardice, thy name is Sebastian.

He sighed and petted Apollonia's nose where it rested on his shoulder. He loved horse noses. So soft and velvety.

In the last forty-five minutes, he'd gained a new appreciation for Colton's baby pain in the arse. She'd gotten so excited when she saw Sebastian, he couldn't help but go to her. One thing led to another, and she'd coaxed him into letting her out like Colton always did. "Come on, pest. Let's put you back in your stall. I've got to go grovel to your human daddy. Maybe you can put in a good word for me tomorrow?"

He gave Max one last pat and shrugged Apollonia's head off his shoulder. Turning, he caught her halter and led her to the empty space next to Apollo. She seemed to be doing fine away from her mother. Unlike a lot of foals, she'd really bonded with her father and he with her.

Sebastian opened the stall for her.

She went inside, turned around, and licked his hand as he was shutting the gate.

"I can't believe you did that. At least you didn't try to eat my hair today, I suppose." Sebastian headed out of the stables and into the cold night air. The snow whipped around, blowing furiously. The ground would be covered by morning. *Brrr....* Huddled in his coat, he hurried to the mansion.

The door opened for him, and Berkley greeted him. "Good evening, my lord."

"Good evening, Berkley. Don't disturb me unless it involves fire or death."

"Very well, my lord. Have a good evening."

Sebastian put away his coat and gloves and headed up the stairs. Admittedly, he took each step a little slower than normal, but he had no idea what to say to Colton. An apology was definitely in order. He should've never stormed off like he had, but how did you go about imparting information that could ruin you and the person you were telling?

Making it to his door, he hesitated, wondering if Colton would be asleep. Would he be furious if he was awake? Sebastian cracked the door open, unsure of what he'd find.

Colton sat on the edge of the bed staring out the window at the blizzard. "Hi," he said without looking at Sebastian.

Sebastian relaxed a little. "Hi. How was your evening?"

"It would've been better if you'd come with me. I missed you."

Oh thank galaxy, Colton wasn't mad. Sebastian closed the door and crossed the room. "I'm sorry I left."

"About that…." Colton didn't turn away from the window. "I'm sorry too. I shouldn't have read your correspondence. It was none of my business."

Sebastian breathed a sigh of relief. He could do this. "I agree. You shouldn't have, but you aren't the only one at fault. I should've told you my suspicions about Plume and about my meeting with Leith." Wanting—no, needing—the physical contact with Colton, Sebastian toed off his boots, shrugged out of his evening coat, and crawled onto the bed.

Colton's posture relaxed. He glanced over his shoulder. A slow, hesitant grin eased onto his face. "Thank you."

Sitting down on the bed, Sebastian put his legs on either side of Colton's and wrapped his arms around him. He let Colton's warmth bleed into him, dispelling his fears even more. "What for?" Closing his eyes, he inhaled the scent of his consort and rested his chin on Colton's shoulder. He wanted to keep this for eternity.

"For being understanding and forgiving me. I don't want a typical ton marriage, Sebastian." Colton stood and turned to face him, the distance between them like a chasm at the moment.

Colton had given him the perfect opening. All he had to do was reach out and take it. He hesitated for only a moment, then said, "Neither do I."

Giving no indication of hearing, Colton paced in front of the bed. "If that's all you're interested in, then we should call it quits now because I can't— What did you say?"

"I said neither do I. I've had that, and it did nothing but make me miserable." Sebastian couldn't go through it again. Which meant he needed to get his secrets out in the open and deal with them. It wasn't fair to Colton, especially when it was something Sebastian himself wouldn't tolerate. He would not abide secrets in their relationship. Not significant ones that could impact both of them, anyway.

Stopping a few feet away, just out of reach, Colton smiled and shoved Sebastian.

Gasping, Sebastian fell onto the bed. *What the—*

Colton came down on top of him and plastered his lips to Sebastian's. He was wild, his hands everywhere, stripping Sebastian of clothes.

Oh yes. Oh no. They needed to talk, not fuck.

Sucking on Sebastian's tongue, Colton skimmed a hand down Sebastian's chest to his groin. His lips red and moist, Colton rose and stared down at Sebastian. The look sent Sebastian's heart pounding and blood rushing to all the right places.

Sebastian was a goner. He did some tugging on clothes of his own. He got Colton's shirt over his head as Colton removed his. It took some effort, but they helped each other until they were both naked from the waist up. They were on fire. When Colton grabbed the falls of Sebastian's pants, Sebastian caught his hands. "Slow down." Sebastian panted. He needed to stop this and tell Colton about his past.

"Yes." Colton didn't slow down in the least. In his haste to open Sebastian's trousers, a button flew off.

Sebastian rolled them until he lay on top. "Colton, I have to tell you—"

Colton bit his neck.

"Ahhh…." A current of pleasure arced through Sebastian. They could talk afterward. He ground his hard prick into Colton's hip. Sebastian felt like a green boy with his first lover every time with Colton—fumbling, grunting, and uncoordinated. Not entirely a bad thing but a little disconcerting.

He rolled to Colton's side. Both their trouser-encased legs hung off the side of the bed. Colton still had his boots on.

Sebastian opened Colton's trousers. Colton reached for them too. When Sebastian chuckled and batted Colton's hands out of the way, Colton tried to help by lifting into the touch. Groaning, Sebastian gave in and ripped at the fabric. Colton's cock came free already moist at the tip.

Was there anything more exciting than being wanted so desperately? It was empowering and inspiring. Sebastian's cock was so hard he ached, and his heart raced. His hands were shaky and his breath uneven. He shoved Colton's pants down his hips. Colton was so beautiful, his muscles almost as firm as his prick.

Sebastian slid off the bed and shimmied out of his trousers. Naked, he climbed back on the mattress and got some lube from the dispenser. He couldn't wait.

"Roll onto your stomach." Coating his cock with the warm slick liquid, he stared at the luscious backside Colton presented. Sebastian couldn't help himself. Bending, he sank his teeth into one muscled cheek.

Colton started and groaned. He scooted backward until his boots hit the floor, and he lay across the bed with his pants around his knees.

Nuzzling the base of his spine and stroking his cock, Sebastian slipped two fingers into Colton's tight hole.

Colton's muscles rippled as he pushed back, impaling himself further. "Yes."

Sebastian worked his fingers in, watching them glide in Colton and out. Sebastian had to squeeze his cock to keep from coming. Throwing his head back and staring at the ceiling, he composed himself. He counted to ten until the need to climax subsided. When he got himself under control, he pressed the tip of his cock into that tiny rosy hole, using his fingers to stretch as he entered.

Colton stiffened and clamped down on his cock and fingers.

"Shh.... Easy, sweeting."

Colton nodded and pushed back.

"Oh bugger." The grip around Sebastian's dick sent shivers up his spine. He pressed his groin to his consort's arse and draped his body over Colton's. Bracing his hands next to Colton's sides, Sebastian kissed Colton's shoulder blades while taking little stabs with his hips.

Sebastian rocked, sawing in and out until Colton grunted and bucked beneath him. It was too much. Sebastian tried to hold back, but there was no use. He stood up and thrust into Colton's willing body as fast as he could and came so hard he grew dizzy.

He braced himself to keep from falling on Colton. "I'm sorry. I didn't mean—"

Colton stood and turned around. Pressing his lips against Sebastian's, Colton urged Sebastian to the bed. They kissed for several long moments.

Breaking the kiss, Colton tipped his head toward the lube. "Get me some."

Bonelessly, Sebastian tried to reach the dispenser. Blasted thing was too far away. Colton's hands landed on Sebastian's thighs and shoved him up the bed until he got several dollops of lube on his palm.

Colton pulled Sebastian back to him and scooped the lube from Sebastian's hand. Sebastian should help, but it was like the energy had been sucked right out of him.

Fortunately, Colton didn't seem to mind. He slicked up his dick. And galaxy, what a sight. The engorged head of his cock poked out of his fist on each stroke. Sebastian pulled his feet onto the bed. Oh bugger, he still had his stockings on.

Colton needed no other cooperation. He sank into Sebastian's arse with one smooth stroke. He gripped Sebastian's hips and threw his head back. The corded muscles in Colton's neck strained as he fucked Sebastian, racing toward his own orgasm.

The hot brand in Sebastian's arse was both exciting and overwhelming. If he hadn't just climaxed, he'd have gotten hard again. The pleasure was mind-numbing regardless. And watching Colton's face contort in pleasure was even more rewarding. "That's it."

Lowering his chin, Colton met Sebastian's gaze. Colton's eyes widened a split second before he closed them again. His body tensed, but he kept thrusting. A low growl escaped his throat, and he froze.

Finally, Colton pulled out of him and flopped onto his back next to Sebastian. The warm trickle of fluid slid down Sebastian's arse.

Fingers tickled his hand, and then Colton gripped it.

Sebastian squeezed and caressed with his thumb. Rolling his head to the side, he smiled at Colton.

Colton smiled back.

Sebastian was so at peace at the moment, he doubted anything could bother him. Rolling to his side, he touched Colton's clean-shaven cheek. "I need to tell you something."

"Okay." Colton nuzzled into the touch, rubbing against Sebastian's hand like a cat.

"Colton, I'm—"

"Lord Wentworth?" Berkley interrupted.

Sebastian growled. Hadn't he said he didn't want to be disturbed? "Berkley, something better be on fire."

"There is, my lord. The stables are on fire."

PANIC HIT Colton so hard if he'd been on his feet, it would've knocked him off them. Springing from the bed, he stumbled and his vision whited out for a moment. Without waiting for it to fully clear, he jerked his trousers up and grabbed his shirt.

"Colton, wait." Sebastian hopped around trying to get his pants on. Something crashed to the floor, but Colton didn't wait around to see what.

The horses. Colton had to get to the horses.

Bloody hell. Apollonia is in those stables. She was just a baby. Colton barreled out the door and down the stairs, taking four steps at a time until he reached the bottom.

Servants raced about the foyer like a mad swarm of bees. Shouts echoed along with a dull roar. An orange glow came from the open front door. Snow—or was it ash?—blew inside, whirling around the undulating knot of people screeching and carrying on.

"Get outside! Get hoses, buckets, and anything that will hold water." Afraid of what he'd find, Colton shoved his way through the crowd and out the door. *Please don't let it be a big fire.*

It was huge. Horses darted around the front lawn with their heads and tails high. Max skirted a stableboy trying to catch him. Dazz had run to the paddock and was whinnying to be let inside. A few other horses dashed away from the fire and staff, but no Apollonia and no Apollo.

Colton sprinted toward the barn. The blizzard wind slapped him in the face.

Someone grabbed his arm. "No. Your Highness, it's too dangerous," one of the stableboys pleaded.

Shrugging him off, Colton yelled over his shoulder, “Round up the horses. Calm them and check them for injury.” The barn door stood open, clear of flames. The roar of the fire drowned out the shouts of the servants and agitated sounds of the horses. Ten yards from the blaze, the heat grew so intense Colton stumbled back. It dried his eyes and blasted his cheeks. He threw his arm in front of his face. “Apollo! Apollonia!”

A distressed whinny answered him. There was movement within the black plumes of smoke.

“Colton,” Sebastian shouted.

Holding his breath, Colton dashed toward the barn as fast as he could. The heat inside was nearly unbearable. Sweat poured down his face, and the smoke stung his eyes. It was so painful he couldn’t help but cry out.

Apollo paced back and forth in the aisle in front of Apollonia’s stall. His ears were flattened against his head, and his eyes wild. He whinnied and squealed at Apollonia, who was still in the stall and pawed the ground. His gate hung on to the wall by one hinge, the wood busted through in several places. He’d stayed for Apollonia.

Colton’s heart sank. He had to get all three of them out of here. “It’s okay, boy. I’m here. We’re gonna get her out.” The smoke and soot invaded Colton’s throat, scorching his lungs. He coughed, and his eyes watered, leaving him barely able to see through the tears as the heat bombarded his body and drenched him in sweat.

Apollo turned back toward the door, snorting and throwing his head wildly.

Ignoring him for the moment, Colton dashed to Apollonia’s stall.

Her eyes darted around erratically, and her ears were pinned back. She whined, and it sounded like a scream. Running at the gate, she tried to get out.

“Shhh….” He opened the gate and leaped out of the way, expecting her to bolt from the stables, but she didn’t. She plowed into him, nearly spilling him to the ground, and snorted. She butted him with her head in an attempt to bury her face under his arm. *Poor baby.* “It’s going to be okay, hoyden.”

Apollo began rearing and whinnying louder.

Coughing, Colton clutched his chest, but the spasms persisted. Oh, it hurt.

Flames raged across the open door, creating a wall of fire. A loud crack resounded over the roar, and sparks rained down on them. The beams overhead began to buckle.

Pulling his shirt up over his nose and mouth, Colton hurried back to Apollonia's stall, grabbed her lead rope, and clipped it to her halter. "Please follow me." He had no doubt Apollo would go through the fire for him, but Apollonia…? He'd never been so scared in his life.

The smoke pressed down on him, and the waves of heat distorted his view. Colton coughed continuously despite having covered his face. His limbs weighed a ton. Lethargy beat at him. Time was running out. The heat was too intense. Holding the rope, he made his way to Apollo.

Apollonia tugged against the rope, trying to back away from the fire. *Oh galaxy, no.*

"Come on, baby. You have to trust me." He coughed so hard he could barely talk.

Apollo sneezed and thrashed his head around. His muscles flinched, looking as if they moved separately from his skin.

Still holding the rope, Colton made his way to Apollo's side. He tried to whisper encouragement but couldn't do so over his hacking. Hoping Apollo understood, Colton held his hand out. If he didn't get them out of here now, he wasn't going to be awake to get them out. Lack of oxygen was taking its toll, and he couldn't catch a deep enough breath. He should be crawling to avoid so much of the smoke, but he couldn't get them all out if he were on the ground. "Shhh…. Boy. Calm. Down," he choked out.

Apollo settled, putting his nose in Colton's hand. *That's right. You have to trust me, old friend.* Grabbing a handful of mane, Colton attempted to haul himself onto Apollo's back and missed. The normally easy task was hampered by the stallion prancing around and Colton's lethargy.

It took three tries, but when Colton finally got on the horse, Apollo seemed to be waiting for instructions.

Crack, pop. A beam exploded and crashed to the floor behind them.

Apollo reared again, and Colton struggled to hold on. He slid sideways, endeavoring to reel Apollonia in by her lead rope, but she dug her heels in. *Oh, please…. Please.* Colton couldn't wait any longer. Turning Apollo, taking him as far back into the barn as he could, he positioned the rope so Apollonia wouldn't get tangled in it.

She'd followed when they moved and stood next to him. He reached out and petted her face. "Come on, baby." *Please.* "Ha!" He kicked Apollo in the flanks and leaned over his back. "Ha!"

There was a soft tug on the rope as Apollo bolted toward the door and the wall of flames in front of it.

"Ha," Colton yelled again and dug his heels in.

Apollo never even paused.

Colton white-knuckled the rope in his hand, ducked his head, closed his eyes, and prayed.

The roar of the fire, the popping and cracking, blared around him. His burning lungs ceased to hurt, and his senses sharpened. The scorching temperature seared his body, and pain lanced through the hand holding the rope. Cold air washed over Colton like a bucket of ice water and stole his breath. His heart hammered, and Apollo's gait evened out as he hit his stride. It was like flying.

Colton began coughing and couldn't stop. A cacophony of noise surrounded them. Shouts. Voices. Sebastian screaming his name. Apollo was still running.

"Whoa, bo—" Coughing, Colton picked up his hand and glanced at it as Apollo slowed. He unfisted it.

The rope was gone, and in its place was bloody, serrated skin. Crimson trickled down his palm and landed on his thigh. *Splat. Splat. Splat.* It spread out on the sooty tan fabric in jagged circles. His hand was empty, his connection to Apollonia gone. *Noooo....* He stared at the hand until tears concealed it from sight.

Apollo finally stopped, and Colton leaned over and vomited.

In the next moment, he was jerked from Apollo's back.

"Colton! Sweeting? Say something."

Colton clung to Sebastian. Clawed at him, really. He had to make the pain in his heart go away. Another series of coughs racked his body. *Safe.* He was safe. Apollo was safe, but—

This is my fault. He should've left her with her mother.

Sebastian pulled back, looking him over, but Colton dove back into his arms.

Rubbing Colton's back, Sebastian kissed his temple. "We're not done with this, but we have things to do. Go calm Apollonia down so you can check her out, and I'll take a look at Apollo. The rest of the horses seem to be okay. All of the staff is fine. Galaxy, I've never been so glad there are no rooms over the stables."

"What?" Colton pulled back and studied Sebastian's face. "What did you say?"

"I said—"

Colton turned and searched the grounds.

Apollonia ran in circles several yards from the fire, with her rope dragging on the ground and three stableboys chasing her. She sneezed, shaking her head, and black smudges marred her beautiful sorrel coat.

A sob escaped Colton's throat and turned into another coughing fit. The weight in his chest dissolved, and his knees buckled. *Oh galaxy, thank you!* His baby was okay.

Strong arms wrapped around his waist. "Are you okay?"

Colton turned back to his consort, grabbed him by the face, and kissed him. "I've never been better."

Chapter Twenty-One

SEBASTIAN HAULED Colton back into his arms and whispered against Colton's ear, "I love you." Now that he'd said it, he felt almost relieved. Like something he'd needed to get off his chest.

For as long as he lived, Sebastian would never forget the sight of Colton barreling out of the wall of fire on Apollo's back. Nor would Sebastian get over the sheer terror that had gripped him when Colton ran into the barn and the flames closed in behind him. Sebastian had been too far away to stop him. He was convinced he now had ulcers, the way his stomach wrenched and churned, and the tingling in his head was no doubt from the sudden explosion of gray hair. He squeezed Colton tighter, trying to calm his racing pulse, but the ash and soot clinging to Colton choked him, making him cough nearly as loud as Colton.

"Crazy little twit." Sebastian shook Colton's shoulders. "If you ever do anything so foolish again, I don't care how much I love you, I'll beat you black-and-blue, then lock you in the highest tower of Townsend Castle and throw away the key. Do you hear me?"

"You love me?" Colton's voice was quiet and scratchy.

Where's the bloody doctor? "Yes, more than you can possibly know." Sebastian moved back but didn't let go of his consort. He couldn't; the fear of losing him was still too close to the surface. The chaos around them barely registered as he rubbed Colton's arms.

Good galaxy, with black smudges all over his face, Colton looked like a chimney sweep; even his hair was singed. Sebastian fingered the locks, and a wrenching pain twisted in his gut. "I've loved you for a long time but refused to admit it to myself. I think I realized it when you tried to ignore me. I really don't like you ignoring me." The skin around Colton's ears was red, swollen, and hot to the touch.

"I promise not to ignore you anymore. Well, maybe if you make me mad, since you've just revealed that it would be effective punishment…." Colton grinned. "I love you too, but then you knew that, didn't you?"

It was too much to hope for. Could Colton really love him? Colton had had a crush on him for ages, but things were different now. If he could feel any love after living with Sebastian the past few days.... "I wasn't sure." He grabbed Colton's hand, reluctant to break contact. Colton's right forearm was bright red and blistered. His sleeve was partially missing. "You're burned."

Colton glanced down at his arm. "I can be burned later. I don't have time right now. We've got to get the horses settled and help with the fire."

At the gentle reminder, Sebastian's training kicked in. Life and death. Colton was not mortally wounded at the moment, but the fire still posed a huge threat and they had work to do.

Although the snow completely covered the ground and began to catch in drifts, the wind was high. The servants dumped and sprayed water on the surrounding area.

"It's too cold for the horses to be left out in the paddock. We need to take them to the castle stables." Which should be interesting, considering all their tack was gone. At least Apollonia had a rope attached to her. She'd follow Colton, so they could use the rope on some of the other horses.

"I'll get them." Colton put his fingers to his mouth and let out an ear-piercing whistle. He immediately began to cough.

Sebastian frowned and looked toward the street. What was taking the doctor so long?

Apollo, Apollonia, Max, Dazz, and Lisette, one of the other horses Sebastian kept, trotted toward Colton. The other three horses, Hockley, Dancer, and Yvonne, continued to scramble about. Under the circumstances, five out of eight was impressive. Colton was like the pied piper of horses.

Sebastian waved the staff off. "Carry on." To Colton, he asked, "What do you suggest? Are you just going to walk and let them follow you?" Sebastian scoffed.

"No, smartarse. I'm going to go get my coat on, ride Apollo, and herd the rest of them." Colton grinned, let go of his hand, and wrapped his arms around Apollonia's neck, who had come over and head-butted Colton. "Then I'm going to get the grooms to check them all out and make certain they're okay."

The filly snorted and nickered, still anxious.

Sebastian shook his head. After how close he'd come to losing Colton tonight, Sebastian hated to admit it, but he suspected both horses would have perished in the blaze if Colton hadn't rescued them. He was glad they were both all right too. "You took a big risk."

"I had to. They were worth it."

"Not worth you." Sebastian touched his cheek and patted Apollonia. He gripped Colton's hand again to get him moving.

"Ah." Colton winced.

His hand was wet and crusty. Sebastian lifted Colton's hand to the light. It was bloody and torn to shreds. *Bugger.* How had Sebastian forgotten about Colton holding the rope and Apollonia darting away as they'd cleared the stables?

"Come on. We're going to go patch up your hand. And where in the hell is that *damned doctor*?" Sebastian's voice climbed on each word. Sliding his hand to Colton's wrist, Sebastian tugged him toward the house.

The horses followed.

"Sebastian?"

"What?"

"Who're those people?" Colton pointed toward the far end of the lawn.

Two men approached on foot. They were too far, about a hundred yards away, and the snow was too heavy for Sebastian to make out anything other than silhouettes, but one of them kept stumbling.

"What in the devil?" Sebastian grabbed Colton's arm and tugged him up the steps and inside the house. He needed his fragger from the office. He had an odd feeling about their prospective visitors.

The *clip-clop* of horse hooves echoed off the marble.

Without turning, Sebastian groaned and let go of Colton. Sebastian knew exactly who had followed them inside. "Get her out of the house."

Colton chuckled and began talking to Apollonia.

Sebastian went to the wall safe behind his desk and moved the picture out of the way. "Berkley, what can you tell me about the men on the edge of the lawn?"

"One of them appears to be the man who started the fire, my lord."

"What?" Sebastian froze in the process of pressing his thumb to the scanner. Damn it, he'd suspected as much, but hearing it out loud.... "Are you telling me the fire wasn't an accident? Like a stable lad smoking or some such?"

"No, my lord. A man set the fire."

"Why didn't I hear about someone being on the property before they got close enough to start a bloody fire?" The safe opened, and he removed the fragger, then closed the safe and the picture over the safe.

"You said not to disturb you unless there was a fire or someone was dead, my lord."

Sebastian ground his teeth together. "Damn it, Berk—never mind. We'll discuss this later." He jogged out of the office.

"My lord, Jeffers has inquired about the fire. What shall I tell him?" Berkley asked.

"Tell him everything is under control and for Their Majesties to stay there. Tell them Colton and I will be at the castle momentarily." After Sebastian found out what these men wanted.

Colton stood outside the front door with the horses gathered around him.

The arsonist and the other man were closer now, almost upon them. The man in front nearly fell. The other, bigger man was pushing him.

Sebastian moved off the steps and waited for them with his fragger by his side. "Colton, get inside."

"Not on your life."

A few of the servants gathered around, putting themselves between the men and Sebastian and Colton. Digby actually backed into Sebastian. "Sorry, me lord."

Sebastian patted the boy on the back and walked around him without taking his eyes off the approaching men.

One man was dressed as a gentleman in a gray coat and nice polished black boots. The other was rough, scruffy. He too had on a coat, but it was a ragged wool that had seen better days. His hair was overlong and shaggy. His face blazed red where the wind had chapped it.

"Durant?" the gentleman called out. He was using brute strength on the other man. "I mean Hastings. Is that you?"

A chill snaked up Sebastian's spine. He hadn't been called by his birth name in ages. "Yes?" Sebastian stepped closer. There was something familiar about the man. He looked like…. "Robert? Lieutenant Robert Jenkins?"

"Yes." Robert Jenkins, Admiral Carl Jenkins's missing son, stepped into the light and shoved the man in front of him toward the servants who had surrounded them. "Tie him up. He's responsible for the fire."

COLTON'S TEMPER flared to life hotter than the fire now burning itself out. He wanted answers, and he wanted them now. Pushing through Sebastian and Robert Jenkins, Colton ignored their protests and locked gazes with the arsonist sitting on the ground against the wall of Wentworth Park. "What did the guy who hired you look like?"

"'E 'twas a gentleman. Dark 'air, dressed nice. Paid me a hundred pounds. Does this mean I can go? I told ye who hired me," the scraggly man declared.

"Hell no," Sebastian half shouted. "Your sorry arse is going to jail." To his underbutler, he said, "Go call the constable."

Robert Jenkins stuck his hands in his pockets. "Tell them what he said." He kicked the man's foot.

"Ow," the arsonist complained. "'E said 'e was yer younger brother, and 'e was tired of yer father throwing ye up in 'is face."

"Bullshit!" Colton saw red. He grabbed the man by the throat. "You lie. Tarren would never—"

Two arms wrapped around Colton from behind, dragging him off the man. Colton struggled. No one accused his little brother of something like that and got away with it.

"Colton, calm down," Sebastian whispered in his ear.

Colton rounded on his husband. He was tired, he hurt, he and his horses had been nearly killed, and this arsehead was accusing his family of wrongdoing. "Don't tell me to—"

"He was talking to me."

"—to calm down."

"It wasn't Tarren who sent him. It was Plume."

"What?" Colton shouted. Plume? That didn't make any sense.

Sebastian grabbed Colton's uninjured hand. "Come on. We need to talk." He looked over Colton's head. "Robert, don't go anywhere. I've a ton of questions for you."

"I'm not going anywhere."

"You'll take care of this?"

Robert nodded.

Sebastian pulled Colton into the house and toward the study.

"Don't you find all this a bit odd?" Colton jerked his hand out of Sebastian's. He was in no mood to be placated.

"Damn it, Colton. I'm trying to tell you something. I tried to tell you this earlier." Sebastian grabbed his hand again, pulled him into the study and shut the door. "Viscount Leith is my father."

Colton froze. He couldn't have been more surprised if someone had told him he was adopted. But Sebastian had a mother, didn't he? Why didn't the viscount and viscount-consort recognize Sebastian as their son? "I don't understand."

Sebastian slouched against the door and ran his hands down his face. "My mother was his mistress."

A lump formed in Colton's throat. His anger evaporated, and he backed up until his legs hit the chair in front of the fireplace. He sank down into the seat and stared at his consort. *Well, that explains his birthmark.* His father was born using Regelence's procreation technology and passed the mark on to Sebastian even though he was conceived naturally.

Sebastian moved to the sideboard and poured himself a drink. He tossed it back and continued without turning around. "She'd worked for his parents, the Earl and Earl-Consort of Marborough, since she was fifteen. When Leith moved out of his family home, he took her with him to Dogwood House. Everything was great then. She shared a room with him and acted as lady of the house. I stayed in the nursery with my governess, but I got to go outside and play when my studies were done. My parents doted on me. I even ate dinner with them in the dining room and.... It was wonderful. Nothing like life at Plume House had been.

"Then Leith's parents threatened to cut off his funds if he didn't marry. They picked his husband and everything. I was only six, but I can remember him complaining about it. When he married, my mother and I were moved into our own house on Hamilton Street, but not much changed. We continued to live the life we were accustomed to. Mom still had pretty dresses; I still had a governess and plenty of toys. My fath—Leith stayed with us more often than not, only returning to Dogwood House to get things he needed. We were happy.

"She died when I was ten, and Leith moved me back into Dogwood House with him. I didn't see him for days. After a week, I was put to work in the stables for a few days, and then finally I was thrown out onto the streets. I lived on the streets for years, picking pockets to survive. As luck would have it, one day I picked Admiral Jenkins's pocket—he was a captain then—and he caught me. I still don't know why he did it, but he took me home, fed me, and offered to buy me a commission in the IN. The rest of it you know." Sebastian turned around and met Colton's gaze. Sebastian's shoulders were held high, but his face.... His eyelids drooped. His face was pale.

It tore at Colton's heart. He stood, wanting to go to his consort, but Sebastian held up a hand.

"If you want out, I understand. I should've told you all of this before I married you. I'm sorry." He inhaled and let it out. "Giles was disgusted after I told him. He kicked me out of his bed and out of his life. A week later he died of a heart attack."

No wonder Sebastian had not wanted to tell him. Colton started forward again.

Sebastian turned his back. "File for an annulment."

"What?" Colton froze, his anger rising.

"I said file for an annulment. I won't contest it."

"Of all the—"

There was a crash from the foyer and a shout. It sounded like Robert.

"Sebastian!" Yes, definitely Robert.

"Colton," a familiar voice called out.

Colton frowned. "Cony?"

CHAPTER TWENTY-TWO

SEBASTIAN STEPPED into the foyer and froze. King-Consort Raleigh sat in the middle of Robert's back, and Nate stood over them with a fragger trained at Robert's head.

Steven, Rexley, Aiden, Tarren, Trouble, and Ashbourne were just inside the front door with three armed guards at their back.

Robert turned his head and met Sebastian's gaze. "Help?"

Great. This was all Sebastian needed. A perfect end to a perfectly horrid day. "Your Majesties, this is Robert Jenkins."

"We know who he is. We chased him tonight," Nate growled. "What I want to know is why he's following our king."

What? Sebastian looked at Robert. "What're they talking about?"

Robert grunted. "I can explain."

"Everyone come into the study and let's get this straightened out. I'm in no mood for more drama." The raspy voice barely sounded like Colton.

Sebastian winced. Colton needed to be in bed, healing.

"Good galaxy." Steven's face blanched. "Berkley said everything was fine. Colton is obviously not fine."

Raleigh furrowed his brow. The struggle to remain where he was or go to Colton played across his face, but he stayed put.

Nate finally lowered his fragger and stuck it in his shoulder holster. The Royal Guards who'd accompanied them still held their rifles trained on Robert, though.

Colton held up his hand. "I'm okay."

"You look terrible." Steven hurried around Raleigh and Nate.

Colton hugged him. "I'm okay. Robert caught the man who set the barn on fire."

Patting Colton's back, Steven nodded and reluctantly released Colton. Steven glanced down at Robert Jenkins and up at Sebastian.

Sebastian nodded. "I trust him." Turning to the guards, he said, "You're dismissed. Go back to your duties. I'll escort everyone home."

"Raleigh, get off of him. Everybody into the office." Steven ushered Colton into the study.

Everyone fell in line behind them as they squeezed through the study door, then fanned out and began talking among themselves.

Steven led Colton to the loveseat and pushed him into it. "Were you in the stables?"

"I went in after Apollo and Apollonia, but we all got out okay."

Once again Sebastian winced. He should've tackled Colton before he ever got out of their bedroom, and Sebastian would have if he'd had any idea what Colton was going to do.

Raleigh, who'd just stopped next to them, sucked in a breath.

Sebastian didn't need anyone to tell him he'd failed in his duties as a husband and Royal Guard. He was responsible for this whole debacle. The best thing he could do was to let Colton go. Galaxy, Sebastian's chest hurt.

He slid into the seat next to Colton but didn't look at him. Sebastian didn't want to. He knew Colton would stand beside him, but it wasn't fair to expect it. "Berkley, we'd like privacy. Stop recording in this room."

"Yes, my lord," the butler intoned.

"All right, then. What in the world is going on?" Raleigh moved to sit on Sebastian's desk and addressed the room in general.

Nate and Aiden stood by the fireplace. Rexley and Trouble sat in the chairs opposite the loveseat. Tarren and Ashbourne dragged seats from the side of the room and joined Rexley and Trouble. Steven leaned on the desk next to his consort. Everyone was staring at Robert, who stood inside the door.

"I'm sorry, Your Majesty." Robert cleared his throat. "I didn't mean to worry you. I just needed to know if I could trust you. With the admiral joining your family, I wasn't sure I could." He glanced at Nate, and a blush crept across Robert's cheekbones. "No offense, Hawk. My father counted you as a friend, but you're also a big part of the IN."

Nate nodded. He'd put the fragger away, but the butt of it was visible since his evening jacket was unbuttoned. "I understand." He waved his hand in a circular motion. "Continue."

Swallowing so hard his throat bobbed, Robert turned his attention to Steven and Raleigh once again. "I knew I could trust Lieutenant Dur—I mean Wentworth." He focused on Sebastian. "Apologies. Old habit."

Sebastian dipped his head.

Colton slid his hand into Sebastian's. It was warm and solid. Sebastian squeezed gently. Did he want to give this up? *No.* But he'd give Colton the choice. Sebastian owed him that much.

"Then why didn't you go to Sebastian first instead of spying on Steven?" Raleigh asked.

"I didn't realize who he was. I knew him as Lieutenant Sebastian Durant. I've been off planet for the last ten years on one mission after another. My father never mentioned that the lieutenant married. I would've never imagined him working as head of castle security."

"So what made you go to him?" Nate asked.

"After you all chased me tonight, I ran into an old acquaintance of the lieu—er, Wentworth's. We talked and he told me where to find Wentworth. You have to understand, I had to be certain. I'm a wanted man. If the IN finds me, they'll kill me like they did my parents."

The entire room started talking at once.

"Shhh.... Quiet." Raleigh sliced his hand through the air. "Robert, we were afraid of that, but how do you know for sure?"

"It's just a feeling. I got a message from my dad three months ago while I was on a training mission. The note said something about remembering my childhood and how I used to hide under the stairs when we'd play hide-and-seek. It was an odd note because I never hid under the stairs. That was always his hiding place." Robert shook his head. "He and my mom always wrote to me, but never like this. Their previous letters were about goings-on, what they were doing, my aunt Mary's new puppies, my cousin Henry's gout, asking about my health, and that sort of stuff. The reminiscence and inaccurate memories weren't right. It was strange enough I took an emergency leave and came home. When I got here, the house had been ransacked, and there was no sign of my parents or my aunt Mary. I located my cousin, and he suggested I look more closely at the house."

Robert dragged his hands down his face and sighed. There were bags under his eyes. "Then I remembered the note. I thought it might be a clue to their whereabouts, so I started searching. I tried under the stairs and found nothing, but then I realized he didn't mention my favorite hiding spot in the note, so I went there." He grinned. "The butler's pantry. Taped to the top of the dumbwaiter was a letter and this." He reached into his coat and pulled out a tiny metal box about the size of a human thumbnail. A hard drive.

Robert tossed the hard drive to Steven. "The note said if I was reading this, my parents were probably already dead. It was pretty cryptic. He said get this into King Steven's hands, but to be careful who I trusted. He made a point to add that I should assume the IN was watching King Steven, and I shouldn't trust the IN or anyone affiliated with them without finding out where their loyalties lie." He looked back at Nate. "I took that to mean you, Hawk. I think he wanted me to make sure your loyalty was to your new family rather than the IN."

"What's this?" Steven asked.

"Hugo, my parents' butler. Anything my father knew will be in Hugo's memory."

Townsend Castle

FRESHLY SHOWERED and bandaged, Colton sat on the edge of his bed in only a nightshirt and watched the doctor place a vial in the bio injector. Father and Cony had insisted they stay at the castle tonight. The room was the bigger bedroom in their newly appointed suite. The staff had moved in all of Colton's old furniture, including the artwork on his walls.

"Will that make me sleep?"

"It should. Unless you're like your brother." The doctor smirked. "In which case, I'll be leaving as soon as I give it to you."

Colton chuckled. Tarren was notorious for having idiosyncratic reactions to medicines. Painkillers that put most people to sleep made Tarren bounce off the walls. Since Tarren already tended to be on the hyperactive side, the results weren't conducive to harmony in the household… especially among the older residents. "Can I give it to myself in a while? I want to check on some things before I go to sleep."

Doctor Tebaldi raised one bushy red eyebrow. He was a nice man, close to Father and Cony's age, with bright red hair, side whiskers, and a ton of freckles. He'd been their doctor since he was out of medical school. "Okay, but no longer than half an hour. You need your sleep so the nanomites can do their job and heal the burned skin and the rope cut on your hand."

"I promise." Colton held up his bandaged hand and tried not to wince. The blasted thing was beginning to hurt now that his adrenaline had worn off.

The door clicked open as the doctor put the injector on the nightstand. Sebastian stepped inside and looked around. He met Colton's gaze and smiled.

Colton smiled back. They were going to be okay.

Dr. Tebaldi closed his bag, glanced toward the door, and back to Colton. "Thirty minutes, Your Highness. No more. I'll come check on you tomorrow."

Colton pressed his uninjured hand to his chest. "Thirty minutes, I swear it." Dropping his hand, he placed it in his lap. "Thank you, Dr. Tebaldi."

"You're most welcome." He bowed, turned toward the door, and bowed again to Sebastian. "My lord."

Sebastian dipped his head. "Thank you for coming, Doctor."

"No problem at all. Call me if you need me before tomorrow, and make certain he takes the pain meds."

"I will." Sebastian closed the door behind the doctor and leaned against it. He let out a deep sigh and gave Colton a soft smile. His hair was wet, and he wore a clean white shirt and black trousers. He yawned.

Colton could identify with the feeling. He, too, was exhausted. It had been a long night. They'd gotten the horses put away, and Robert had settled in a guestroom and was now officially receiving sanctuary from the Townsends. Colton had seen a doctor, Apollonia and Apollo had seen the vet, and just ten minutes ago, they'd gotten word that the fire was out.

"How's your arm?" Sebastian asked.

"It hurts a little. What was on the hard drive?"

"Don't know. It's encrypted and no one has access. Your sire and Winstol are both taking a crack at it, but we may have to call Payton to get the information off it." He pushed away from the door and strode forward to stand in front of Colton. "You should take your pain meds."

"I will in a few minutes. What about the arsonist?"

"In jail, and the constable is picking up Plume as we speak."

"Good." Colton patted the bed. "Come on. You look like you're about to fall over."

"Yes, well, about that…." Sebastian sat down and gripped Colton's good hand. "We need to talk."

Colton kissed him on the lips. "We can talk in bed. Strip."

Sebastian chuckled. "Let me talk first. You might not want me in your bed after I say what I have to."

Colton scoffed. "It's *our* bed." He noticed the somber look on his husband's face. "You're serious?"

"Yes."

"I can assure you, whatever it is, I do want you in my bed, so you might as well get undressed and get under the covers with me." There was nothing Sebastian could say that would make Colton kick him out of bed. Not after tonight. Not after Sebastian had told Colton he loved him. Colton grinned and kissed Sebastian's hard, pinched mouth. "I love you. Remember?"

"I do. And I love you."

"Then get in bed."

Sebastian shook his head. "Not yet."

Colton sighed, but he knew the look. He'd seen it for years. He wasn't going to win, so he might as well comply. He waved his good hand. "Very well. Talk."

Sebastian got up from the bed and stood in front of Colton. "Before our wedding, Plume threatened to make my past public. I talked to Leith, but I don't think he can control Plume. Do you understand what all this means? I'm much worse than a bastard. I'm an abomination. My father is supposed to prefer men to women. Not only am I a freak, but I'm the son of a freak. There may be another scandal."

Colton stood and wrapped his arms around Sebastian's neck. The silly man hadn't figured it out yet, but he would. "Then we'll weather it together, like we did the last one. You do know that Giles never loved you, don't you? If he had, he would've stood by you. I, on the other hand, have loved you since I was thirteen."

Hugging him tighter, Sebastian buried his face in Colton's neck. "I've loved you about as long."

"No, you haven't." Colton pulled back, frowning at his consort.

Sebastian chuckled and ran his finger down the bridge of Colton's nose. "Yes, I have. But I will admit it wasn't till the last couple of years that love changed to something more… romantic." He kissed Colton and leaned back, looking him in the eye. "No more secrets, sweeting. For as long as I live, I'll share them all with you. And everything else I have to give."

Oh yes, Sebastian was finally starting to understand. Colton closed his eyes, resting his head on his consort's shoulder. Maybe Tarren's romance novels weren't so farfetched after all.

EPILOGUE

December 14, 4830: Olympian Stables

"ARE YOU sure about this?"

Colton smiled at the uncertainty in Sebastian's voice, but he did not look away from the scene out the window. He had the perfect view up here. Building his office on the top floor of the barn was a spot of genius. It was usually reserved for stableboys, but he'd built Brooks a cottage just next door, and he'd included a large freestanding apartment building for the stable hands on the other side of Brook's cottage, so someone was always close by. "I'm positive. Are you certain?"

Sebastian wrapped his arms around Colton's waist and nuzzled his chin onto Colton's shoulder, leaving a trail of warmth along Colton's cheek. Galaxy, he loved this man. He wrapped his own arms around Sebastian's, locking them to his waist to keep him there as he tipped his head back and kissed Sebastian's cheek.

"I think so." Sebastian stared out at the stable yards, and wrinkles formed on his forehead as he furrowed his brow in thought. "I just wonder if you are doing this for me."

Colton chuckled. "Of course I am, but I think it needs to be done."

"What if it hurts your reputation as a breeder?"

Ahhh, so that was it, then. He was still trying to protect Colton. Colton sighed and raised his head back up. "Look out there. Do you see all of that?"

The scene was amazing. More than anything Colton could have imagined. Olympian Stables was simply smashing. The grounds were covered in a foot of snow, and there was more coming down, but it didn't distract from the beauty of it. Christmas had exploded at Olympian Stables, complete with a fifty-foot blue spruce, decorated with white lights, red ribbon, little gold horseshoes and silver stars, right in between the three hundred by two hundred foot indoor riding arena and the four thousand square foot barn. Lights strung around the outdoor paddock reflected off the snow, making the entire grounds a sparkling winter wonderland. Tarren had even threatened to string mistletoe everywhere. Only threat of losing life and limb and a warning that mistletoe was toxic to the horses had kept him from doing so.

Sebastian nodded. "It's beautiful. You've done an amazing job, and I hate to ruin it."

"You won't ruin it. My point was, look what we've built. What has come of our relationship so far. Whatever happens, we will handle it together. We've weathered scandal before, remember?"

Sebastian chuckled, vibrating Colton's back and filling him with warmth. "How could I forget. As much as I hate to admit it, I think I owe Barnaby."

"Well, I wouldn't go that far." Colton frowned, not even liking the jest.

Another chuckle sounded, and Sebastian kissed his cheek. "No, I don't suppose I should have anything to do with him, considering he's in jail and a bastard. That would only add to the scandal."

"I don't care about the scandal. I was referring to the fact that maniac nearly killed my horses. I'd like to have him hanged instead of sitting in a cell."

"Sweeting, you are a ruthless man."

Colton grinned. "I try."

A lone black lift came down the drive toward them, and Colton's stomach churned with a mix of excitement and nerves. He was really excited about this grand opening, but he was nervous too, and not for the reason Sebastian was. He knew everything would work out just fine. Love had a way of seeing to that.

Colton turned in Sebastian's arms, looking into those deep blue eyes. He smiled and kissed those perfectly rakish lips. "Come on. We have a grand opening to attend and a guest to greet." Without giving his consort a chance to second-guess himself, yet again, he grabbed Sebastian's hand and tugged.

As Colton opened the office door, the scent of evergreens, sweets, and Colton's favorite scent—hay—hit him. He inhaled deeply and hurried his pace.

They went down the stairs to the barn and were immediately greeted by Apollonia, who he'd let out as soon as he'd gotten here. She had her front feet on the second step up and was bobbing her head in greeting.

"She will be climbing these stairs within a week," Sebastian said behind him as Colton reached out to Apollonia.

"She will not." Colton sighed. Honestly, he wouldn't put it past her. Maybe he should have built her a stall up in his office. Putting his hand in the middle of her forehead he pushed, making her back up.

She stepped back and… jingled. What in the…?

He got out of the stairwell and walked to her side. Around her neck was a red-and-green jester-type collar with a gold jingle bell at each point. He touched it, and she turned her head toward him, trying to see what he was doing. "Where did you get this?"

"I gave it to her. She needed party clothes."

Colton glanced toward the entryway as Muffin skipped in followed by Rexley, Trouble, and Payton.

Muffin stepped right up to him, then turned in a circle, showing off her outfit. She was dressed in a green dress with red-and-white ribbons striped like a candy cane. The bow in her red hair had a sprig of holly tucked into the knot. "Me and Nia match."

Sebastian chuckled and rubbed her head. "Indeed you do. You both look splendid."

"She insisted that we come and add more decorations to the horses." Payton pointed past Colton to Apollo's stall, which was right next to the stairs. "I decided to leave Simon with the baby and come too."

"He needed the break. Babies are a handful," Muffin added.

They all chuckled, knowing she'd heard Payton say exactly that. He'd come back for the birth of his son, but he and Simon where only staying until Christmas, which was probably a good idea. Garrett was a colicky baby, and Father and Cony were helping out quite a bit. Even now, Pay had bags under his eyes from lack of sleep.

He grinned at Colton, shrugged, and gestured toward Apollo. "We couldn't let him go to his own party without dressing up."

Apollo had a red halter with felt antlers sticking out to the sides of his head right behind his ears. "He looks… er…."

"Festive?" Trouble sidled up next to Rexley.

"I was going to say…," Colton said, "Christmasy," at the same time Sebastian said, "like a nickninny."

In truth, Apollo looked miserable. He rested his chin on the stall gate and stared at them. Colton made a mental note to take the ridiculous halter off as soon as it got busy and Muffin turned her back. He didn't want to hurt her feelings. She loved the horses and was quite good with them. He'd been right when he'd thought she might just be a natural. She definitely was. Already she was able to ride and control Apollo on her own. And Apollonia, or Nia as Muffin called her, followed Muffin around nearly as much as she followed Colton and Sebastian.

"What are all of you doing here? We saw the lift but were expecting someone else." Colton petted Apollonia, who had started trying to raise her head up under his hand.

"If you are talking about Leith, he's here too. He stopped by the castle, and we rode with him. Father and Cony are on their way, and there was a whole string of lifts behind them." Rexley glanced back at the open door.

Colton followed his gaze, still absently petting Apollonia.

Leith walked in and smiled at them, dipping his head in greeting. "It looks marvelous."

"Thank you." Colton started to step forward to greet him, but Sebastian beat him to it, and Colton inhaled and held it. The two were getting along much better, but he couldn't help the little hitch in his breath at the memory of their first couple of meetings, which had been rather nasty and accusing on both sides.

Sebastian strolled forward with the ease of comfort. He gripped his father's hand, then bumped shoulders with him. "Father."

"Good afternoon, son." Leith smiled again, but this smile was brighter, so much more at ease and… proud? Yes, definitely proud. He'd made no qualms about telling everyone how proud he was of his oldest son, even when he and Sebastian could barely speak to each other without yelling. They still had a ways to go to get back to where they had been when Sebastian was a child, but they were definitely headed in that direction.

"They seem to be getting along now." Rexley stepped beside Colton and started petting Apollonia.

Payton, Trouble, and Muffin had gone off somewhere. He could hear them, but not what they were saying; the barn was four thousand square feet, after all.

Colton nodded but kept watching as his father-in-law chuckled at something Sebastian said and his skin crinkled at the corners of his blue eyes. It was odd that no one had seen the resemblance in father and son before, but Colton suspected that would change now they were appearing in public together. "Leith talked to Father about announcing Sebastian as his heir."

Rexley sucked in a breath beside him and ducked into Colton's line of sight. "Is that wise? I know that he was actually married to Seb's mother, but won't that cause the talk of bigotry to start up again? And this time with Seb at the center."

Colton nodded. "Probably, but I think it's the right thing to do for both of them." During one of Sebastian and Leith's many shouting matches, it had come out that Leith was actually married to Lucy Durant, Sebastian's mother, when he married Leo. When he found out Leo threw Sebastian out while Leith was mourning Lucy's death and that he'd met with the detectives Leith hired to find Sebastian and paid them off, Leith went public with the knowledge and had his and Leo's marriage declared invalid. The rumors were vicious, and Leo was playing the martyr and trying to make Leith into the villain. Sadly society was on Leo's side.

"Are you okay with all this?"

Colton nodded and slapped his brother on the arm. "Absolutely. I'm a sucker for a star-crossed lovers story, and Sebastian's parents were certainly that."

Rexley raised a brow at him. "Tarren is the romance novel aficionado."

Colton shrugged.

A cacophony of voices echoed into the barn as a group gathered in the doorway.

"Are you ready for this?" Rexley asked.

"Absolutely."

Lord Conway walked in the door first, then Cony, Father, Rourke, and Tarren. After that it was a steady stream of people. Gareth Fareweather and his father came in, followed by Edmund and the rest of Colton's new acquaintances. As the senior Fareweather wandered off to look at the horses, Gareth and Edmund came forward.

"Colton, this is smashing. You have outdone yourself," Gareth said in awe.

Edmund nodded his agreement, looking all around.

Just past them, in the doorway, Lord Conway gripped the shoulders of an unsuspecting Lord Hapshire, pulled him close, and bussed him right on the lips.

Hapshire, a big burly man twice Conway's size, glowered at Conway, doubled up his fist, and planted Conway a facer.

Conway grabbed his nose, staggered backward, and groaned. Finally he pointed up.

Right inside the door hung a sprig of mistletoe.

Rexley stifled a chuckle behind his hand.

Colton frowned at him. That was not in the least bit funny. All he needed was for a fight to break out at his grand opening. “I told Tarren no mistletoe.”

“You told him mistletoe was toxic, so he used silk. That is a fake plant,” Rexley said.

Aurgh. Colton was pretty certain he actually said the words no mistletoe. He strode forward but not before Lord Rumpledust stopped in the doorway and puckered his lips at Percy Edmonstone.

Rexley caught Colton’s arm. “Where are you going?”

“To get rid of that mistletoe before someone gets hurt.”

Rexley smirked at him.

“What?”

Rexley didn’t say anything. He just pointed up at the ceiling.

A sense of dread washed over Colton, telling him not to look up, but he did it anyway.

Hanging from the rafters were strings with mistletoe spaced about every three feet. They were all over the place. He was going to kill Tarren.

“Well, that was odd.” Sebastian walked up to Colton as he lowered his head. Rexley was nowhere in sight. Coward.

“What?”

“Lord Higginbottom tried to kiss my father.” Sebastian shook his head, but there was a sardonic grin tugging at his lips.

Colton grinned at the idea of another man kissing Leith, who was unequivocally heterosexual. He wondered what the ton would think when they found out about that.

Dismissing thoughts of his father-in-law, Colton pointed upward and watched as Sebastian raised his head. He expected the same reaction he’d had, but instead Sebastian chuckled, grabbed him behind the neck, tipped him backward, and kissed him.

Smiling against those warm lips, Colton decided there would be plenty of time to kill Tarren… later.

Exclusive Excerpt

Diplomatic Relations

A Sci-Regency Novel
Sequel to *My Regelence Rake*

Dalton Fairfax, Lord Ashbourne, has always flaunted the rules of Regelence high society. Despite being the heir to the Marquess of Ravensburg, and cousin to the Townsend princes, Dalton found his calling in the military, first in the Intergalactic Navy and now the Regelence Special Regiment. Finally home, and in the same city as the parents he seeks to avoid, Dalton jumps at the chance to help his planet by taking on the role of bodyguard to the heir of the Duke of Eversleigh.

Blaise Thompson, Viscount Redding, strives to prove himself worthy of carrying on the Eversleigh legacy as the next Regelence IN council member. Maintaining his stellar reputation isn't easy for Blaise, especially while keeping his outrageous younger brother in line and foiling his rival's personal attacks. Ever conscious of living up to his responsibilities, Blaise has no time for romance, not even with a lusty special forces soldier.

But opposites don't just attract… they sizzle. And when the only way to stop a scandal that threatens them both is to compromise their principles, Blaise and Dalton are forced to confront the risk of losing everything… even each other.

GROANING, DALTON Fairfax huddled farther down into his peacoat as he ran. Damn the luck, letting Ravensburg spot him leaving the IN base on the very day he returned to Regelence. His father, the Marquess of Ravensburg, was a pain in his arse. His parents had been making a fuss for weeks now about him moving back home and selling out his commission. Not bloody likely.

The wind whipped his cheeks so hard he'd lost sensation in them two blocks ago. He glanced back at the mass of people on the sidewalk from which he'd just escaped, but kept going. It was a little like trying to swim up the Bordo River on Lerdra. Shouldn't these people be sleeping off last night's excess? Dodging a nanny pushing a pram, he almost plowed into a young lord.

"Watch out!"

Dalton leaped over a frozen puddle before glancing back again.

Ravensburg had his arm in the air, as if hailing Dalton, as he shoved through a mass of people on the sidewalk. If his face got any redder, he'd look like a tomato. When had Father gotten that out of shape? Or perhaps he was a victim of wind chill as well?

A stab of pity, mixed with something that felt suspiciously like guilt, niggled at Dalton, but not enough to make him stop. Eventually he'd have to talk to his father, but not now.

Skirting a trolley filled with oranges, he peeked over his shoulder again, and bam! He splatted up against a rather squishy body. *Oomph.* "Meteor dust!"

"Whoa!" The squishy body flew backward in a flurry of puce and flapping arms. A hat sailed forward off the man's head.

Dalton shot out a hand to grab the man, but the man's walking stick came flying toward him. He snagged the stick out of midair, but missed the owner's arm.

The man landed on his arse with his legs spread and his gray beaver hat between his knees. He brought to mind a toppled bowling pin as he floundered around.

Several fellow pedestrians stopped to gawk.

Dalton seriously considered resuming his escape, but how callous would that be? He wasn't a complete scoundrel, even if it meant his father caught up with him. Sighing, he planted the walking stick on the sidewalk and offered his free hand. "Terribly sorry, ole chap."

"Oh, I say, Ashbourne. Is that you?" The bowling pin, er… man, blinked bright blue eyes up at Dalton. His lips flowed into a grin, making his jowls more prominent. Lifting his hat from between his legs, he plopped it on his head, turned his face upward, and took Dalton's hand in a warm clammy grip.

Oh stars. It was Viscount Tyndel. Of all times to run into a former paramour. Dalton pulled and failed to help the viscount rise. Galaxy, the man had packed on some pounds. He'd never had the toned physique Dalton preferred in his lovers, but the man had a talented mouth, so Dalton hadn't cared overly. Now? There were practically two of Tyndel.

Putting his back into it and using the walking stick for leverage, Dalton tried again to help Tyndel up.

Slowly, Tyndel rose to his feet, staggering a bit. He dusted off his chocolate-colored trousers and rearranged his waistcoat, jacket, and puce greatcoat. "When did you get back in town? Last I heard, you were serving in the IN on Lerdra."

"Right. Um…." Dalton chanced a glance behind him. Was that Ravensburg? The man certainly seemed in a hurry, and the hat appeared the right shade of brown, but Dalton couldn't get a good look at him otherwise. An IN soldier kept pace in front of him and a much smaller blond man directly beside…. "Damnation!" The blond was his sire. Where had he come from?

Arthur Fairfax's body lurched back in recognition. He said something to—yes that was definitely Ravensburg—and pointed in Dalton's direction. Great, now both his parents were on his tail. He'd managed to avoid them while on leave last year, because they'd been in the country at Windswept Abbey, but evading them while they were in town was already proving more difficult.

Dalton sprang into a jog. Bloody hell. He'd forgotten all about Tyndel. He turned over his shoulder toward the now slack-jawed viscount and walked backward. "My apologies, Tyndel. We'll catch up later." His gaze strayed a few yards back. *Eep*. His sire was quick for such a small man. "Family emergency." Which wasn't a lie—it was an emergency that he get away from his family. He fled without another word.

"Oh, I say, how undignified," someone called out behind him.

Dalton grinned at the absurdity of the situation and kept going. How very undignified indeed. Both Lords Ravensburg running down a crowded sidewalk in the middle of downtown Classige. Dalton chuckled. He couldn't wait to tell Uncle Raleigh.

After bolting into an alley, he came out on Green Street and looked both ways. There was a jeweler, a tailor…. There. The haberdashery. Maybe he could hide out and do some shopping.

He sprinted across the road, narrowly avoiding a lift. Glancing behind him, he made sure his parents hadn't made it out of the alley yet, and then he flung open the door and hurried inside.

The bell tinkled, and…. *Ah warmth!* His frozen face and burning lungs approved. Dropping his hands to his knees, he took a deep breath and then another. He really needed to get reaccustomed to the higher altitude in Pruluce. Having been stationed on a planet with nothing but plains for the past year had not done him any favors today. Thank goodness for the last six weeks of special training to go into the Regelence Special Regiment, or he'd be in worse shape.

"Ahem."

Dalton raised his head as a tall thin man in a dove-gray morning coat and charcoal trousers came around the corner toward him. The pinched expression on his face clearly declared Dalton beneath him. The establishment did cater to the haute ton, but still… a solider wasn't exactly riffraff. Besides, how could the salesman even see with his nose that high in the air?

Straightening to his full height, Dalton lifted his own chin; he could do haughty when necessary.

"How can I help you, lieutenant…?" The man looked as though he'd bitten into something quite sour, and the way he made Dalton's rank sound like the equivalent of horse droppings was very impressive.

Dalton barely suppressed a twitch at the corner of his lips. Staring down his nose at the man, he lifted a brow. "Lieutenant Lord Ashbourne." He wasn't above playing the lord card to keep from getting tossed out of the shop.

Normally that was all it took, and this proprietor was no different.

Mr. Lemon Sucker's entire demeanor changed, and the poker up his arse seemed to have disappeared. "Welcome, my lord. I'm Humphreys. How may I serve you? Please allow me to take your coat and…." He looked at Dalton's head.

Bloody black hole, he'd lost his cover in the mad dash to get away.

Humphreys quickly divested Dalton of his peacoat. "What can I help you with today, my lord?"

"I'll let you know. I'm going to browse around." Dalton stepped past Poker Arse, completely dismissing him, then felt guilty for it. But the man was rude to him first, he reasoned—not to mention he needed out of the doorway. Even though the bottom part of the door was wood, the top had panes of glass and a clear view to the street.

"Very well, my lord. Please let me know if I can be of service. I'll check back with you in a moment?"

Waving his hand behind him, Dalton continued walking. He did need a new civilian wardrobe more fitting to Regelence for when he was off duty. Though he was loath to give up the shorts and sandals he'd worn on Lerdra during his time off.

Studying the shelves of cravats to his right, he decided to browse while he let his esteemed parents get farther away.

"Bannon, get down from there right this instant. What if someone sees you?"

Dalton froze.

The furious whisper had come from somewhere to his left. Whoever the speaker was, he whispered louder than Dalton's cousin Tarren, which was quite impressive.

"I mean it, Bannon."

Wait. A flutter racked Dalton's stomach. It couldn't be. Bannon was the name of his cousin Aiden's friend. And his brother…. Could that be Dalton's Adonis calling his younger sibling?

Before he'd gone into special training, Dalton had been home on leave and spotted the most angelic, gorgeous creature he'd ever laid eyes on. The man had starred in every one of Dalton's fantasies since then. That lovely face had even gotten him through those long nights in the surf while he'd suffered from hypothermia and starvation. He could still picture the man clearly. A real diamond of the first water. Lord Redding, Blaise Thompson, heir to the Duke of Eversleigh, had brown hair and the most brilliant green eyes Dalton had ever seen—like emeralds in the sunlight. He had kissable lips and a grace of movement that made him appear ethereal. He was beautiful, elegant, and very, very beddable.

Only Dalton hadn't been able to arrange an introduction. Somehow their paths had not crossed again, which wasn't surprising, considering that Dalton was a rakehell and Blaise was… well, respectable. None of Dalton's cousins had taken him seriously when he'd asked to meet the viscount.

Footsteps came from behind him. "My lord, can I—"

"Not now!" He waved his hand without looking at the man.

"Hrmph. Very well, my lord."

Bloody hell. Dalton swiveled around. "Pardon me, Humphreys. My apologies. I was deep in thought, and I'm still deciding, but I'll let you know."

"Very well, my lord." Humphreys dipped his pointy chin, turned on his heels, and left.

Dalton hurried to the very end of the aisle and glanced down the next one. Empty. Standing perfectly still, he closed his eyes and listened. *Where are you, lovely?*

"Eep." The shelving unit cattycorner on his left rattled. A black beaver hat fell from the shelf, bounced onto the navy blue carpet, and rolled in a circle before landing crown up in the middle of the floor. "Oh stardust! Blaise, let go of my feet and stop pulling…." A pair of dazzling green eyes peered down from the top shelf under a shock of bright red hair. "Oh, hallo."

"'Ello." Dalton grinned. Not only was it Aiden's friend, Bannon, but Bannon's grousing confirmed that his gorgeous brother was indeed on the other side of that wall of hats as well. "Can you get that for me?" Bannon asked.

"Certainly." Dalton snagged the hat from the ground, and warmth spread through him as though he'd drank a shot of whiskey. Alas, he was about to meet the breathtaking Viscount Redding. Finally.

"Bannon…," Blaise hissed from the other side.

"I have him." A female hissed back. "Bannon, get down."

The shelving teetered.

"Oh!" Bannon's eyes widened, and his head began to sink below the shelf.

Three more hats dropped from the top ledge, and one from the middle—right about where Bannon's foot would be—and hit the ground. Unlike the first hat, these didn't roll but instead pelted the ground like darts.

Dalton had a vision of the shelf falling and knocking over the rest like dominoes. He raced around the corner with his arms outstretched, intent on catching the hellion, and plowed right over the man of his dreams.

It was nothing like running into Tyndel, because Blaise was not at all squishy, and he never saw Dalton coming. He fell like a chopped tree—straight down.

Dalton reached out, but the impact had sent him reeling backward as well. The cuff of Blaise's soft wool morning coat flitted through his fingers, followed by a small current of air that sealed the deal. All he could do was watch with his mouth ajar as Blaise hit the blue carpet. The breath knocked from him was little more than a hiss.

Clutching his chest, Blaise gasped for air. The agony and surprise on his face hit Dalton so hard he might as well have fallen himself. Those beautiful green eyes went wide and unfocused. His chestnut hair fell in an attractive tousle over his forehead, and those smooth alabaster cheeks grew blotchy with spots of color, but for all that, he was still the most beautiful man on Regelence. Like an elven prince from one of the storybooks Grandfather used to read at bedtime.

Before Dalton could move forward to check on his hapless victim, Bannon screeched.

Hanging from his fingertips, the redhead dangled four feet off the ground. The shelving unit swayed back and forth as if hit by a gale force wind.

A woman tried to steady the shelves but had no success whatsoever. It was only a matter of seconds before the whole thing toppled, and who knew which way it would actually fall.

Dalton rushed forward through the rain of hats peppering the ground around him like tiny missiles and caught Bannon with one arm. After setting the young man on his feet, he used both hands to steady the shelf. The girl helped, and it stopped swaying, but most of its contents had crash-landed onto the carpet.

Dalton's lips twitched up into a big smile as he studied the turbulent sea of hats. Some on their sides, some upside down, others right side up, one or two still rolling. In their stuffy society, a little harmless folly was a godsend. Well, almost harmless. He supposed Blaise might disagree at the moment, but still it tickled Dalton.

Somehow all but one hat missed Blaise, who was now trying to sit while gasping for air and clawing at his cravat.

Dalton rushed to him, tossed the green hat from his abdomen, and helped him sit. Sinking down behind Blaise, he propped the viscount's back against his chest and couldn't help but feel tenderness. "Easy, sweetheart."

Galaxy, he smelled divine. Like cold nights around a campfire and the inside of a sweet shop all rolled into one.

Blaise leaned back into Dalton's arms, so warm and trusting, and despite the situation, Dalton's cock stirred. Gritting his teeth, he willed his body to behave and intercepted Blaise's hands. Pale, elegant hands that would look splendid on Dalton's slightly darker skin. And thoughts like that were definitely not a good way to get control of his body. Geez, the man couldn't breathe, and here Dalton was lost in a fantasy.

Unknotting the cravat, he pulled it free. "That's it, sweetheart, easy now. Try to slowly let the air back in."

Little by little Blaise began to relax and inhale. Soon he was breathing easier, and so did Dalton.

"There now. Much better, yes?"

Blaise nodded and snuggled, moving his back side to side, against Dalton's chest. He leaned his head back on Dalton's shoulder and closed his eyes with his face only inches away.

A charming sprinkle of freckles dotted his cheeks, and his slim neck begged to be bitten. The strong pulse throbbing there taunted Dalton's tongue. Would he taste salty or sweet? Or a combination of both?

"Oh bother." Bannon stood a few feet away with the black hat he'd risked life and limb to get, wringing it in his hands. His pale skin blanched nearly white. "Father is going to throttle me."

Humphreys appeared behind him with his mouth ajar. *Wonderful!* There was no telling what the very uptight man would say about this. Frankly, Dalton couldn't believe he wasn't already shrieking and calling the law on them.

The girl bit her bottom lip and shook her head at the damage before turning on Bannon. "I told you it was a bad idea."

"You did not!" Bannon shouted at her. "You said the hat would be dashing on me."

"I didn't mean for you to climb up and get…." She trailed off, looking over at Humphreys.

With a sigh and a prayer to anyone who'd listen that Humphreys didn't have an apoplexy right on the spot, Dalton met the older man's gaze. "I'll pay for everything, but allow me to revive Lord Redding first."

Surprisingly the proprietor did not explode. Standing up straighter, he closed his lips and dipped his chin. "Very well, my lord." With a glare at Bannon, he lifted his chin, sniffed, and walked away.

Like a bolt of lightning had struck him, Blaise jerked forward and scrambled to his feet. He spun around and locked gazes with Dalton, his mouth gaping open. For several seconds, they stared at each other.

Dalton couldn't have moved if he'd wanted to. He sat there transfixed by those grass-green eyes and the most profound feeling that his life had just irrevocably changed. He shook his head, trying to clear the insane thought, and hopped to his feet. It wasn't like he was a lad with his first infatuation. He didn't even believe in love at first sight, but there was… something… some strange pull he couldn't deny. The shock in Blaise's eyes made Dalton wonder if he felt it too.

Blaise swallowed hard enough to make his Adam's apple bob. A small, shy smile teased his lips, and those gorgeous eyes peeked out from under fluttering lashes. Pink tinged his neck and face as he bit his bottom lip. He took a step forward, and the color drained from his face.

Maybe it was the widening of his eyes or the jerky way he moved, but Dalton read his intent to flee and said, "Blaise, wait."

But he didn't wait; he took off at a brisk pace, kicking hats out of his way as he went.

Bollocks! Dalton reached out as if he could somehow stall the retreat, but Blaise increased his pace.

Bannon and the girl stumbled along behind him. After a few seconds, Bannon peered back over his shoulder with a sheepish expression. "Sorry. And thank you."

Dalton nodded. *Bloody hell!* What had he done? Well, other than knocking the man on his arse, of course. Rolling his eyes at himself, Dalton groaned. He watched Blaise disappear around the corner with his coattails flapping behind him.

Ugh. That had not gone at all like Dalton envisioned their first meeting. So much for a first impression. He'd just have to make a better second one. Glancing around at the hats littering the floor, he chuckled.

That shouldn't be too hard.

J.L. LANGLEY said her first words at six months of age. By the time she was a year old, she was talking in complete sentences and, as most of her family and friends will tell you, she hasn't shut up since. After becoming an accomplished motormouth, J.L. set out to master other avenues of self-expression, including art, and dance.

She attended the University of Texas, where she majored in art and worked as a dance instructor on the side. Her love of artistic expression in dance landed her a career in which she taught and performed for over twenty-five years. After marriage to her junior high school sweetheart and the birth of their children, J.L. decided to try her hand at writing. To date, she has several successful novels and a handful of novellas to her credit.

She lives in Texas, where she was born and raised, with her real-life hero, their rowdy two boys, two even rowdier German shepherds, and ten goldfish, one of which is named Jaws. When she's not writing, she can usually be found with her nose in a book appreciating the communication skills of other writers.

Facebook: www.facebook.com/authorjllangley
Twitter: @jl_langley

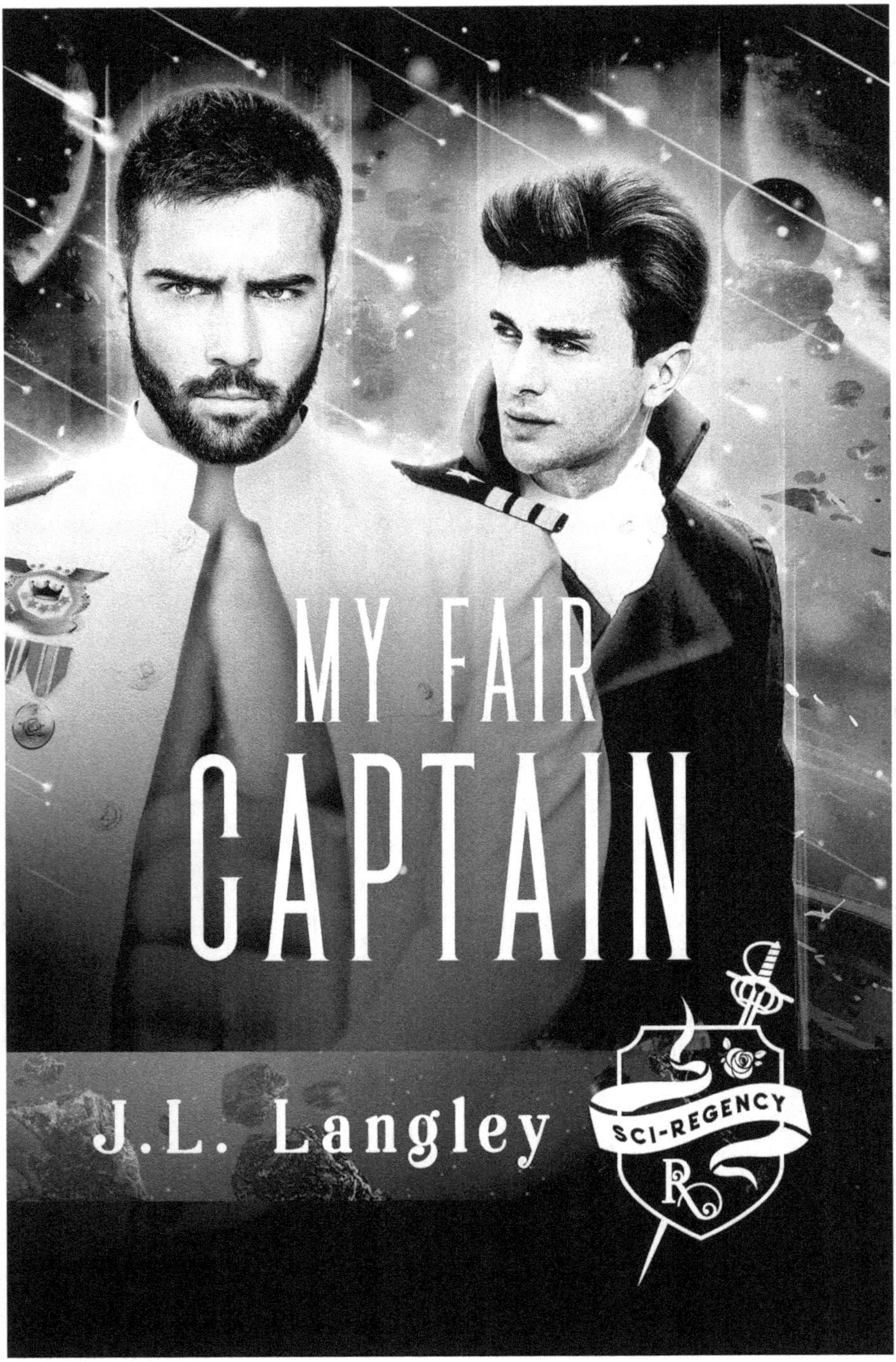
MY FAIR
CAPTAIN
J.L. Langley
SCI-REGENCY
R

A Sci-Regency Novel

When Intergalactic Navy Captain Nathaniel Hawkins goes undercover to investigate the theft of an IN weapons stash, the mission raises painful memories from his past. Using a title he fled nearly two decades earlier, Nate once again becomes the Earl of Deverell, heir to the Duke of Hawthorne, in order to navigate the ins and outs of a Regency world. But planet Regelence—where young lords are supposed to remain pure until marriage—has a few surprises for Nate, not least of which is his attraction to Prince Aiden.

A talented artist, Prince Aiden Townsend isn't interested in politics and the machinations of society gentlemen, and he adamantly rejects the idea of marriage and a consort. Aiden wants the freedom to pursue his art and determine his own future. But the arrival of the dashing and mysterious Deverell awakens feelings of passion and longing the young prince can't deny.

As Nate uncovers a conspiracy reaching far beyond the stolen weapons, his future is irrevocably altered by the temptations of a life he never thought he could have. Drawn into the web of intrigue, Aiden is in danger of losing his life… and his heart.

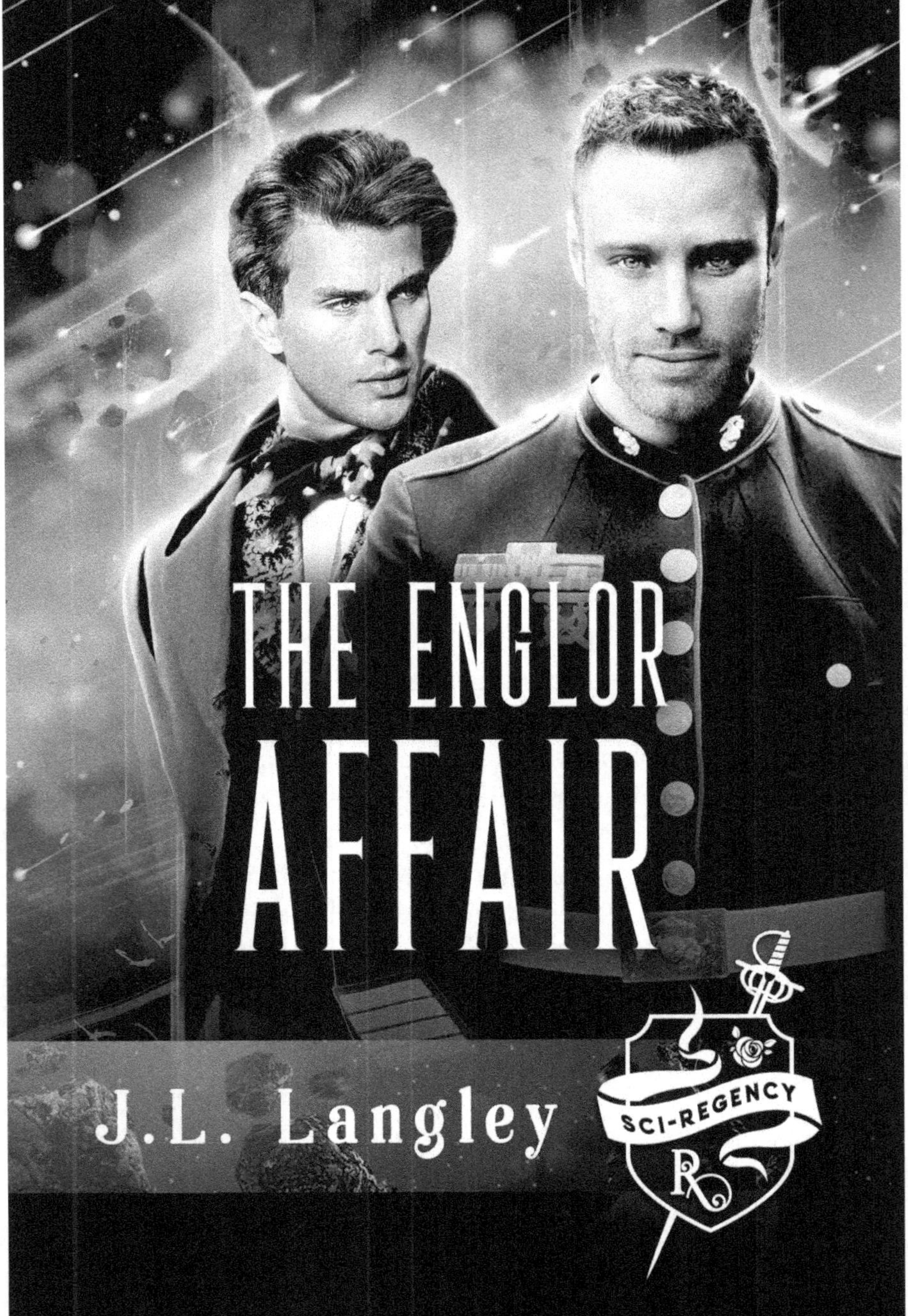
THE ENGLOR
AFFAIR
J.L. Langley
SCI-REGENCY
R

A Sci-Regency Novel
Sequel to *My Fair Captain*

Anxious to escape the confines of Regelence society, if only for a little while, Prince Payton Townsend poses as an admiral's aide to further investigate a dangerous conspiracy. Payton plans only to use his computer skills to help navigate the tangled web of mystery and deceit on planet Englor, then return home, but he finds himself drawn to the charismatic Colonel Simon Hollister.

Simon, however, is no mere soldier—he is heir to the throne of Englor, and his life is meticulously planned to include a bride and heir. Unlike Regelence, the Regency society on Englor disapproves of same-sex relationships, and Payton and Simon's attraction plays out in a daring secret affair, one Simon never expected would grow into love.

Risking scandal and certain ruin if they are discovered, Payton and Simon uncover more about a common enemy and a deadly plot that imperils both their worlds. But in this game of interplanetary intrigue, love might be the ultimate casualty….

CPSIA information can be obtained
at www.ICGtesting.com
Printed in the USA
LVHW021134251118
598196LV00023B/2400/P

9 781640 806917